# Across the Great Ocean

## Book I: Desolation

## Virginia Mary

ISBN 979-8-9898034-0-8

eBook ISBN 979-8-9898034-1-5

Book Cover Design Copyright © 2024 by Virginia Mary

Book Cover Design by EbookLaunch.com

Map by Virginia Mary

Edited by Louisa Klein, Lost In Fiction LTD, contact: louisakleinuk@googlemail.com

Published by Virginia Mary

www.virginiamaryarts.com

*Across the Great Ocean* is an exhilarating adventure fantasy series that unfolds in a dystopian world. As the narrative unfolds, it traverses themes that encompass war, violence, attempted sexual assault, and death. For those who may be sensitive to the aforementioned themes, please read with care.

*Dedicated to those I love.*
*For without you,*
*I would have no words.*

NORTH OCEAN

THE SACRED FOREST OF AKTA

SORNIENO

EASTERN CHAO BINH

Brvery

MOUNTAINS OF SHIREN

EMPIRE OF GALA

Capital

ZHAO

Port of Gala

KINGDOM OF KAHR

Levar

Fisher's Port

Bay of Shiren

WESTERN CHAO BINH

THE GREAT OCEAN

Island of Zlara

SOUTH OCEAN

Eura's Harbor

Eko

PORT OF YANA

KINGDOM OF YANA

Rost

Huang

REPUBLIC OF TERLU

Bay of Suhai

Toto

THE LOST LANDS OF ONUMI

Port of Terlu

Nun

QARA DESERT

SUHAI EMPIRE

TINSHE

NIJIN

# BOOK I:
# DESOLATION

## CHAPTER ONE

# THE PLAGUE

W HEN I WAS YOUNG, I would sit on my mother's lap and watch the ducks dance in the pond from our balcony. She would braid my hair and teach me about the great gods, goddesses, and spirits that once roamed the Earth. My mother taught me that we are all interconnected- humans, spirits, even the ducks and water that flows beneath them. She pointed to the moon, to show the goddess Eura, who was always watching over us.

"Look at the moon, Nyla. No matter what problems plague our world, she always shines through the darkness, casting her beautiful light for all to see."

My balcony may have been small, but it was a sacred place to me. Looking back, there wasn't even enough space for a chair, yet it felt so vast to my tiny body. I saw many strong mother ducks over the years, protecting their babies from the world around them. As long as they stayed swimming in the pond, nothing could harm them. I watched them grow and change, until they flew away. I don't know where they went, maybe to another pond- a better pond. But I wish they stayed.

If only I could have stayed there forever. Not just on the balcony, but to be young and mindless of the death and darkness that consumed my world.

During my tenth year of life, a plague ravaged my home, Tinshe, which made up the southern half of the Suhai Empire. Unfortunately, Tinshe was already suffering through a fifty year economic depression that left many people jobless, homeless, and hungry. The plague came from across the world and attacked with great ferocity, an untamable beast.

Many wealthy nations not only survived, but thrived. The northern half of the Suhai Empire, Najin, had advanced science and medical fields that prepared them to effectively handle the plague, but they turned their backs on the rest of us, who could not afford the hefty price of the medicine. They claimed it was the great spirits cleansing the world of impurities.

The New Plague claimed my mother and my two sisters, Luchi and Dalia, within months of breaching our walls. My friends, neighbors, and most of my people perished with them. I do not know why the plague took whom it did. For years, I cried to the moon goddess, Eura, asking why she took them and not me, but she never answered. In the wake of the devastation, all I had left to do was to take care of my two brothers, Benjin and Luka.

Though my father, Daath, survived the plague, he was no longer with us. Despite being just a city sweeper, he was once my hero. He was as smart as a golden eagle, as strong as a fuji ox, and as silly as a koala monkey. He always joked that he did not know why my mother settled for him.

She was a strikingly beautiful woman, with sharp features and sparkling blue eyes that could captivate anyone. When she walked, people looked. When she spoke, people listened. My father claimed she was his first and only love, a wild and unpredictable flame he couldn't resist. He would never attempt to tame her, but instead aimed to fuel her fire, helping her become her brightest and boldest self.

My father was deeply grounded and humble. Around us, he was cheerful and goofy, but around others he was quiet- always listening and examining. He acted carefully and calculated, while my mother acted fearlessly and instinctively. He was the moon to her sun.

Once he lost his wife and two of his daughters, he lost himself. Benjin, Luka, and I seemed to have lost him too. At first, he stopped eating meals with us, and then he stopped coming home entirely. Now, I only see him in my dreams.

After losing so much, it pained me to lose him too, but I tried to understand. My father was strong his whole life for us. It was not just because he was one of the tallest men in my city- his real strength shined in his actions: skipping meals so his family could eat, working as a sweeper all day, and then picking up hours at the mill overnight. I understand that the New Plague broke him. Through my memories of him, my mother, and sisters, I found strength. If the world had once been so pure, I believe it could be again. But for now, it was our turn to be strong.

I do not know where I would be without my two brothers. Though Benjin may have only been nineteen, he reminded me more of my father than my actual father did. In fact, even though it had only been a few years, when I thought of my father- I just saw Benjin.

Although Tinshe had no formal universities like Najin, Benjin was still smarter than anyone. Being born on this side of the Suhai Empire had many setbacks, but Benjin always had a way to keep our family fed and safe. I wished he would let me work more hours to take some of the burden off his shoulders, but he wouldn't let me stop my studies, even though I could not attend university. He believed that one day things would change, and he wanted us to be ready.

I worked at a factory, where I put one screw in a seeder on the assembly line. Or, at least, I was told it was a seeder. I had only ever seen the screws and the metal sheets that I put them into, as well as the thick plumes of black smoke that bellowed out of the pipes and into our already polluted air. Whatever we were building was sent north to Najin before we could see it. Benjin always told me to stop questioning things and I knew he was right, because I had seen what the militia did to those who ask too much, but that only made me have more questions.

As soon as the strong winds of the plague settled, our emperor approved Najin's militia to be stationed south in Tinshe to help rebuild and provide resources, in an attempt to re-establish our economy. Instead, they behaved like vultures, seizing what little remained in the already desolate city.

For countless generations, our people were defended by the sacred Protectors- a strong family line of warriors who were believed to be just as much gods as they were men. They kept our side of the empire safe and represented us in times of war. They never resorted to using violence in over two hundred years, as they were spiritually connected to both the Earth and the gods who protected it, always finding a path for peace.

As Tinshe progressed, the world's Civil Council even granted a Protector a place among them to voice the needs of our side of the empire. The Civil Council sits on the Island of Aara, which lies in the middle of the Great Ocean, to keep the councilmen free of corruption from any one side. It sits between all of our empires, kingdoms, and ports.

When the Upper's militia moved in, they tore our community apart. Their General, Ahkpi, lied to Emperor Nahkon of the Suhai Empire, as well as the Civil Council, claiming that he was moving troops into Tinshe to help support us through the plague. Our Protectors could not reason with General Ahkpi and his hatefulness. As he sent more troops in to rob us, he rallied across Najin, bragging to his followers of his generosity. Meanwhile, it was he who coined the term 'Others' to blame us for the plague and any other hardship Najin faced. It quickly became clear that no amount of spiritualism could protect us.

About six months into Tinshe's militia occupation, our representative Protector returned home from the Island of Aara. He was sent to see the conditions of Tinshe and was to report back to the council with his findings. When he arrived, the Protectors revealed the atrocities that brewed in Tinshe during his absence. Outraged, he and the Protectors went to confront General Ahkpi of Najin to demand his troops leave our side of the empire. But when they faced him, Ahkpi ordered his militia to execute them. With the Protectors gone, people quickly lost hope.

# CHAPTER TWO

# THE SUN'S RAYS

"BENJIN, LUKA, DINNER!" I called out to my brothers, once I returned from four hours of hunting. I had finally found a tiger rabbit and enough dandelions to last us the week, which was no easy task with a bow as flimsy and worn down as mine. I cooked the rabbit in salt water stew and brewed a bowl of dandelion tea. I heard Luka barging up the apartment's stairwell, which was five stories high.

"Rabbit stew again?" He groaned.

"Let's see you find us something better, Buba." I swooped Luka up and tickled him, before he squirmed out of my arms. "Have you seen Benjin?"

"I dunno." He took a big swig of stew before he even sat down on his floor cushion.

I watched the apartment door swing open and there was Benjin, covered in dirt and grime. After my father left, he took over his job as a city sweeper. He was sent all over Najin to scrub and clean everywhere, from roads to alleyways and the buildings that lined them. We didn't have city sweepers on our southern side of the empire, so sometimes he had to travel up to six hours to get to work. If he had a long project up north, we wouldn't see him for days because it would be impossible for him to come back after a midnight shift and make it back to work before dawn the next morning. Those were always the worst times, because Benjin was the only one who protected us from the militia. He had an innate sense of where to hide and what to do when trouble arose.

"Hey, you two. What's for dinner?" Benjin always spoke with his famous grin.

Girls always flock when he walks me to the factory, especially in the summer, when it hits over a hundred degrees and the sweat glimmers down his face. I pretend not to notice the girls, because it makes me feel like an Upper to have attention like that. When I am alone, no one notices me.

Before the plague, Juu and Tasi were my best friends. Well, they were my only friends, but they were still my best friends. We did everything together. When I had them, I never noticed how invisible I was to the world. But when you're alone, it's hard not to notice. I suppose it doesn't matter; I should just be grateful for being alive.

"Tiger rabbit stew!" Luka pretended to throw up.

"Very funny, Buba, but you know how hard it is to find meat nowadays." Benjin patted Luka's head and sat down, before pulling off his black work boots. Chunks of mud fell onto the floor beneath them. "How were your studies today, Nyla?" He pulled up the sleeves to his gray work jumpsuit, revealing his tanned forearms. His hands were stained black from work.

I was hoping he wouldn't ask. Hunting for dinner took so long that I barely got through my day's work and reading took me long enough as it was. "Easy, as always," I lied, but I already knew Benjin would see right through me.

"How about I help you after dinner? The sun is still up, we might as well make use of it."

With the sun's setting rays gliding through the balcony, Benjin looked just like our mother Lee. His strong jawline was accentuated by his razor-sharp blue eyes, and you could never tell what he was thinking, because his eyes masked his mind. He was never one to complain or talk poorly of others, but instead always found something positive to say. His soft black hair was trimmed short on the sides, but sat like a mop on top of his head, only to fall in front of his face whenever the wind blew through. He whisked it back without a second thought. Though he may have my father's stature and resourceful personality, he had my mother's beauty, something I was lacking.

While Benjin was tall, strong, and charming, I might as well be from a different kin. I was the tiniest girl on my block and barely weighed more than Luka, who was nearly a decade younger than me, but I never let my size hold me back. I had my father's big brown eyes and his long, wavy brown hair. My skin was as pasty as the snow that never falls anymore, while Benjin and Luka had my mother's natural golden glow. Benjin always said I was just like our mother, but when I looked at my reflection, I just saw a scrawny girl with eyes bigger than her head.

"Alright... But don't be mad if I didn't make it very far through my reading," I mumbled.

"When General Patten of the Kingdom of Yana brought his army to the outer walls of Shiren, the goddess of life fell from the clouds and rained a storm so powerful that it flooded the entire valley outside the great empire," Benjin's voice drifted over the fire, as the sun set. Luka was snuggled up on his lap, quietly snoring with his thumb in his mouth. "This was how the Great Ocean was formed, to protect the peaceful empire from the kingdom's military. Shortly after, the Empire of Shiren was renamed to the Empire of Gala, in honor of the goddess."

"In all of my readings, the gods and goddesses always came to save the people. Why did they not come to us during the New Plague? Or when the militia came and raided our side of the empire?"

"If only we knew, then maybe we wouldn't be in this mess!" Benjin laughed. He rubbed his head, pulling his hair back. I sighed and stared at our crumbling fireplace.

Our mother used to read us passages every night and the five of us would marvel at the gods and goddesses who stomped out all the evil in the world. She taught us about Qalia and Urliq, the afterlife realms that were depicted by the first oracle of Qara. She warned us that if we didn't eat our vegetables, we would end up in Urliq, which in the common tongue translated to the End- a place ruled by Shadow. Only by doing our chores, excelling in our studies, and honoring the gods would we reach Qalia, or Beyond, where the gods lived.

My sisters, Luchi and Dalia, and I would even dress as goddesses and play make believe in admiration of them. I once felt deeply connected to the spirit world, but now, it all felt so fake. I wasn't even sure if I believed in the gods anymore. Benjin locked eyes with me and let out a heavy sigh. He knew his answer was not enough for me.

"A thousand years ago, when Gala created the Great Ocean to protect the Empire of Shiren and its people, the bond between humans and the spirit world was much stronger. After General Patten's army was decimated, the world lived in relative peace for almost a thousand years. Sure, there were some civil wars and hiccups along the way, but overall, the world was good. During that time, people forgot how much we needed the gods. At first, people forgot to pray. Then, the festivals for our gods stopped being focused on our connection to the spirit world, but instead on wealth and gluttony."

"And during the plague, the festivals stopped all together."

"I guess you could say the gods never abandoned us, it was us who abandoned them." He threw his hands up in defeat. "But really, Nyla, who knows. Of course, I wish the gods would swoop down and save us, but at this rate, I am losing faith. There are talks about an uprising- for us to fight for equality in this world, for us to take hope into our own hands. I believe change is coming. We just have to get by until it does." Benjin rose to his feet. "Come on, it's time for bed."

Our apartment had two tiny bedrooms. My parents used to share one room, where Luka would sleep nuzzled between them. The rest of us piled onto one big bed in the other room, which was the only piece of furniture in our bedroom. Once we lost our sisters and Benjin moved into my parents' old room, we threw it out. It felt too empty. Now, Luka and I shared a smaller mattress. As I carried Luka to bed and dozed off, I heard the front door click open.

When I awoke, Benjin was already gone. He usually left for work well before dawn, so I often only saw him later in the evening. I gently woke Luka up and warmed some dandelion tea on the stove. We would have to get ready quickly if I was to make it to the factory on time for work. Since Benjin was at work too, our Nonna would watch Luka.

Pola was not our actual Nonna. My mother's mother, who I was named after, passed during the New Plague. She was a sharp-talking immigrant from the Republic of Terlu, which hugged the coast a few hundred miles north of the Suhai Empire. My father's mother, Daara, fortunately passed away before the plague.

Sometimes, it was hard for me to remember life before the plague. Nonna Daara passed without ever having to see the darkness that swept the world. I was thankful for that, because she loved my father, her only son, more than anything. My father never really had a father to call his own. Without a husband to help support her, Daara's life revolved around her son. I think she would have died of a broken heart if she saw all the suffering her son would endure over the years.

"Luka, get some tea. I have to go to work," I called out, as the tea boiled and bubbled over.

"Let me sleep, let me sleep!" He wailed.

"Come out here before I dump this hot bowl of tea on you, Buba!" He quickly jumped to his feet and scampered over.

"Why do I have to go to Nonna's? Can't I stay here and sleep?" He cried.

"Don't bother me with questions you already know the answer to. You know Benji's rules. If the militia conducts a sweep and you're here alone, you won't know what to do. Besides, you're six. You can't even tie your own shoes."

"I know what to do! Keep my nose to the ground and to stay quiet," he said, mimicking a line that Benjin had repeated to us a hundred times before.

Luka was only one year old when we lost our mother. He was born six months before the New Plague hit, so he never had a normal childhood, whereas I was ten and Benjin was fourteen, so at least we had some years of normalcy. At times, I feared Luka would only ever see a plagued and war-torn world.

I gathered his toys and our only snack, Tinshe's infamous dried and tasteless wheat strips, and took him down the three flights of stairs to Nonna's. As I knocked on her door, Luka leaped out of my arms and barged in.

"Nonna, Nonna, Nonna!" He yelled. So much for him not wanting to come here. I heard Nonna's classic laughter erupt through the house.

"There's my little string bean." She creaked over and gave him a kiss. She had short, curly gray hair that bounced on her shoulders as she talked, framing her chubby face. "And how's my beautiful princess?" I felt my face blush, Nonna knows how to make a person feel loved.

"I'm alright, but I have to get to the factory. If I am late again my paycheck gets taken."

"Alright, princess... Always in a rush, that one... You go on out there and I'll see you later." Nonna wrapped her arms around me like a big warm blanket. It reminded me of my mother. Sometimes, I closed my eyes and pretended that it was.

"Thanks for watching Luka, as always. I don't know what Benjin and I would do without you, Nonna." I knelt down and gave Luka a tight hug. "Behave. I'll pick you up after work."

"Oh, please. I don't know what I would do without you kids. You keep me young. Give Busy Benjin a hug from Nonna when you see him." She took Luka's toys and snacks from me. "Now, run along, Nyla."

I ran out of Nonna's apartment and down the stairs. As I got outside, I realized it was pouring, but if I turned back to get a tarp, I would be late and my pay would be docked. I couldn't miss a whole day's pay just to stay dry and besides, a little rain never killed anybody. I ran down the street and three blocks over to the factory gate. I didn't have time to wait for a guard, so I squeezed between the fence posts and ran through the door.

I jumped into my station and got straight to work, with only a minute to spare. I was soaking wet- my boots were walking puddles. Brisa, my seventeen-year-old coworker, handed me a metal piece. Without thought, I put a screw in and passed it along to the next worker in the assembly line.

"Heya, Nyla. You're a wee bit wet," Brisa spoke with a grin on her face. Her coiled black hair was pulled into a low bun, with curls that slipped out and fell in front of her face.

"Am I? Didn't notice."

Since the New Plague, Brisa was one of the few girls that I could connect with. With her by my side, these long shifts went by far quicker. Brisa was the oldest of twelve kids, but lost seven siblings to the New Plague. She was born in Fisher's Port, a small coastal town in what was now the Kingdom of Kaar, though it remained unrecognized by the Civil Council, as well as by the other nations' leaders. Fisher's Port was known to be an impoverished and dangerous city, as was the kingdom as a whole, so I doubted Brisa ever went to school at all. I assumed that was why she talked oddly. I knew very little else about her life, because we only really had small talk.

Since the plague, it became difficult to truly talk to people. Conversations dredged up memories and history, so it was difficult to avoid sensitive topics. It also felt like people were hesitant to form new attachments, as if the pain of losing so many had drained their capacity to start anew. Instead, we just grazed by, as if trapped in a half-dream state.

"You haveta be careful. Boss sees you runnin' in all late and wet, he'll throw a fit."

"Well, I wasn't late and I can't control the weather. He can take that up to the gods."

"Alright, alright. I'm just sayin'. You haveta be careful. Honest work is hard to come by nowadays. Best to keep the one you got."

"Okay, mother," I said as I passed my metal pieces along.

"How's Benjin?" Brisa asked, changing the subject.

"Benjin's Benjin."

"Can't ya entertain me a wee bit?" Brisa slapped a metal piece into my hand.

"Benjin said he is in love with you but doesn't know how to tell you," I gushed.

"Really?" Her eyes widened and she grabbed my hand.

"No, Brisa. He doesn't even know who you are."

"Well, geez. Can't blame a girl for dreaming."

"Yeah, you and the rest of the south side girls."

I left the factory as the sun was setting. Benjin did his best to walk me to and from work whenever he could, but he was stuck in Najin more often than not. If it was dark out, I knew to walk close to the buildings. The more hidden, the better. My gray work jumpsuit helped me travel unnoticed as well. I stepped carefully in my boots, careful not to make a sound.

As I was turning onto my street, I saw three militants circling around a lump on the sidewalk. I stayed in the shadows, tip-toeing through, but I couldn't help but watch. Once I got closer, I realized the lump was a man, beaten badly and sitting in a puddle. He was crying out to the goddess Gala as the militants kicked him. One of the militants spit down on him, with his boots harshly dug into the poor man's forearm. I squinted my eyes, only to realize the puddle was blood. The man's voice faded to silence.

I ran down my street as quickly and quietly as I could. I bolted up the stairs to Nonna's without taking a moment to breathe. I slammed on her door, calling her name. The door whipped open and she stood before me with a sour scowl on her face.

"What is with you, Nyla? It's late, people are sleeping!"

My eyes grew big; I realized there was no point in telling her what I saw outside. There was nothing to be done and it would only sadden her. These sorts of things happened all the time anyway, but still, every time I saw a man die, it felt like the first time.

I carried Luka's sleeping body into bed. He had dozed off at Nonna's and with money tight, meals were scarce, so it was a blessing for him to sleep through dinner. I opened the balcony door and sat down with my legs hanging over the edge between the fence posts.

Faint whistling floated through the wind. I looked at the little pond, illuminated by the moon's glow. It was drying up and empty of life. I hadn't seen a duck land in it in years. I used to skip lunch and save my wheat strips so I could throw them off the balcony, even though I could never throw them far enough to reach the pond. I heard the door unlock and I snapped back to the real world, where ducks and ponds are a thing of the past.

"Hey, you!" Benjin took his coat off and walked over to me. "What are you doing out there all alone?"

"Luka fell asleep at Nonna's and I didn't want to wake him."

"The moon looks beautiful, huh? Shining its light through the dark sky." Benjin wrapped his coat over my shoulders, fitting me like a dress. It was warm and smelt like him. Something about Benjin's smooth and secure voice immediately brought me to tears.

"I saw a man get beat to death by three militants today. I thought he was in a puddle of water, until I realized it was blood. He was so helpless. I was the only one that saw and I hid like a coward- the moon goddess would look down on me."

"Woah, easy there. Eura would never look down on you. There was nothing you could have done, don't blame yourself." He put his arm around me, like a wall protecting me from the world. "If you got involved, you would have only gotten yourself hurt."

"That's the problem, Benji. I hate that there's nothing I can do. There's never anything I can do. I hate feeling so helpless. You always know what to do- I never do." I buried my face in his chest.

"The moon can't take away all the darkness, but she can shine her beautiful light. I know sometimes we feel helpless, but we just have to redirect our energy. We have to be like the moon and shine in the darkness, Nyla. Eura helped you fight by cloaking you in shadows so you could slip away unseen by the militants. She knew it was not your battle to fight." Benjin stood up, and held out his hand to me. "Come on, let's go heat up some dandelion tea."

I laid in bed that night, hugging Luka tightly in my arms. I played with his bouncy brown curls, sticking my fingers through them, until I drifted asleep and dreamt of my family. We were sitting around a beautiful pond, one that I had never seen before. The pond was filled with ducks and lilypads, and there was a giant willow tree towering over us. My father was telling one of his famous jokes that we all heard a hundred times over. We had a picnic of food, all cooked by my mother. We even had fruits: bongamelon, honeydews, and tartar berries. I laid in my mother's lap as she petted my hair. Almost as soon as the dream started, I awoke to the creaking of the front door opening. I slipped out from under Luka and crept out of our room.

"...Benji?" I whispered, my eyes struggling to adjust in the dark. He nearly jumped in surprise. "Where are you going?"

"Don't worry, I just need some fresh air. Go back to sleep," he answered, slipping out the door. I stood in the bedroom doorway for a moment, blankly staring where he once stood, but I was too tired to think, so I turned around and went back to bed, careful to not wake Luka.

# CHAPTER THREE

# THE TRUTH

T HE SUN HAD JUST barely risen over the horizon when I woke up. I rolled out of bed and stumbled into the main room to boil some tea. Our apartment was modest, with two bedrooms, a tiny bathroom, and a main room, where we had little beyond a stone stove and a low table with three cushions around it. The main room led to the front door, and our little balcony sat on the opposite side. It might be small, but it was all we needed... And we barely scraped by to pay the rent every month anyway.

Benjin was sitting on a cushion, reading the paper. We did not get actual newspapers like the northerners did. Instead, a local man named Muri created his own over fifty years ago and continued to make a weekly edition to keep us in the know. Muri was seventy-nine, but his brain was as sharp as a young man's. Without him, our side of the empire would be completely cut off from the rest of the world. He was the glue to our community, connecting us all. He had three sons: two of whom worked in the mill and the third who would steal newspapers from garbage cans in the north. Muri used to gather the newspapers, but he was far too old now, especially considering it often ended in a chase by the militia. Although they tried to prevent Muri's son from gathering news sources, they never interfered with Muri himself.

"Hey, Benjin, why doesn't the militia just stop Muri from writing newspapers if they hate it so much? He's just one old guy- it's not like he could stop them." I sat down on a cushion. Benjin looked up at me,

I could tell he was deeply thinking. He poured some tea into a cup and slid it over to me.

"Muri may just be one old guy, but he is the town's eyes. He shares news with us, making everyone feel connected. Without him and his newspaper, many would lose hope, and I am sure the militia understands that people need hope- we cannot function without it." He picked his newspaper back up and let out a heavy sigh.

"If everyone lost hope, no one would go work in the Upper's factories and clean their side of the empire."

"Now you're getting it." Benjin grinned. "Besides, the militants wouldn't be able to find him, even if they tried."

"How? The militia seems to know everything." I sipped my tea.

"No one knows where Muri lives, not even his sons. Once the militia came, Muri left his family for the greater good. It is said that one of his sons hides coins and the newspapers for him somewhere, then Muri collects it when no one is around. He uses these newspapers to create his own, then leaves a stack for his son to distribute."

"What if they capture his son?"

"Then other people will stand up and replace them."

"Wow, Muri is like the moon... Shining light in darkness," I pondered aloud, as I went to wake Luka. Out of the corner of my eye, I saw Benjin crack a smile.

When Benjin and Luka walked me to work, we passed the now dried puddle of blood on the street. When Luka asked what it was, Benjin told him that a man was so happy that all the love in his body poured out onto the road. Luka paused for a brief moment, then continued skipping ahead and singing a song that only he understood. I wondered who the man was and why he got beaten to death. He was probably just in the wrong place at the wrong time. Benjin put his arm around me and kissed the top of my head.

"Are you ever gonna grow, Nyla?" He laughed. I playfully shoved him, but he didn't even budge.

We got to the factory a few minutes early. It was a beautiful spring day, the warmest one of the year thus far. There were little better feelings than when you finally feel the sun's rays melt against your face after a numbing winter. As we sat and waited, three girls approached us. Or, I should say, they approached Benjin.

"Hi, Benjin. Isn't it a beautiful day out?" The girl asked. He put his hand up to shield the sun and squinted. She was average looking, one of those girls that always happened to be around. I could tell Benjin had no idea who she was.

"Uh, yeah. Beautiful day outside," he said with a polite smile. His gray-blue tunic brought out his eyes. I could tell he had no interest in talking to her, but he was too polite and had no excuse. Fortunately for him, it was already time for us girls to go into the factory. The guards swung open the tall iron fences and waved us in.

"It was nice talking to you, Benjin. See you around!" The girl squealed, as she walked away. Her friends circled back around her and I watched her glance back over her shoulder to see if he was checking her out, but Benjin seemed to already have forgotten her.

"Benji has a girlfriend!" Luka shouted, running in circles and tugging on Benjin's pants.

"Absolutely not, Luka. Don't spread rumors!" He grabbed Luka and threw him up onto his shoulders as if he was as light as a feather.

"Why are you never interested in any of these girls, Benjin?" I asked as I walked up the steps to work.

"When would I have time for a girlfriend? When I am cleaning the streets all day? Or when I am trying to wrangle you two?" He shrugged and walked away, as Luka pulled on his hair and bounced on his shoulders.

I hated that he had to sacrifice his life for us, and I knew he did so much for us, but I didn't believe that we were the reason he had no interest in these girls.

Before the New Plague, Benjin had a girlfriend whose name was Luna. She was raised down the hall from us and always came over to play. My brother had a crush on her since they were small. Luna was a beautiful girl, with long hair so blonde that it was almost white. It contrasted against her dark skin, like stars in a soothing night's sky. No one in Suhai really had light hair, as it was a northern trait, but Luna's parents were immigrants. They moved to our empire from Kosi, which was a small port town on the northwestern outskirts of the Republic of Terlu, once belonging to the Kingdom of Yana. I bet everyone from Kosi was as beautiful as Luna. She had a natural free spirit that always kept Benjin on his toes.

Once news of the plague reached the south, Luna's parents took her and fled without warning anyone. We never found out what happened to them, or whether they made it out before the militia stormed into our side of the empire. All Luna left behind was a letter with a red string tied around it, addressed to Benjin. She wrote that she loved him and asked him to wait for her. Although five years have passed, he still wore the red string around his wrist.

When I left work, Benjin was sitting on the steps. His gaze was fixed down the street, where the setting sun painted the horizon. I wondered what he was thinking. It was his one night off and here he was, chaperoning his little sister home from work. A wave of guilt washed over me. Despite being only nineteen, he looked many years older. He was taller than any adult, towering well over six feet. He had never been lanky either, having filled out his frame since his teenage years. None of the other neighborhood kids, or even the adults, dared to mess with him. Even still, I could not fathom him ever hurting anyone, even if the need arose.

"Hey, Benji!" I shouted as I skipped down the steps. "Where's Luka?"

"He was at Nonna's for the day. We have to pick him up on our way home. Let's go before the sun goes down."

"Did you have a nice day off?"

"Met up with Laago for a bit. We went fishing and caught enough baby willow sharks to last us a week."

We quietly walked down the street, careful not to chat about anything beyond small talk. You never knew when militia was listening, so it was safer to assume they always were. I was boring Benjin with work stories when he covered my mouth and pulled me into an alley. We ducked down in the shadows just as five militants walked down the street. I held my breath.

"Yeah, we got some guy last night. He had that old man's newspaper on him. Such bull."

"Surprised the general allows these people to have newspapers. 'Muri's Hope', ha! I light those papers up whenever I see 'em."

When we picked Luka up, he was already asleep, so Benjin carried him to our apartment and laid him carefully in our bed. He seemed so peaceful, blissfully unaware of the world around him. I dreaded the day he would see the world for what it truly was. Benjin and I sat on the balcony, listening to the gentle whistles that danced in the air and eating sea-salted cookies that Nonna had baked for us.

"Tinshe is growing more dangerous every day. In the past, the militants were stealthy and would only strike at night. When I was walking home from the coast with Laago earlier, we witnessed a militant beat a man in broad daylight- there is no way he survived. We had to take alleys the whole way back." He handed me a cookie. "With me being at work a lot, I think you should quit the factory. The thought of you walking home alone at night makes me sick to my stomach."

"Benjin, I am not a child anymore. I am almost sixteen," I pouted. "Plus, you're barely four years older than me. You don't have to take care of me, I know how to stay safe."

"Nyla, I don't want to fight with you," Benjin pleaded. "We have to stick together. You have to understand, we need to take every precaution to stay safe and avoid conflict."

"I am sick of the militants controlling every aspect of our lives. What's the point of living if we can't actually live?"

"Please, Nyla. We need to be patient and wait."

"Okay, okay. I'm sorry." I leaned against him. The sound of utter defeat in his voice nearly broke my heart, even more than watching that man get beat to death did. "Can I ask you something, Benjin? And please be honest."

"Oh, gods, what?"

"Where do you keep going at night?"

Benjin looked off to the moon. It was the only sense of reliability that we had anymore. No matter what happened on our side of the empire, the sun always set and the moon always rose. I silently pleaded with the moon goddess, Eura, to protect what remained of my family.

"Nyla... I understand why you want to know, but I think it is for the best to keep things how they are," Benjin whispered so quietly, almost as if he didn't even want me to hear him.

It felt like he carried the weight of the world, but he did not need to bear that burden alone. I could help; he just had to let me. I needed an opportunity to show him that I could hold my own. I was no longer the little girl I once was.

"Like you said, Benjin, we need to stick together." I put my hand on his shoulder and locked eyes with him. "I need to know. I deserve to know." He let out a famous Benjin sigh, stood up, and walked inside.

"You coming?" He called over his shoulder. I quickly jumped up, and as I followed him in, he shut the balcony door behind me. "Sit." He pointed to a cushion on the floor.

Benjin crept to the front door and peered out of it to see if any militants were patrolling, before he shut and locked it. He then walked over to the sink and lifted the lever up. Though water flowed from the tap, its only use to him was to cover the hum of our voices. He clasped his hands together and let out another deep sigh, once he finally took a seat across from me.

"Four years ago, the militants raided our city and executed the Protectors-"

"Please not another history lesson that I already know..."

"Well, they never found all of the Protectors."

"What do you mean?" I was always taught that all the Protectors were executed, that none survived.

"General Ahkpi and his militia may be smart, but the Protectors were wise. Throughout history, there was always one Protector who hid from the outside world and lived in secrecy. They knew that to keep the people of Tinshe safe, they needed to keep one of them casted away for life, in case of treason against their lineage," his voice grew in excitement as he spoke. "With the rest of the Protectors executed, an underground resistance group quickly formed. It was founded by revolutionary men and women who knew that Tinshe would never prosper as long as it was occupied by Ahkpi's forces. They took an oath to forever serve the remaining Protector. As time went on, the resistance force grew. Four years have passed and now, there are hundreds of us."

"...Us?" Goosebumps grew down my spine as I feared the words he would say next.

"Yes, us." Benjin looked down, unable to make eye contact. He knew I understood the jeopardy it put our family in. But, as upset as I was, I did not harbor any anger. I put my hand on his.

"Mother and father would be proud."

"I always wanted to tell you, Nyla, I did. But with great knowledge comes a heavy burden. You must not tell a soul," Benjin said.

"Never," I declared. I paused for a moment, there were so many thoughts flooding my head. "I just don't get... if there are hundreds of resistance fighters, how did I not know? How does the militia not know?"

"I am sure they are aware of the strong sense of dissent in our community, even a fool would know. I would even assume they are aware there is a resistance force too, but they would never guess how powerful we are. They think we are weak, broken people. But as our numbers grow, so does our strength."

"So what's the plan? When do we strike?"

"Strike? Don't you know the peaceful ways of the Protectors?" Benjin laughed and leaned back. "No violence unless there is no other option. We do not need more bloodshed. Besides, most of our fighters died in the plague. For now, we quietly grow in numbers, spreading like the plague. We are the invisible army. When the Protector thinks we are ready, we will do as he commands."

"How long could we possibly wait for? Like you said, the militia is getting more aggressive every day."

"Who knows, some wars last a lifetime. It is not my duty to say, I only do what I am told."

The thought of a lifetime of war stung my brain. How could Benjin just accept this? My mind drifted to thoughts of my little brother. I did not want him to only know a world of desolation, I wanted him to see a world of peace, one where he had the opportunity to follow the song of his soul.

"You never really answered my original question. Where do you go at night?"

"You are relentless, aren't you? Just like mother." Benjin smiled. "It is my duty to track the movements of the militants on our street. The resistance has men and women scattered throughout Tinshe documenting their every move. We work in short shifts, most only a few hours long. For the most part, it doesn't change. Like the moon rising and falling every night, the militants stick to their routes."

"What if they catch you?"

"They won't."

The next morning when I awoke, the world looked different. It wasn't as black and white as I remembered it being, but instead full of countless shades of every color imaginable. I always thought people were either fighters or do-nothingers, but now I realize that sometimes doing nothing is fighting.

As I was brushing Luka's hair, there was a knock at the door. I quickly picked him up and hid him in the cabinet. I walked towards the door, avoiding all of the squeaky floorboards, careful to not make a single sound. As I peered out the peephole, a sense of relief flooded my body.

"Hey, Laago," I said as I opened the door. "Benji's at work already."

"Oh, shoot. I always miss him in the morning," he said, walking himself in. He was wearing a gray short-sleeved linen shirt that never seemed to be buttoned all the way up and his only pair of pants, black trousers with a small paint stain on his hip.

"You would have better odds if you came by at night." I lit the stove and put a bowl of dandelion water on it.

"Yeah, yeah. Where's Luka?" As Laago dropped to sit on the cushion, Luka ran out the cupboard with a pot on his head.

"Here I am!" Luka jumped into Laago's lap.

I had always been fond of Laago. He had been around for a long time and always had Benjin's back. Or should I say, Benjin has always had Laago's back. He lived in the apartment's basement and worked as the building's maintenance keeper. I wondered if he knew about the resistance.

"Oof, look at you, big guy. When did you get so strong?" He tousled Luka's hair.

"Hey, I just brushed that!" I went to my room and tossed Laago the brush. "You're fixing it." Laago caught it with one hand and started tearing through Luka's hair.

"Ouch, ouch! Nyla does it gentle!" Luka cried.

"Alright, alright, Luka!" Laago laughed and looked up at me. "How's work? Any new pretty factory girls you want to set me up with?"

Laago and Benjin may be best friends, but their personalities couldn't be any more different. While Benjin only ever dated Luna, Laago's had so many girlfriends that I lost count years ago. He might not be as good looking as Benjin, but he sure knew how to sweet-talk a lady.

"No, Laago. They're all waiting in line for Benjin." I poured myself a cup of tea and sat down.

"Yeah, but once they realize Benjin is a prude, they'll come crawling to good ol' Laago." He swiped my cup of tea and took a sip. His shaggy brown hair rested on his shoulders, which were sculpted from all the manual labor he did for work.

"Benjin's not a prude, he just doesn't like wasting his time on girls that don't matter." I got up and poured myself a new cup.

"I wonder how long it's gonna take him to get over Luna."

"Why are you still here anyway? I have to go to work." I went to my room to pack Luka's things to bring to Nonna's.

"I'll walk with you."

"I can walk myself!" I shouted over my shoulder.

"Boss's orders. You know I don't make the rules," he joked. I stormed back to the table, grabbed the brush, and took Luka off of his lap.

"Did Benjin seriously send you here to be my babysitter?"

"Hey, I thought we were friends, Ny. Either way, it's not a big deal. Let me walk with you," he pleaded.

Over all of the years I had known him, Laago was rarely serious. He sat there with his eyes glued to mine, his brown eyes twinkling in the sunlight that beamed through the balcony door. It was clear he would not take no for an answer.

"Then let's get going, I don't want to be late," I surrendered. Laago took Luka from my hands and threw him on his back, running out the door.

"Come on, Ny, you're making me late!" He mocked, running down the hall with Luka bouncing and giggling on his back. I rolled my eyes and locked the door behind me.

"How do you always have so much energy?" I sighed, chasing them down the stairwell to Nonna's.

"It's all the weird gases that leak in my basement apartment!" He shouted, jumping down the stairs.

"You're crazy."

"Yeah, you are crazy, Laago," Luka squealed.

"I'd rather be crazy than boring!" He smirked, looking back at me. I darted behind him and kicked the back of his knee in, causing him to almost fall over. I kept running, not giving him a chance to strike back. "Let's get her!"

"Charge!" Luka yelled, bouncing on Laago's back. I got to Nonna's door and knocked vigorously, knowing as soon as she opened the door, I was safe.

"Hello?" I heard her soft voice call as she opened the door, causing Laago to stop dead in his tracks. Luka jumped off him and into her arms. "There's my little string bean." She kissed his forehead.

"Hi, Nonna!" Laago reached over for a hug.

"Why, hello there, stranger..." She squeezed him tightly, crushing Luka in the middle. "Long time, no see."

"I know, I'm sorry. Work has been crazy."

"Oh, you... I know you're always off with the ladies." She winked. I rolled my eyes.

"Me? Never... On my time off I go worship the gods in the temples."

"Yeah, right, you know less about the gods and goddesses than a tiger rabbit."

"You kids..."

"Thanks for watching Luka, Nonna. I have to get to work." I gave her a hug and ran down the hall as fast as I could in an attempt to get rid of Laago.

"See you soon, Nonna!" He shouted, chasing after me. Just as I reached the stairs, he grabbed me by my waist and threw me over his shoulders. "Just because I don't believe in the gods doesn't mean I don't know about them."

"Put me down!"

"Or what, Eura's going to come after me?" He ran down the stairs, as I slammed my fists on his back.

"You're such a jerk!"

"Watch your mouth, or you'll have to live out eternity in Urliq," he mocked, before putting me down on the ground. "You know, you should grow a little more if you don't like being carried so much."

I rolled my eyes as dramatically as I could, but as we stepped out of the apartment building, his eyes were distracted by the bright blue sky. It was a beautiful day out, which made it so much harder to be stuck inside a stuffy factory. I thought back to when I used to spend all day outside with my friends, playing games and laughing. Now my days were wasted working or scavenging for food.

"How about that Brisa girl?"

"What about her, Laago?'

"She's cute, right?"

"Too young for you," I said, walking faster.

"What? How old? I'm only twenty! You make me feel like an old man sometimes."

"Seventeen," I snapped. I watched him count on his fingers.

"Eh, that's barely three years- and it was only just my birthday! That's not so bad."

"Either way, all she talks about is Benjin."

"Benjin talks to her?"

"Nope."

"I'll help her forget all about him then!" He playfully pushed me, as I ran up the steps to the factory.

"Later, Laago."

"Yeah, see ya around, kid."

# CHAPTER FOUR

# THE FIGURE IN THE SHADOW

I FINALLY STEPPED OUT of the factory's gate and took my first real breath of the day. All of the workers scurried around me and rushed off to their homes, exhausted from a long day of work. I looked up to the moon and admired how it aligned perfectly with the street as it slowly rose into the dark night's sky, illuminating the road and captivating me. The moon's glow could make even the dirtiest city look beautiful. It felt like she was guiding me home, calling me into her warm arms.

My mind was flooded with thoughts of my father. No matter how tired I felt, I remembered how hard he consistently worked to support our family. He spent his days sweeping Najin and his nights at the mill, but he never complained. Instead, he came home with a smile on his face and a hug for each of his children. Some people assumed that positivity was something you were born with, but it was not. It was something that you had to work for every single day. I had to remind myself how fortunate I was. I had a job, a home, and two loving brothers.

As I continued down the road, something felt off. There wasn't another soul in the streets. How long was I standing there, mesmerized by the moon? Silence consumed the air, not even a gust of wind broke through. I quietly snuck down the main road and headed down the block when I felt the hairs on the back of my neck stand up. I was being watched.

"Hey, you!" I heard a militant howl. "Stop where you are!"

Without hesitation, I dashed down the street as fast as I could. I ran towards the moon, as far as I could away from him. He blew his deafening whistle, signaling to other guards. Why was he bothering me? I hadn't done anything wrong!

As I went to turn the corner, a massive figure emerged and pushed me against the wall. I wanted to scream, I wanted to cry, but he forced his hand on my mouth. I fought with all my might, but he didn't even budge. The militant turned the corner, huffing and wheezing. He was fat, with balding hair.

"You- I told you... To stop running...You disobeyed direct orders."

He raised his lantern to see my face, blinding me with its brightness. But before I could react, the figure who grabbed me threw me onto the ground and lunged at the militant, stabbing him in the chest. He struck him again and again, until the militant fell lifeless onto the cold ground.

"Benj-" I sputtered, but he quickly held his hand up.

Silence. I covered my mouth, I could not believe what I saw. My brother... My innocent, warm brother. He just killed a man.

Benjin dashed over to me and grabbed my arm, his hands trembling. Without uttering a single word, he began to pull me home, practically dragging me along. I was speechless, frozen still. The sound of his knife piercing the man's chest made me feel nauseous. But the mere thought of what could have happened if Benjin had arrived a moment later sent shivers down my spine.

We sat at our table in silence. Luka was deeply asleep in our bedroom, completely unaware of the treason his brother had committed. Our apartment was dark, but through the moon's light I could see Benjin was shaking, his skin coated with wet blood, and splatters staining his shirt. I reached to touch his hand, but I was trembling too. By now, the streets were echoing with commotion and the city's bell tolled. They found the body. Benjin covered his ears with his hands, as if he was trying to block reality.

"Benji... We need to clean you off and figure out a plan." I lit the stove to heat a bowl of water. "You need to take your shirt off, it is covered in..." I shook my head, unable to even say the word.

I treaded wearily into his room and found him a clean shirt and pants. When I came back, he still hadn't moved. He was just sitting there, glowing in the moonlight with an empty stare. I brought the heated bowl of water to the table and grabbed a clean rag. As I slowly lifted his shirt off, I saw a tear fall from his face. It was the first time I had seen Benjin cry since he lost Luna.

"When I got home from work... You weren't here. I thought something happened, so I ran to you, as quickly as I could... But it was too late. He was already chasing you. Had I been there to pick you up from work like I should have..." His voice cracked. He shook his head in disbelief and whispered, "I had no choice. I was not going to lose you too."

"It's okay, Benjin. We are here and we're okay. Let's get you cleaned up." I wrapped my arms around him, stroking his hair like our mother used to, before I began washing the blood off of him. The rag quickly turned as red as bitter wine.

"I'm sorry you had to see that, Nyla. I just wanted to protect you."

"There was no other choice. Had you not been there... I don't know what would have happened. I'm so glad you were there for me." I grabbed him by the shoulders and forced my eyes onto his. "Look at me. You and I both know what happens when the militia stops people, especially girls."

"I know..." Benjin pushed me away. He abruptly stood up and threw a match in the fireplace. "We have to burn these clothes."

"If anyone asks, you picked me up from work and we saw nothing."

I didn't sleep that night and I would bet Benjin didn't either. The sun slowly crept through my dusty window, as I laid there petting Luka's head. I slipped out from under him and crawled out of bed. When I left my room, I noticed Benjin sitting on the balcony whistling a solemn tune.

"Did you sit out here all night?" I asked, but he didn't respond. "Let me boil a bowl of dandelion water." As I brewed the tea, Luka rolled out of bed and ran towards Benjin.

"Benji! Benji! Benji!" Luka squealed. "I thought you had work?"

"Luka, leave him alone!" I shouted, swatting him back, but Benjin looked over his shoulder with a tired smile.

"It's okay. Get over here, Buba." He looked exhausted. I poured a cup of tea and handed it to him.

"Didya take off today so we could play, Benji?"

"No, my shift starts in an hour. I was about to head out, but I figured I would wait up for you kiddos." He kissed the top of Luka's head.

"Are you sure you want to go in today?"

"Why wouldn't I?" He countered with a grin. And just like that, it seemed like everything would be okay. "Besides, I have a short route today. I'll be home before you know it."

Benjin left for work, leaving Luka and me at home. Normally, I spent my off days hunting. Even though I felt physically and mentally drained, if I didn't go, there would be no meat for the week. I had to hurry up and get going, because I was already having a late start. I turned off the stove, saving my dandelion tea for later. The thought of eating made me feel sick anyway.

"Come on, Luka. You're gonna spend the day with Nonna." I gathered some of his things and we headed out the door.

"Nyla?" Luka asked, skipping down the hall. His feet bounced off the cold, gray tiled floor. The walls were painted a musty yellow, stained from years of tenants overcrowding these narrow halls. "Why is it called the New Plague? Was there an Old Plague?"

"General Ahkpi coined that term, because he thought the plague was cleansing the world of its impurities. Kind of like the world was starting over."

"Was mommy an impurity?" He stopped and turned to me.

"No, Luka."

"What about Luchi and Dalia?"

"No." I knelt beside him and put my hands on his small shoulders. "General Ahkpi was wrong to call it the New Plague and the Uppers were wrong to go along with it. If it was up to us Others, maybe it would have been named the Plague of Death." He looked at me for a moment as he processed the words I spoke, before he threw his hands up in fists and began to run down the hallway.

"Plague of Death! Plague of Death!" Luka chanted as we approached Nonna's door.

When the people of Najin officially named it the New Plague, riots broke out across Tinshe. It occurred shortly after General Ahkpi was promoted to his new position of power. He toured the northern half of our empire, parading his hateful opinions. While mothers, brothers, and daughters were dying, he had the audacity to claim the world was 'cleansing' itself. His supporters loved it, it fueled their egos and pushed the world's misfortunes onto us. The Uppers always thought of us as pests, nothing more than the dirt on their shoes, but to call us impurities that the world needed to rid itself from? The plague came from the other side of the world, we did not cause it. We just suffered from it. I took a deep breath, trying to calm myself down, and knocked on Nonna's door. As always, she greeted us with her big smile and another tray of her famous steaming sea-salted cookies.

"Perfect timing! I just pulled the cookies out of the oven. I'm sure little Luka's nose could smell them from his room." She pinched his nose and motioned us to come in. "Is Busy Benjin at work?"

"Yeah, he just headed out." Even simply hearing Benjin's name made me sick.

"Oh, that boy... Always working, just like your father," Nonna said, bouncing Luka on her lap. I rolled my eyes. Benjin is a much better man than my father. He didn't leave us when things got hard.

"Yeah, just like my father," I retorted. Nonna heard the irritation in my voice and reached her hand over to mine.

"I understand the pain you feel of being left behind." She looked around at her empty apartment, the walls coated with fading photos. "It hurts, but try to understand that Daath was not only your father, but he was human too. He loved you kids so much... But the gods gave him more than he could handle. Daath didn't want you to see him fall apart." Nonna paused and squeezed my hand. "Maybe it was for the better that he left when he did, when your memories of him were pure and good."

"Well, we fell apart too, only we didn't have the choice to run away." I pulled my hand away and headed towards the door. "I have to go hunting. Thanks for watching Luka."

As I ran down the stairwell, tears blurred my vision. How could she say such a thing- that my father leaving was for the better? We needed him and he deserted us. He left his infant son fatherless and his other children to pick up the pieces. We had no money, no food, no guidance. I understood his pain and why he felt the desire to leave, but we needed him. I collapsed onto the ground, slamming my fists on the stone floor. How could he just leave? He was supposed to protect us.

"Nyla?" Laago shouted up the stairs as he ran over to me. "What's wrong? Are you hurt?" He fell to the floor beside me and grabbed my hands.

"Let go of me!" I cried. I tried to rip my fists out of his hands, but Laago was too strong.

"Please, calm down, your hands are bleeding. I don't want to attract any attention from the militia. Let me take you to my place and we'll have some tea."

"It isn't fair. It isn't fair!" I wept, surrendering myself. Laago picked me up and I cried into his chest as he carried me down the staircase. My body went limp in his arms; I knew struggling was futile.

When we got to the basement, he gently kicked his door open. Not only did he keep it unlocked, but he rarely even closed it all the way. Laago sat me on his bed and wrapped me in a tattered gray blanket. His room was dark, dusty, and damp. The ceiling was covered in pipes stretching every direction. I thought of how sad it would be, to live alone in this cold and dull basement. He slipped off his black shoes and tossed his jacket on the table. His gray shirt was freshly stained with oil, he must have just gotten off work.

"I know what you're thinking, Ny. This place is fit for an emperor, huh? Well, it's actually a lot better than where I grew up in the northwestern outskirts of Terlu. That place was a real dump!" He laughed, as he rummaged through his cabinet. He pulled out a roll of fabric and motioned for me to come over. My legs shook as I stood up. He put my hands into a pot of water, and gently rubbed the blood off. "Wow, you really beat yourself up. I don't think you broke anything though. Does this hurt?"

"No, I'm fine," I mumbled. The day was wasting away and I hadn't even started hunting. Maybe Benjin was right to think I was no help.

Laago pulled my hands out of the pot and gingerly dried them with a cloth. His hands were rough and calloused over. I sat back down on his bed. It was small and sat pushed against his wall so it could be used as a couch too. He lit his stove and began mixing a bowl of tea.

"I used to be like you; I would keep my emotions in until they erupted. The problem was, I would usually explode on some poor soul who was at the wrong place at the wrong time." He laughed. Laago had a way of speaking so deeply yet simply.

"What made you change?"

"It was after one of those days my pops beat me real bad. That man knew two things: how to drink and how to hit. I guess it's how I learned to fight."

"You've never really spoken about your father."

"Because he never really was one." Laago shrugged. "Well, I ran out of the house, down the street, and kept going until I turned a corner and saw this kid. He kinda looked like me, except he was wearing nice, clean clothes. It made me furious. So I grabbed him and started beating him. Why did he get to have nice clothes and money, while I had to skip meals and get the brains beaten out of me every day? It wasn't fair." He paused for a moment and bit down on his lip. "By the time someone pulled me off the kid, I had beaten his face so hard that you couldn't recognize him. He started crying, asking what he did to deserve it, and I guess that was when I realized I was just as angry at myself as I was at my pops. I was becoming the man I swore I hated. I couldn't even apologize; I just ran."

"Where did you go?"

"I ended up all the way at the Port of Eura before I collapsed. I sat on the water all night. I wanted to change, but I didn't know how. I remember I watched the moon shine over me, pushing and pulling the waves, when I realized... it was that easy."

"What do you mean?"

"The moon doesn't think to push and pull the tides, it just does." He poured tea into two stone cups and sat next to me. "So I left. I continued south, following the only main road there was. I ended up in Tinshe and started a new life. That's when I met Benjin. I'm still a scrapper, I always will be, but now, I'll only hurt someone if they hurt me or someone I love."

"Thanks, Laago."

"Of course, I make the best ginger tea in town."

"No, I mean really. Thank you."

"I know." He blew on his tea. "So, talk to me."

I told him everything, from the rage I felt towards my father, the loneliness I felt from losing everyone, and even to Benjin stabbing the militant. I told him how resentful, miserable, and full of despair I felt. I ranted to Laago for hours, but no matter what words spewed from my mouth, he did not bat an eye. Instead, he respectfully listened, only stepping away to boil fresh water to refill my cup when it emptied.

It felt liberating to finally speak freely to someone, because even around Benjin, I censored myself. It wasn't that I didn't trust him, but rather, I didn't want him to have another thing to worry about. So I always kept my emotions inside, afraid of burdening anyone else with the pain I felt.

When my mouth finally ran dry and I had no more words to say, Laago took a deep breath. He stood up and began to pace, while his fingers rubbed his chin anxiously. He stepped carefully around a pile of dirty clothes that looked to be a permanent fixture in his apartment and swerved out of the way of a dripping pipe above him without conscious thought.

"How sure are you that no one saw what happened that night?"

"It was the middle of the night, pitch black out-"

"But you said it was a full moon, you were following the moon. It could have been light enough for someone to be able to recognize you," he countered. "I don't want to needlessly worry you, but this empire is full of people, someone had to have seen. It's not safe here anymore- it's only a matter of time before the militia finds out. Where's Benjin?"

"He's at work, but he should be coming home soon," I said, my panic rising. "Where would we go? We can't just leave!"

"Leave what? There's nothing to leave! There's nothing for us here, just memories we are clinging to. There's a whole world out there, Ny."

"But Benjin and I both have work, you know how rare that is. What about Nonna? We can't just leave her... And my studies-"

"Your studies aren't going to help you if the militia executes you. And Nonna would want you to do whatever it takes to survive."

"I don't know..." My heart was pounding and I couldn't think straight.

"You're being naive! The militia will not stop searching until they find out who was responsible for the murder. I will not let your innocence get you all killed. Not every problem just disappears when you ignore it," he argued. Though his words were brutal, they were honest. Laago grabbed my hand and began to pull me out of his apartment.

"This isn't happening," I whispered to myself.

The plague had taken everything from me. My mother, my father, my sisters... Now it was robbing me of my home too, the only physical connection I had left to those whom I lost. It all must be some messed up nightmare, leaving me shaking in my bed. Soon enough, Benjin would wake me and bring me back to reality.

"We will make it through this, we have been through worse."

He tried to encourage me, but I felt hopeless. Laago had no reason to be involved in this, he should stay far away from the mess Benjin and I created. Dark thoughts began to consume my mind, nearly drowning out any glimmer of light. Though somewhere, deep down, I still knew that I could not give up. I couldn't do that to Benjin and Luka.

I followed Laago up the stairwell to Nonna's, but once we reached the first floor, I looked down the hallway and saw two militants knocking on doors. Laago grabbed my hand and dragged me the rest of the way to Nonna's apartment.

"Where's Luka? We need to go!"

"He's in my bed, taking a nap. Is something wrong, princess?" Nonna asked, hurrying to her feet.

"The militants are knocking on doors, they might be looking for Benjin. We need to leave the empire immediately," I whispered. Without asking a single question, Nonna shuffled into her room and woke Luka.

"Wait just a moment. Let me gather some things for you children to take." As she spoke there was a loud bang on the door. We all froze. Nonna hastily motioned us towards the bathroom. There was another set of bangs. "Just a minute now... Give an old lady a moment to get on her feet," she innocently shouted.

Laago, Luka, and I hid in the bathroom. I covered Luka's mouth as Nonna opened the door. Though I couldn't see, I heard the voices of two militants.

"Looking for a Benjin, no last name noted. Believed to be 6'7, black hair, blue eyes. Records show he lives in this building."

"My goodness... Benjin... That sounds familiar." Nonna paused. "Oh, yes! Benjin. Charming boy, I believe he moved across the street, above the mungbean stand... He didn't do anything wrong, did he?"

"Classified. Carry on." The militants left as quickly as they came.

As soon as we heard Nonna shut and lock the door we came out of the bathroom. She grabbed the bag she was packing and filled it with a few more things.

"That should buy you some time."

"Nonna, you lied. They're going to come back for you once they realize. You have to come with us."

"I have lived my life, Nyla. I have done what I wanted to do. The last thing there is for me to do is to protect you kids. Here, take this bag and go! It won't get you far, but it is all I have. Don't worry about Nonna, I will be fine." She gave me and Luka a hug. "I love you kids like my own. Now go, time is short."

"All clear!" Laago whispered as he peaked his head out the door. We all dashed up the stairs, headed towards our apartment. We barged through the door, out of breath and frantic. Benjin dropped his cup of tea and jumped up from the cushion.

"They know." He immediately realized.

"We need to leave now!" I ran into my room to gather some things for Luka and myself.

"Laago, you shouldn't get involved," Benjin urged. "You should go back to your apartment and forget about all of this."

"There is nothing for me here. You guys are the only kin I have. Besides, I am the only one here who has ever been outside Suhai. I can navigate us to the Republic of Terlu; we should be safe there." His voice was stern and unwavering. Benjin knew Laago meant what he said, and there was no use in arguing with someone as stubborn as he was.

"Okay, then we leave in five." He dumped his work bag out and began filling it with necessities.

"Meet me outside my apartment. I have to get something." Laago ran out the door as quickly as we came.

"What's going on?" Luka cried.

I grabbed the only painting of my family and put it in my bag. It was the size of a small book cover, made shortly after Luka's birth. He sat swaddled in blankets in my mother's arms. My father's smile stretched across his face, his eyes barely open. Happiness was radiating from him, and even now, I felt his warmth.

Nonna gave us enough dried wheat strips and sea-salted cookies to last us a week. Not only that, but she gave us a bag of coins as well. I threw an extra pair of clothes and some of Luka's belongings into my bag and ran into the main room.

I stared out the balcony, into the darkening sky looming over the empire. The air was still, as the whistling that always chimed through Tinshe bellowed. It sounded much louder than usual. My hunting bow! I ran to my room and grabbed that too- we had to be ready for anything. I only had ten arrows, but it was better than nothing.

"Alright, let's go!" Benjin ordered. As he flew out the door carrying Luka, I looked back at our home with a heavy heart.

"Goodbye, everyone. Maybe I'll see you at the next duck pond," I whispered as we ran out the door.

Nonna's distraction worked. As we ran downstairs to Laago's apartment, we didn't pass a single militant. Nevertheless, we had to be cautious. Not only did we have to hide from the militants, but we had to hide from everyone. If someone saw us, they would have to report it. Otherwise, they could lose their life. I wouldn't want to put that decision on anyone's conscience. Once we reached the basement, Benjin knocked twice gently on Laago's door. Without a moment's hesitation, Laago stormed out.

"Let's go."

"What did you have to get?" Benjin asked.

"Just a few toys." Laago pulled out an axe and tossed it to Benjin. "And two daggers for me." Benjin smiled. The boys hid their weapons under their clothes, as there was no need to attract any unwanted attention.

All Laago brought beyond the weapons was an extra shirt. It was nearly identical to the linen one he wore, only it was somehow even more worn-down. Both were provided to him by his boss as work shirts, because he was famous for walking around without one if it was laundry day. The old ladies of the apartment loved it, but the landlord did not.

Laago was never known to be materialistic, and even if he was, he would have no money to indulge the urge with. All that he earned went towards rent and food, everything else he had was owned by his boss, even the bowls he ate from.

He shoved the shirt into Benjin's bag without asking and we crept out the building, following my brother's lead. Since the sun had already set, the streets were clear of people, but the militia were always lurking. If we treaded carefully and stayed in the shadows, we could potentially make it undetected.

"Follow me. I know where the militia is stationed on the next two streets from my work with the resistance. Laago knows the route the next few after that, so he'll take charge then and bring us north towards Terlu," Benjin ordered. Laago nodded in agreement. I couldn't help but grin, because it confirmed my suspicion that he was a part of the resistance too.

We all ran down the street, as silently as possible. To escape the Suhai Empire, we would have to travel to the Port of Eura, which was the northeasternmost point of the empire. Once we made it past there, we would be within the outskirts of the Republic of Terlu and safe from the militia's grasp. Though to get there, it would be at least a ten day journey. For us to run that far without being caught would be close to impossible. We needed a plan.

We continued running through the streets until sunrise, with Laago leading us most of the way. Though our path intersected with some militia, we were careful enough to avoid detection. I wondered why there were less militia patrolling than usual, especially after one of their men got killed, but I was too delirious to question it.

As daylight broke through, we needed to find a place to hide. My legs began to give out, but I had no choice but to keep moving forward. I watched Luka's little body bouncing against Benjin's chest as he ran. He had carried him nearly the entire way, without complaint. Laago motioned us to veer down an unlit alley. We huddled against the wall.

"There's probably half as many militia out there as usual. I wonder where they all are?" Benjin whispered.

"Who cares? The less the better. If we can find a member of the resistance, we can find a place to stay," Laago sputtered between breaths.

"How would we do that?" I asked, eating a dried wheat strip.

"It's easy, if you know how to look." Benjin held his hand up to us, asking for silence. After taking a deep breath, he began to whistle a tune to an old Tinshe folk song.

'A garden once bloomed so lush,
All the townspeople came.
They danced in thrill
Until the rain began to drop.'

When he finished the melody, he fell quiet. We listened to the wind roar through the buildings. The empire felt eerily still for a moment, until a faint whistle began to ring. I looked up in awe. For years, I had heard beautiful whistling float through the wind throughout the night and thought nothing of it. Goosebumps grew down my body as I learned it was the resistance communicating. Benjin whistled the tune once more and suddenly, a choir of whistles flowed through the air, dancing in the sky around us. I looked at Benjin, speechless.

"Beautiful, isn't it?" He laughed.

I felt warm tears begin to flow down my face. All of these years, I thought we were alone... For the first time in a while, I felt hope. Each of the whistles represented someone, no different than Benjin or me, who was determined to not surrender to General Ahkpi and his militia. A beautiful whistle began to glide down the alley, calling for us. I looked to Benjin, whose eyes were already scanning the buildings in front of us.

"Let's follow it!" Laago insisted.

Benjin tossed Luka into my arms. We all scurried down the narrow alley, following the whistle. About halfway down, a door crept opened.

"Here!" A mysterious voice commanded.

I looked at Benjin, who moved his hand towards his axe. Laago was quick to follow suit. They nodded to each other, silently agreeing that we would trust this mysterious person. Benjin entered through the door of the dingy building first, with Laago following closely behind. The door opened into an unlit hallway. We plodded through, silently and cautiously, with Benjin leading the way.

"Show yourself!" Benjin demanded, his voice firm and intimidating.

"An axe, two daggers, and a bow. I see great unrest engulfing your auras. Fear not," the voice loomed over us. I clenched Luka tightly.

"This is it... It's a dead end!" Benjin shouted, pounding at the cement wall.

"No, it can't be," Laago stammered. He knelt down, running his hands along the wall. "Get behind me, Benjin."

"Do you think there's a door?"

"The voice has to be coming from somewhere." Laago continued knocking on the wall. "Here! This wall is hollow. Give me your axe." As the words hissed from Laago's mouth, the voice laughed. Even with our weapons, I felt defenseless.

"Smart boy!"

A wall began to rise behind me, blocking us from leaving. But before we could react, the wall in front of us began to fall. Suddenly, light poured through. We all stumbled through, shielding our eyes from the blinding lights.

"Drop your weapons, they have no use here," a voice commanded. I squinted, trying to adjust my eyes.

"Not until I know we are safe," Benjin demanded. I was slowly able to make out figures around us. We were outnumbered. Luka began to cry.

"They're just kids, it's okay," one of the voices called. I hid behind Benjin and Laago, shielding Luka.

"Why did you whistle that tune, boy?"

"We need help!" Benjin shouted.

"From who?"

"The militia," Benjin honestly replied. I held my breath, but to my surprise, the bright lights flashed off and my eyes were finally able to adjust to the room around me.

As the light faded, I realized we were in an apartment. It was laid out similar to ours, but a bit nicer. It had a main room with walls covered in faded yellow paint, a bedroom and a cramped bathroom off to the side. There were five people in the room with us. Three men, two women.

"Take a seat," one of the men said. He had sloppy brown hair that fell in front of his unshaven face, but a warm toothy smile. His tunic was stained and ripped.

"Who are you?" Benjin asked firmly, not budging.

"My name is Bao. We are the resistance."

## CHAPTER FIVE

# THE LIGHT IN THE TUNNEL

W E TOOK A SEAT on the floor around the low table. Behind us, four of the resistance fighters were playing cards and joking, not seeming to have a care in the world. They looked like Others, dirty and poor. How were these shoeless slobs the resistance?

"Here's some tea." Bao handed me a stone cup as I sat down on a cushion next to me. Honey scented steam slowly rose from the cup and filled my lungs. "Why are you kids running from the militia?" He questioned, blowing on his tea.

"Two nights ago, Nyla was walking home from work when a member of the militia stopped her. He chased her down a few blocks before I found her. I grabbed her and we tried to hide, but I was too slow, he already saw us. Before his backup arrived, I stabbed him," Benjin confessed. The room went quiet.

"Don't say anymore." Bao's eyes widened. "Follow me." He abruptly stood up and motioned us over to the bathroom. He squatted down, grabbing the bottom of the bath and lifted it up, revealing a staircase. "This way."

We followed Bao down a neatly packed-in dirt staircase, as the bath closed back down behind us, shutting us from the apartment. He lit a torch, the only light source in the darkness as we stepped underground. The air was cold and musty.

"These tunnels connect the whole empire, from the most north-western tip of Najin to the southern point of Tinshe."

"Wow... Who built these?"

"The resistance began building these four years ago. They were created as a pathway for us to steal medicine from Najin and transport it to the sick people of Tinshe. At first, it was one single path, but now, there are hundreds of miles of tunnels, all intersecting each other. Most of them lead to dead ends. This way, even if the militia accesses them, they will be lost forever. The only people who can survive down here must know every twist and turn."

"Is there a map?"

"No." He shook his head. "A map could fall into the wrong hands, but a memory cannot."

"This is brilliant!" Laago exclaimed.

"Ah, it is," Bao said. "When men unite their minds, they can forge wonders of beauty. However, more often than not, they opt for destruction over creation."

We spent an hour following Bao, traveling through what felt like an endless maze. The tunnel was tight, making me feel claustrophobic. I couldn't imagine how someone as tall as Benjin must have felt; he had to awkwardly crouch to not bump his head. My hands grew numb from the cold and my boots were damp- the wet dirt floor was scattered with puddles. Every time I tried to step around one, my foot would inevitably stomp in another.

"How did you become a part of this, Bao?" Benjin inquired.

"I served in Suhai's army, before the New Plague, back when it actually meant something. Once empty-headed Emperor Nahkon legitimized Najin's treasonous militia, I left."

"Isn't it punishable by death to leave the army without permission?"

"Smart girl. A lot of the resistance is made up of men and women who left the Empire's army once the militia was officially established.

No one wanted to answer to those tyrants. And, if you ask me, Emperor Nahkon is just their puppet. He doesn't even leave his palace anymore."

"That's very noble of you," Laago admired him.

"Never thought of living in dirt as noble." Bao chuckled. His face had wrinkles left behind from years of smiling. "I am taking you to someone very important. I think you kids are exactly what we were looking for." I wondered how a bunch of wanted kids could possibly help the resistance, but I kept my mouth shut and followed Bao through the endless labyrinth of tunnels.

"Here!" Bao declared.

"It's just another dead end..." Laago said.

"Ah! Another dead end or another beginning?" Bao whistled, mimicking the chirp of a city frog. There was a whistle back, from the other side. The wall began to fall.

We walked into a large open room. Its walls were made of native stone slabs, pushed into the dirt and haphazardly cemented together. Candles were lined up against the perimeter, their tiny flames providing the only light beyond Bao's torch. There were inscriptions carved all over the walls, ceiling, and floor, engulfing the room in neat columns. It was of a different language, one I have never seen.

"These kids claim they killed a member of Ahkpi's militia," Bao casually explained.

"Ah, these aren't children, they are young warriors," a voice echoed, it was the same one we heard in the alley and the hallway. A frail older man with dark leathery skin was sitting in the middle of the room. He wore a deep red robe with no shoes. "Welcome, I have been waiting for you all." He motioned for us to join him, swaying his trembling hand. Bao disappeared back into the tunnels, leaving us alone with this mysterious man.

"Who are you?" Laago asked, as we gathered around him on the cold dirt floor.

"Who am I?" The old man contemplated, stroking his long white beard. He paused between each word he spoke. "Who are you?" He turned his head and looked into my eyes.

"I... I don't know."

"You will know soon enough, my child." He paused, before turning his gaze to Benjin, who kneeled directly in front of him. "You will all endure great hardship, suffering, and loss..." His eyes locked with Laago's. "But once you are through, you will be better men and women." The man glanced back at me, his eyes smiling. He felt welcoming and warm. I looked over to Benjin, who was staring deeply at the man, studying him. I wondered what he was thinking.

"That's a long beard," Luka said, reaching out to touch it. I smacked his hand down, but the man laughed.

"Wait! I know who you are," Benjin declared, jumping to his feet.

"My name is Amu, the one they claim to be the last Protector," the old man revealed. Benjin dropped back down, bowing before him. "Please, my child. I am no god." He reached his hand out, putting it under Benjin's chin and raised his head. "There is great strength within you. You are strong, like your father."

"You knew my father?" Benjin stammered.

"He was a founding member of the resistance. I sent Daath to the Island of Aara shortly after Ahkpi's treachery unfolded. Even a fool could discern that the militia was not sent to help but to conquer. Every message we attempted to send to the Civil Council was intercepted and blocked by the militia. Daath was tasked with personally delivering an urgent message to the Council of Five, warning them of the atrocities that brewed. With the remaining Protectors already executed, he was our only hope, but Daath never reached his destination. Thus, the people of Tinshe never received aid from the Civil Council."

"What happened to him?" Benjin asked.

"It is beyond even me." Amu shook his head, his face twisting with grief. "One day, I stopped sensing his energy."

"Your father didn't give up hope, he was the hope!" Laago cheered, his voice bubbling with excitement, but Benjin fell silent for a moment. I looked into his eyes as he processed this.

"I should feel better, knowing this. I have learned my father was a hero." His head fell like a weight into his hands. "But it pains me even more now to not know where he is or what happened to him."

"Just because Amu stopped sensing his energy, doesn't mean he is dead, Benji. Our father is strong. If anyone is out there fighting, it's him," I said. "We can't give up hope."

"The girl is right. It is time for you to stop searching elsewhere for light and to create it within yourselves. This is the purest form of hope and it will take you much farther than any other form could."

"But how? We are powerless. We have nothing, not even a home to call our own." Benjin sighed.

"Ah, these are lies you tell yourself. Look at me, boy. I am old, barefoot, and free of any material possessions. Yet, I am the richest man in the Suhai Empire. My wealth may not be gold or silk, but it is something even more valuable." He pointed to his head and tapped his temple. "This is something that even the strongest army in the world cannot steal."

"If I may ask..." Benjin pondered aloud. "Why are you here, of all places?"

"Our paths did not cross accidentally. When the last Koba moon occurred, where both the moon and the spirits of our world were closest to us, I received a message from the moon goddess herself. Eura answered my prayers and led me to this very spot. I knew then that it was my destiny to wait here for her to bring me what the people of Tinshe needed," Amu said. "She brought me you."

"Why us?" Benjin pried.

"I am not the keeper of that truth, I am a mere holder of it. The duty bestowed upon me is only to guide you towards your destiny. In due time, the rest will fall into place," he assured us. "You are the ones chosen to deliver a message to the Council of Five."

"How will we get there?" Laago asked.

"When you are ready, you will know. But in the meantime, you must begin training immediately."

"Laago and I know how to fight."

"Fight, perhaps, but to survive this journey it will take much more. You may have noticed the streets have been filled with less members of the militia. My spies have uncovered Ahkpi's plan. The militia is moving troops northeast to invade the Republic of Terlu in thirty days, when the moon is hidden from the sky. You must warn General Pago, the leader of the republic's forces. You will then continue east to the Island of Aara to inform the Council of Five. You will leave here in six days, once your training with Bao is complete. He is our highest regarded warrior. Bao!" His voice raised to an abrupt shout and Bao was quick to re-emerge from the tunnels.

"This way!"

I reached my hand out for Luka to hold. I felt uneasy bringing him around for all of this. How could I be sure we would be able to protect him? If anything, Luka would be a liability. He was only six, he couldn't fight. He could barely spell his name.

"How do you navigate through all these tunnels?" Laago asked in astonishment.

"To you, it may seem like an endless maze of paths, but to us, we are traveling through the veins of the Earth. She will keep those who are pure at heart safe, while those who are filled with evil will disappear forever." Bao dragged his hand affectionately along the wall of the tunnel, his fingers dancing along a crack in the tightly packed dirt.

We followed Bao for many hours. It felt like days had gone by, because there was no concept of time underground. I slowly trudged behind Laago, practically dragging Luka. The only escape that I could find to distract me from my aching feet were thoughts of my past. Memories of my two sisters flooded my mind.

Luchi passed when she was eight from the plague, with Dalia following her shortly after, who was only five. She was inseparable from my father, always clinging to his side or sitting on his shoulders. While he was at work, she sat on the balcony stalking the streets for him. As soon as he turned the corner onto our road and was within her vision, her tiny body would jump up and she would babble for the whole neighborhood to hear. Dalia would have been ten years old now. She would be proud to hear the sacrifice our father made for the people of Tinshe. She always viewed him as a part god and truly believed he could do no wrong. At five years old maybe, she knew more than me.

Luchi was a beautiful girl with straight black hair. She was deeply spiritual for an eight-year-old, something I never really understood. She was stubborn too. Ever since she was young, she refused to eat meat. Once, she hid my bow so I could not hunt. I remember I tore through the apartment, screaming that she did not understand we had to eat, there were no other choices. I called her naive and innocent, saying she could starve if she wanted to. I tried to remember pleasant memories instead, but none came to mind.

After following Bao for what felt like an eternity, the tunnel began to widen, until it opened completely. My jaw dropped as we walked through, as the tunnel led us to an enormous underground forest. There were lush green trees for as far as my eyes could see. I finally was able to feel the cold crunch of grass beneath my feet, replacing the miserable sloshing of mud. Emerald green moss rose from the base of the thick cedar pine trees and up the branches, covering some of them completely. Thick vines draped over, some hanging onto the branches by a thread, others securely fastened on, appearing to have been sitting in place for a lifetime.

There was no natural light this far underground, but there were brass lanterns carefully placed throughout, illuminating the forest's beauty. Some hung off branches and others rested on the ground, lined along a gentle stream that flowed by. Their light twinkled in the water as it gently glided downstream.

I looked over to Bao, who seemed to find our speechlessness entertaining. His face was covered with a wide smile, so genuine and pure. Even Luka was silent. Benjin stood over me with his hand covering his mouth. His ocean blue eyes glimmered from Bao's torch as they flickered around in awe at the beauty surrounding us.

"This is the Forest of Earth. We discovered it when we began building these tunnels. It spans throughout the center of the Suhai Empire, from Tinshe to Najin. The animals that live here have remained untouched from mankind, living separately underground since the beginning of time."

"It's incredible..." Benjin stammered.

"Put your hand here," Bao said, placing his hand against the bark of a mossy pine tree. "Feel the energy that radiates through this tree and into you. We are all connected, from this tree to the grass, and even the dirt, the birds, and us. By understanding this, we can harness the energy that flows through the Earth and use it, just as the trees do. There may be no natural light here, yet these trees grow. They are able to sift through the energy radiating out of the Earth and channel it through their roots to their leaves. We are no different, we possess the same power." Bao bent his knees and raised his arms, creating a firm fighting stance. "You, try to knock me," he ordered Laago.

Laago jokingly looked behind him, as if Bao was calling to some other person. He then looked at me and shrugged, before stretching his arms. He lowered his stance, charging at Bao. He pulled his arm back and shot it forward, directing his blow at Bao's face, but just as his fist flew inches from his target, Bao shifted ever so slightly, leaving Laago to tumble over.

"No single hit should use too much energy, otherwise you leave yourself vulnerable. Do not underestimate your opponent. Rise and try again," Bao commanded. His demeanor had completely shifted from earlier. His eyes glared at Laago with a serious intensity.

Laago rose to his feet, wiping dirt off his face. He widened his stance and began to circle Bao, who stood there unfazed. Laago stepped forward, but before he could raise his hand to throw a punch, Bao extended his arm out, jabbing Laago in the chest and sending him tumbling onto the ground.

"It is not how hard you hit, but how you hit. By hitting a man like so, you can knock the wind out of him, without causing permanent damage. Rise and try again," Bao said.

Laago stumbled to his feet, still clenching his chest and wheezing. He stood hunched over with his hands on his knees before he cracked his back and was ready to try again. I could see in his eyes that he was becoming frustrated, but his sheer determination overruled it. He found his stance and lunged at Bao. This time, he sent a left jab forward, before winding back to administer a strong right hook. Bao crouched down, grabbing Laago's body and swiping his legs out from under him in one slick move. He fell onto his back, shaking the ground beneath him. My hand covered my mouth as I gasped; there was no way he could get back up after that.

"You are thinking too much, which gives your opponent time to predict your every move. Free your mind and try again." Bao stood firmly in place, his eyes focused on Laago. To my surprise, Laago got up without hesitation, with sweat dripping down his body and dirt on his hands. "Do not allow your frustration to consume you. Let it flow in and out of your body like the air you breathe."

Laago closed his eyes and exhaled. He swiftly lunged forward, ducking and turning behind Bao, giving him the ability to put Bao in a chokehold.

"Good work. Next time I won't let you off as easy!" Bao shouted as he harshly jabbed his elbow to Laago's stomach, freeing himself.

"I did it!" Laago exclaimed, trying to catch his breath. "I could puke right now, but I did it." He dropped to the ground next to me, clenching his chest.

"Don't celebrate yet, Laago." He motioned to Benjin, who immediately rose to his feet as commanded, sinking into a strong stance. "Connect your body to the Earth you stand on," Bao declared. Benjin inhaled, eyeing him down.

"Go, Benji!" Luka jabbered. I watched Benjin as he slowly circled Bao, like a golden eagle stalking its prey. A single droplet of sweat dripped down his face. He thrust forward and spun around Bao, who quickly turned to face him. A flock of birds flew away, abandoning the tree they were resting in.

"You move quickly and quietly. Good," Bao said, but Benjin didn't break concentration. He took a step back, smoothly slid to the side, and leapt towards Bao before he could readjust. With a swift motion, he aimed his fist directly at Bao's chest, yet refrained from making contact.

"Got you!" Benjin smiled.

"Or, do I have you?" Bao countered, grabbing Benjin's arm and twisting it behind his back in one fluent movement. "Every moment is an opportunity to strike. Try again."

Benjin and Bao sparred for hours as Laago, Luka and I sat there watching. They fought with great ferocity, shaking the Earth around them with every move. Sweat dripped down both of their backs.

Benjin's hair struck to his forehead, his shirt damp. Their feet crushed the lush grass beneath them, flattening it out.

"Benjin is a better fighter than I ever knew. Look at him go, he's keeping Bao on his toes!" Laago admired, his eyes following Benjin dance around the forest, evading and advancing on Bao.

"Yeah, he's a natural." I laid on my back and sighed. "A natural at everything."

"I bet you're a good fighter too, Ny," Laago said, elbowing me in the arm.

"All hundred pounds of me."

"I wouldn't doubt it and you shouldn't either."

I ignored Laago and continued watching Benjin. Amu wasn't waiting for me all these months. He was waiting for Benjin and Laago, true fighters. I was just dead weight, like Luka. Watching Benjin's sheer power sparring with Bao filled me with more jealousy than it did pride. His abnormally tall height gave him an advantage against anyone who had the audacity to get in his way. I was over a full foot shorter than him and half his weight.

"I am impressed with your abilities, Benjin. That is all for today. Nyla, stand up."

"Thank you, Bao." Benjin dropped his arms and relaxed his body. He walked over to us and high fived Laago before dropping to the ground.

"I'm beat," he admitted. "Go get 'em, Nyla."

"I don't think I can fight you..." I mumbled as I slowly rose to my feet.

"And why is that?"

"Because I am small and weak."

"Small, perhaps, but not weak. You must learn your strengths and weaknesses. If you accept and adapt to your shortcomings, no one can use them against you."

Bao spoke so simply, but his words shot into me like a dagger. I looked over to Laago, who was laying in the grass, smiling at me. If he believed in me, why couldn't I too?

"I... I may be small, but I am quick."

"There! Use your size to your advantage. I see you have a bow with you. I will train you to be able to shoot a golden eagle from the sky n one shot. But what if the militia is close? You must be prepared to defend yourself. A member of the militia may look at you and put his guard down, thinking you are nothing to fear. Use that to your advantage."

I found my stance, digging my feet into the Earth. As I inhaled, I thought of all the roots that spanned the Earth, connecting us. As I exhaled, I felt a surge of energy that bellowed from the ground and through my body. I dashed towards Bao, leaped over him, and spun around onto his back, wrapping my arms around his neck.

"That was incredible, Nyla!" Benjin stammered. Laago jumped up and cheered, as I slid off of Bao's back, landing on my feet.

"You used your size to your advantage." He turned to face me. "When Laago put me in a chokehold, his body was too big and bulky, leaving him vulnerable. You are small, so I could not strike you once you were on my back. I hope now you see the great strength that surges through you too."

"You were just going easy on me," I said with a smile too big to hide.

"Perhaps," he said with a wink. "Though it does not diminish your success."

"Me next!" Luka shouted from the sidelines. Bao gestured to him to come over.

"You are done for the night, Nyla. Now it will be Luka's turn." Luka skipped over to Bao, giddy with excitement.

"Will you teach me to fight?" He asked, throwing his best punches into the air. Bao smiled and sat down, crossing his legs.

"I will teach you how to protect yourself and your kin."

"I can't protect Benjin! I am too tiny, tinier than Nyla!" Luka dropped onto his butt, sitting in front of Bao.

"You may be little physically, but mentally, you are as big as any of us."

"Mentally?"

"Yes, mentally." Bao tapped his temple twice. "Look around you. The Forest of Earth is filled with animals, some so small you wouldn't even notice them. It doesn't mean they are weak, it just means they utilize different strengths than someone big like Benjin. That's how Nyla was able to successfully fight me."

Luka looked up around him in awe. His little mouth hung agape at the wondrous forest around him. I was so impressed that at six years old he was able to understand the significance of Bao's words. He sat before a true master, a man who trained alongside the last Protector. I never felt so proud to call him my brother.

"Just by taking care of yourself and being an extra set of eyes and ears on the road, you will help more than you will ever know," Bao explained.

"So Benji can't carry me?"

"Every now and again we all need a little support from others. But maybe, instead of him always carrying you, you can start by having him carry you less. Then as time goes on, you will become stronger. A day will dawn where you won't need him to carry you at all."

"Maybe one day I will be stronger than Benji!"

"I think if you train hard enough, one day you will be. Most kids your age are sheltered from this world. Instead, you are willingly walking into the crossfire. By the time you are Benjin's age, think of all the lessons you will have learnt, ideas you will create, and the light that you will shed."

We slept that night huddled on the cold forest floor. With no sunlight, the temperature dipped well below freezing. Luka and I slept nuzzled between Laago and Benjin to stay warm. I don't know when I awoke or if I even really fell asleep, because constant darkness made it impossible to get my bearings. Laying there nuzzled between Benjin and Luka reminded me of when we were younger, when all of my siblings slept in the same cozy bed. So much had changed since then. Just as I began to drift back to sleep, Bao woke us up to start training.

"You kids look like you slept well," he said with a grin.

"I don't think I have ever been so sore." Laago sighed, as he sat up to stretch.

"Yesterday was just a warm up. Wait and see how you feel tomorrow." Bao laughed. "Well, come on now, we have no time to waste."

Everyone reluctantly rose to their feet, including Luka, who may have just been sleepwalking. We followed Bao through the underground forest. The grass was crunchy beneath my boots, covered in a morning dew. Everywhere around us was flooded with life, the lively forest was bursting at its seams. At first glance, an overwhelming deep green blanketed my view. Perhaps some people wouldn't even take a moment to look closer, but the forest was far more than just trees and greenery.

I crouched down and my eyes got lost on the forest floor. Small fungi and flowers sprouted up under thick fern bushes. A vibrant orange mushroom speckled with pink flakes caught my attention. When I pushed back a fern leaf to get a better look, a black mole squirrel darted out. Shocked, I fell back on my butt. When I examined the mushroom, I noticed tiny chunks missing from it. I think I may have interrupted the little critter from his breakfast. I jumped onto my feet and ran ahead to the boys, not wanting to get lost in this dense forest.

"From now on, every morning we train physically. During the afternoons, I will train your minds. Every evening, we train with weapons," Bao ordered.

"Sounds simple enough..." Laago nervously laughed.

We traveled through the lush forest, stepping over vines and walking through puddles. I carried Luka in my arms as he cuddled into my chest. He was getting too big to carry, he had been growing like a weed lately. I watched the birds fly from branch to branch, their squeaky chirps echoing through the trees.

"Here!" Bao decided. "This is where we will train." It was a large clearing in the midst of the trees, surrounded on one side by a small stream. "Benjin, you first."

The next couple of hours flew by. We rotated every set, with each of us collapsing to the ground in exhaustion the moment Bao was done with us. In just one day, Benjin and Laago had made significant progress as fighters. Benjin moved like the wind, dodging Bao with ease and striking with great ferocity. Laago hit Bao with such powerful intensity that I was shocked he didn't injure Bao, let alone break his own hand. Watching them move was captivating, but it was clear they still had a lot to learn.

Bao then brought us over to the stream and ordered us to sit alongside it. It was a small, clear runoff flowing from a much larger creek. The water glimmered from the lanterns' light. He sat at the other side of the water in his tattered clothes, breathing deeply. His chest raised and lowered with every breath. He picked up a rock and placed it in the stream.

"Watch the water as it flows. Even when something attempts to block its path, the water still finds a way around- smoothly, devoid of thought or hesitation. When you leave here, many men will try to stand in your way. It is up to you to move like water, free and without hesitation." Bao placed another rock in the stream. "I want you to close your eyes and become one with the water that flows before you. Allow your body and mind flow into one, seeping into the Earth around you." His words carried both weight and lightness, closeness and distance.

Even Luka closed his eyes, to truly soak in Bao's words. We all sat there in silence, listening to the stream flow, but I could not focus. My mind was overwhelmed with thoughts. I wondered if Benjin felt like he was flowing into the Earth. I just felt hungry and cold.

"Breathe in, then exhale and let your cluttered thoughts drift out with every breath. There is no need for them," Bao advised. It was almost like he could read my mind.

I tried to focus on my breathing. I inhaled slowly and thought about my mother. She would've hated meditating, she could never sit still. I exhaled. I wondered if my father went through the same training when he met Amu. I inhaled.

"Can we eat?" Luka interrupted. I opened my eyes, but Bao sat there and ignored Luka's plea.

"Yes," Bao replied, hours later. He stood up and motioned for us to follow him. Benjin scooped up Luka, who fell asleep shortly after asking for food. I worried about how our journey would be, dragging Luka along everywhere.

Bao seemed to know every inch of this forest. It was his hidden oasis, free from the suffering that engulfed the world above us. He casually told us stories while looking behind at us, not even watching his step over all of the branches, puddles, and vines. I watched his feet, they never missed a step. Without even looking, he would step around a mushroom to avoid crushing it.

In Tinshe, people lived disconnected from nature. Our empire was full of stone buildings and roads built atop of what were once rivers and forests. The sky turned black with thick smog from all of the factories. If you sought the tranquility of nature, you had to journey all the way to the coast, but even then, you were still surrounded by people and litter. Even the ocean that hugged the coastline had islands of trash floating through.

As we walked through the forest, Bao told us stories of his time in Suhai's army. He even briefly mentioned his wife, Ona, whom he lost to the Plague. It seemed he would gradually grow more comfortable with us and loving words would slip out, before he would catch himself and change the subject. Before then, I viewed him as mentally and physically unbreakable, but now I recognized that he was just another broken man, clinging to hope.

"Here." He pointed to a tree. "This is my home."

"Uh, are you sure?" Laago asked, scratching his chin.

Bao jumped up and grabbed a tree branch, flinging himself up. He climbed as quickly as a koala monkey, flowing from one branch to the next with great ease. Though he was an adult, he moved as weightlessly as a child.

"Hold on tight, Luka," Benjin ordered, lunging towards the tree himself. He propelled himself from branch to branch, shaking the tree with every pull. Golden leaves fell and sprinkled onto the floor.

"Need a boost, Ny?" Laago asked.

"No." I rolled my eyes and dashed at the tree, springing up to the branch. I missed, almost slamming my face into the thick tree trunk.

I wasn't even close to reaching it, but I hated how Benjin and Laago always had to help. I could do things on my own too.

"Are you sure about that?" Laago laughed.

"I'm sure," I hissed, getting into a better stance to try again. As I went to launch myself up, Laago grabbed me by the waist and flung me up. I grasped the branch and swung myself onto the next, glaring down at him.

"Yeah, yeah. You're welcome," he shouted, jumping up behind me.

As I climbed up through the layers of branches, a tree house made of rough dark wood that blended into the forest around us appeared. The higher I climbed, the more light leaked down, slipping through the thick branches. I pulled myself through the small square opening on the floor and held my hand out for Laago.

"Seems like you forgive me?" He smirked, grabbing onto my hand. I pretended to let go, but he didn't even flinch.

Bao's home had multiple rooms, some sitting independently on separate trees, but still connected by shaky wooden bridges held together by thick rope. Long windows stretched along three of the walls showcasing the towering trees around us. There was a small porch attached to the main room, where we entered from, with only flowing curtains separating it from the inside. Wind glided through, spreading the crisp clean smell of the forest throughout Bao's house. It smelt so fresh and natural, so different from the polluted air of Tinshe.

"This house seems so high up, yet we are still underground..." I gushed.

"I wanna live in a treehouse, Benji!" Luka exclaimed, bouncing off the walls with energy.

"I know, I've never seen something like this, Buba. But you have to relax, we are guests in Bao's home," Benjin said, rustling Luka's hair.

Bao called us for dinner from the next room over. It was a small kitchen with a wooden low table and no cushions. It was clear everything was handcrafted. His home was simple, yet beautifully unique. There was minimal furniture and no decorations, but it allowed the architecture of his home itself to shine through. We all gathered around, practically salivating.

"Hope you kids like vegetables." Bao placed a steaming bowl of an assortment of vegetables on the table. He grabbed a plate of bread and brought it over. "Most of us down here don't eat meat. The animals here are our neighbors, it never felt right to harm them."

"How many people live in this forest?" Laago asked.

"Oh, I don't know. Most of the more involved resistance divide their time between under and aboveground. I typically only get to come home once a week, so the forest tends to remain quite empty. There is too much to be done up there for us to be able to stay down here frequently. It is better for the natural environment here anyway."

"I am surprised by how untouched the forest down here is. If I didn't know better, I probably wouldn't have even realized people lived here."

"These forests are the backbone of our Earth. If people exploit her land and animals, she will revolt. For the last hundred years, the population has risen exponentially and empires have expanded. More people necessitate more resources, and there's no sustainable way to continue pillaging our already exhausted and depleted land." Bao bit into a piece of bread. "And then there are those who support tyrannical leaders like General Ahkpi, who would set the world ablaze if it made him a coin richer. That's why I hold us accountable for the plague. I believe it was Earth's reaction to the real disease spreading across the globe- the people."

The men and women of the resistance seemed to have a deep respect for our Earth and her creatures. Most people extorted the land and its resources, but the resistance fought to protect it. If the wrong person discovered the Forest of the Earth, it would be stripped away. I realized this burden now fell upon our shoulders as well, it was up to us to help hide this precious land from those above.

Bao didn't waste a moment. As soon as we finished eating, he ordered us out to begin weapon training. He jumped out the opening in the main room and caught a vine mid air, swiftly swinging down the tree like an animal. We all filed down the tree behind him, with our stomachs full and bloated. I thought of my warm and comfy bed back at our apartment. I longingly wondered if we would ever return.

We headed back to where we slept last night. I already felt myself growing accustomed to the forest, knowing where to step and where to avoid. I walked through, gazing up and admiring everything around me. I wanted to soak in every detail of this hidden world. Once our training is completed, I doubt we would ever have a chance to come back here. I watched a mole squirrel climb up a tree and into a tiny hole, where her babies were waiting with open mouths.

We got to our site and grabbed our weapons. I felt relatively confident with my bow, considering I have been using it to hunt since I was seven or eight, but it was old and cheap. Unless I got close to my target, there wasn't much accuracy. Hunting a tiger rabbit with it was one thing, but if I am going to defend myself from the militia, I have a lot of training ahead of me. Bao held his hand out, stopping us. He stood strong, with his feet always firmly planted into the Earth, as if he was just another tree in the forest.

"Do not think of your weapons as separate entities. Instead, they are an extension of yourself. Allow your body to flow as one. Nyla, I would like to start with you."

As I stepped forward, the boys collapsed onto the grass, relieved to not be his first victim. I stood there for a moment as Bao stared at me. His eyes were narrow, he was analyzing me. I felt my anxiety grow as I tried to figure out what he was thinking. Finally, he spoke.

"Show me your stance," Bao ordered. I immediately widened my legs, lifted my elbow, and pulled my bow back, but my arms trembled knowing I was being critiqued.

"Relax your body. Raise your elbow and inhale. I want you to aim at the next leaf that falls. When you exhale, release."

I watched the wind swirl through the trees, shaking leaves down. I closed my eyes for a moment and tried to forget that they were all watching me. Instead, I pretended I was just hunting a tiger rabbit, something I had done a thousand times over- I had nothing to fear. But still, my bow was shaking as my heart raced. I inhaled, raised my elbow, and stalked a red leaf that floated down. Finally, I released, but I missed.

"An arrow is launching into the future. If you aim where your target was in the past, you will surely miss. Whenever you launch an attack, whether it be a punch or through a weapon, do so with anticipation of where your opponent will be, not where they are. Getting caught up in the past is a dangerous thing for a warrior." Bao swiftly pulled a bronze blade that was tied against his bicep by a leather strap and threw it forward, launching it through a falling leaf and straight into a tree. Even Benjin gasped in astonishment. "I want you to keep trying until you hit ten leaves. Benjin, up."

I waited for the next leaf to fall, eager to prove myself to Bao and the boys. It was early spring, but down here it didn't seem like seasons affected the trees, which I suppose made sense because the forest was cut off from the weather above ground. The trees were all full of leaves and life, as if it was mid summer. The thought of spring reminded me that it must almost be my birthday. I would be turning sixteen. I stalked a leaf as it slowly drifted down. Anticipate where it will be, not where it is. I exhaled and launched my arrow, missing even more than I did the first time.

Behind me, I heard Bao training Benjin. "Your axe is strong and heavy. For you to be an effective fighter you must balance it, being nimble and light. You cannot succeed with such a powerful weapon if you put all your strength into one blow. Instead, use a series of blows. The head of your axe, too, can be a weapon. By jabbing it forward, you can break a skull. For the rest of your time here, your axe will not leave your side. This way, it will morph into one with your body. But for now, try to strike me." I turned around to watch- did Bao really expect Benjin to try to strike him with an axe?

"Are you sure?" Benjin cautioned.

"I have fought many men in my life. I will not start fearing them now," Bao declared. "Nyla, focus on your training," he said, without even looking towards me.

I just had to hit ten leaves and I could call it a night. I raised my bow and inhaled, studying the trees. I tried to imagine the invisible wind that flowed through the forest. Instead of watching the leaves, I just needed to focus on the wind! The leaf itself wasn't moving, it was just being carried by the air as it pushed and pulled it. Instead of waiting for a leaf to fall, I waited for the wind to blow.

Moments later, a gust flew through, shaking a handful of leaves off trees. I held my breath and took focus on a single leaf as it detached from its branch. Following the wind currents, I exhaled and released.

The arrow flew through the air and into the leaf, stabbing it against the tree. I got it! I jumped up with glee and Laago swept me off my feet, spinning in a circle.

"I knew you were gonna nail that leaf!" Laago cheered.

"Thanks!" I blushed, "I didn't realize anyone was watching."

"Laago! You're up."

"Well, only nine more to go, kid," he shouted as he walked away.

"Show me your weapon," Bao said. Laago pulled out his daggers. The handles were leather, with eight-inch blades. Bao carefully took them from Laago's hands and studied them. "Not many people successfully master dual weapons. They forget that these are two halves to a whole, balancing each other. Treat them as extensions of your arms, like blades at your fingertips. If you were in a fist fight and only struck with one fist, you would leave half of your body exposed and vulnerable. Neither dagger can be favored."

It took me hours to hit all ten leaves. I lost track of how many times I missed, but no matter how badly I was tempted to quit, my paralyzing fear of the militia kept me going. Everytime I threw my bow down in frustration, I thought of the man lying in a puddle of his own blood, surrounded by militants kicking him. I thought of my father, either dead or imprisoned for life by these tyrannical men. I thought of the militant who chased after me, throwing us into this whole mess to begin with.

My arms were sore, my legs tired, and my mind was asleep. Bao had already returned home, leaving the boys to relax for the rest of the night. Benjin was sound asleep with Luka, who was curled into him for warmth. I trudged over to them and collapsed into the soft grass. I never wanted to touch my bow again.

"Hit all ten?" Laago asked, laying on his back.

"Finally."

"I knew you could," he reassured me.

"How was dagger training?"

"Wanna see?" He laughed, raising his shirt. His chest was covered in bruises. He pointed to another big one on his bicep.

"I thought you were supposed to be the one hitting him?"

"Yeah, that's what I thought too."

"Looks like you have a lot of training ahead of you," I teased, before I drifted off into sleep.

I woke up to the sound of birds chirping as they twirled in the sky above us. The viridescent grass was coated in a thin layer of white frost. This morning was even colder than the last, but Bao must have dropped off blankets for us at some point during the night. Despite sleeping on the ground, I was actually quite comfortable, though it was likely due to my sheer exhaustion. Luka's curly brown hair was tangled in my face so I rolled my body over, pulling the blanket over my face and nuzzling into Benjin, in an attempt to steal some body heat.

"Good morning, sunshines," Benjin called over. I jumped up, smashing my head into Laago's chin. Benjin's laughter roared through the forest, turning my face crimson red. "I figured you thought that was me."

"What a good morning! I feel like I just got rocked in the face." Laago clenched his jaw, still half asleep. "What happened?"

"Nothing!" I insisted, grabbing some dried wheat strips from my bag.

"Ooh, Nyla's getting red!" Luka babbled. Laago sat there rubbing his chin, completely unaware of the teasing.

"Good, everyone's already up. Let us begin training," Bao said, walking over towards us from the forest.

"Already?" Laago moaned, pulling the blanket over his head.

# Chapter Six

# DREAMS AND REALITY

T HE NEXT THREE DAYS consisted of nonstop training. Our bodies were worn-down, beaten, and bruised. By nightfall my muscles cried and when the sun rose my head pounded. Everyday we awoke to Bao's commands and fell asleep to them. He was relentless, incredibly particular, but full of wisdom. He took a lifetime of army and resistance training and submerged us in it throughout the six days of training. Only instead of drowning, we survived.

It was our last night in the forest before we were expected to continue our journey. Bao invited us to his home for a farewell meal. As we walked through the forest to his tree, a sense of melancholy washed over me. In this forest, we were safer than we had been in years. I yearned for a life spent entirely here, with the protective embrace of the towering trees and the glistening streams that meandered across the forest floor. If I could, I would never return to Tinshe.

I walked in silence, trailing behind the boys. They laughed and exchanged stories, seemingly without a care in the world. Strangely, their laughter deepened my sadness. My mind was preoccupied with concerns about our journey to come. I had dark fears of losing them to the militia, thoughts that felt like an arrow through my heart. Listening to their laughter choked me up, but I held back my tears. The last thing I wanted was to make them worry about me.

We finally got to the base of the tree and Benjin effortlessly flung himself up with Luka hanging onto him. He was so tall that he could skip every few branches. Luka squeezed him tightly and buried his face in his back. Laago turned around and held his hand out to me.

"Let me help you up, Ny." I reached out my hand and held onto his when he paused, his eyes narrowing. "Are you alright?" He inquired, stepping towards me.

"Yeah, I'm fine. Just tired. Here, give me a boost," I stammered. I walked past him, avoiding eye contact, but Laago pulled me back.

"Hey, you don't have to act tough around me. Either way, I see right through it. What's going on?" He asked, letting go of my hand.

"I don't want to leave here. I feel safe for once and I am scared about what may happen once we go," I whined, with my voice quietly trailing off.

"Want to know a secret?"

"What?"

"I'm scared too and so is Benjin, I'm sure of it. But being afraid won't help us. Instead, we have to use that energy as motivation to be cautious and strong."

Laago's voice soothed me. Before this week of training, Laago was just a friend of Benjin's that was always around cracking jokes. I never knew this side of him existed. Suddenly, I wanted to know more.

"Hey!" Benjin shouted from above. "Are you coming up?"

"We'll be right there!" Laago responded. "Ready?"

"I think so."

Laago grabbed me by the waist and tossed me up into the tree. I swung myself up to the next branch and looked down, watching him grab the branch and pull himself up. I shook my head and looked back up, trying to just focus on climbing the tree.

I lifted my body through the opening in the floor into the main room of the tree house. A delicious smell wafted through the house. It reminded me of Nonna and her constant array of baked goods. I walked over into the kitchen, where my brothers were already sitting at the table.

"Hey, hey. What smells so good?" Laago rumbled, slipping behind me in the doorway. He went over towards Bao, who was finishing up cooking. "Need a hand?" He asked, but Bao just shooed him away. I took a seat at the table, but couldn't take my eyes off Laago. I never noticed how muscular he was.

"Are you hungry?" Benjin looked over his shoulder to Laago and back at me with a puzzled look on his face. "Because I'm starving." He cracked a grin, as if he knew I was admiring his friend.

"You're always starving," I joked, hiding my blush.

"You would be too if you were as big as me!" He laughed, flexing his arms. Laago turned around and put him in a playful choke hold.

"Yeah, you wish," he countered, flexing. "Benj wishes he was as big as me."

"Alright, big guy." Benjin slapped the table. "Arm wrestle. Right now."

"Oh, you're on," Laago retorted, dropping to the floor.

"Dinner is ready. Compare muscles after," Bao declared, winking at me. He carried plates of food over. He made a fresh loaf of bread and an assortment of baked vegetables, steaming hot and tossed in herbs.

We ate and laughed, then we ate some more. It reminded me of when I was young and my family would have picnics. We would gather around the pond, huddled together on an old quilt, passed down from my father's mother. It was stained with life and love, all fond memories. For once, my memories did not pain me, but instead warmed my heart.

"I can't believe we only met you a week ago, Bao," Benjin exclaimed. "I feel like you're a long lost family member."

I felt a lump form in my throat. I thought of my father, who sacrificed everything for our people. I wish he could see us now, his own kids following in his footsteps without even realizing it. An unfamiliar feeling began to bubble inside of me- one that I could not quite put a name on. I looked around at the boys and cherished their smiles and laughter. Bao stood up and raised his wooden cup.

"To the resistance."

"To the resistance!" We raised our cups and cheered.

"I may not know much, but I know a good fighter when I see one. The three of you are true warriors, and any man who crosses your path will regret it." Bao sat back down. "I hope when this is all over, you come back and visit me so I can hear about your journey."

"We would want nothing more than that," Benjin earnestly replied. "Thank you, Bao, for everything. Truly."

"Hey, now, don't get soft on me yet. I said once this is all over!" Bao smiled. He lifted himself onto his feet and walked out of the room.

"I never knew vegetables could taste so good," Luka babbled, reminding me of our sister Luchi.

She would have loved it down here, living off vegetables and existing in peace amongst the animals. I would like to think she was reborn into one of these chirping birds that fluttered through the Forest of Earth, where she would live out her days in tranquil land surrounded by ethereal beauty.

"That's because mother never knew how to cook 'em." Benjin chuckled.

Moments later, Bao returned to us and laid out a map so large across the table that we had to move our dishes onto the floor. It was a map of our known world, with each empire and kingdom marked, along with any major cities or capitals. I had never seen one with this much detail.

"This is where we met, the apartment that I was stationed at," he said, running his finger along its wrinkled and worn paper. "The Forest of Earth is here, directly beneath the River of Suhai." I studied the map, my chest sinking to the sight of how far we had to travel just to reach the outskirts of Suhai. His finger glided across the map. "General Pago is currently stationed in Huang, on the coast of the republic. We have tunnels that will bring you to the Port of Eura. From there, you will walk to Huang."

"That'll take us forever! Can't we just take a boat?" Laago interrupted, practically jumping up from his seat in protest.

"A boat in open waters? You will be as vulnerable as a fish flopping on dry land. Like sitting ducks! You must walk," Bao urged. His voice was stern and unwavering, like a wall that would never fall.

"Well, I always knew I would go home to Terlu. I just never imagined this would be why." Laago sighed, his eyes following Bao's finger as it traced our route.

"Ahkpi's invasion of Terlu is in twenty-four days, when the moon is hidden from the sky. This is more than enough time for you to reach Huang to warn General Pago."

"Let's say we make it to Huang in time, how do we even find him?" Benjin questioned.

"The Republic of Terlu has a well-established military, you will not miss it."

"So we just run into a general's tent and tell him that Ahkpi is transporting his militia to Terlu's southwest border for an invasion? Is he really gonna believe a bunch of kids?"

"Amu created a scroll for you to give to General Pago. It is sealed shut with the Protectors' emblem in wax. You must give it to him directly- no exceptions. No one else is to be trusted with this information." Bao pulled the scroll from his bag and extended it towards Benjin.

"Okay." Benjin took a deep breath and accepted the scroll, delicately studying it in his hands. "We can do this." I could tell he was nervous, despite how strong he was trying to act. He bit his lip.

"I have a strong vine to secure the scroll to your chest. You are to not remove it from your body until you can physically place it in General Pago's hands," Bao reiterated. "You will sleep here tonight and at dawn, we will embark on our six-day journey through the tunnels to reach the Port of Eura. From there, you will follow the coastline to Huang. Though it is the same distance we will trek underground, you may encounter some delays. If all goes as planned, you should reach General Pago within fifteen days, giving him and his troops nine days to prepare for the invasion. The longer you take, the less time the republic has to prepare themselves."

"No pressure..." Laago rubbed his forehead anxiously. "Just the fate of the republic in a couple of kids' hands."

"You are no longer just kids. You are warriors, protecting the world from Ahkpi and his tyranny. This great journey would not be bestowed upon you if the gods did not deem you capable. I believe in you all. I have seen you fight, you are mentally and physically prepared," Bao consoled us. Sitting here, I did not feel like a warrior. I looked down at my scrawny body, praying Bao was right. "Benjin, I want you to have this." He pulled a leather belt with an axe holster out of his bag. It had a golden eagle beautifully etched into it, its wings spread out to intimidate its prey.

"How could I accept such a gift? I have nothing to return." Benjin graciously waved the offer off.

"By opening your hands and taking it," Bao plainly spoke, tossing it onto Benjin's lap. He ran his fingers along the etching, before he fastened it around his waist and attached his axe onto it.

"Our father always said a golden eagle serves as a sign that one is on the right path."

"It is a saying known in many cultures." Bao nodded his head, before he abruptly stood up. "The hour is growing late. It would be wise for everyone to get some sleep."

We got up from the table and headed back into the main room. Bao gathered some blankets for us, before he disappeared to his bedroom. We all situated ourselves on one side of the room, away from the opening in the floorboards that dropped to the bottom of the forest floor.

"No one roll over there..." Laago joked. A cool breeze drifted in from the porch, flowing through the curtains.

"Yeah, Luka and Nyla, you're sleeping between Laago and me," Benjin said, as he arranged the blankets for everyone.

"I'm not going to roll through the opening... You don't have to be so protective," I rebuked.

"We haven't even started our mission, I am not trying to slip up now," Benjin urged. I rolled my eyes and stormed out onto the porch, leaning against the railing.

"All I do is try to keep everyone safe and I just get argued with all day," he complained to Laago.

"I don't argue! I love you Benji," Luka gushed.

"I know, I know. I think sometimes she just needs to know you trust her. You can't protect her forever, Benj," Laago reasoned.

"Yeah, so I might as well protect her while I can. Whatever, I'm going to sleep," Benjin mumbled, settling into his bed for the night. "Come here, Buba. Let's go to bed."

I watched the tall trees swaying in the wind, their branches creaking. I missed the moon. Without it, darkness engulfed the night. Soon enough, I would finally get to see it again. As exciting as it sounded, I knew that also meant we would be above ground, where the militia was.

"Hey, can I join you?" Laago asked, walking through the curtain.

"You'll probably do whatever you want anyway," I muttered, gazing off into the distance.

"You know me too well."

"Are you here to tell me to do whatever Benjin says? That he's only doing what he thinks right? That he's just trying to protect us?" I hissed. Laago leaned against the railing and let out a heavy sigh.

"I know it can be hard to have someone act so overprotective."

"He acts like he's my father. Meanwhile, he's barely four years older than me. I'll be sixteen soon, I'm not a child."

"When I met Benjin, you were maybe three. I never had any siblings, I only ever had my pops. And he was horrible. Beat the life out of me pretty much every time he stumbled home," he recounted, staring into the trees. "Honestly, your family was more of a family to me than my own. Losing your parents hurt me more than leaving Terlu and my old man. I was eight when I left my whole life behind. I figured I was safer on the streets than in my own home."

"I am so sorry, Laago," I said, immediately regretting my outburst. I put my hand on his shoulder.

"I ate from people's trash, slept in alley ways... I didn't even have shoes." He looked down. "Then one day, I was digging through garbage when I turned around and saw a kid staring at me. As soon as our eyes met, he bolted. I remember collapsing onto the ground, sobbing. I felt utterly unwanted and alone. I was so dirty that even kids ran from me. I was scared and alone. I knew I wanted to be a better person, but I didn't know how. Then, as I am feeling sorry for myself, the kid came back. He set a dish of hot food beside me, before he slid off his shoes and placed them by my feet. He sat against the alley wall opposite of me and eventually, he introduced himself. Benjin was the first person I spoke to since I left home."

"Wow... I never knew how you two met."

"So, I'm sitting there with this kid, eating my first hot meal in ages. I finish and go to put the shoes on, but I don't even know how to tie them. Then Benjin told me his father knew how to and invited me back to his place, but my bad history with my pops made it hard for me to trust people, especially men. But something about Benjin, I don't know, he made me feel safe, even though he was just a scrawny seven-year-old. We walked into your apartment and I'll never forget your mother's face. Here I was, this random kid covered in dirt and smelling like trash, wearing her son's boots. Benjin says, 'this is my friend, he eats trash', all matter-of-factly!" Laago laughed. "But she didn't bat an eye. She gave me a bath and made me a little bed. It was the best day of my life. I lived with your family for a year, until I got the opportunity to move into the basement apartment. At first, your mother didn't want me to live on my own; after all, I was only nine. But your father trusted me, he supported whatever I chose."

"I didn't even know you lived with us."

"Yeah, you were practically a baby when it happened and Luka wasn't even born. Daath taught me everything a father was supposed to teach his son. He swung by my apartment pretty much every day to see how I was. He was a god among men, strong and decisive, yet loving and soft. Your mother always made sure I had food, no matter what." His voice cracked, before falling quiet. "When the New Plague hit and it was just us, I felt like I was eight years old again, running through the streets with no direction or hope. But Benjin, he manned up. He could have crumbled, but he didn't. That kid was fourteen years old and stronger than most men."

We gazed into the depths of the forest, lost in contemplative silence. Laago had spent his entire childhood yearning for guidance and support, while here I stood, surrounded by all the guidance I could wish for, yet failing to fully appreciate it.

"I guess I take Benjin for granted."

"Sometimes we get caught up in the little things and forget about the big picture," he sympathized. "Let's go to bed, we have a long day ahead of us."

That night I dreamt I was laying on my mother's lap, watching the ducks play in the pond from our balcony. There were four baby ducks, all swimming in circles. I wondered where their parents were. My mother stroked my hair and softly hummed. The pond glistened from the moon's intense glow, illuminating the ripples in the water.

"It's a Koba moon, Nyla. That means the moon is at its closest point to Earth, which is when I am closest to you," she whispered. Her body slowly faded, leaving me alone on the cold balcony. I jumped up and called for her.

"Mother? Come back!" I ran into the apartment to find her, but as I entered my body suddenly dropped into the streets of Tinshe. I hit my head on the hard ground, blurring my vision. As I stumbled to my feet, clenching my head, a militant called to me.

"Hey! You! Stop where you are!" He yelled, dashing towards me. I tried to run, but my legs wouldn't move. I screamed for help- for my mother, my father, Benjin, anyone. The militant grabbed me and shook me. I kept screaming, punching and kicking him with all my might.

"Nyla, wake up!" Benjin pleaded, shaking me. My eyes shot open, my whole body trembled. Benjin was trying to constrain me. Laago held Luka, his face filled with concern. "I am here, Nyla. It's okay." Benjin stroked my head and hugged me tight.

"I-I'm sorry, I thought..." I stuttered, eyes wide with fear.

"I know, it's okay. I get nightmares too," Benjin whispered, as Bao walked into the room.

"Is everything okay?" Bao asked.

"Yeah, just a nightmare," Benjin replied. "Nothing to worry about."

"Ah, nightmares..." Bao pondered. He sat down in front of me. "They can be terrifying things. What was it you dreamt of?"

"I was sitting on my balcony with my mother watching the ducks in the pond, like we used to. She was in the middle of talking to me when she disappeared, so I got up to find her. But when I ran inside, it was just a black pit. I fell through and landed in the street. Then all of a sudden, the militant Benjin..." I paused, shuddering at the thought. "The militant Benjin killed was there, except this time, Benjin wasn't there to save me from him."

"I would never let them hurt you, Nyla," Benjin promised, his eyes wide.

"Over my dead body," Laago chimed in, holding his hand over his heart.

"We live in a world filled with distractions that separate us from the spirit of the Earth. For many, their minds are only blank when they sleep, and so these spirits will often use dreams to communicate with us." Bao rubbed his chin and looked at me. "I understand your dream felt overwhelmed by darkness, but we may be able to learn something from it. You mentioned your mother was talking to you. What did she say?" He questioned. I closed my eyes and tried to remember, but the image of the militant muddled my mind.

"I'm sorry, but I don't know..."

"The next time you find yourself in a dream, I want you to try to take control. Pay attention to the little things. Listen to what the spirits may be telling you," Bao explained, rising to his feet. "Now that we are all up, we may as well begin our journey." As he walked into the kitchen, Laago reached over and put his hand on my knee.

"How are you feeling, Ny?"

"Better," I lied.

We all rose to our feet and began packing the few belongings we had. I only had the bag Nonna gave me, still filled with dried wheat strips and coins. It held an extra pair of clothes and some of Luka's things I had stuffed in it. I pulled the small painting of my family out and held it against my lips for a moment, before I clipped my arrows on my belt and threw my bow over my shoulder. I lifted Luka to his feet and combed through his hair.

"How is my little Buba?"

"Tired..." Luka rubbed his eyes. "When can we go home?"

"Unfortunately, not anytime soon."

Benjin pulled up his shirt and tied Bao's vine around his chest, slipping the scroll through. He checked over and over again until he was positive it was tightly secured. I felt his anxiety bubbling inside of him, ready to explode, but Benjin was too strong for that. I didn't know what it would take to break him, nor would I want to know. He threw his work bag over his shoulder and picked up his axe.

"Ready?"

"Ready as I'll ever be," Laago responded, stretching his back.

Bao reentered the main room and tossed Benjin a paper bag filled with bread, before jumping through the opening in the floor. Benjin stuffed it in his bag.

"Luka, get on my back," Benjin ordered, ready to climb through the opening behind Bao. Laago and I followed him closely behind.

Bao wasted no time once we reached the forest floor. He hit the ground running and we did our best to follow him as he quickly weaved through the forest. I tried to soak in the beauty around me, aware that I may never come back to the Forest of Earth. The air was so pure down here, undisturbed by the empire's pollution.

I began to think of what life could be like outside of Tinshe. Were streets lined with dilapidated apartment buildings, never renovated since being built? Was the sky gray from all the smoke that wafted through the air from the factories, suffocating and burning our throats during the dry season? I had never even been outside of the Suhai Empire, let alone out of Tinshe. Was the Republic of Terlu truly better? It had to be. I refused to believe the whole world was as doomed as my hometown.

"Laago, what was the Republic of Terlu like when you lived there?"

"Terlu is vastly different from Suhai. The Republic of Terlu doesn't have an emperor or a royal family. Instead, we elect Presidents," he explained. "It sounds good and all, but where I grew up in the northwestern outskirts, it was a dump. Most people lived in shacks. I never saw any wealth until I fled my home and reached the southern border along the coast, where there are food markets, stores, and more money than I could imagine at eight years old. That's because the port towns profit greatly from fishing and are trade hotspots."

"What's the President like?"

"The President of Terlu is Suin. He's pretty much been President for as long as I could remember."

"How's that any different from an emperor?"

"Well, he's always reelected because the people really like him. President Suin is a good and honest man. He seems to care about the working people, not just the rich."

"Maybe one day Suhai can have an elected President as well." I couldn't even imagine having the ability to freely choose the leader of my empire. Could anybody run to be elected?

"It's possible, but for that to happen, the people of Suhai would have to collectively rise together and fight for it. There would need to be a complete upheaval of our current system. The Republic of Terlu had a ten year long bloody revolutionary way before the traditional government surrendered to the people."

"Benjin told me that it didn't end until their emperor and his family were assassinated."

"No transfer of power occurs peacefully," Benjin chimed into our conversation. "Leaders are given power, then suddenly believe they are godly. But, in reality, they are no greater than the people they serve, because it is us who gives them the power to begin with."

"What about General Pago, what is he like?"

"I'm not really sure." He shrugged. "I was just a kid when I left, so I never really learned much about him. But I know he started off the lowest rank in Terlu's army and worked his way up. That sounds pretty honorable to me," Laago concluded. I nodded my head in agreement.

We followed Bao for hours until we finally reached the end of the forest and began our way through the narrow tunnels. I envied Luka who slept soundly on Benjin's back. We were slowly trying to build up his stamina. Today, we made him walk for three hours before Benjin allowed him to have a break. I felt sorrowful that he was six and on a life-threatening journey. He should be playing with friends or going to school.

"Are we almost there yet?" Luka groaned, finally waking.

"Not yet..."

"I want to go home, Benji."

"You know we can't, Buba."

"Why can't we?"

"Because we want to help make the world a better place," Benjin replied, but his words sounded desperate, as if he was trying to convince himself too.

"Why do we have to? Why can't someone else?"

"What if everyone argued that?" He countered. "Then no one would stand up and fight for a better world. We have to lead by example, Luka."

"Fighting for a better world is tiring," he mumbled, as he drifted back to sleep.

"It sure is..."

"Laago, remember that girl, Uma?" Benjin laughed.

"Oh boy, I forgot about that one. I call her *Mistake Number Three*." Laago shook his head in shame.

"Who was the mistake? Her? Or you?" Benjin joked.

"Remember she followed me all day because she thought I was cheating on her? She was crazy!"

"Laago, you were cheating on her. It's not crazy if she's right."

"Wait, Uma? Uma from the mung bean stand?" I asked.

"Only Uma I know," Benjin replied, his axe handle bouncing against his leg with every step.

"Is there anyone from our town you haven't dated?"

"Dated is a strong word, I like to call those daycations."

"You're a pig, Laago."

"Come on, Ny, I'm a changed man! Those days are behind me."

"Since when?" Benjin roared, waking Luka.

"Not everyone's perfect like you, Benj," Laago jabbed.

"Well, of course not, but you can at least try." Benjin ran forward, dodging Laago's push.

"What about you, Ny?" Laago asked, turning around to me. "Tell us about your boyfriends."

"Leave me out of this conversation!" Benjin covered his ears, then covered Luka's, then covered his again.

"Never had one." I blushed.

"What? Never? Not one?"

"Laago, she's fifteen."

"Almost sixteen," I corrected.

"That's no different," Benjin argued.

"Benj, you can't be talking, you had a girlfriend since you were like five. I'm sure Nyla's had some boyfriends but just doesn't want her big brother to hear!" Laago nudged my arm. "You can tell me later, I won't rat you out to Benjin." I rolled my eyes.

I was always very shy growing up. Juu and Tasi were my two best friends, and once I met them, I never felt the need to make any more connections. The three of us had so much fun, and besides, I had my two sisters to play with. Dalia might have been young, but Luchi was only two years younger than me. There were cute boys around town, but they never really crossed my mind. I was content with my life as it was.

Once the plague hit and I lost everyone, I quickly became unfathomably lonely. Time moves so slow when you are alone. It wasn't until then that I even thought about boys. Either way, I was too shy, no boy would ever notice me. There were plenty of pretty girls to keep them distracted, so I decided to just keep to myself. Why would I want to open myself up to someone new, just to end up losing them?

"That's different," Benjin countered defensively. "Luna was different."

"I think that's the first time I've heard you say her name since..."

"Since she left? What more is there to say?" Benjin clenched the red string that wrapped around his wrist.

"I didn't mean to be a pain, Benj," Laago earnestly expressed. "I just feel like ever since she left you gave up on girls. Any girl in Tinshe would go crazy for you."

"I don't want just any girl; I want Luna. Just because you bounce around from girl to girl doesn't mean I have to. You live your life, I'll live mine," Benjin scoffed.

"Benjin, I hate to admit this, but I agree with Laago. She left five years ago. Eventually, you will need to give love a chance again. I don't want you to live your whole life alone."

"Do you think I want to be alone? I was with Luna for the majority of my life. When I was five I walked down the hall to her apartment door with flowers I picked by the pond and asked her to marry me. It's almost fifteen years later and I would still marry her today."

"I'm sorry, Benj. I know it's hard to talk about, but I have been waiting for you to let this out since she left." Laago put his hand on Benjin's shoulder. "You know you can tell me anything."

"I know."

"You and your sister are always internalizing everything. It isn't you versus the world. It's us. If we are going to make it through this, alive, we need to be open with each other."

"Since when did you become so wise?" Benjin smirked, swatting Laago's hand away.

"Honestly, I don't know. Maybe it was something in those vegetables Bao kept cooking!"

"The boy is right," Bao interrupted. "Communication is everything. The moment you start to internalize your fears, the group will fall apart. You must be honest with one another."

"Honestly, I forgot you were even here." Laago grinned.

That night, we slept huddled against one of the many dead ends of the tunnels. When Bao extinguished his torch, darkness swallowed us. I felt as if we were sinking into a pit of emptiness. The silence was ear piercing. I tried to focus on the quiet hums of Benjin's breathing, but it was fruitless. I longed to be back on the ground, where the night sky illuminated the world around me. It astonished me how much we take for granted. Each day, the sun rises and sets, the tides push and pull, and the seasons change.

As I tried to fall asleep, I thought about all of Laago's past lovers. I wondered what he even saw in them. I tried to accept him for who he was, without judgment, but it felt ingenuine. Even trying to ignore it didn't work; it only made me obsess over it more. I knew he was a good person with a genuine heart, but I struggled to understand him as much as I wanted to.

Was he trying to find the love his parents did not give him in random girls? Was he trying to fill a void within himself? I wondered if he was lonely deep down and trying to mask it. Like Benjin, Laago never complained. My mind became overwhelmed with worry. I found myself desperately praying to Eura for his sake, begging her to help him find what he was looking for. I prayed for him to know he was loved. I finally drifted to sleep in the midst of my prayer, with a sunken heart.

"Who's ready for another day of walking?" Laago mumbled as he rolled onto his feet.

"Not me!" Luka groaned. "Carry me, Benji."

"No, you need to walk on your own, at least for a little bit."

"I want to go home!" Luka began to cry, stomping his feet. Benjin dropped down onto his knee and put his hands on Luka's shoulder.

"Do you want to grow up to be big and tough, Buba?"

"...Yes," he whimpered, wiping his tears.

"How will you be big and tough then, if you aren't now?"

"I don't know."

"Be tough for me. You can do it."

"Let's go!" Laago replied, throwing his arm around my shoulder.

"I never knew walking could be so painful," Benjin complained, as he turned around and smacked Laago's arm off me.

"You'll get used to it," Bao retorted. "Or you won't. Only time will tell," he grinned.

Bao had a dark sense of humor. It was hard for me to tell whether he was serious or joking by the tone of his voice until I checked to see if he was smirking. We pressed on through the tunnels, enduring our frigid and dreary surroundings.

"Hey, Benji?" Luka tugged on his hand.

"What's up, Buba?"

"Is daddy dead?" He blurted, unaware of the intensity of his question.

"We don't know."

"Why don't you know?" He innocently questioned.

I watched Benjin, I could tell his mind was flooded with thoughts. How do you explain to a six-year-old that his father disappeared? He heard what Amu said, what more is there to say? I was relieved he asked Benjin and not me.

"Well, one day he went on a really important mission and never came home."

"Why didn't he come home?" Luka pestered. "Do you think he's mad at us?"

"Absolutely not!" Benjin scooped Luka off the ground and held him on his hip. "If daddy could, he would come find us. He loves us all very much. Sometimes, you have to do something even if it hurts those you love most." Laago put his hand on Benjin's shoulder.

"I'm hungry!" Luka decided.

"Me too, Buba."

"When we get back to land, we have to find a good meal!" Laago drooled.

My heart warmed as I thought of my father. Every night, no matter how late he got home, he would quietly sneak into our room and give each of us a gentle kiss goodnight. Even if we were causing trouble or not listening, he would tell us he loved us. I never had to question my father's love, because he always made it abundantly clear. Even now, with so much fear and uncertainty plaguing my life, I still feel his love, radiant as ever.

As we walked through the tunnels, a flickering light appeared from the other end. Bao immediately unlit his torch and signaled for us to get down. The tunnels were narrow, so there was nowhere to hide if someone crossed our path, unless there was a dead end we could quickly slip into. We could now hear two distinct voices, one belonging to a man and the other a woman's. I could not make out exactly what they were talking about, but I heard the man laugh. Soon, their torch light would capture us. We all sat silently behind Bao, waiting for him to give us an order. Instead, he began to whistle.

They stopped dead in their tracks, holding their light still. I held my breath, waiting to judge their reaction. Suddenly, they began to whistle the same tune back. Bao quickly rose to his feet and walked over to greet them. I collapsed my body onto Laago, hugging him.

"I was terrified," I whispered, relieved.

"One step closer and they were going to get a dagger to the face," Laago replied. We got up and followed Bao, our hearts still racing.

"Long time no see, Bao!" The man exclaimed. He reached forward and shook Bao's hand. "What brings you here?"

"Long time indeed. I was sent to bring these lost kids home," he lied.

"Demoted to a babysitter?" The woman laughed. Benjin and Laago glared at each other.

"What brings you two here?"

"We finished up this week's tour and are heading back home to the forest," she responded. Her voice was deep, more masculine than an average woman.

"Any news from the ground?"

"A lot of militants weren't on their usual routes. Not sure what's going on there, but it looks like they are moving north," the man answered.

"Interesting... It sounds like they may be planning something," Bao determined. "Well, stay safe. We best be on our way." The man and woman gave us a nod and began walking away. Without hesitation, Bao continued on as well. Finally, their light faded into the distance.

"Who were they?" Benjin asked.

"Members of the resistance."

"Weren't you the same guy telling us about the value of communication last night?" Laago joked. Bao turned around sharply.

"I told you to communicate to each other, not to the whole empire."

"Do they not know about Ahkpi's invasion plans?" Benjin pried.

"There is no reason for them to know. Just as there is no reason for them to know who you are. I am the only one Amu informed of your mission and it was for the sole purpose of me to guide you. The less everyone knows, the better. This way, if someone is captured there are no secrets to share."

"We should make up fake identities. I'll be Zhao, traveling the world in the circus," Laago decided. Even though it was dark and I couldn't see, I knew Benjin rolled his eyes.

"Can I be in the circus?" Luka babbled.

"Having an identity is not a bad idea, but let's create a more practical one," Bao pondered. "You kids are traveling from the outskirts of Terlu to work on a fishing boat at Huang."

"That's not fun..."

"I want to be in the circus!" Luka whined.

"It's okay, we can be in the circus another time," Laago said with a wink.

Our conversation slowly dwindled, leaving us to suffocate in silence. Traveling in such a boring place made it difficult to find new things to talk about. We spent every single waking moment together, what more could we have to say? Walking through the dark tunnel was immensely monotonous. I kept catching myself counting my steps. Forty, forty one, forty two... Fortunately, the pain in my legs began to settle, as my body became accustomed to walking for long periods of time.

"Bao, what are you going to do once we reach the Port of Eura?" Benjin asked, stretching his back as he walked.

"I will return to Amu and see what he has planned for me next."

"You seem so dedicated to the resistance. It must be hard for you to make time for yourself," Laago sympathized.

"Without the resistance, I would have nothing. What good is free time anyway?"

"Doesn't it get lonely?" I whispered, regretting asking as soon as the words left my mouth. Benjin turned around and shot me a look.

"I often have to travel through these tunnels for days at a time to reach my next destination. I am used to it now, though spending days alone in darkness once filled me with grief. I thought of my wife nearly every minute. She consumed my mind so heavily that at times, it felt as though she was walking with me. I could swear I even heard her voice, clear as day, a handful of times."

"How did you overcome your grief?" Benjin inquired. Bao looked forward, deep in thought.

"One especially tough night, I dreamt I was laying in our bed. I rolled over and there my wife was peacefully sleeping, her body intertwined with the white blankets that draped our bed. I gently brushed Ona's soft hair off her face and admired her beauty. I laid there, tearing up over how fortunate I was to call her mine. When she finally woke, she hid her face into a pillow, embarrassed by my gawking. I told her she was more beautiful than any goddess and I meant it. She leaned closer and whispered that she loved me deeply, but I had to let her go." He let out a heavy sigh. "For whatever reason, I didn't fight it. I understood she was right, even if it broke my heart. Part of me believes she visited me in my sleep and that it was not just my imagination. The other part of me doesn't care whether it was just my imagination or not, because it was what I needed to hear."

"I always struggled with letting go too," Benjin confided in him.

"That is because in life we are always taught to never surrender. You and I are born fighters, Benjin. When I heard you speak of your girlfriend yesterday, you reminded me of myself. Giving up is not in our blood. So even when it is best for us to let go, our brains may acknowledge it but our hearts cannot connect and follow through with it. This disconnect is the cause of so much pain and suffering in our lives."

"So what do I do? I want to move on from Luna. We spent our whole lives together and then she just left me with nothing more than a red string! I'm sure she has moved on and forgotten about me, yet here I am still dreaming of her every night. How do I connect my brain to my heart?" He agonized.

"There's no one solution- what works for one may not work for another. For me, it was not until I broke down into my worst self that I was freed from my suffering and renewed."

"I feel like I have been through so much in my life. If I haven't reached my worst yet, I don't know if I will make it through when I do."

"True character forms during hardships." Bao looked back at Benjin, whose face was sunken with defeat. "Let's call it a night," he decided, turning towards a dead end.

# CHAPTER SEVEN

# BLOOD AND DIRT

THE NEXT DAY WAS uneventful. As expected, we walked from the moment we woke up until the moment Bao allowed us to stop. The boys all told stories and jokes, keeping the energy much lighter than the day before. Benjin seemed happier. I think him admitting the pain and betrayal he felt from Luna leaving lifted a weight off of his chest. We talked more about her in these last few days in the tunnels than in the entire five years since she left Tinshe. He was less brooding and more of his charming, quick-witted self.

That night, I dreamt of my mother again. Only this time, we sat at the low table in our apartment and sipped dandelion root tea. Though I heard my other siblings playing in the background, I only saw her. Everything beyond her was cloudy. I admired her long and untamable hair, falling down her back and shoulders. She studied me with her spirited but soft blue eyes as she blew on her tea.

"I am so proud of you, Nyla. You and your brothers have come so far. I am sorry I am not there to protect you, but I know that you are strong enough to take care of Benjin and Luka for me."

"I miss you, mother. I wish you could be here with us, I feel so lost and scared. We are supposed to go on some journey to save the Republic of Terlu and Tinshe, but I worry we will fail, like father."

As I agonized my fears to my mother, her face began to melt. Her striking features began to mush, her long hair fell. Before I could muster a word, my mother had dissipated before my very eyes and a militant took her place.

"Hey, you! Stop where you are!" He shouted, lunging across the table towards me.

I screamed in peril, running into my bedroom and moving my bed in front of the door to block him from entering. He slammed on the door, shouting and cursing as I sat in the corner of my room sobbing and covering my ears. Suddenly, Bao's words filled my head. It was my dream; I was in control.

I took a deep breath and closed my eyes, then slowly exhaled. It was just a dream, nothing could hurt me. I was safe, sleeping between Benjin and Luka. I was in control, the maker of my own dreams. When I opened my eyes, I was back at the table with my mother.

"I miss you too, Nyla," she reassured me. "But I need you to stay strong. Under the next Koba moon, we can be together again." I heard Luchi and Dalia laughing on the balcony, their squeaky voices floating through the house.

"The Koba moon? Amu... He mentioned it too."

"It is when our worlds are closest."

"I don't want to wait until then... I wish I could stay here forever. It seems so nice here, it reminds me of life before the plague."

"Your life is too valuable. You are a beacon of hope to the Tinshe and the Republic of Terlu, whether the people know it or not."

"I definitely don't feel that way," I faltered. "Where's father? I need to speak with him," my eyes darted around the room. He always gave the best advice. Maybe if I knew why he failed, I could learn from his mistakes.

"This is why I came to you. Daath is not here," my mother declared.

"What do you mean he's not here?"

I jolted up to Benjin shaking me, motioning to me to remain quiet. I adjusted my eyes and noticed Luka hiding against the dead end behind Laago, who tightly gripped his daggers. As I turned around, I saw Bao crouched in front of me staring off into the distance at a light that was approaching us. I immediately knew it wasn't a member of the resistance. We were sleeping in a dead end, a path no resistance member would have a purpose for taking. It had to be an intruder.

As the light approached us, I was able to differentiate two distinct voices. Within a minute we would be within their light's reach, making confrontation inevitable. I quietly picked my bow off the ground and placed an arrow against the string. I raised my elbow and pulled back, but did not release. Bao let out a whistle and the two voices immediately quieted, stopping dead in their tracks.

"Who goes there?" One of the voices commanded. These were not friends. "We command you to show yourselves."

"Reveal yourself, otherwise, we will make you," the other voice ordered sternly, but I felt fear in his voice as he trembled over his words. Bao seemed to pick up on this too.

"There are more of us than there are of you, boy. Lay down on your stomachs and surrender!" Bao shouted, his voice echoing in the narrow tunnel. None of us dared to move or even breathe.

"We are soldiers of Najin, commanded by General Ahkpi. We will not surrender," he retorted.

Bao turned his head to me and nodded, signaling me to release. I closed one eye, focusing on the faint figures in the distance. As quickly as I released the first arrow targeted for one of the militants, I prepared and released a second for the other. I nocked a third arrow, if needed to finish the job. I did not want to inflict suffering. I heard a blood-curdling screech and two thumps. I dropped my bow and covered my ears, but it was too late. Bao immediately got up and ran over to the bodies.

"Please- Please... Spare us. I'll give you anything!" The man pleaded, bleeding out and gasping for air, as his friend laid still. The arrow punctured his heart.

"Why are you in these tunnels?"

"It was an accident- I swear... We- We were patrolling and found a hole. So we went through it... Please. We didn't tell anyone. No one knows." The man sobbed, clenching the arrow that was lodged in his stomach.

"It's okay, boy. Take a breath." Bao circled behind him and put a comforting hand on the militant's shoulder before abruptly slitting his throat. I gasped, covering my mouth. Blood poured out of the man's throat as he dropped onto the cold ground. Benjin put his arms around me.

"He had no choice, Nyla. They would've informed the militia of the tunnels," Benjin insisted.

"We have to bury these men before we continue on," Bao ordered, already digging into the dirt with his hands. "Hurry now, we still have many miles to cover today."

He sounded completely unphased, as if we were digging holes to plant carrot seeds. Benjin immediately jumped up and joined Bao. I turned around to see Laago holding Luka into his chest, covering his ears to protect him. Laago just stared blankly down the tunnel, ignoring me. I slowly rose to my feet, my body trembling as I inched towards the bodies. A stench flowed through the air, filling the tight tunnel. I couldn't help but gag.

As I got closer to the bodies, I noticed how young they were. They couldn't have been older than Laago. One had a scar across his face, from his chin to his cheekbone. Now an arrow was pierced through his heart. Just like that, I took his life. I didn't know his name, where he came from, or who his mother was. I didn't know him, all I knew was that he happened to walk down the wrong tunnel. Why did they have to find the hole that would lead them to their death?

"Nyla, can you hear me?" Benjin repeated, his hands gripping my shoulders. I slowly nodded my head. "You weren't answering when I kept calling your name. Did you hear me?"

"Yeah," I lied.

"We have to dig." Benjin dropped back down onto his knees and teared through the dirt with his hands. I fell onto the ground next to him, digging as I stared at the bodies of the young men whose lives I took. I wondered what they were like and if they had partners waiting at home for them. Maybe if we grew up on the same side of Suhai we could have been friends.

Benjin and Bao dropped the bodies into the ground and quickly covered them. Laago sat with Luka, singing and telling stories to distract him. I wondered if Luka had any idea what just happened. I hoped not and prayed to the goddess of life, Gala, for forgiveness. But as I prayed, I realized it was in vain. It was only the beginning of our journey and I had already taken two lives. I could not seek forgiveness for a crime I knew I would commit again. Instead, I asked her to protect us and help us make the right decisions.

Before we continued our trek, Bao knelt over the graves and whispered a few words. Benjin came over to me, covered in dirt and sweat, and put his hands on my shoulders. I could not look up at him. Just as easily as I took these two lives, someone could take ours. During the New Plague I thought I learnt how fragile life was, but I now realized I was only beginning to truly understand.

"We had no choice," Benjin whispered, as I stared at the ground. "Nyla."

"I know," I said, walking past him and continuing forward with Bao leading the way.

Though our day had just begun, we all seemed to unanimously decide to keep to ourselves. No matter how far we walked, I still felt like I was standing over those two bodies, with blood forming into a puddle beneath my feet. I stared down at my hands, hours had passed but the trembling remained. Though my hands may have been covered in dirt, I envisioned them stained with blood too.

I trailed behind Laago, blankly gazing into the ground. I thought about the vivid dream I had abruptly awoken from earlier this morning. Just as I was able to control it, I was pulled back to reality. The last time I dreamt of my mother, I awoke recalling only vague bits and pieces: glimpses of us laying on the balcony and her petting my hair before it spiraled into a nightmare.

This time, I remembered everything as clear as day, more so than I could recall many of my actual memories. My mother claimed our father was not there with her. Was she trying to tell me that he was alive? I desperately wanted to confide in Benjin about my dream, but every time I opened my mouth, an immense pain gripped my chest. Instead, I took a deep breath and wearily continued on.

Once we covered our distance for the day, we sat clustered in another dead end eating dried wheat strips and Bao's home cooked but aging bread. With each bite, I was reminded that those two militants would never eat another morsel in their life. I robbed them of that. I felt nauseous, my stomach in knots. The food tasted like nothing, just mush, but I knew if I did not eat it would gain me unwanted attention. The last thing I wanted to do was worry anyone.

"We appear to be ahead of schedule. If we continue at our current pace tomorrow, we should make it to the Port of Eura before evening the following day."

"That's great news!" Benjin responded, but his wavering voice did not match the words he spoke. Arriving at the port meant our journey with Bao would come to an end.

"Once we reach the Port of Eura, we will wait until night falls for you to continue so you can travel through the port under the cloak of darkness. If we reach the end of the tunnel quickly, you will have a few hours of rest before you must leave. Otherwise, you cannot stop until you reach the outskirts of the republic. The militia will not be within Terlu's territory, as their plan to invade is a surprise. If you move quickly, you should be far beyond their reach by dusk."

"I can't believe I am finally going back home to Terlu after twelve years. I wonder if it has changed much since I left." Laago laid on his back and looked up at the dirt ceiling.

"Can we go to your apartment?" Luka wondered.

"I don't think so. I lived in the northwestern outskirts, which is too far out of our way. There's nothing to see there anyway. We can save that trip for another day." He took a long, thoughtful pause. "Besides, I wouldn't want to go home unless I had something to show for it."

"What do you mean?" I asked.

"I just don't want my first time seeing my pops to be me as a refuge on the run from the militia." He chuckled. "I refuse to return home until I make something of myself."

I looked up at him, but Laago's eyes remained zoned out on the dirt that surrounded us. I wanted to tell him that he already made something of himself, simply by forging his own path and refusing to tread in the footsteps of his terrible father, but all of the words swarming my heart were lost before they made it through my throat.

"Aw! I hate tunnels and walking," Luka groaned, interrupting the heavy silence.

"Me too, Buba." Benjin sighed as he laid down beside Laago, motioning Luka to come over. He waddled over to Benjin and collapsed on his chest. Bao rubbed his torch into the dirt, allowing darkness to fill the tunnels.

I laid still all night, covered in sweat regardless of the crisp tunnel air. My body and mind were paralyzed by the lives I had taken. I kept my eyes open, for every time I closed them, I saw those boys' faces. I tried to think of anything but them- my mother, my father, my sisters, even work at the factory- but nothing could overpower the fact that I was a murderer. When I thought of my mother, I immediately agonized over the boys' mothers, whose sons would never make it home.

Who was I to decide who lives and who dies? I am no god. It was not for me to pass judgment down onto others and take a life. I allowed the guilt and pain to consume me, as a punishment for my actions. There was no doubt in my mind that I would end up in Urliq, suffering an eternity in the Shadow with all of those who have committed such treasonous acts.

After what felt like years, Bao rolled over and relit his torch. It was a new day. I laid still, my eyes blankly staring at the dirt above me. I felt like I was in a grave, six feet underground and suffocating. What's the point of living, if everything could be taken from you so easily?

"Were you up all night?"

"I couldn't sleep," I mumbled, my voice cracking with dryness. Bao sighed and slowly sat up.

"To take a life feels very conflicting..." He trailed off in thought, joining my eyes in gazing at the ceiling. "I would be more concerned if you showed no remorse, than I am with you fretting over it."

"Is it morning already?" Benjin stretched his arms, finally awake as well. He reached his arm over and smacked Laago.

"No... One more hour..." He groaned, shielding his face from the light with his arm.

"Yeah, one more hour!" Luka mimicked.

"How'd you sleep?" Benjin asked, but I didn't know how to respond. The last thing I wanted was to give Benjin something else to worry about, yet I couldn't lie. Like Bao said, if we were to make it through all this, we needed to communicate.

"I couldn't," I said. Benjin's natural smirk faded, leaving behind a worried expression.

"I wish I could take your pain. I should have taken care of those militants, I was supposed to protect you. I am sorry you have to go through this."

"It was bound to happen sooner or later." I sighed, already feeling a little weight lift off my shoulders.

"We're here for you, Ny. You did a brave thing. I'm sorry I wasn't a better friend yesterday, I should have been there for you. Instead, I let myself get stuck in my head," Laago said. His honesty meant a whole lot more to me than if he just put on a fake brave face and ignored his own pain. Though it was not his hands who took the boys' lives, it just as easily could have been.

"I don't know what I would do without you guys," I said, rising to my feet. I looked at Bao, who stood there proudly. He nodded his head to me, which said more than any words could. I knew he understood the pain that riddled my heart and mind.

"Everyone up. Let's go!" Bao ordered, already walking away with our only light source. Benjin jumped up, swooping Luka off the ground and following Bao closely behind. Laago rolled onto his feet and threw his arm around me.

"You're one tough girl, Ny!" He remarked, as we strolled along. I pulled some dried wheat strips out of my bag and handed him one. "Great, wheat sticks. Remember what your father used to say?"

"They are so dry, that your tongue will shrivel up and fall out of your mouth-"

"Before you can finish chewing a single one," Laago said, finishing my sentence. Though my heart warmed at the thought of my father, it was quickly overtaken by a deep sense of sadness.

"I can't wait to get out of these tunnels," I muttered as I munched on a strip.

"I think you'll like Terlu. Or at least the coast. The first thing we should do is visit a market. They sell every food you could imagine, all fresh. There are even street performers, dancers, singers, magicians…" Laago's eyes lit up as he imagined the colorful streets of Terlu. "And if you know how to bargain, you can get some great deals."

"Do you think there will be bongamelons?"

"Bongamelons, tartar berries, honeydews… You name it."

"I haven't had a bongamelon since I was a kid." I drooled over the thought of my favorite fruit, fiercely sweet and juicy.

"Remember when your parents would take us on picnics?"

"How could I forget?"

As we walked through the tunnel, Luka babbled to Benjin and Bao about everything from his favorite color to pondering why people wear socks. He spoke a mile a minute, clearly with no intention of stopping. Every few minutes Benjin would respond with a short response, feigning enthusiasm.

"Benji, why do we have to wear socks and shoes? Can't we just wear shoes?"

"Why do you think, Buba?" Benjin sighed, too tired to deal with another day of Luka's endless array of questions.

"Because feet are stinky?" Luka suggested after a long thoughtful pause.

Benjin picked up his pace, perhaps eager to get ahead of Luka, but instead he sped up as well, talking as fast as he skipped through the tunnels. Laago and I drifted behind, both of us uninterested in keeping up with them. Luka gave up on Benjin, who resorted to whistling instead of responding to his questions, causing him to instead barrage Bao. 'Why do you hold that torch? Are we almost there yet? Why is it so cold? Why is it so hot? Why, why, why?'

I wanted to scream, but Bao was far calmer. Instead, he took time to thoughtfully answer each and every question Luka had for him. Laago and I abruptly stopped walking, unanimously deciding to let the three of them get ahead of us.

"It's too early for this." Laago looked at me and chuckled.

"If I hear the word 'why' one more time…" I joked. After a moment, we both began walking again, following the torch light through the tunnel.

"I don't know how Benjin does it." He sighed. "Luchi was the same way, always asking questions."

I thought of my little sister, her straight black hair always falling in front of her eyes. Among us girls, she looked the most like my mother. I wondered what she would be like today if she was still alive. Growing up, Luchi questioned everything. She never accepted that things were what they were. Whenever my mother cooked any meat, whether it was duck or tiger rabbit, Luchi would argue endlessly with her. My mother would try to help her accept our culture's traditions, but Luchi would always argue that it was not an excuse and that simply because we were accustomed to doing something, didn't make it right.

"I miss her."

"She was more stubborn than Benjin," Laago said, breaking the silence. I couldn't help but chuckle. My sweet sister… My mind wandered, as it often did as we trudged through these endless tunnels.

"Laago?" I asked, but before he could respond, I faltered. "Never mind."

"What?" He turned his head curiously to me, but I regretted even considering asking him such an invasive question. We continued moving forward, following Bao's dimly lit torch.

"No, really, it's nothing."

"It was obviously something."

"I was wondering what your mother was like… You only ever mentioned your father." My voice trailed off more as each syllable drifted from my tongue. Laago heavily sighed. "I am so sorry. I shouldn't have asked, I-"

"No, no…" He interrupted. "I just can't even remember the last time I thought of her. I have only ever told your parents and Benjin about her."

"What was she like?"

"My mom was a harlot. My pops was one of her regulars and he knocked her up," he casually spoke, as if none of this was abnormal. Though, I suppose 'normal' is subjective, because this was his normal. "She never wanted to have me, but my pops did. I honestly think he was in love with her, even though he never admitted it. Maybe he thought if she had the baby they would become an actual couple. I don't know. After I was born, she left. I don't even know what she looks like. My pops rarely ever spoke about her, unless he got really drunk. One time when he was about to pass out he told me that I reminded him of her, but I don't know if he even knew what he was saying."

"I had no idea." My mouth dropped open.

"I used to be ashamed of it. Of her, my pops, of myself..." His words trailed off, before he found his voice again. "But I am not anymore. I don't blame my mom. She was young, poor, and homeless before she became a prostitute. She did what she had to do to survive."

"That is really mature of you, Laago. Most people wouldn't be so understanding if they were in your position."

"It took me years, but I finally realized why waste my time being ashamed of something that I have no control over? If my mom wasn't a harlot and my pops wasn't her client, I would have never been born. I would have never felt the cold ocean waves crashing against my legs, the grainy sand on my feet... I would have never met Benjin, Daath, Lee, or you," he reflected. "Whatever mistake my mom and pops made, I am glad they did. I am glad to be alive."

I couldn't imagine my life without Laago. He had been a part of my family for my entire life. I wanted to tell him that his parents were missing out, that they didn't deserve such a selfless and loving son. But sometimes, even when my heart knew what it wanted to say, something within me stopped it.

"I am glad you are alive too, Laago." I finally mustered the strength to say. He threw his arm around me and we continued to walk through the dingy tunnel together.

The rest of the day was uneventful. In the past, that would bore me, but I had a newfound appreciation for the mundane. I hoped the rest of our journey would be uneventful too. I didn't want to experience any more surprises, because if I learned one thing, it is that surprises tend to be a bad thing.

As we collapsed to the ground at the end of the night, Bao confirmed we would reach the Port of Eura by the following evening. Though the boys cheered, I felt my stomach turn. We would be entering new territory. I tried comforting myself by focusing on Laago's positive words of republic's markets, but I couldn't shake my fears. He had not returned to his home country in twelve years. A lot has changed, especially since the New Plague. I wondered if the markets would even exist anymore.

"I wish you could come with us, Bao," Benjin admitted.

"I cannot leave Amu or the people of Tinshe. It is my duty to serve and protect them," he declared, ripping into a piece of bread. He glanced over at Luka, who was sprawled out on the dirt. "I never had an opportunity to have my own kids. Ona and I always planned to, but our time together fell short. I will miss you all deeply." His eyes sullenly drifted onto the warm flame of his torch. Though his words may have appeared simple and light, they carried great weight. "But I know our paths will cross again, one day, and I look forward to it."

"To Bao." Benjin raised his pouch of water, and we all followed suit.

We all took a drink and Bao bowed his head in response. He would have been a great father. He taught me that my small size wasn't a disadvantage, but a strength. He showed us the importance of letting go, even if it caused pain. But most importantly, he showed us that no matter how strong and wise a man is, he will experience suffering. Bao was a warrior, but was still brought to his knees when he lost his wife. I used to look at my parents, soldiers, emperors, and kings as if they were indestructible. Now I understood that they could feel just as scared and lost as kids.

"I had another dream about mother, but this time I was able to control it and talk to her. She said she was proud of us, but the reason she came was to tell us that our father isn't there."

"What do you mean he's not there?" Benjin stammered.

"I don't know, I asked to speak to him and that's all she told me. Before I could find out what she meant, the dream was interrupted by those two militants." My eyes wandered from the boys and into the finicky flames of Bao's light. "I think he's alive," I declared, as I looked back at Benjin. His eyes widened in shock, but quickly narrowed in focus. His hand was slowly rubbing his chin.

"That's a bold claim to make from a dream," Laago pointed out.

"I know," I mumbled, feeling defeated already. Part of me wished that I never mentioned it.

"Bao, if our father was captured by the militia, where would they take him?"

"The Suhai Empire has many prisons..." Bao pondered, thinking aloud. "I suppose, if General Ahkpi's militia caught your father he would have arrested him and charged him for conspiracy or perhaps even terrorism. For such a high crime against the empire, Daath would have been banished from Suhai and imprisoned for life."

"What are you getting at?" Laago interrupted.

"Suhai does not keep high threat prisoners within its walls." Bao's eyes darted from his flame to Benjin. "Instead, they are sent to a maximum-security prison. I am not sure, but I believe it is in the Mountains of Shiren, which divides the Empire of Gala from Chao Binh."

"That has to be where our father is!" Benjin exclaimed.

"Possibly," Bao speculated. "It would explain why Amu stopped sensing Daath's energy. The Mountains of Shiren are as tall as they are vast. It could act as a barrier, preventing his energy from flowing to us."

"Let's break Daath out!" Laago declared, throwing his fist up.

"No!" Bao sharply dictated.

"We can't just leave him there to rot!" Benjin argued. "He sacrificed his whole life for us. Now we will do the same!"

"You will report to General Pago of Terlu and then head east to the Island of Aara to inform the Council of Five. That is your mission."

"Our father would do anything to protect us. We cannot abandon him. It has been years since he has gone missing. Now that we know he may be wasting away in some prison, we can't just do nothing."

"I understand your pain, but this is what Daath would want. As it stands, we have no way to rescue him. The prison is impenetrable and to even find it could take months. It would be a suicide mission." Bao sighed. "Empress Jhena of the Empire of Gala has the most powerful and advanced army in the world. It is her most elite soldiers who guard the prison. Once the world's armies are informed of the atrocities that Ahkpi's militia is committing, we will hold much more leverage. We will save your father, but we need to focus on the greater good here. Empress Jhena is an honorable ruler. She may even personally pardon Daath once she hears the truth."

"I hate imagining him there. I hope he isn't suffering." Benjin leaned back against the wall, sunken with defeat.

"Daath is an unwavering man, he will persist. While you continue your journey, I will use every resource I have to track down your father. Amu and I will find him."

# CHAPTER EIGHT
# THE OUTSKIRTS

T HE AIR FELT DIFFERENT this morning. I drearily dragged my body upwards and sat on my butt. I was the first one awake. As I stretched my arms, I tried to imagine the Port of Eura. By the time the sun falls through the sky, I would be further than I had ever been from home. Home. What was home? I glanced down at Benjin, whose body was draped over Luka like a blanket. Luka's curly brown hair almost fell past his shoulders and was draped over his chubby cheeks.

"Home," I whispered, to nobody but myself. Benjin and Luka were my home, not some dilapidated apartment.

I heard Bao rouse, yawning and stretching his body. Today we would be parting ways with him. I dreaded the thought of not having his expertise and advice to support us through the journey. Without him, I felt vulnerable and lost. It didn't make sense why he couldn't just come with us.

"I hope you didn't have another sleepless night?"

"No, I just woke up too."

"Is it that time already?" Benjin moaned, rolling over and waking Luka.

"We have a lot of ground to cover today. It would be best if we started moving."

Although Bao spoke as if it was a mere recommendation, he was already rising to his feet. I leaned over and tapped Laago on the shoulder. He groaned in disdain without even opening his eyes.

Without skipping a beat, we all rolled to our feet and began to follow our leader.

"What's the first thing you guys want to do once we get out of these tunnels?" Laago asked, rubbing his eyes.

"Eat a hot meal," Benjin responded, rubbing his stomach.

"I can't wait to take a shower..."

"I can't wait for you to take a shower too."

"Like you smell any better. What about you, Ny?"

"I want to eat as much bongamelon as I weigh." My mouth salivated at the thought of the fiercely sweet fruit tingling my tongue.

"Once we get to Terlu's markets, you'll eat so much bongamelon that you'll never want to eat it again!" Laago promised.

"Are you paying?" Benjin retorted.

"You don't have to pay when you're quick like me."

"Great, so we won't have to find General Pago, because we'll end up in prison."

"We still have the money Nonna gave us," I said.

"It has to last us our whole trip. If we run out of money before we reach the Council of Five we are screwed." Benjin always acted like I was a child.

"We know, Commander Benjin. Let us at least dream!" Laago complained.

"We have a decent amount of wheat strips leftover too," I mentioned, shuffling through my bag.

"I hate dried wheat strips!" Luka stomped his feet.

"I bet you hate starving more than you hate wheat strips!" Laago scooped Luka up and threw him on his back.

"I gathered some money as well, for your journey." Bao reached into his bag and tossed Benjin a sack of coins. "I wish I could give you kids more, especially for all you are sacrificing for our cause."

"This is more than enough. Thank you." Benjin tucked the sack into his bag.

"Maybe once we get to General Pago he'll reward us for saving the republic!" Laago exclaimed.

"General Pago is an honorable man, I expect he will take good care of you all. Send him my regards when you meet him."

"You've met Pago?"

"Met? We are kin," he casually revealed.

"How are you just telling us this now? Were you ever planning to tell us?" Laago was astonished, well, we all were.

"It is painful to think of. Roan is Ona's brother."

"I'm so sorry... I had no idea," Benjin stammered.

"That makes you guys practically brothers. I can't believe you're related to General Pago! He's a living legend," Laago bellowed.

"If General Pago is your brother, why didn't you just go warn him?"

"When Ona passed, things became complicated. I did not handle things as I should have, I see that now," he admitted. "At the time, I was drowning in grief. I took a lot of my anger out on those around me. Because of how I acted, I lost many people in my life."

"I'm sure he would understand... You lost your wife, of course you would be upset," Benjin reasoned.

"And Roan lost his sister. I had no excuse to take out my pain on him, when he was just as much of a victim as I was."

"Why don't you just apologize?" Laago said.

"I can't."

"You can't? Or you won't?" Laago grilled him with questions, but Bao just kept walking and ignored him.

"Laago, enough..." Benjin scolded, smacking him on the back of his head.

"I was just trying to help!"

"I can't apologize to Roan because I can't bear to see him. He is the spitting image of Ona. It took me ages to get her out of my head and I fear if I see him, I will descend right back to where I was. Seeing him would remind me of the old times, when Ona and I would travel to Terlu for holidays," Bao's voice wavered.

As he spoke, I felt a pain in my chest. My heart ached at the thought of his suffering. Not only did Bao lose his wife, but he had to abandon the people who cared about him, because they reminded him of painful memories.

"I understand." Benjin reached over and placed his hand on his shoulder.

"We should pick up the pace if we want to make it before sundown," Bao said, not able to bear the truth.

Silence engulfed the tunnels. Bao must feel so lonely when he travels through here alone, but I suppose when you experience a loss as severe as he has, even the most crowded of rooms can feel like a dark and empty tunnel.

I felt everyone's anxiety heavily weighing the air down as we marched through our final day underground. Our future was muddled with uncertainty and we sloppily covered our fears with light conversations and empty jokes. I longed for the past, where even though life was riddled with suffering, I at least had certainty. Every night, I laid in the same bed. Every day, I drank the same dandelion root tea and went to work at the same factory. Since we left our home, each day had been filled with more uncertainty than the last. We spent days sleeping on the floor of the Forest of Earth and then in the dead ends of these tunnels. I knew for certain we would not be sleeping tonight, as Bao instructed us to not stop moving until daylight hits. But what about when the sun begins to rise, where would we sleep then?

"Why can't I have a weapon?" Luka asked, to no one in particular. Benjin looked down at him, considering his request.

"I don't know if you're ready for one, Buba," he finally decided, leading to Luka stomping his feet.

"I am ready! I'm not a baby!"

"Wow, you're starting to sound like Ny!" Laago laughed, nudging my arm. I, however, didn't find it funny. I rolled my eyes.

"How about this? If I can find you a weapon in the markets of Terlu that I think you can handle, we'll get it."

"Fine!" Luka resigned, then quickly lost interest anyway as he started to skip ahead.

"Buying a blade is going to be too expensive. The markets are a rip off for anything weapon related. How about next time we catch a militant we give Luka their weapon?" Laago sharpened his dagger against a rock as we walked.

"As much as I don't want to give Luka a weapon, it might not be a bad idea. What do you think, Nyla?" Benjin turned to me.

"Oh... I don't know," I said, surprised he even bothered asking for my opinion.

"Do you think Luka can handle his own?"

"I wouldn't trust him with a blade, he's too little to understand it isn't a toy. What about one of those batons all those militants carry?"

"That's perfect, Ny!" Laago exclaimed. "He can't really hurt himself with a baton, but if a militant gets close to Luka, he can hit 'em hard with it. It would buy us time if our hands are full."

"Too bad we didn't think of this before. We buried two perfectly good batons with those militants," Benjin commented.

"I'm sure there will be plenty more opportunities for us to pick one off."

"I wonder how many militants are going to be at the port," I worried aloud.

"Well, if the empty streets on our way to Bao's were any sign..."

"I suspect about half of Ahkpi's militia will be stationed at the port," Bao declared. "They will most likely be scattered about, to not raise any suspicion."

"How are we going to sneak by half of Najin's entire militia?" Laago fretted, rubbing his forehead.

"We just have to fly under their radar. We are just four kids traveling from the outskirts of Terlu to work on a fishing boat in Huang." Benjin took a deep breath.

"Here!" Bao stood before a dead end. We all looked up in confusion.

"I think these tunnels might have made you lose your marbles, Bao!" Laago joked, but Bao ignored his comment and dropped to the ground.

"We will rest until the sun goes down."

"We are really here?" Benjin exclaimed, but as the thought sunk in, so did his expression. "So, I guess this is the end of our journey together, huh?"

"I suppose it may be the end of this journey, but your real journey has barely begun. Our paths will cross again, I am sure of it, and when they finally do, you will be heroes of the west and protectors of peace."

We all sat around Bao, resting our legs for the time being. I laid on my back, staring up at the dirt ceiling. In just a few hours, I would be looking up at the stars and feeling the cool sea breeze. I wondered if it would be a full moon.

"Nyla, it's your birthday in two days! You've never spent a birthday outside of Tinshe, let alone outside of the entire Suhai Empire." Benjin rustled my hair and laid down beside me. I would finally be sixteen.

"We have to celebrate!" Laago threw his arms up in excitement. "Little Ny is gonna be a woman!"

"Hey, she's sixteen, not eighteen," Benjin argued.

"I don't need two men telling me whether I am a woman or not. That's my choice. And guess what, you wouldn't know a real woman if she came and hit you in the face!"

"I love it! You're a strong girl, I mean woman, Ny!" Laago roared. "I remember when you were just a baby," he reminisced. I turned to Benjin, who was staring at me with a toothy smile.

"What's so funny?"

"Nothing, I am just proud."

Almost as soon as I drifted off to sleep, Bao declared it was time for us to go. Immediately, my heart began to pound. Benjin clipped his belt on, situating his axe on his side. His hand clenched his chest, where the scroll was tied tightly around his body with a vine. I threw my bow over my shoulder and took a deep breath. Bao began to whistle the familiar tune. I wondered if this is how it felt to head into war.

Suddenly, a whistle reciprocated Bao's call from the other side of the dead end. The dirt wall began to fall and in shined light. I immediately smelt an overwhelming stench of fish. As my eyes adjusted, I realized we were in a small closet. A fat man stood in the doorway.

"Welcome to the Port of Eura!" He bellowed.

The man led us out of the closet and into the back of his fish market. The stench was overwhelming; I could barely breathe. Luka dramatically held his nose and pretended to puke. I hit the back of his head and shot him a look.

"My name is Bachu. I am the most northeastern member of the resistance." His voice was rough, rumbling over each syllable. His once white apron was covered in fish guts and blood.

"Nice to meet you, Bachu." Bao reached over and shook his hand. "I am Bao. I was ordered by the resistance to deliver these kids to the port." *He was always vague when sharing information with fellow resistance members. Amu, the last Protector, sent us here, not the resistance.*

"Where are they headed?"

"To the markets of Terlu," Bao responded, not technically lying. Bachu's eyebrows raised, clearly not buying it.

"The resistance sends a couple of kids all the way to the markets of Terlu. I bet you kids have some serious shopping ahead of you!" Bachu didn't just laugh, but he roared. "Well, don't let me keep you," he pointed towards the door as he went back to work behind the counter.

"Well, this is it," Bao declared, crossing his arms. "I wish you all great luck. Remember all that I taught you. You are warriors, any militant will be sorry to cross your path." He smiled. Luka ran into his legs and swung his arms around, hugging Bao tightly. I looked at Benjin and Laago, then we all jumped in and embraced Bao in one big hug. I held back my tears as I nuzzled into his chest.

"We are going to miss you, Bao," Benjin gushed.

"It's time for you all to go and continue your journey. Follow the coastline as far north as it stretches, then continue following it east until you hit Huang. Remember, do not stop until daylight breaks and you are out of the militia's reach."

"Got it!" Benjin promised as we headed to the door. I looked over my shoulder to get one last glimpse of Bao, but he was already gone.

The cold sea breeze hit us as soon as we left the fish market. I immediately looked up to the sky, which was oversaturated with bright twinkling stars. I longingly gazed at the moon, it was just rising over the horizon. Eura, the moon goddess, was closely watching over us. She will keep us safe, she always has. I listened to the waves crashing in the distance. It felt so good to be above ground.

"Let's move!" Benjin led us towards the water, using the darkness as a shield to protect us from any unwanted attention.

We cautiously followed him, jogging quietly through the port. There were a couple of other shops surrounding the fish market, but they all had their lights off for the night. We stayed close to the buildings, using them as cover. The street was not paved, it was just tightly packed in dirt. It must have rained today, because every other step I was sinking into mud. I turned my head to the left and saw two militants sitting against a shop on the other side of the road. I quickly reached forward to Benjin, tapping him on the shoulder. As I pointed to them, we all dropped to the ground and froze. I focused my eyes on the militants.

"I think they're asleep..." Benjin whispered, slowly rising back up.

We all followed his lead and slowly crept down the street. I anxiously looked around, knowing there had to be plenty more guards. As we were about to pass the last shop, I noticed there was a bright light shining in the distance. Benjin stuck his arm out and stopped us dead in our tracks. He crouched down and motioned us to come look.

I peered around the corner and saw about thirty militants all gathered around under a single light post. Most of them were sitting around and eating. Many were loudly talking and laughing, clearly drunk. Some were playing a game with a ball, while others were napping on the dirt. At the other side of them there was what appeared to be a huge abandoned warehouse. That must be their temporary barracks. If it was night and there were that many militants casually relaxing outside, I imagined the warehouse was full of many more sleeping soldiers. We all huddled together.

"How are we supposed to get past them?" Laago worried aloud. We had reached an intersection in the road and the only way we could continue forward was to cross it.

"We can head back a little before we cross the street. That way we can sneak behind those buildings and crawl across the road towards the water undetected."

"There's two militants sleeping right there! What if they wake?"

"We'll just have to be quiet. Ready?" Benjin asked, but he already began hurrying back along the buildings. I followed him closely behind, holding Luka's hand tightly. Benjin took us about fifteen feet back from where we came, then crouched down and examined the road. Once he confirmed the coast was clear, he bolted across. We walked along the shops, hiding in the shadows and staying as low to the ground as possible.

We finally reached the end of the block, where the two militants were sleeping. They were sitting on a ledge with their backs leaning against the building. Benjin glanced back at us and scooped up Luka. He cautiously stepped around them, holding his breath.

They didn't budge.

Next, Laago treaded around them, avoiding sinking into the mud. I quickly followed, stepping carefully into his footsteps. I stepped into the first footprint, then the second, but when I lifted my foot back up, the arrows on my hip ever so slightly shifted into each other, making a clang.

I immediately looked over at the militants and realized one was drowsily waking. Before he fully opened his eyes, I flipped my bow around my body and nocked an arrow. Out of the corner of my eye, I saw Benjin shield Luka. Just as the man's eyes widened, I released. The arrow quickly pierced through his chest, causing him to slap his arm back, hitting the other guard who sat sound asleep beside him.

Laago leaped over and covered the injured man's mouth before he could let out a wail and slit his throat with his dagger. He then swiftly ran it across the sleeping man's neck, who was passed out so drunk that he remained unaware there were even trespassers. I hoped that if I got killed, it was in my sleep, while I dreamt of my family.

I lowered my bow and glanced down the road at the drunken militants lounging outside the warehouse. Few of them even had their weapons on them. But although they were oblivious, it was only a matter of time before we would be caught. We had to move fast if we wanted to make it out of here alive.

"We have to hide these bodies," I ordered, running behind the building. "Here, in this pit!" I motioned Laago over. He threw one body over his shoulder and jogged over to me.

"This is just dehumanizing…" He shuddered, shoving the man's body into the trash-filled pit. He ran back, grabbed the second one and tossed it in like a bag of garbage.

It wasn't until we covered the bodies with trash that I finally took a breath. We huddled behind the shop, parallel to the barrage of militants, but hidden in the darkness. Laago's shirt now had blood stains stretching from his chest to his shoulder. He stood next to me, his hand shaking as he tightly gripped the bloody dagger.

"I think we just have to make a break for it. We are only about thirty feet from the coast. The ocean will serve as good cover, the crashing waves are loud and it is dark. Once we get there, we will run along the coast and not stop until we reach the outskirts of Terlu," Benjin decided. I looked over at the army of militants and shuddered.

"The sooner we do it, the sooner we will be away from them," I whispered, mostly just to comfort myself. My stomach was churning and my hands were shaking. I had gruesome thoughts of us being captured.

Benjin got down on the ground and began to army crawl across the street. I dropped to the floor, along with Luka and Laago, and we began to mimic him. Then, just as we were about halfway across the street, I began to hear voices. It was a group of men walking down the street towards the warehouse, their swords hitting against their legs as they marched. We all picked up our pace, gliding across the street. I prayed the darkness shielded us from their sight. Benjin reached the end, where the road dipped and hit the sand. He rolled over the edge and poked his head back up, watching us. Moments later, Laago slid over, then Luka, followed by me. Our eyes all followed the group of militants.

"Hey!" One of the men shouted. I grabbed Laago's hand and squeezed it. "So much for keeping lookout!" He laughed, noticing the two militants were not at their posts.

"They probably headed back to the barracks early for a drink. We'll rat 'em out in the morning," another concluded. We all sighed in relief. Had they even taken a moment to check, they would have seen their fellow militants' blood splattered against the wall.

"Let's move!" Benjin whispered after they passed, grabbing Luka's hand.

We all rose to our feet, but stayed crouched, and began running towards the ocean. The waves crashed and receded, following the moon's orders. I can't remember the last time I saw the ocean. The Port of Eura sat nestled on the coast of the Bay of Suhai, which poured out into the Great Ocean. I squinted my eyes and looked south down the coast where the actual port was. In the darkness, I couldn't make out much, but I could tell it was enormous. The dock protruded into the water, its bright lights sending a twinkling shimmer across the ocean waves. It was probably two miles away, but I could clearly see large boats surrounding it.

The Port of Eura had a strip of stores and warehouses that ran along a wide dirt road which hugged the sandy coastline and connected the Suhai Empire to the Republic of Terlu. Although it was the most direct route to the republic, it was technically a backroad. When shipments came into the Port of Eura, they were taken northwest, along a well-traveled trade route, and then taken either west to the Suhai Empire or northeast towards the republic.

Since that was where the goods were headed, most civilians in this area lived north of the Port of Eura. The eastern outskirts were less populated and more industrialized. But fortunately for us, it was not too long of a journey before you reached the empty land between the Port of Eura and the Republic of Terlu's great walls.

I kicked up sand as I ran eagerly towards the ocean. Laago was already standing ankle deep in the water with Benjin. He dunked his head into a wave and washed his face off. It was the closest thing we had to a bath in nearly two weeks. I jumped towards them and splashed Laago with a handful of water. I felt a thick layer of dirt and grime drift off my legs and into the ocean.

"Oh, you're going down, Ny!" Laago joked, but careful to keep his voice down.

"Quiet! We need to keep moving," Benjin snapped, already continuing on. For almost a moment, it felt like old times, when in reality, we just took the lives of two men. I knew Benjin was right, one slip up could cost us our lives. But when you constantly feel the threat of death looming close by, it begins to feel normal.

We all jogged along the coast, our feet sinking into the sand with every step. I stared up at the moon. It was much brighter than I remembered, towering over the sky. I looked at her darkened craters, contrasting the lighter areas. Every crater that marked her surface was left behind by a meteor, but she did not hide her scars. She wore them proudly, knowing they only showed the world what she has endured, and she was beautiful for that.

"I missed you," I whispered.

I looked back down and watched Laago stumble over something and come tumbling down. As Luka and I caught up to the boys, I realized it was a militant that he tripped over. He must have passed out drunk on the beach! Before I could even process it, Benjin instinctively jumped on top of him, sitting on the man's chest and firmly covering his mouth.

"You need to pay attention, Laago! What are we supposed to do now?" Benjin scolded Laago, who stumbled back to his feet. The man squirmed under Benjin, but stood no chance at freeing himself.

"We have to kill him," Laago responded nervously. The man began moving frantically, but his screams were muffled into Benjin's hand.

"Take off your shirt. When I move my hand, stuff it in his mouth."

"He's gonna bite my hand!"

"Do it, Laago!" Benjin commanded.

Laago quickly pulled his already bloodied shirt off and shoved it into the militant's mouth as Benjin lifted his hand. Benjin moved his weight off the man's chest and spun him around. I covered Luka's eyes. The man began wailing his arms and kicking frantically as Benjin grappled him from behind, securing a chokehold. I closed my eyes, but the image of the man's body flopping in the sand burned in my mind, like a fish pulled out of the water. I heard his body thumping on the ground, trying to break free. It persisted for about two minutes, which were easily the longest seconds of my life.

When I finally opened my eyes, he laid still. Benjin slowly released the man, whose limp body then dropped into the sand. Benjin rose to his feet, then leaned over and began rummaging through the militant's pockets. He took his baton, some food packets, and coins. He walked over to Luka and swiped my hand off his eyes.

"Here you go, buddy," Benjin said as he handed Luka the baton. Luka's eyes widened, then he looked over at the militant in the sand.

"Why is he sleeping?" Luka innocently asked.

"He probably had a long day." Benjin began walking along the coast. "Let's keep moving."

"Why didn't we just have Ny hit him with an arrow? Would have been quicker," Laago whispered.

"I am hoping when the militants find him, they will think he just got drunk and drowned," Benjin casually explained, tossing Laago his spare shirt from his bag.

It was almost eerie how nonchalant he acted. I felt tremendously nauseous and I was not even the one who took his life. Plus, Benjin did it with his bare hands. He felt the man fight for his life and waited for his last breath to fall, his face turning red and then ghost white.

"I don't know... They're going to find three dead militants tomorrow. No way they'll think it's an accident," Laago worried.

"We'll be in the outskirts of Terlu before anyone finds them anyway," Benjin reassured him, picking up the pace. Laago looked back at me and frowned.

"We'll be fine," I promised, even though I did not believe my own words.

The moon was directly above us now, meaning it must be midnight. We had been running for hours and I felt my guard dropping. I tried to keep my mind awake, because we would still be in militia land until the sun rose. But every time I shook my head, my eyes began to drift off again without hesitation. Luka was fast asleep on Benjin's back, his body bouncing with Benjin's stride. I pulled out some dried wheat strips from my bag and tossed some to Benjin and Laago.

My eyes traced the dirt road that hugged the coast, there was about a quarter mile of sand before it met the ocean. I stayed on the lookout for militants, keeping my hand hovered over my arrows. Every time I felt my guard drop, the mental image of all those militants huddled around the warehouse shot adrenaline pulsating through me. The other side of the road was lined with warehouses and shops, with their fronts facing the ocean. The street almost looked abandoned at this hour of the night, as there were no lights or people.

The Port of Eura didn't have many permanent residents beyond the shop owners and fishermen. Any goods that were shipped into the west from the east either entered here, at the Bay of Suhai, or in

Eura's Harbor, which is north of Terlu. But because of this limited access and the need for so many imports, I always imagined the Port of Eura to be a high energy and bustling town. Instead, it kind of looked dull and depressing. I ran up towards Benjin.

"Shouldn't there be more people?" I questioned.

"I have been thinking the same thing. This side of the port is more industrial though. More people live north, along the trade route," Laago guessed.

"I bet there are more soldiers camping out in those buildings," I assumed.

"Let's not stick around long enough to find out."

The moon began to fall behind us in the sky. I prayed to the moon goddess, Eura, for protection. Part of me felt it was worthless, the only thing that could protect me was the arrows that bounced on my hip. We were truly on our own. The other part of me was too tired to care.

As we ran through the sand, my eyes continued to study the buildings. A sudden feeling of being watched sent a shiver down my spine. I anxiously scanned our surroundings. I thought I was growing delirious, but then, faintly in the distance, I spotted the light of a tobacco pipe softly illuminating outside one of the store fronts. I smacked Benjin and pointed, then swung my bow around and prepared an arrow. But we did not slow our pace.

I prayed the dark sky and crashing waves hid us from his view. I watched the mysterious figure slowly lower the pipe and exhale a large cloud of smoke. My arrow was locked in place, ready to launch if he made a noise to warn the other militants. As we crossed in the distance parallel to him, I could have sworn I saw his hand slowly raise, as if he was waving hello. I shook my head in disbelief, my mind must be playing tricks on me. He was too far to really see anyway. Once we were far enough that the pipe's light was no longer visible, I lowered my bow.

"Did he wave to us?"

"What?" Benjin asked, his eyes focused in front of him.

"It looked like he waved to us," I mumbled, doubting myself.

"I thought I saw that too, but I figured I was just seeing things," Laago admitted.

"I'm sure we are just tired," Benjin said, adjusting Luka's sleeping body on his back.

The sun slowly began to rise over the horizon and as it did, the heat intensified. Our running had turned to jogging, which now faded into a brisk walk. Benjin was practically dragging Luka by the arm, after carrying him most of the way. My eyes continued to trace the dirt road that hugged the coast, waiting for signs of Terlu. We were far enough past the Port of Eura, so there were no more buildings. At the other side of the road I could make out tall grass fields speckled with colored flowers.

"Why can't we run on the road? My feet keep sinking into this sand," I complained.

"I'd rather stay out of sight," Benjin mumbled faintly. We were exhausted and getting on each other's nerves.

"Shouldn't we be there by now?"

"Well, these technically are the outskirts, so I guess you can say we are here. But we can't stop until we find shelter. Pretty soon we'll start seeing some homes and more signs of life," Benjin spoke with confidence, but I knew it was all wishful thinking, because he had no idea where we were either.

"We have to find a lonely old lady. They're suckers for company," Laago planned. "Plus, old ladies love to cook."

"Oh, yeah, is that a rule?" I retorted. "To qualify as an old lady you have to love to cook?"

"I'm not an old lady, so I wouldn't know. When you get old, let me know, Ny."

"You're an ass."

"Woah! Never heard Ny curse before. Benj, you hear that?"

"You're an ass, Laago," Benjin agreed, too tired to even listen.

I don't know if it was my starvation, exhaustion, or the heat, but I saw a reddish-brown ball hurtling towards us. I watched as it flew over the tall grass, darted across the road, and jumped into the soft sand. At this point, I was too exhausted to even say anything. I just watched the mysterious blob sprint towards us.

"Is that a dog?" Laago stopped and squinted, holding his hand above his eyes to block the sunlight. Before I could respond, the animal leapt up and jumped onto Laago, knocking him onto his back. Benjin tossed Luka to me and went to go pull the beast off him, when Laago let out a howl. The animal was licking his face. "Hey, relax! Off!" He spurted between laughter.

"Is that a foxdog?"

"Huh, I think so," Benjin agreed. "Its snout is too narrow and its coat is too red to be a dog, but it's far too large and outgoing to be a fox."

"I think she likes me!" Laago chuckled, finally pushing the dog off him. "You look too well fed to be a stray... Where'd you come from?" He rustled the animal's face, kissing it.

I had never seen a foxdog before, they were not native to the west and my empire certainly did not have exotic animals like these. We had boring ones, like tiger rabbits, frogs, and ducks.

"Come on, Laago. We gotta keep it moving if we want to find somewhere to sleep."

"I think we might have found somewhere and this little girl is gonna take us there, Benj!" Laago's eyes followed the fox dog as she ran towards the road. She stopped about halfway over and looked back at us, whining.

"Puppy!" Luka cheered, chasing after the animal.

I looked at Benjin, who shrugged in defeat. We all followed the foxdog across the road and into the high grass field. As we hiked our way through, I noticed a plume of smoke drifting into the air somewhere in the near distance. It did not come from a fire of death, but life.

"That's gotta be her home!" Laago shouted.

The grass field was coated in flowers of all colors. Hues of fuschia, violet, gold, and indigo were woven throughout. I plucked every dandelion I saw and shoved it into my bag. My lips were dry and cracked; my mouth watered for a cup of dandelion root tea. The foxdog scurried back and forth, impatiently waiting for us to catch up.

The smoke billowed out of a stone chimney attached to a dilapidated wooden home. Outside, there was a small fenced in enclosure surrounding the home with tomato plants that towered over. Looking around the field, I didn't see any other buildings. The foxdog jumped over the fence and through the open doorway, which was left open. Her loud bark rattled the house.

"Who's a good girl? Who's a good girl, Shaba?" A voice echoed through the home and drifted back into the field. We all stood outside the fence, unsure of what to do.

The foxdog bolted back outside and jumped over the fence and landed straight on Laago, knocking him off his feet yet again. For some reason it seemed to really like him.

"Hey! Hey! Be careful!" Laago squirmed underneath trying to dodge the foxdog's tongue.

"Foxdog's have a natural ability to read people," the voice claimed. I looked up from Laago and saw a woman standing in the doorway. "I do not see travelers in these parts often. What brings you kids here?"

Her gray hair was sloppily pushed into a bun on top of her head. She wore a long loose fitting dress that waved in the wind as she walked towards us. It was made up of large colorful patches, some with flowers, others just spotted. Her dark brown skin glowed in the unforgiving sunlight, wrinkled from years under its intensity. She was barefoot and covered in dirt, but her smile was bright, almost too perfect.

"Hello!" Benjin waved. "We are traveling to Huang to work on a fishing boat."

"Where are you coming from?"

"The northern outskirts," Benjin lied. Again. The woman stared at Benjin, before turning her gaze to me. I let out a smile, but broke eye contact and looked down at the ground. Her eyes shifted to Laago, who laid on the ground playing with her foxdog and Luka.

"You kids look like you could use a nice meal."

"Please! We're starving." Laago sat up, the foxdog's head resting on his lap.

"I have a table in the shade around back. It's too hot to be in the sun. You kids will get sick," she said before heading back inside. The foxdog jumped up and ran around to the back, as if she understood what the woman had said.

We walked along the tiny house. There couldn't be space for more than one room inside. Behind it, there was a wooden table covered in grime. A bushel of wilted flowers rested in a clay pot on the center of it. A few feet away stood two cows, munching on grass. I sat down next to Laago, letting my body melt into the seat. It was the first time we stopped moving since yesterday evening and I was afraid I wouldn't be able to stand back up.

"I could fall asleep here." Laago dropped his head into his arms on the table.

"Me too!" Luka mimicked him, dropping his head down too.

"What a precious place to live," I marveled. I had never witnessed anything quite like this. I grew up in the city, where everyone lived on top of each other. Here, this woman lived with her foxdog, encompassed by acres of solitude and surrounded by the natural beauty of the Earth.

"It's a beautiful place that I am grateful to call home," she responded through the open window that overlooked the table. She was standing in her kitchen, cooking, yet able to converse with us outside.

"Do you live out here alone?" I asked.

"No, no. I have Shaba. She has enough energy for a full village!" I looked over at the foxdog, who was running circles in the grass. I admired her shiny red coat.

"Do you grow all of your own food?" Benjin questioned.

"Most of it. Tomatoes, carrots, potatoes, blue peppers, string beans... My cows provide me with milk. I head to the markets every now and again to stock up on wheat and meat. Those are two things I can't grow," she replied. "How about you go collect some milk from the cows?"

"I've never milked a cow," I admitted.

"Aren't you from the outskirts?" She questioned, clearly doubting our story. Fortunately, her inquisitive glare was quick to fade. "Well, I hope you kids like vegetables. Shaba is the only one here who gets to eat meat. It's too expensive. Can you believe it? I feed my foxdog better than I feed myself. Ah, it is what it is," she rambled on.

"I picked some dandelions on our way, if you want to use them for tea," I offered. She motioned for me to toss them over to her through the window.

"Smells delicious already!" Laago shouted over to her.

"Don't get too excited. I know my strengths and cooking isn't one of them." She laughed, clattering and clanging pots. I elbowed Laago and he chuckled. There went his theory that every old lady was a great cook.

"I just realized, we never asked for your name," Benjin blurted out. "How rude of us!"

"My name is Kiuyah, but you don't have to tell me yours. It seems to me like you are running from something. Shaba isn't the only one around here that can read people."

Benjin looked down at the table. He wasn't a liar, especially to a good person like Kiuyah. She welcomed us into her home and offered us a warm meal... Would we be any better than the men who overthrew Tinshe if we lied to good and honest people?

"Thank you, Kiuyah," he finally responded.

"You're safe here. If you want, you can spend the night. I know it's not much, but it's a roof over your head." Kiuyah walked away from the window and disappeared.

"We would love to!"

"I am so glad Shaba found us,"' I remarked, looking over to the foxdog, who was now tantalizing the cows.

"I'm an animal whisperer!" Laago boasted. Kiuyah walked around to the table and placed steaming dishes of vegetables. It made me think of Bao. My heart sank. Although I barely knew Kiuyah, I had a feeling that she would get along with Bao.

"Dig in, kids!" She handed out plates and took a seat next to Luka.

"I love food!" Luka shrieked.

"Me too!" Kiuyah laughed.

"This place is beautiful," Benjin complimented. "Have you lived here your whole life?"

"I have lived just about everywhere, I only settled down here about ten years ago. I grew up in Soknan, a small city in Eastern Chao Binh," Kiuyah said with a smile, as she scooped a handful of potato wedges into her mouth.

"Wow, that's across the world."

"It is. I left home when I was fifteen, because I was supposed to be married off to some man. I would have been his seventh wife," she revealed. "In Eastern Chao Binh, religion and government are woven together, inseparable. There, men are to be respected. They own their wives, most men have upwards of ten of them. The man I was to marry was in his sixties, he was older than my father."

"I'm so sorry... That's horrible," Benjin said.

"It is horrible. I refused to waste my life away slaving for some fat old man, so I left my family and I never looked back."

"You must have seen some amazing things."

"I traveled to every corner of the world. I left Soknan and followed the coastline north until I reached the Empire of Gala, where I settled in the city of Bivery for a few years," she reminisced. "I arrived long before Empress Jhena came to power, during her father's reign. Gala is the wealthiest and most progressive empire, boasting the world's most powerful army. Even more impressively, the soldiers never exploited the people, or at least I never noticed it. There are even recent rumors that their military engineers are developing metal war ships."

"Metal ships? How would they float?" Benjin asked, but Kiuyah just shrugged.

"I never saw them, that's just gossip I heard at the markets of Huang."

"If the Empire of Gala was so great, why did you leave?" I asked.

"I worked there for years as a house cleaner and saved a lot of money. Though I had the stability I yearned for, I decided I wasn't ready to settle down. It was almost as if something was calling my name to continue on, so I continued north until I reached the Sacred Forest of Akta."

"I've heard so many stories about that forest!"

"And I bet all are true," she mused between bites of potatoes. "It was there I learned spirits are real- gods and goddesses roam the Earth just as we do, even if we cannot see them. The forest holds many secrets, and many who enter do not return. It was actually there where I found Shaba."

"I was wondering how a foxdog made its way to the outskirts of Terlu."

"I stumbled upon Shaba with her leg stuck in a forgotten snare. She was trapped and injured, much like I once was. After freeing her, I couldn't just leave her behind. I set up camp and nursed her back to health. It took weeks, but soon enough, she began hunting and was so adept that I didn't need to scavenge anymore. She caught the food, and I cooked it. We make a great team." Kiuyah called for Shaba, who immediately came barreling through the grass, only to stop right before her.

"She's so loyal!" Laago gushed.

"Foxdogs are phenomenal beings- wise and instinctive, but also loving and protective. Shaba once bit three fingers off a man who tried to steal from me. That's why I didn't stay in Fisher's Port for long." She let out a hearty laugh. "So I fled south, eventually traveling so far that I reached the southern tip of Western Chao Binh."

"I would've thought you'd never return."

"When I first left Eastern Chao Binh, I could never have imagined willingly traveling to the western half. I assumed they were the same, just two halves to a whole. But Western Chao Binh is as different to Eastern Chao Binh as the Qara Desert is to the Mountains of Shiren. People live more freely in the west- men do not take ten wives, let alone child brides. Women have rights and are allowed to work," she explained. "While it wouldn't be a bad place to settle down, I began to have night terrors there. I would wake up in the middle of the night screaming, fearing that my arranged husband would find me. So, I left. I snuck in a shipping boat and ended up in Kosi."

"That's where my girlfriend is from!" Benjin exclaimed.

"Ex..." Laago corrected. I glared at him.

"Kosi is the land of beautiful men and women, who all have ethereal hair so light that it is almost white... I don't get it. Maybe it's something in the water!" Kiuyah laughed. "I, too, fell in love with a woman in Kosi," she revealed with a heavy breath.

"How'd you meet?"

"Some guy who always hit on me at the markets invited me to this party and wouldn't take no for an answer. I never had many friends, since I was never in one place for too long. I figured I had nothing to lose. I thank the gods every day that I went that night. Leaving Shaba behind for the night, I went to the beach party. I remember feeling so awkward standing alone among all the groups of friends. I sat down by the blazing bonfire and contemplated leaving, when I looked up and saw this woman dancing." Kiuyah shook her head. "The way she moved embodied freedom, like a leaf in the wind, she was bound by nothing. If there was such a thing as Qalia, she was it."

"So what did you do? How'd you get her?" Benjin asked, sitting on the edge of his seat.

"Well, she eventually stopped dancing and she sat in the sand. I remember she wiped the sweat off her forehead and brushed her long blonde hair off her face. Without knowing why, I got up, sat right next to her, and told her the truth- I had traveled across the eastern half of the world, yet I had never seen someone as beautiful as her."

"There you go, Kiuyah!" Laago cheered.

"At first, she just stared at me, and inside, panic set in. I thought she might consider me mad! But then, she started to laugh, and all my fears melted away. She asked if I really traveled around half of the world. I told her I had been to every corner of the east. That's when she said, 'Let's travel to every corner of the west.' And we did- from Kosi to the Kingdom of Yana, through the Qara Desert until we settled in the Republic of Terlu."

"That's beautiful," Benjin admired.

"I don't mean to pry, but what happened to her? Where is she now?" Laago asked.

"Ani's life was taken long before she was ready to go. We were living here on our farm when the plague hit. I didn't want her going off to the markets, I knew it wasn't safe, but she said she'd rather die than to live her life in fear. A week later, she passed. Now, it's just me and Shaba."

"I'm so sorry. We lost our mother and two of our sisters to the New Plague," Benjin related.

"I hate that name. The 'New' Plague. The only thing the plague cleansed this world of was my love and happiness, along with many others. The fact that those damn Najin snobs call it that makes my blood boil."

"Me too! Then they used the plague as an excuse to move their murderous militia into Tinshe, only to crush our side of the empire even more!" Laago fumed.

"I knew you weren't from the outskirts." Kiuyah smirked.

"Actually, I am from the northwestern outskirts," Laago responded, technically telling the truth.

"We are from Tinshe," Benjin admitted. "I am sorry we lied."

"No need to explain." Kiuyah's smile was warm and inviting, almost motherly. She stood up and began collecting our plates. "There's a bath under that oak tree behind those cows, feel free to wash up. It's attached to the well so the water will be ice-cold. You'll get used to it though. I'm gonna clear some space inside for you kids to sleep."

"That sounds wonderful!" Laago jumped up and headed to the bath. It was a large metal box with a pump attached to it. "I finally get to shave this itchy beard!" He crowed, as he scratched his chin.

Normally, he was clean-shaven, especially during the warmer seasons, but lately he had no choice but to let his facial hair grow. For the first time in a while, his brown scruff was beginning to develop into a beard. It fit his face well, almost making him look older. His hair was so long that he tied it into a small bun with a thin brown leather strap to cool his neck off.

"Wake up, Buba. It's bath time." Benjin picked up Luka.

"I like being stinky..." Luka mumbled, half asleep.

"Speak for yourself. Phew yew!" Benjin made a sour face.

"I wish our parents could be here. They would love Kiuyah and her house." I sighed, walking alongside Benjin.

"Who knows, maybe one day we can take our father here." Benjin threw his arm around my shoulder and pulled me in. Shaba bolted past us to Laago. "But I think mother's spirit is here with us. I believe she goes wherever we do."

"I think this is the longest I've gone without bathing!" Laago called over to us, stripping his clothes off.

"Laago!" Benjin quickly covered my eyes. "At least give us a warning!" At first I closed my eyes dramatically, but then I found myself squinting through in curiosity.

"Gods, this is cold!" Laago groaned, sinking his body into the tub. Benjin dropped his hand once Laago was submerged. He lathered the soap bar down his arms and onto his chest. I plopped down onto the grass next to the tub with Benjin.

"Hurry up, I'm tired!" Benjin whined. The sun was still shining bright in the sky, but we were all understandably exhausted.

"Get my back."

"There is no way I am washing your back!" Benjin laughed, laying on his back with his hands resting under his head. Laago playfully splashed water at him.

"Come on, I'll be quicker."

"Not in a thousand years. I already have to wash Luka too."

"Ny, get my back."

"Over my dead body!" Benjin sneered. I watched Laago's biceps flex as he rubbed the soap bar down his arm.

"It's your birthday tomorrow, Ny!" Laago remembered.

"I almost forgot..."

Turning sixteen filled me with mixed emotions. Though it showed I was nearing womanhood, it also served as a painful reminder of how much I missed my family. Where I was raised, sixteen was considered an important milestone for girls. My mother had promised we'd have a party when my day came. Now, I had no interest in a celebration. All I truly longed for was my family.

"No towels, huh?" Laago stood up and stepped out of the tub. My mouth dropped open. I had never seen a naked man before. Our eyes met, but I quickly looked away.

"Laago, turn around!" Benjin snapped, jumping to his feet.

"Whoops! You told me to hurry," he laughed as he covered himself. "Kinda seems worthless to put dirty clothes back onto a wet body," Laago complained as he dressed himself.

"It's better than nothing," Benjin retorted as he pushed over the tub and emptied the dirty water. "Your turn, Buba."

"I'm going to see if Kiuyah needs any help cleaning. Call me over when you are done so I can bathe." I rose to my feet as Laago laid on the ground next to Shaba.

I took a deep breath and walked over to the house. I made a futile attempt to push Laago from my thoughts, but with each blink, the image of his body in the sunlight that shimmered through the oak tree leaves flickered in my mind.

"Kiuyah?" I called through the doorway. "Would you like any help?"

"Come in! I'm pretty much done, but it's nice and cool in here. Feel free to relax." She was hovering over the sink, scrubbing dishes.

There was a cramped kitchen in the back corner of the room and a warm looking bed in the adjacent corner. A small table with chairs separated the two different areas. She had laid out pillows and blankets for us in the front side of the room. A nest of coziness, large enough for four of us. A bookcase engulfed the wall to the left of the door.

"It's so cozy in here."

"It's the only true home I've ever known." Her gaze drifted to an oil painting that hung proudly above her bed. It depicted two women who faced an ocean of tumbling waves, one with sun-kissed hair and a golden complexion, the other a dark-skinned brunette whose skirt fluttered in an endless breeze. Though only a painting on canvas, it held within its strokes an eternal bond of love, frozen in time for all to see.

# CHAPTER NINE

# FEELINGS IN FIELD

W E ALL FELL ASLEEP before the sun went down, cuddled together in our nook. It was far more comfortable than sleeping in the tunnels or on the floor of the Forest of Earth. I laid between Luka and Benjin. They smelt fresh and clean for once, a pleasant surprise. Shaba slept practically on top of Laago, her head resting on his shoulder. It reminded me of the big old bed in our apartment, where we used to sleep with Luchi and Dalia.

Once the sun began to rise and glimmer through the window, Shaba rolled out of bed and out the door. My mind was awake, but my body still felt exhausted. Soon after, Kiuyah got out of bed and stepped outside as well. The boys laid beside me, deeply asleep. No one tossed or turned, instead, a soft rumble of snores drifted through the tiny wooden home.

After much debate, I finally rose to my feet and joined Kiuyah and Shaba outside. The sky was a blend of orange and pink, with some blue sprinkled throughout. It contrasted against the tall green grass and speckled flowers, as if it was a painting. Kiuyah was in the dirt tending to her crops and Shaba was running laps around the field, burning off her morning energy.

"Morning, sunshine!" Kiuyah tossed me a plump tomato. "Grab a basket and start harvesting."

I took a bite of the tomato and its juice poured down my mouth. I had never tasted anything so fresh, it bore no resemblance to the tomatoes we had back home. I took a basket and began picking.

"You seem like a quiet girl," Kiuyah said, plucking weeds from the dirt.

"I suppose I can be."

"Tell me about yourself," she asked. Though it was a simple inquiry, my mind went blank. I began to stutter, so she cut me off. "I always hated answering questions like that too, but what is the first thing that came to mind when I asked?"

"I guess I am small..."

"Your long hair might weigh more than your body!" Kiuyah laughed. "Come on now, I'm just teasing. Men love small women, it makes them think they're the strong one," she turned her head to me and winked. "But we both know the truth."

"Men like women with weight to them."

"Eh, or so people say. I suppose everyone has their preferences."

I nodded my head in agreement, filling my basket up with tomatoes. Some were large, others small. Some were more red, some more orange. But regardless of their size or color, I was sure they all tasted delicious.

"Just like these tomatoes."

"Exactly." She smiled. "So, what's with you and your friend?"

"What do you mean?" I pretended to be unphased, as if I didn't know what she was insinuating, though my face was as red as the tomato I bit into.

"He has a good heart. Shaba has never reacted so welcoming to a man, she has a natural ability to read people. All foxdogs do."

"He's much older," I whispered, afraid the boys would hear, though I knew they were inside and deeply asleep.

"How old are you two?" She pried, as she wiped sweat off her face.

"Well, I'm fifteen and he's..." I paused. "Wait, today is my birthday! I almost forgot!"

"The big sixteenth birthday. This calls for celebration!" She reached over and wrapped her arms around me. She smelt like a meadow. "I'll make flapjacks for breakfast."

"I haven't had those since I was a kid!" My mouth watered.

"I'll get cooking after we finish." She let go of me and continued to tend to her plants. "Anyway, four years is nothing. Ani was six years older than me."

"Really?"

"Once you hit a certain age, I don't think it really matters. As long as you are both adults and consenting, who cares?" Kiuyah shrugged her shoulders. "To think when I was fifteen my parents expected me to marry a man in his sixties... Now, that's bad. But if two adults truly love each other, I say let 'em be!"

"I don't know... He's had many lovers before, real pretty ones too. Besides, I am sure he just thinks of me as a friend. Benjin and him have been inseparable since before I was even born."

"I think you should stop underestimating yourself," Kiuyah said, looking up from the weeds. "To me, you are a beautiful, wise, and compassionate young woman. And I have only just met you. Don't be so hard on yourself, it only creates unnecessary stress and insecurities."

"Thank you, Kiuyah. It has been really hard trying to become a woman without any guidance. I miss my mother," I admitted. I turned back to the tomato bushes, my eyes tearing up. "I don't know how you did it. You willingly left your home when you were my age and traveled so far."

"It didn't happen overnight, that's for sure. I had to grow up the hard way, on my own. You share that in common with me."

"Birthday girl!" Laago bursted through the door, shouting into the air.

"I'll start cooking breakfast." Kiuyah grinned and shook her head, rising up to her feet.

"How's it feel to finally be a woman?" He asked, holding his arms out for a hug.

"It doesn't feel any different." I smiled as I sunk into him.

"Happy birthday, sis!" Benjin called from the doorway. Luka ran between his legs and jumped onto me, almost knocking me over.

"Nyla's a teeny-tiny big girl!" Luka blabbered. I picked up my basket that was beginning to overflow with tomatoes and slipped past Benjin in the doorway. He rustled my hair and stepped outside.

"Hey, Buba. I bet I can run to the tree faster than you!" I heard him shout before he bolted out.

"I bet I can beat both of you with my eyes closed!" Laago yelled, chasing after them. I set the basket on Kiuyah's table.

"So that's the one, huh?" She laughed. "I never understood the appeal to men, but it's funny how when you fall for someone... It just happens, nothing can control it."

"Believe me, I've tried." I chuckled, before my thoughts turned serious. "I used to think Benjin was drawn to him just because he was a funny guy, always cracking jokes. He'd stop by, share some laughs, and be on his way. At least, that's all I noticed. He really is such a caring, hardworking, and positive person. It's only recently that I've caught a glimpse of this side of him. It feels like he always knows what to say and when to say it. I wish I could be that person for him too."

"Why can't you be?"

"I've never been known for my words and even if I was, he doesn't really seem to get upset." I thought back to when I had to kill those two militants in the tunnels. He barely said a word to me all day after that. "Maybe he just internalizes everything."

"Everyone likes to talk about their feelings, but some only will if you pry." Kiuyah winked at me, as she mixed her batter. "I'm glad you're opening up. I guess I get lonelier out here than I even knew."

"I'm glad Shaba introduced us."

The house was slowly filled with the delicious aroma of flapjacks. Kiuyah kept stacking them up on a big plate, creating a mountain. She hummed a tune as she cooked and swayed her hips. Though she appeared at great peace, I could not help but feel pain for her being out here all alone. Her home in this colorful field may appear picturesque, but she had to get lonely. Of course, she had Shaba, but that's different.

"What is that smell?" Laago roared, running inside with Luka glued to his back. Benjin soon followed. They were all drenched in sweat.

"Alright, kids! Help me bring breakfast to the table."

I grabbed a bowl of fruits and a pitcher of water, but Laago swiped them from my hands with a wink. Benjin was already halfway out the door with the tower of flapjacks in his hand, so I followed them outside empty-handed. Kiuyah laid out plates on the table and began to stack flapjacks onto them.

"They smell delicious!" Benjin assured her as he plopped down next to me on the bench.

"And they taste delicious!" Laago shoved half a flapjack in his mouth with his hand.

"You're an animal." Benjin laughed. "I can't believe my little sister is sixteen. I remember when she was born!"

"Me too!" Luka babbled.

"No, Buba, you weren't born yet! I was four. I remember I thought our mother had a bongamelon in her shirt because her belly was so big. When she told me I was going to have a little sibling, I cried because I was jealous. Then, she said I would be a big brother so I cried because I was so excited that I couldn't wait! A few weeks later, mother gave birth to you in our bath. I had all my toys lined up on the kitchen table, ready to show you them all."

"Remember when Nyla didn't speak for a week because she was mad you didn't let her come fishing with us?" Laago's laughter roared through the field, as he crammed more flapjacks into his mouth. Kiuyah tossed one to Shaba.

"Or the time she said she was going to run away because she wanted a giant turtle whale but mother said she couldn't get one!" Every story they told my face grew redder.

"She packed her bag with her toys and said she was leaving! Your pops sat with her all night, explaining that they were native to Eko and they needed an ocean to live. She was so mad!"

"Like you guys don't have any embarrassing stories..." I grinned, stabbing a flapjack with my fork.

"Laago is one big embarrassing story!" Benjin teased. He had a slight sunburn on his nose and cheeks, but a dark tan was already setting in. He brushed his hair back out of his face.

"Watch out! Mister perfect coming through. I had to teach this kid the ways of the street! He thinks he's all tough now, but who taught him?"

"Hey, man. Who was always saving your ass when you got into fights you couldn't win?"

"Definitely not you!" Laago threw a tomato chunk at Benjin. His brown shaggy hair bounced on his shoulders. In the outskirts, that style is common. In Suhai, all the men shave the sides of their hair, only allowing the top to grow long, a style that originated in the Republic of Terlu.

"I haven't laughed this hard in ages... I'm glad you all spent the night," Kiuyah professed. "You kids are a delight, you are welcome to stay as long as you would like." She reached her hands across the wooden table and squeezed mine and Benjin's hands. I only knew her for such a short period of time, yet she felt like kin, as though I had shared a lifetime with her.

"We'd love to stay, but we have to get to Huang. I think we should leave before sunset tonight." Benjin pulled his hand back and picked up his fork.

"Are you sure you want to travel at night? Why not leave at first light?"

"I think it would be safest. The less people we encounter, the better."

"People in the outskirts don't bite! I've rarely run into trouble on the path to the markets."

"I'd love to stay, but..." Benjin bit his lip and looked over to me.

"It is good to follow your instinct. Shaba knows the way to the markets, let her lead you there. I can't guarantee she'll take you kids all the way, since she doesn't like to stray too far from me, but she can at least get you on the right path," Kiuyah offered, biting into a tomato. Its juice dripped onto the table.

"That would be wonderful!" Benjin exclaimed. "Perhaps one day we can make our way back here."

"My door is always open."

We spent the rest of the day lazing around in our makeshift beds and listening to Kiuyah's endless array of travel stories. I admired her fearlessness. I thought of how much courage it had taken us to make

it this far on this journey. Kiuyah has traveled further than anyone I had ever met, each wrinkle of her face told a story. Each gray
hair represented a different village, city, or empire she traveled to.

I wondered if her parents ever realized they pushed her away,
by forcing her into an arranged marriage. My parents would have
done anything for me. I never lived a day feeling unloved, because
I always had my family. Kiuyah's own parents betrayed her. Her
community, by encouraging such an archaic ritual, betrayed her.

As the sun sank into the sky, my heart did as well. It would soon
begin to set, meaning it would be time for us to continue on our
journey. I imagined that was how Kiuyah may have felt, when she
left all of her temporary homes behind. Though I suppose she did
not have the pressure of the world weighing on her shoulders.

"Alright, everyone. I hate to say it, but we should get going."
Benjin rose to his feet.

"Shaba, are you going to show us the way?" Her face rested on
Laago's stomach as he stroked her lush red fur.

"Let me at least pack you kids some food to hold you over
until you reach the markets. You have many miles to go." Kiuyah
climbed to her feet and started rummaging through her pantry.

I leaned back and stretched my arms. My eyes drifted around
the room, before they landed on the painting of Kiuyah and Ani,
overlooking the ocean. I wanted to remember everything. Already, I feared I was forgetting the details of Bao. He told us so
many stories of his life, from his service in Suhai's army, losing his
wife, and him finding peace. It almost felt disrespectful to forget.
But just as the feeling of melancholy began to overtake my mind,
I suddenly felt a pang of excitement thinking of all the beautiful
people we have yet to meet and all the inspiring stories we have
yet to hear.

I rolled to my feet and threw my bag over my shoulder, followed
by my bow. I clipped my arrows to my waist and situated them
on my side. Benjin unconsciously placed his hand on his chest,
checking to see if the scroll was tied tightly enough around his
chest. His axe was hanging from his hip.

"Don't forget your baton, Buba." He pointed over to the ne-
glected black baton wedged between two pillows.

"Here!" Kiuyah tossed Benjin a bag of tomatoes, carrots, and string beans.

"Kiuyah, I don't know how we can ever repay you." Benjin looked at her in admiration, his eyes reflecting his gratitude.

"Come visit me one day and bring some of the fish that you catch in Huang." She smiled warmly and extended her arms out towards us. "Come here."

We all took a moment to bid Kiuyah a warm farewell. I held her tight for an extra moment, savoring the embrace. As I turned away, I saw a tear glistening down her cheek. Shaba dashed out the door and into the field, like a bolt of lightning. Luka held Benjin's hand and skipped along, singing an old folk song.

"Ready for our next adventure?" Benjin grinned, looking over his shoulder.

"Ready as I'll ever be..." Laago trotted behind with me.

"We are supposed to reach Huang within seven days. We ran through the night, from sunset at the port to the late morning at Kiuyah's. That probably knocked out almost eighty miles. Huang is about four hundred miles from the Port of Eura, so we've still got quite a journey ahead."

"Benj, I don't even want to think about how far we have to go. That doesn't even include us getting to the Island of Aara. We are on a journey that will never end," Laago groaned.

"My point is, if we maintain a good pace, we will arrive on time. That's manageable."

"How many days would that leave General Pago to prepare his troops?" I asked. Shaba ran to Laago, jumping and barking, then ran back ahead into the distance. I wished we moved as fast as her, we would have already been in Huang.

"I think we spent six days traveling through the Port of Eura. So if we make it to Huang in another eight, General Pago will have ten days to prepare."

"Do you think that's even enough time?" Laago worried.

"That's out of our hands," Benjin said, swinging Luka onto his back.

We quickly arrived back at the dirt road that followed along the sandy coastline. It was low tide, which filled the air with the ocean's stench. I stepped through the last of the tall grass and onto the smooth dirt. My legs were red from being scratched as we weaved through the sharp blades of grass.

"Benj, do you see that?" Laago squinted down the horizon, looking east towards the port. Multiple plumes of black smoke drifted into the air in the distance. Benjin's mouth dropped open.

"Do you think it's the militia?" I stammered.

"It looks like they advanced out of the port and set camp up closer. They may invade sooner than we thought."

"Well, come on. Let's start moving!" Laago anxiously shouted.

"Wait." Benjin's eyes scanned the road. "Everyone get off the road!" He commanded.

We all jumped into the grass and hid behind a lone tree. Shaba bit Luka's shirt collar and began pulling him back further into the field. She knew danger was upon us. My eyes caught two militants walking up the road in the distance.

"Luka, go with Shaba." Benjin pushed him up onto his feet so he wasn't being dragged by the foxdog.

"Do you think they saw us? What are they doing?" I asked.

"They're scouts," Laago said. Benjin let out a heavy breath and shook his head.

"Nyla, once they get close enough, you are going to hit one with an arrow."

"What? Why? We should just run."

"You're going to kill one and we will capture the other. We need to know when they are arriving in Huang. If we don't know, what use are we to General Pago?"

Although his words were true, they did not settle the feeling that gripped my chest. Glancing over my shoulder, I watched as Luka's head disappeared into the distance, heading back towards Kiuyah's house. I trusted Shaba to protect him. I slid up behind a tree, using it as my shield. The tall pale grass rose past my knees. I notched an arrow on my bowstring and held still, waiting for the men to come closer.

"Laago, you and I will crawl closer to them. When Nyla hits one, we will immediately jump out and grab them. You get the man Nyla hits, cover his mouth and pull him into the grass. I will get the other and do the same."

"I'll kill him quickly if the arrow doesn't." Laago nodded.

"Let's move!" Benjin and Laago began to crawl west along the dirt road, hidden in the tall grass. They assumed their positions moments before the men came within my arrow's reach. I held my breath, focused my arrow, and released.

But I missed by a hair. The arrow breezed between the men, causing them to duck out of instinct. I swiftly nocked another arrow on and let it loose, this time striking one of the men before they even knew where the arrows came from. The arrow pierced through the man's chest and he quickly fell to the ground. Before the other man could react, Laago and Benjin emerged from the grass, weapons in hand. Laago grabbed the injured man and dragged him into the field, disappearing from the road. The other militant dropped to his knees in surrender, raising his arms.

"Please... Mercy..." The man stuttered, his eyes darting around in fear.

"When are the troops invading Huang?"

"I... I don't know. The generals don't tell us soldiers that information!" The man cried. Benjin stood in front of him and reached his axe out, so the tip was resting on his forehead.

"When are the troops invading Huang?" He repeated. I sat still behind the tree, with a third arrow resting on my string, ready to be launched into the scout's skull without a moment's notice.

"In ten days! In ten days... Please, I swear it. Don't kill me. I have children... My wife!" Tears streamed down his face.

Just as I felt an ounce of pity for him, I heard Laago shriek in pain from beyond the grass. Without even meaning to, I released my arrow and it flew into the man's eye, knocking him onto the ground. He rolled around, screaming in pain, with blood pouring out. Benjin lifted his axe and swung down powerfully, slicing his head clean off, to finish the job. I ran over to Laago, who sat with his dagger in the other man's neck.

"What happened?!"

"He sliced me good- I thought he was dead!" He cried. I threw my bow and dropped to his side. Laago's bicep was gashed open. I tore my bag open and pulled out my only spare shirt and wrapped it tightly around his arm. Laago cursed under his breath.

"Are you okay?" Benjin shouted, as he threw the other scout's body into the grass.

"Yeah, I think I am okay," Laago grunted, tossing the dead militant's body off of him. Blood poured from his bicep and down his arm. I couldn't discern what was his and what was the militant's.

"I'm going to hide these bodies and find Luka. Nyla, stay with Laago." Benjin grabbed the men's collars and began dragging them deeper into the grass field. I sat hovered over Laago, applying pressure to his wound. The shirt turned dark, stained with blood.

"How are you feeling?" I gingerly wiped the sweat that poured down his face with my hand.

"My arm is on fire," he grimaced. "I should've stabbed him as soon as I grabbed him. I'm an idiot."

"You're not an idiot, Laago. Everything happened too fast. I missed my first shot, I could have gotten us killed. I need you to just focus on your breathing." I placed my hand on his chest. I felt his heart pounding, like it was trying to break through his chest.

"Ny..." He grabbed my hand and squeezed it. "I'm glad you're here with me."

As I calmed him down, I grew more anxious. Once the militia realized the scouts were missing, they were bound to send out more to track them down. Benjin was still out of view, either disposing of the bodies or tracking down Luka.

"Tell me about Terlu's markets." I stroked his hair off his face and tried to mask my own emotions.

"The streets are paved with stone and spotless. There are performers that dance through the crowds, wearing colorful fabrics that float through the wind as they sway..."

"That sounds beautiful. I can't wait to see it."

"Me too," he said, wincing in pain.

"Laago!" I shook him. "You need to stay awake. Tell me more about the markets," I pleaded. Benjin was still out of sight and we were running out of time. If the bleeding didn't stop, we would have to cauterize it. The sun began to set, leaving behind an array of colors. But its beauty did not calm me, it just made me anxious of the darkness that follows.

"Fruits... Vegetables... Meats. So much food. And people, people from all over. Talking to each other, eating together, living together... No Uppers versus Lowers. Sure some people are wealthy and others aren't, but there's no needless class war."

"Maybe once we warn the Council of Five they will send troops in to rebalance Suhai, then we won't have a north and south, but instead one unified empire."

"Yeah... That does sound nice. Or we could just leave," he mumbled.

"To where?"

"Anywhere. Forget the militia. Forget General Ahkpi. We can travel the world, like Kiuyah. I want to see the Sacred Forest of Akta... The volcano of Eko... and the Lost Lands of Onumi..." He kept trailing off, unable to muster more than a few words at a time. I looked back and saw Shaba darting through the tall grass to us.

"Nyla!" Benjin shouted, trying to catch up with the foxdog. Shaba dropped a pouch by my feet and ran back towards Kiuyah's to get Luka. "Put that on Laago's wound!"

I opened the pouch and pulled a handful of the ashy gray powder out. Benjin dropped to Laago's side, untying the shirt that was firmly wrapped around his bicep. The gash was deep, but I didn't see any bone.

"Bite down on this!" He put a thick stick in Laago's mouth.

I began to carefully sprinkle the mysterious powder onto his cut, afraid to cause him any more harm, but Laago groaned anyway. Benjin impatiently grabbed the pouch out of my hand and dumped the rest onto his bicep. Laago bit down so hard he broke the stick, cursing under his breath.

"Kiuyah said that should stop the bleeding and clean the wound. If it doesn't work, we have to cauterize it." Benjin took the bloodied shirt and wrapped the wound tightly.

"No, I'm not doing that. No way!" Laago tried rising to his feet but fell back down. Benjin placed his hands on Laago's shoulders.

"Laago, look at me. You are okay. We are here for you," Benjin maintained. "I want you to try to stand up."

"I think he needs time to rest, Benjin."

"We don't have time, Nyla! If Laago can't get up, I'll carry him to Kiuyah's and he will stay there while we head to Huang," Benjin snapped.

"You aren't going to Huang without me. I'm coming."

"Laago, if you need rest-"

"I am coming!" He interjected. He slowly shifted his left arm to the ground, using it to lift his body. He muttered profanities under his breath as he pushed upwards, rising to a crouch, before he fell forward onto his knees. I went to catch him, but Benjin pushed me back.

"He's in pain!"

After losing all that blood, Laago needed to rest. It wasn't safe for him to push himself, and the risk of developing permanent damage was far too great. Even if he could muster the strength to walk, he still couldn't fight, given his arm's near uselessness. He would be more of a liability than help, but Laago was the most stubborn person I knew, rivaled only by Benjin. No amount of reasoning would sway him. There was no way he would give up.

"You can do this, Laago," Benjin affirmed.

Laago lifted one foot up and firmly planted it on the ground, then used his good arm to push himself all the way up. He stumbled forward, but caught himself before he fell. He stayed on his knees for a moment to catch his breath, his body trembling.

I heard Shaba barking in the distance and turned around to see Luka on her back, holding on for dear life as the foxdog flew through the grass. Shaba slid to a stop at Benjin's feet, dropping another brown knitted pouch.

"Kiuyah said it's a pain reliever!" Luka explained. "Are you okay, Laago?"

"I'm fine, Luka," Laago reassured him. Luka ran into his legs and wrapped his arms around, hugging him tightly.

"Here, Laago, chew on these roots." Benjin tossed him the pouch. "I think it is called holiva root," Laago poured the contents of the pouch into his bag and chewed.

"It tastes like dirt." He choked them down and wiped the sweat off his face.

"Holiva root... That sounds familiar," I wondered aloud.

"Let's get moving!" Benjin commanded, already heading back to the dirt road. Shaba followed, with Luka still sitting on her back. Not only did she seem to not mind carrying him around, but she actually appeared to enjoy it.

"Are you sure you are okay?"

"I'll be fine, Ny," Laago promised, placing his hand on my shoulder for support.

We began trudging along the dirt path, as Laago was not in any condition to run. Even with the sun setting, the hot air felt suffocating, sending sweat dripping down our bodies. Occasionally, the cool sea breeze would sweep over us, but the relief was only temporary. I worried about Laago, who wobbled step after step silently. I tried to fill the time by telling stories, but it wasn't my strong suite. So instead, I brought myself to silence and just listened to the sound of the distant waves crashing. The waves swirled over one another, before collapsing into the soft sand, only to recede again. I watched the cycle repeat, over and over again.

Suddenly, Laago bursted into laughter, interrupting the silence. We all turned in unison and looked at him, but our confusion only seemed to make him laugh harder, until his laughter roared so loudly that he struggled to catch his breath. His laughter roped in Luka, who began to bellow as well.

"You good, Laago?" Benjin stopped walking, allowing us to catch up. Shaba stayed close to Laago's side, his hand often rubbed her ears affectionately as he walked. She was very protective over him.

"I- I was just thinking..." Laago sputtered between laughter. "We are going to Huang!" He began to laugh so hard he was keeling over.

"Uh, yeah? We are going to Huang." Benjin looked at him, his eyes narrowed. But Laago's face suddenly dropped, ending his laughing bout. "What's wrong, Laago?" Laago's head dropped down, looking at the ground. He stood there for a minute, before bursting out into laughter again.

"I got worried I wasn't wearing any pants, but they're on my legs!" His laughter calmed to a chuckle. Benjin walked over and put his hand on Laago's forehead.

"He feels hot, but not any hotter than I am. I don't think it's heat exhaustion, we haven't been out long enough. Besides, even though it is hot out, the sun is practically set. It has to be from blood loss."

"But he was talking fine before..." I looked at Laago, not only was his face red with sunburn, but his eyes were red as well. "Wait... Holiva root! Laago's high!"

Benjin bursted into laughter, perhaps mostly from relief. Suddenly, we all stood in the middle of the dirt road howling. Shaba sat there with her head tilted to the side, probably thinking we were crazy.

"Do you feel pain anymore?"

"Benj, I feel fantastic," he replied, his face beaming with a wide grin. "What are we waiting for? Let's go, we gotta get to Huang." Laago began to march down the street, swinging his arms wildly. Benjin looked at me and shrugged.

"I'm just happy he isn't in pain," I admitted.

"Yeah, but I kind of wish he saved some of the holiva root for us too." Benjin nudged my arm and began following Laago, before his voice turned serious. "Let's just make it to the next village and call it a night. There is no use in forcing him to travel in this state."

"After we get to the big and brave General Pago we need to find ourselves some ladies, Benj!" I rolled my eyes at his words. "I say we throw a party."

"Oh yeah? Maybe we'll just skip out on the whole Island of Aara and saving the world?"

"Exactly! Wait..." He paused. "What were we talking about?"

"You were saying something about owing me money?" Benjin winked at me.

"I never noticed how much hair I have." He brushed his hands through his thick wavy hair. "I feel like a cloud. Do I look like a cloud?"

"You look great, Laago," Benjin responded.

"Everything's great..." Laago's mouth fell agape as he stared upwards at the sky and slowly walked forward.

"I wonder how long it's going to last?"

"Probably until he gets some sleep," Benjin guessed.

"It's going to be a long night."

"It's going to be a long week..." Benjin grinned, somehow able to find humor in all of this.

And while I admired that about him, I could not stop worrying about Laago. If he was in trouble, being high off roots just prevents his body from communicating with his brain. We still had many miles ahead of us, without any certainty of where we would be able to sleep. I tried to focus on the waves, crashing and receding. Laago would be okay; I should just join Benjin in enjoying him high.

"I love you guys," Laago gushed.

"We love you too." Benjin threw his arm over Laago's shoulder.

"I love soup too," he firmly stated.

The evening's walk may have been brutally hot, but Laago served as entertainment, distracting us from our sticky sweat and aching feet. There was no such thing as one fluent conversation, but instead just random thoughts having no relevance to, well, anything. He rotated between laughing at the dirt on the ground to questioning his existence. All we could do was support him, because worrying benefitted no one.

Not too far ahead of us, I saw plumes of gray smoke drifting into the air just beyond a sparse patch of trees. It smelt like a wood fire, meaning there must be a town somewhere in the near distance, and more importantly, somewhere for Laago to sleep off the holiva root.

"I think we finally made it to the outskirts!" I shouted.

"Well, technically we have been in the outskirts of Terlu since we crossed the border of the Port of Eura. But this is just the first major settlement. I'm sure we passed many homes like Kiuyah's, but they were just hidden beyond the tall grass."

"Okay, mister know-it-all!" I rolled my eyes and ignored him, but his laughter made me smile. At least he embraced being a know-it-all. "Hopefully one of these villagers will let us stay the night."

By the time we reached the village, Benjin was practically drag-ging Laago down the dirt road. To even call it a village was an overstatement. It was a collection of five stone houses all gath-ered around a depressing wheat field. There were some children outside playing, but they didn't seem to notice or care about us. Luka jumped off Shaba's back and joined them. He was naturally charismatic, a quality I never had. I felt bad he never got to make any friends in Tinshe, because the plague ruined our community. He would have been so popular.

With Luka finally off her back, Shaba decided to sit under an oak tree and take a well-deserved nap. Laago began to wander over to some chickens to ask them how their day was. I grabbed his hand and pulled him back over, following Benjin over to a young man with sunken eyes who sat on his front stoop.

"Hello! We are traveling to Huang for work. Is there anywhere we can stay in this village tonight?"

The man did not even respond, instead he just pointed to-wards another stone house that laid deeper in their village. Benjin thanked him and we headed over. As we passed his house I saw two girls, who looked around my age, poke their heads out the window and giggle. The boys didn't seem to notice.

Benjin walked up the two slanted stone steps in front of the house and knocked on the door. He stepped back down and stood with us. He was awfully tall, so he had to be careful to not intim-idate anyone with his size. We heard some scampering and then the door swung open.

"Yes?" A woman stepped forward, probably in her thirties. She clearly ate well.

"Hello!" Benjin smiled cheekily at the woman. "We are travel-ing to Huang for work. A man over there mentioned you may be able to help us with finding a place to sleep tonight?"

"I've never seen a boy so tall. Let alone so handsome!" She smiled back a bit too wide.

"His name is Benjin. He's my friend," Laago rambled, still high. I elbowed his side, hinting him to shut up before he weirded out our potential host for the night.

"You kids can stay in my barn tonight. It's right behind my house, you won't miss it."

"Thank you so much, miss! We appreciate your generosity." Benjin clasped his hands together.

"Let me know if you need anything, hun," she said with a flirtatious wink, before she turned back into her house and shut the door behind her.

We headed behind her house to a small wooden barn that was filled with bales of wheat stacked high against the walls. Though the doors sat wide open, the air was hot and stuffy inside. Benjin began stacking the wheat piles on top of each other to clear space for us to sleep. Laago ripped off his shirt and dropped his body onto the floor, laying there with a goofy smile glued to his face.

"I never want to get up!" He moaned. Just as I dropped my bag on the ground, the two girls from earlier approached the barn. Their giggles drifted through the thick air, grabbing Benjin and Laago's attention.

"The lady in that house said we could stay here tonight," Benjin defensively explained, though it was no concern to them.

"I'm Atheti and this is my sister, Jumi. What's your guys' names?" She stepped forward, clasping her hands behind her back.

They both had the same narrow faces. Atheti had long black hair that was braided to the side with a yellow bow that matched her tattered dress. Her sister had similar thin black hair, but it was much shorter. Her deep brown eyes hid behind her heavy bangs. She had a big nose that stuck out and her cheeks were covered in freckles.

"I'm Benjin, that's Laago, and Nyla," he responded, barely paying attention. Laago struggled to sit up, his eyes glazed red and barely open.

"What brings you to our village?" Atheti asked, her eyes locked onto Benjin. She had long eyelashes that fluttered as she spoke.

"We are traveling to Huang for work," he said, turning back around to pile more wheat.

"What type of work?" She walked over and sat on a stack of wheat, her legs playfully bouncing against it.

"Fishing."

"You're not much of a talker, huh?" She persisted. Benjin sighed and sat down next to Laago.

"I'm sorry, I don't mean to be rude, but I'm awfully tired. We had a long day."

I knew Benjin more than I knew myself. He hated when girls fawned over him for his looks. It was as if he was some porcelain doll for them to admire and play with, not a person with a heart and soul. Atheti sat down next to him and her sister, Jumi, was quick to follow. They were both barefoot, their feet black.

"You look like a big strong man. It must take a lot to make you tired," she flirted. I rolled my eyes.

"It's hot out today, even with the sun all set," her sister finally spoke. Her voice was soft, her face hidden behind bangs.

"The sun..." Laago laughed, falling back down.

"What's his deal?" Atheti asked.

"He had to take some holiva root for an injury," Benjin explained.

"Gee, he should probably switch that bloody rag with a clean one. His wound will get infected," she declared, matter-of-factly.

"We don't have one," I retorted, in an attempt to get her to drop it. Instead, Jumi jumped to her feet.

"I can take care of him," she said, skipping out of the barn. I felt my blood boil. Laago didn't need some dirty village girl to help him.

"Anyway, tell me about yourself, Benjin," Atheti asked, but he was distracted by Laago's wound and oblivious to the desperate girl next to him. I watched her lower her dress, to show off her bust.

"There's not much to tell." His eyes drifted to Shaba who was wandering just outside the barn doors, sniffing the ground. Jumi came back into the barn and dropped to Laago's side.

"Here, let me do it." I reached out my hand for the white cloth. I untied my shirt that was wrapped around his wound and peeled it off. The gray powder Kiuyah gave us seemed to work, there was no fresh blood and it didn't look infected, though it could still develop in time.

"You have beautiful brown eyes," Laago complimented Jumi. I wrapped the cloth around his arm and tied it tightly.

"Thank you..." She blushed.

"So how do you all know each other?" Atheti pried, as she excitedly twirled her braid in her hand.

"Nyla's my sister and Laago's been my friend since we were kids. My brother is out playing with those kids by the wheat farm."

"Aw, how cute. You take your little sister and brother around with you. You must be such a good older brother." If I could roll my eyes to the back of my head, I would. I could not wait to leave this village.

"I'm tired," I declared, grilling Atheti.

"Yeah, I think we should call it a night," Benjin agreed. "I'll go get Luka and Shaba."

"But the sun only just set!" Atheti whined.

"Come on, Benj, let's live a little!" Laago chimed in.

"You do you, but I'm going to sleep," Benjin called over his shoulder as he walked out towards the farm. Atheti slid off the pile of wheat and plopped next to Jumi, who was hovering over Laago.

"What happened to your arm?" She asked, but Laago only shrugged. I wondered if he even recalled what happened, with this fog overtaking his brain. "Oh, so mysterious!"

"If you like mysterious, I can be mysterious." Laago sat back up, his eyes drifting down to her chest. The girls blushed and giggled.

"I made friends!" Luka shrieked as he ran at full speed and jumped on Laago.

"Be careful with his arm, Buba!" Benjin called over, though his warning was a bit too late.

"You're pretty!" Luka gushed.

"Aren't you a little cutie?" Atheti rustled his hair.

"Well, it was nice to meet you girls, but we are going to call it a night. We have to be on the road early." Benjin sat down next to me, avoiding them.

"Don't you want to hang out a little longer?" Atheti whimpered to Laago.

"Ladies, I'd love to... But I need to rest so my wound heals," Laago declined, until Atheti made a dramatically sad face. "I mean I guess I can stay up a little longer."

"I can show you the prettiest spot in the village!" She jumped to her feet and held out her hand for him. He grabbed it and stumbled to his feet, with Jumi following them out. I rolled over onto my side to hide my tears from Benjin. Luka plopped on the ground, resting his head on Shaba's stomach.

"Nyla..." He sighed. But I didn't answer, I couldn't. "Sometimes being around someone a lot can make you-"

"I don't know what you're talking about," I interrupted, though I knew I was only lying to myself.

"Laago's just not a reliable guy when it comes to those things. He's a great friend, but a bad partner. I'm sure you'll find someone closer to your own age that values you."

"I'm tired, Benjin."

"I just hate to see you get upset. You're a smart and loving girl. There's no need to settle."

I buried my face in my shirt to muffle my sniffles and tried to distract myself. Why did I care about some stupid boy so much? The world was falling apart, I watched men die bloody deaths right before my eyes. There was war, famine, and plague- we lived surrounded by pain...

Though having someone you love by your side did make all the suffering feel worth it.

I drifted off to sleep reminiscing about my mother and father's eternal love for each other. Up until she passed, my father would weather any storm, because she gave him purpose. He would wake her every morning with a warm cup of dandelion tea, her favorite. He knew her like the back of his hand, always knowing how to calm her down. My mother never took him for granted, she knew how hard he worked for our family. She was always hugging or kissing him, he had her whole heart.

I awoke just as the sun rose over the horizon, immediately raising the temperature in the stuffy barn. I sat up and wiped sweat off my face. Laago sprawled out beside me in his drawers. I shuddered at the thought of him and Atheti. As much as I was curious where the night took them, I knew the truth would only upset me further. I couldn't believe I ever thought he changed or that I stood a chance. I spent every day with him, then he meets a girl and goes out with her after knowing her for an hour. I sat up and stretched my legs, in a feeble attempt to shake my feelings off. But only a moment passed before I looked back over at him and began to worry about his wound. I hated that I cared so much. I leaned over and gently shook Benjin awake.

"The sun is rising, we should head out soon," I whispered. My body was exhausted but I wanted to slip out before Atheti and Jumi showed up. Benjin rolled over and woke Luka up.

"It's morning, Buba."

"Already?"

"Yep. We should get a move on..." Benjin rose to his feet and began to stretch. "Want to wake up Laago?" He asked. I stood up, lightly kicked Laago's side, and grabbed my stuff.

"I'll be outside," I said, as I stepped out of the barn. Benjin walked over and kicked Laago again, this time waking him.

"Morning, sunshine."

"I feel like there's a giant turtle whale on me. What happened yesterday?" He went to sit up, but collapsed after putting pressure on his arm. "I got stabbed!" He remembered.

"Kiuyah gave you holiva for the pain, I didn't know it would make you high."

"I don't remember a thing," he mumbled, groggily rising to his feet.

"That's probably for the better," Benjin said as he stepped outside, with Luka and Shaba following closely behind. I stood by the farm, anxiously waiting to leave. Laago stumbled out, focused on bending and stretching his injured arm. I could tell he was in pain. We started heading towards the dirt road, leaving the village behind us.

"Were you gonna leave without saying goodbye?" Atheti called from her steps. Laago trailed behind us, not even noticing her. She ran up behind him and grabbed his hand. "Hello?"

"Hey?" Laago responded, dumbfounded.

"You told me you would say goodbye." She stepped closer to him, gazing into his eyes.

"Uh, yeah. Sorry." He glanced up at Benjin, unable to hide his confusion.

"Maybe one day I'll see you again!" She kissed him on the cheek and skipped off, back towards her house. Laago turned around, his eyebrows raised, and watched her go, before he headed over to us.

"Who was that, Benj?" He stammered.

"You're joking, right?"

"I have never seen that girl in my life," Laago swore. I walked ahead and tried to ignore them. Luka was chasing Shaba, trying to get on her back again.

"She was all over you yesterday. You literally went out at night with her."

"No way! I was high as a golden eagle and you guys let me go off with some random girl?"

"You seemed fine! I didn't realize you were still under the root's spell, honestly."

"Did we..?" His eyes widened.

"I can't believe you don't remember!" Benjin laughed. I was far enough to seem like I couldn't hear them, but I could. Laago put his hand on his forehead and shook his head. Suddenly, he froze in his steps.

"Did Nyla see me with her?"

"Why do you care?" Benjin's eyes narrowed, analyzing him. I held my breath, not wanting to miss his response.

"She doesn't need to see that," he mumbled after a moment, clenching his bicep with his hand. "I'm never having holiva root again."

"Good, because I can't deal with carrying you fifty miles while you're off your rocker and asking me if you are a cloud."

"Did that really happen?" Laago laughed, covering his face. "Please tell me I didn't do anything else embarrassing..."

"Depends how you define embarrassing!" They stepped onto the dirt road and broke into a jog to catch up to me, Luka, and Shaba.

"Morning, Ny!"

"Morning." I avoided eye contact and kept walking, my footsteps heavy as my heart. I knew I wouldn't be able to hide my disappointment. It wasn't Laago's fault, he didn't have to like me, but knowing that didn't make it sting any less.

# CHAPTER TEN
# WHEAT BEER

I T MAY HAVE ONLY been spring, but the sun acted as though it was midsummer. I knew it was midday, because the sun was relentless. I forgot how close the outskirts of Terlu were to the Qara Desert, where you can boil a pot of water by just placing it under the sun. Down south in Tinshe, the summer was mild, but the winter was often harsh. We had the freezing South Ocean pushing cold air across our side of the empire. In Najin, which hugged the southwestern border of the Qara Desert, the summers were more intense, but they still had the luxury of the cold sea breeze.

Shaba was panting heavily, slowly trotting forward. Kiuyah had mentioned that foxdogs were native to the Sacred Forest of Akta, which meant she must prefer cooler climates. She had to be sweltering under her thick fur coat. Shaba let out a rough bark, grabbing everyone's attention.

"What is it, Shaba?" Laago dropped to one knee and petted her head.

"I think she's overheating," I speculated. Shaba licked Laago's face, then walked over to Benjin and licked his hand.

"I wouldn't want to wear a thick fur coat like that in this heat!" Benjin added. Shaba walked over to me and licked my hand too, then darted back towards the direction we came.

"What is she doing?" I worried aloud.

"I think she decided it was time for her to go home..." Benjin pondered. "Kiuyah did say Shaba doesn't like to stray too far from her."

"Do you think she'll know her way back?

"She could probably sniff Kiuyah out from the Kingdom of Yana!" Benjin guessed.

"I miss her already..." Luka sniffled.

"You just liked that she carried you, Buba." He chuckled. We watched Shaba fade into the distance, before we turned our backs and continued down the dirt road.

"I have a blister the size of a bongamelon on my foot," Laago groaned, his hand clenching his injured bicep. "And my arm is killing me."

"My whole foot is one big blister. My work boots weren't made to travel across the world!" Benjin complained.

"My whole body is a blister!" Luka squealed. Benjin scooped him up and threw him on his back, as if he was as light as the air around us. I realized one day Luka would be too big for Benjin to carry.

"How are you doing back there, Ny?" Laago spun around to face me, walking backwards.

"I'm good," I replied, staring over my shoulder into the ocean.

We passed multiple villages, all similar to the one we stayed in last night. A few stone homes, with some type of farm, but all eerily quiet. It was almost as if we were walking in circles. Had we not been following the coast, I may have actually second guessed our route.

Finally, the sun began to drift behind us, sparing us from its heat. My skin was stained red from its rays and my feet ached. My mouth was unfathomably dry and my lungs wheezed. Even Benjin was slowing down, so I knew I only had to suck it up a little bit longer.

"That's it, I'm calling it." Laago sighed, as he rubbed his freshly shaven face. "Next village, we find a place to stay. Otherwise Luka has to scooch over on your back because you'll be carrying me too."

"Alright, alright. There's a lot of light coming from the village over there, I'm sure there will be somewhere for us to stay."

There was another small group of stone homes, not too far in the distance. Though it did not appear any more prominent than any of the others we passed, I could see that many people were gathered outside. As we approached the village, I heard instruments blaring.

"It sounds like a festival!" Laago shouted.

We all picked up the pace and jogged over, eager to see the commotion. We turned off the dirt road and stumbled our way through the tall grass until we reached the clearing. There were crowds of people, spread throughout the small village. People must have traveled from all over the outskirts, which explains why the other villages we passed seemed to lack life.

Women were dancing, children playing, and men were gathered around large barrels of wheat beer laughing. I looked down at Luka, whose eyes were wide in awe. It was the first festival he had ever seen. When I was little, there was a festival every Koba moon, but the Suhai Empire banned large groups of people from gathering once the plague hit.

"I think we picked the right village to stop at!" Benjin grinned, already swaying back and forth, bobbing his head to the music. He took Luka and spun him around, before setting him back down. He roared at Luka's silly dance moves, who alternated between jumping up and down and running around and through Benjin's legs. I stood on my toes to try to see over the crowd at the band whose music was echoing through the field, but I was too short.

"Need a lift, Ny?" Laago asked, tapping his shoulder.

"No, thank you," I responded, looking around at the lanterns that were strung across a thin rope, connecting the houses with their colorful lights. "We should probably try to find somewhere for us to sleep tonight before it gets too late."

"Good idea!" He grabbed my hand and led me through the crowd, weaving between rowdy women and drunk men until we arrived at the barrels.

"Need a mug?" One man shouted, sitting on a barrel. He looked older than he probably was, someone that maybe enjoyed drinking a little too much.

"No, thanks! This is an awesome festival though, we are passing through to Huang."

"Nothing like a nice drink after a long day!" The man jumped off the barrel and filled a mug up. "Stay a while," he insisted, reaching the mug out to Laago.

The man was so drunk that he could barely stand up straight, he wavered in the wind like leaves on a tree. Laago grabbed the mug hesitantly, his eyes lost in the amber ale that sloshed about. He was never one to drink because of what he endured from his father and the only person he ever hung out with was Benjin, who never really cared for drinking either. After a moment, he abruptly raised the mug into the sky.

"Cheers!" He shouted, clanking his mug with the other men.

"What brings you to Huang?" Another man asked. He was older, with a big beer belly and gray slicked back hair that was balding underneath.

"My friends and I are working on a fishing boat. We were hoping to find somewhere to stay overnight in this village. Do you know of any?" Laago held the mug in his hand casually, but did not drink from it.

"You mean this pretty lady isn't your wife?" He asked, sending goosebumps down my spine. His smile was petrifying.

"Nope, just my girlfriend. But we are traveling with her two brothers as well." Laago threw his arm around me, only lying to fend off the creepy men. They immediately seemed to lose interest in me, as if the only way they would respect my boundaries was if another man claimed me.

"I've got a spare room!" A third voice called, hidden behind the shadows.

"Really? We are four people, I know it's asking for a lot," Laago said, squinting his eyes to try and put a face to the voice.

"It's just sitting there collecting dust anyway." A man stepped forward. He looked to be in his fifties, his black hair just starting to turn gray and his skin was dark and leathery. "It was my son's, before he enlisted."

"Thank you!" Laago extended his hand out and the man firmly shook it. "I am Laago and this is Nyla."

"My name is Petota."

"It is nice to meet you," I whispered, trying to sound friendly while still partially hiding behind Laago. Drunk men made me uncomfortable. I watched the other man sitting on the barrel glare at me from the corner of his eye. It felt like I was his prey.

"Well, my house is that one over there." He pointed to a small home not too far away from us. "The door is always open. There's a room that's pretty much empty, you kids can stay there." He disappeared back into the crowd, carrying on with his night.

"Let's go tell Benjin!" Laago decided, slipping back into the crowds. I grabbed his hand and followed closely behind him. Music bellowed through, a twelve stringed instrument fiddling away and a drum beating. The singer had a rough and tough voice that melodically captivated the crowd.

"Where'd you guys go?" Benjin shouted over the crowd.

"We found a place to stay!" Laago cheered, still holding his mug.

"Woah, you had holiva root once and now you're drinking too?"

"Had to fit in if someone was going to let a couple strangers stay at their house!"

"How's it taste?"

"It tastes musty... But not bad."

"Let me try!" Benjin grabbed the mug and took a swig. "Not bad." He took another swig and passed it to me. My eyes widened, I never drank before. I looked up at Benjin, who was grinning. He thought I wouldn't dare to drink it, so I snatched it from his hand and took a big sip.

"Woah!" Laago took the mug back and chugged the rest of it, letting out a big belch at the end.

"Let's get another one!" Benjin decided, surprising us all. We all ran over to the barrels and the drunk man gave us another fill. We all took turns drinking from it. I didn't want to admit it, but it tasted disgusting.

"Wanna dance, Buba?"

Benjin grabbed Luka before he could even respond and swung him up into the air. Already girls began to swoon over him. Benjin's more attractive than the average village boy, and definitely has more teeth. Laago looked at me and held out his hand.

I never danced before, I was always too shy. But the festival was full of energy and with my stomach full of wheat beer, I had confidence for once. I grabbed onto Laago's hand and he pulled my body in, our faces inches apart. Our eyes met, but I broke it off, dwelling over Atheti. We danced through the crowds, pushing and pulling like the ocean. Every time I began to feel jealous, he pulled me closer, making me forget about everything.

"Look up, Ny!" He cheered. A single golden lantern was drifting upwards into the darkened night sky.

We danced through the crowd, landing us by the band. There were three men. The singer was wearing a big straw hat that flopped around on his head, as he sang about a woman who ran off into the night, leaving behind her husband and children. She ran through the forest, ran through the hills, only to end up back with him. The other man plucked a twelve string fiddle, his eyes lost in the sky. The third hit a single drum, but somehow made many different sounds that echoed through the field. We danced and sang, twirled and laughed. The song ended with a powerful slam of the drum and the crowd erupted into cheers. Suddenly, the sky became engulfed with golden painted lanterns. I jumped up and down, throwing my hands in the air. I never felt so free.

The crowd began to slowly disperse as the band packed up their instruments. The moon was above us, the goddess Eura reminding us night was here. Parents carried their sleeping children, trekking through the field and back to their villages. Suddenly, it felt like it was just Laago and me.

"Ny..." He studied my eyes. "It felt like you were avoiding me all day."

"I was just tired." I looked down and began to walk away to find my brothers, but he grabbed my hand and stopped me.

"Bao said if we want to make it through all of this, we have to communicate. If it was something that happened yesterday, it wasn't me, it was the holiva root."

"I know. Let's go find Benjin and Luka," I insisted, pulling my hand away.

Thoughts of Laago crashed over me all day, as waves do in an ocean. But when it came time to speak, they all receded. I desperately wanted to be honest with him, but my voice fell dry and barren, like a desolate shoreline. What was there to even say? I felt crushed and embarrassed, hurt and naive. But above all else, I felt dumb. Benjin was right, whatever I thought was there was all in my head.

"Are you guys ready to call it a night?" Benjin called over to us. Luka was wrapped around his back, already asleep.

"Definitely," Laago agreed. We followed him through the field to Petota's house. He sat on the front step, taking a long drag of tobacco.

"Did you kids have yourself a good time?" His voice rumbled. He lifted his mug of beer to his lips, leaving a layer of foam stuck to his thick black mustache.

"That was the first festival we have been to in years!" Benjin smiled.

"Well, don't let me hold you up. Make yourselves at home. Your room is the door on the right," he said as he stood up and leaned against his house, leaving us space to slip inside.

"Thank you, Petota!" Laago smiled. The man nodded his head and pressed his pipe against his mouth.

The house was dark and dusty, as if it was abandoned. The front door led to the main room, which had a small kitchen and table. On the right there were two doors. Laago pushed the right one open, a small corner room with no furniture. It had two windows, one on each wall. Benjin laid Luka down, then dropped his bag on the ground and unhooked his leather belt holding his axe, setting it on the floor as well.

I laid down next to Luka and petted his hair, he was still deeply asleep. Laago pulled open a window, letting a cool breeze flow into the stuffy room. I looked out the window, into the blackness of the night. There was no view of the moon from here. As soon as Laago sat down, he got up and headed back outside. I looked over at Benjin.

"He's probably going to the bathroom." He shrugged, as he collapsed onto the floor next to me. I gazed into the ceiling, exhausted.

"Mind if I join you?" Laago's voice drifted through the window.

"Not at all," Petota rumbled. "I sit out here every night. It's like a ritual to me."

"I was always a night owl too. I feel more like myself when the sun sets."

"You and I both, kid." He passed his mug to Laago. "So what brings you to our village?"

"We are headed to Huang to work on a fishing boat. We have to get there within four days." He took a long swig.

"Huang, the capital of the republic," the man grunted.

"Do you ever travel there?"

"I'm more of a country man. I never fit into the city scene, always felt out of place."

"I understand that. I grew up in the outskirts too."

"A country boy? I should've known. Where's your village?"

"I'm from the northwest, but I left when I was eight."

"I don't blame you. It's a dump up there. My son has been stationed in the northwest, fighting against the tribes that come from the Qara Desert to steal and ravage the people of the outskirts." He took another long drag of his pipe.

"It wasn't like that when I was young. Well, it was a dump, but it was a peaceful dump. There's nothing there for the tribes to steal anyway, everyone lives in shacks up there." Laago stared into the night. "Have you lived here your whole life?"

"Born and bred, 'til the day I die."

"This village seems like it has a strong sense of community. I'd never leave either."

"You'd think, but the boys always want to get out of here. My son left the moment he could, he enlisted in the republic's army the day he turned sixteen."

"Wow, that's a brave thing to do."

"He was always goin' on about politics, the world, and whatnot. Real bright kid."

"You must miss him."

"Not a day goes by where I don't sit here thinking 'bout him."

"I bet he really misses you too."

"If he did, he'd come home." Petota took another heavy drag of his pipe, the smoke drifting in through the window of our room. "You should get some sleep, kid. Huang is a long ways away."

"Goodnight, Petota."

Laago quietly slipped back into the dusty room and laid down next to Benjin, who already fell asleep. My heart ached for Petota, a man I didn't even know. I imagined him waiting on his front steps every night for his son to come marching home, though his hair would turn gray before that day ever came. Petota was surrounded by a loving and warm community, but he still seemed just as alone as Kiuyah or Bao.

Almost as quickly as I fell asleep, I found myself back to walking down the dirt road. I zoned out on my feet, watching them raise and lower with each step. When I finally looked up, I saw the ocean was lined with war ships, with thick storm clouds engulfing the sky behind them. The war was here and I was alone. Where was Benjin? I began to run down the road, but it just became longer and longer. No matter how hard I tried, I wasn't moving forward.

I jolted awake. It was early, the sun was just peaking over the horizon. Though hours had passed, I felt as though I didn't sleep at all. I rolled over onto my side and admired the boys, who were peacefully sleeping. It was our fourth day on the road since we left the Port of Eura, which meant we should finally be traveling through the walls of Terlu, which stand at the bend in the coast. The walls separate the outskirts from the rest of the republic, where the lifestyle is very different. Once we arrived within the walls, we would officially be protected by Terlu's army.

I rolled out of bed and stepped outside. The air was still cool, not yet oversaturated with the sun's heat. The village was quiet, its people laid hungover in their beds. I wandered around, admiring the stillness. Behind Petota's stone home was a small river hidden behind a rolling hill. I headed over, eager to get a chance to clean myself. My legs were covered in mud from the festival and my body felt stiff from the sweat that dried on me. Feeling like dirt certainly wouldn't help my low self-esteem.

I slipped off my clothes, leaving just my undergarments on and stepped into the cold water. I used to hate cold baths, but I have since learnt to appreciate them. I knew that once I spent another day traveling on that forsaken dirt road I would be yearning for this. I dunked my whole body under and floated peacefully as the sun slowly rose over the horizon. I listened to the birds chirping around me and watched them flutter through the sky above me. If I was Petota's son, I would have never left this village.

"Beautiful mornin', ain't it?" A voice called from afar. I shot up, snapping back to reality. It was the creepy drunk man from last night.

He stumbled down the hill, nearly falling flat on his face. I couldn't help but wonder if he was still drunk.

"Yes, it is," I replied. As he approached me, his eyes caught attention to my clothes that laid on the riverbank. I suddenly felt terrified. I wanted to run back to Petota's, but I couldn't get out without revealing myself. The man smiled, his buck teeth sticking out.

"Mind if I join?" He asked, already stripping off his shirt. I didn't answer. He was paper thin and white as a cloud. As he stepped into the river, I slowly moved further away. "I forgot your name."

"Nyla."

"Oh, yes, I remember now. How could I forget such a beautiful name to such a beautiful face? I've never met a Nyla before. My name is Quacho," he said. Once again, I didn't respond. Fear paralyzed my body. It wasn't what he said, but the look in his eyes as he said it. "Where's your friend?"

"Going to the bathroom," I lied, hoping it would deter him. But Quacho didn't care, instead he slowly drifted closer to me.

"You're not much of a talker, huh?" His eyes squinted, as if he sensed my fear, leading him to smirk in satisfaction. He swam in laps, moving slightly closer to me each time. I kept moving back, deeper into the river, but the further I went, the stronger the current grew. "What brings you to our village? We don't get many pretty young girls traveling through here," he whispered, now no more than within five feet of me.

"We are going to work on a fishing boat in Huang."

"You don't look like a fisher. If you were my lady, you would never have to work. I'd take care of you, like a real man." He reached his hand and placed it on my cheek. "Your skin is so soft." His hand caressed my face and began sliding its way down to my chest, before I screamed so loud that the birds fluttered from the trees.

"Get away!" I shrieked, unable to control my outburst. "Get away!" I threw my fists and splashed water at him, but my feet barely reached the ground, leaving me weakened.

"Hush now!" Quacho snapped, stepping away. "What's wrong with you?"

"Nyla?" I heard Benjin yell from over the hill.

"Benjin!"

"You're crazy!" Quacho hissed at me over his shoulder, as he stumbled out of the river to throw his clothes back on. "You're a crazy witch!" Benjin ran down the hill, straight towards the drunk, with Laago following closely behind. I swam to shore, grabbing my clothes. Benjin decked the man onto the riverbank and pinned his arms down.

"What did you say about my sister?" Benjin pulled his arm back and shot it forward into the man's face. "Is this what you do? Take advantage of someone smaller than you?" He rocked the man again in the face, sending blood flying.

"I said she's a crazy wi-" Benjin hit him again and this time Quacho's nose broke under the pressure. Laago rushed over to me frantically.

"What happened? Did he touch you? Are you okay?" He panicked, and his reaction unnerved me even more, leading me to break down crying. Laago wrapped his arms around me, hugging me tightly. "You're okay, he can't touch you now."

"A crazy what?" Benjin bellowed, hitting him again. "You want to see crazy?" I pushed Laago away, my body still trembling.

"Benjin, stop!" I ran over and tried pulling him off. The man's face was covered in blood. "You're going to kill him!"

"Good!" He kept wailing on Quacho, until Laago was finally able to pull him off. Benjin's knuckles were red.

"Relax! He can't hurt her now."

"Yeah, but he can go off and hurt another girl."

"She wanted it! That witch..." Quacho chuckled, as blood poured out of his mouth. "She was practically beggin'. I said, you're not my type. I only go for pretty girls... But I felt bad. She-" Before he could utter another word, something in Laago snapped. He grabbed the man by the collar and dragged him into the river, holding him under its current. Petota came running down the hillside.

"What's going on down here?"

"That man tried to assault my sister!" Benjin rose to his feet. Petota ran into the river, shoving Laago off of Quacho, who was sputtering for air.

"Get out!" Petota fumed, dragging Quacho to shore. "Get out of our village!"

"You want us to get out? This man is just going to go and take advantage of another girl!" Benjin yelled, standing over Quacho, who laid quivering on the ground.

"Get out before anyone sees you." Petota grabbed Benjin by the shoulders, his voice low. "If his father or brothers catch you, you won't live to see another day!"

I pulled Benjin's arm, begging him to go, but he did not budge. He stood as still as the Earth, but his face as red as a setting sun. He wanted to kill the man, but it would bring him no peace and he knew that. Benjin bent down over Quacho with a disgusted look on his face.

"Touch another girl and I will come back and kill you," he uttered, before he spit on the ground next to him and rose to his feet.

We walked down the dirt road, with the sun beating on our faces. My face stung where Quacho placed his dirty hand, I wished I could burn it off. My heart was still racing, even though an hour had passed. Benjin and Laago walked quietly, still fuming about the events that transpired as well. Luka skipped along in front of us, blissfully unaware.

I hated being a woman in a man's world. I couldn't do anything alone without the fear of being harmed. Benjin could travel across the world and be completely left unbothered, no one would mess with a man his size. It is so unfair. I feel like a walking target.

"How are you feeling, Ny?" Laago asked, breaking the silence.

"Fine," I responded, before even thinking.

I hated that I could not even talk about it, as if I am embarrassed over something I have no control over. I hate that I feel ashamed about what happened, as if it was my fault. In my heart I knew that it wasn't, but it did not stop me from feeling riddled with guilt. I just wanted to take a bath, it was the only thing I could do alone and now I felt like I can't even do that.

"I can't imagine how you are feeling. We're here for you though," Laago spoke compassionately, each word so carefully said. I stared sightlessly into the ocean, avoiding eye contact. Benjin shook his head.

"I should've killed him. I should've taken my axe and wiped that pervert's head clear off!" He swung his axe, imagining Quacho's head rolling on the ground.

"Benjin..." I whispered. The thought made me sick.

"So we just let him go? So he can go after his next victim. His father and brothers will just come to the rescue if he gets caught!" Benjin ranted.

"Hey, Nyla doesn't need to hear all this." Laago put his hand on Benjin's shoulder. "Please."

"I know, I'm sorry," Benjin said, turning his walk into a jog. He needed to burn off some energy. Laago looked over at me empathetically.

"Don't say it, Laago."

"Don't say what?"

"He's just acting like that because he cares! He just wants to protect you," I mocked his usual response. "Well, I want to protect myself. I'm sick of feeling so weak and powerless. I don't want to always rely on you or Benjin to come and save me!"

"You're not weak or powerless, Ny, you're strong. You've taken down grown men with a single arrow. I was just going to say we should get you a dagger." Laago smiled. "You're an amazing archer, but you need something for close range self-defense. We should get you one when we reach the markets."

"I'd like that." I looked up at him and our eyes locked in a shared understanding. "Thanks, Laago. You always seem to know what to say." My heart rate finally slowed, no longer pounding through my chest.

# CHAPTER ELEVEN

# WITHIN THE WALLS

THE DAY DRAGGED BY. For the majority of our walk, everything looked the same: a boring dirt road surrounded by endless tall tan grass plains on one side and an empty sandy beach on the other. Every time I blinked, I saw Quacho's skinny pale body closing in on me. I wished my two best friends were still alive, I could talk to Juu and Tasi about anything. Although the boys were there for me, I couldn't fully open up to them about this, especially since Benjin was such an overprotective brother. Though he always meant well, his reaction only made me feel worse.

As I internally mourned my lost friends, I realized I could barely remember what they looked like anymore. When I thought of Juu, I saw her short black hair and her skinny body, but her face was a blur. I could remember specific memories we shared, but the imagery that was once so clear began to fade. I could see Tasi and the outline of her short and thick body, her matted hair tied back in a sloppy bun, but what color were her eyes? They had to be brown. Did she have freckles? Or maybe Juu did. I felt a pang in my chest, as I realized one day all of my memories of those I lost in the plague would dissolve.

"We made it!" Laago eagerly cheered.

When I squinted my eyes, I saw the outer walls of the Republic of Terlu looming in the distance. The wall stretched from the ocean and deep into the land for as far as my eyes could see. I had never seen something so massive. Its stature made me feel even tinier than I already was. The outer wall laid where the coast began to turn southeast, which meant we were about halfway from the Port of Eura to Huang.

"Not yet," Benjin fretted, anxious to make it safely behind the walls.

In the back of my mind, I knew that no matter what we were not safe. The scout had said the militia was invading in ten days, but that could have been a lie. At any moment, Ahkpi's militia could raid the republic, officially beginning the war. And somehow, it was up to four kids to stop them. I glanced back over my shoulder, scanning the horizon. I worried about Nonna, Kiuyah, Petota, and all the other loving souls we had left behind. Najin's forces would reach the outskirt villages before they reached the walls of the republic, and if the republic's army didn't arrive in time, the villages would be ravaged.

"I wonder how Nonna is..." I worried. The last time we saw her, she lied to the militants to protect us. She was one of the most selfless people that I had the honor to meet.

"Nonna knows how to take care of herself, Nyla. I wouldn't worry. We'll be back home with her soon enough," Benjin assured me. But as much as I missed Nonna, the thought of returning to our dull life depressed me.

"Do you really want to go back to Tinshe after all this?"

"Where else would we go?"

"There's a whole world out there and we've only gotten a chance to see a small portion of it," I argued.

I tried to imagine what the Sacred Forest of Akta's towering trees might look like or the Lost Lands of Onumi's ruins, but I could not even fathom their beauty. What a shame it would be, to live surrounded by such ethereal places but to never visit them.

"That sounds great, but I don't know if it's realistic. Steady work is hard to come by."

"We are young and strong men, we can find jobs anywhere," Laago reasoned. I knew he would get it. "There's nothing for us in Tinshe. Who knows if our homes will even be there for us when we return? We kind of just up and left." Benjin's eyes narrowed to slits as he scanned the outer walls of the republic. I could tell something was on his mind that he wasn't ready yet to share.

The sandy-colored stone wall loomed over us. It was massive, standing about fifty feet high. I couldn't imagine approaching the Empire of Gala, where the walls are said to be double the size. As we approached, I noticed very few of the republic's soldiers stationed at the border. It was clear General Pago had no idea of the invasion.

Since we took the coastline instead of the major trade route, we were entering through the side. Though there were some people waiting to get into the city, it wasn't as chaotic as I imagined the front entrances would be. There were a handful of soldiers patrolling from above the wall and another handful stationed in front of the gate. It sat wide open, its steel gate dispensed above, waiting to drop down at any given moment, closing the republic off from harm.

"State your business!" A soldier called over to us. I grabbed onto Luka's hand and pulled him closely.

"We are traveling from the outskirts to work on a fishing boat in Huang," Benjin said.

"Do you have proof?" The man demanded. He was a young guy, his hair greased back on his head. He tried getting close to Benjin's face, but Benjin was tall like the wall, so the guard had to stand on his toes, which wasn't very intimidating.

"No, sir, it's a family friend's boat. We have never been to the republic and didn't know we needed proof."

"I'm sick of dirty villagers comin' into my clean city and makin' a mess!" The soldier shouted, his spit spraying. Benjin stepped back and held his hands up to show he wanted no harm. I looked over at the other guards, worried they would join in, but instead realized they were holding in laughter.

"We don't mean any trouble!" Benjin was interrupted by the soldier who broke out in laughter.

"Come on through, kids. We just like messin' with ya. Welcome to the Republic of Terlu!" The soldier slapped Benjin's arm and turned back around to his fellow soldiers, leaving him to sigh in relief.

"I like these guys!" Laago smiled, waving to them as we walked by. I followed closely behind Benjin, passing through the enormous gate and officially entering the republic. As we passed the soldiers, I felt a pit in my stomach. If we didn't make it to General Pago soon, those guys were dead.

The dirt road turned into a smooth sandstone path, matching the wall in color. Along each side were homes with white walls and green pagoda roofs. Although they were simple in design, the cleanliness shocked me. An older woman with fine gray hair stood in front of her home sweeping. She wore a long brown dress made of hemp that fell to her calves with cinnamon-colored pants underneath.

"I thought you said Terlu was dirty?"

"I told you, I grew up on the outskirts. Within the walls is a totally different story," Laago explained, his eyes wandering all around him.

Already small vendors were popping up along the road, I could only imagine what it would be like when we dive deeper into the republic. I glanced into my bag. We still haven't spent any of the money that Nonna gave us. Scents of fire grilled meats and vegetables wafted through the air.

"The Republic of Terlu is a lot nicer than the Suhai Empire..." I was pleasantly surprised.

"Every empire has its good and bad parts, but, yes, Terlu does seem nicer," Benjin agreed. As he walked by, people stared. Sometimes I forgot how tall Benjin was. I had never seen anyone compared to him in height, besides my father. I looked down at Luka and patted his head. I wondered if he would end up as tall as Benjin.

As we ventured deeper into the republic, the streets grew more crowded. Apart from the festival, we had not been around many people since we left Tinshe. Benjin lifted Luka onto his shoulders and Laago instinctively grabbed my hand, without even looking back. The wound on his arm was slowly beginning to heal over into a scab.

Tall wooden sticks lined the street, adorned with green lanterns. Potted peonies and golden chrysanthemums sat snugly against the walls. As we delved further into the republic, not only did the surroundings become more appealing, but the people also dressed more elegantly. Many women wore smooth silk dresses that flowed to their ankles and delicate shoes, their black hair wound tightly in buns. I looked down at my clunky black boots. They matched Benjin's work boots that he loosely wore on his feet.

Though Tinshe was a part of an empire, it did not have a traditional culture. Men and women dressed freely, unlike in other empires and kingdoms. Growing up, I always wore old shirts that Benjin passed down to me. Here, young girls wore actual dresses, sewed tightly around their waist to fit their figure and sandals. I looked down at my raggedy clothes and felt self-conscious, before glancing at Laago, who wore the same pair of pants every day, even before our journey. Neither of the boys seemed to mind how dirty we looked. Instead, they confidently marched on, their eyes forward.

The markets of Terlu were truly unlike no other. Decorated stands lined the streets, filled with a wide array of goods. There were produce stands overfilled with leafy greens, beautiful women selling colorful clothing, and even a frail old man selling homemade teapots. Even though I had only seen such a small fraction of the markets, I was already convinced that one could buy anything under the sun here.

A man dressed in all white stood on a balcony above us, blowing through a shiny gold wind instrument, sending deep melodies adrift through the air, entangling with the voices of the crowd. A tall woman with thick black hair down to her ankles hummed along. She wore a rose red silk dress with dainty black thread stitched elegantly throughout. Her face was painted white with brightly colored makeup caked around her eyes.

I imagined how it would feel having money, walking through these streets and running my hand along the different fabrics and tasting the different kinds of delicacies. I would buy a grilled duck skewer just to take a single bite. All of the vendors would smile at me, because they would know I always let them keep the change.

As we passed by an alley hidden behind the overflowing stands, I noticed a small young girl dressed in rags, eating a rotting fruit off the ground. She sat barefoot and covered in dirt, all alone. Her eyes shot up at me, catching me off guard. As quickly as I was sucked into my fantasy, I fell back to the grim reality.

We reached a large open area with an ancient-looking bonsai tree towering over, with white lanterns delicately hanging from its branches. They emitted a soft light, twinkling in the sky as the sun set. Soft honey flowers were just blooming on the tree, reminding us that spring was truly here. To one side was a small park, where families sat on blankets and children played, surrounded by sharp magenta flowers. To the other side were storefronts, many with tables out front, filled with customers. There was a grocery story, a tea shop, and a tailor.

"I think we should buy some food and try to find a place to stay before it gets too late," Benjin decided. "Nyla, you wait out here with Luka. Laago and I will head into the grocery store and try to haggle for a good deal." He picked Luka off his shoulders and set him on the ground.

"Come on, Luka!" I tossed Benjin the coin sack and reached my hand out to Luka. "Let's go sit under the bonsai tree." Benjin and Laago disappeared into the small store.

"This city is so pretty!" Luka babbled, admiring the twinkling lanterns above us. "Can we stay here?"

"I don't know, it's up to Benjin," I stared off into the tea shop.

A handsome boy, around Benjin's age, carried a tray of steaming tea to an outdoor table where a woman, layered in a fine silk dress, sat with her husband. The boy's bright smile radiated as he served their tea. I petted Luka's head and daydreamed about working at the tea shop. Inside, there were about three more tables. The boy stopped at each one, checking on his customers. Without even finishing half of their cups, the woman and her husband got up and left, leaving behind a pile of gold coins on the table. The boy swiftly walked out and expressed his gratitude as he collected the payment. His eyes wandered from the table he cleaned up to mine, but I quickly looked away and blushed. He must have felt me staring at him. Tired of my shyness, I mustered the courage and looked back up at him. He let off a wide smile, before he returned inside with the dirty dishes.

"Look what we got!" Laago beamed, carrying a bag of food. "Bread and cooked potatoes!"

"The man we bought the food from said the tea shop has a room upstairs they may let us stay in," Benjin added. "I'll run in and see if I can work something out."

"I have a surprise for you, Ny." Laago sat next to me with a grin as he pulled a bongamelon out of his bag. "We can call it a late birthday present!"

"No way, this is my favorite fruit!"

"I know! You told me you haven't had one since you were a kid." Laago took his dagger and cut into its hard shell, revealing the bright pink juice inside. He handed me a chunk, then Luka. I bit into it, letting the juice drip down my chin. "Is it as good as you remember it being?"

"Even better..." I took another bite and tried to savor its sweetness, as well as Laago's.

I was taken back by his recollection of such a seemingly insignificant detail. I often felt like no one listened to me when I spoke. I looked up at him, my eyes fixated on his lips as he bit into the fiercely sweet fruit. They looked even more enticing than the fruit itself.

"We can crash here tonight! We just have to do some work for them," Benjin shouted, walking back over to us. "The lady told us to come back at closing time."

"When's that?" Laago asked.

"About fifteen minutes," Benjin plopped down, squeezing between Laago and me. Luka crawled over and sat on his lap, nuzzling into Benjin's chest. I blankly stared into the tea shop, waiting for the last few customers to leave. Benjin took a bite of Luka's bongamelon and smacked his lips.

"I hate how here people laze around in silk sipping imported tea, when the northwestern outskirt villagers are living in poverty, being raided by Qaran tribes, and struggling to survive," Laago criticized. He leaned back and crossed his arms, judging all the people who strutted past us in their fancy clothes.

"No empire or republic is perfect. If there is wealth, there is inequality. At least Terlu elects their officials," Benjin countered.

"Yeah, President Suin. He says he cares about the working people and I want to believe he does, but then why doesn't he do anything?" Laago scoffed. "We pay taxes just like the rest of 'em, except we do not see any of the coin once it leaves our pockets. In fact, it took years for the Republic of Terlu's military to even send troops to protect us from the tribes."

"Well, first off, President Suin is not an emperor, so he only has so much power." Benjin rubbed his chin. "Also, the Republic of Terlu has lower tax rates in comparison to other empires, so even with every city paying up, it may not be enough."

"Looking around here it seems there is more than enough money to be shared." Laago shook his head. "It's greed."

"I don't know, there's always another side to every story," Benjin pondered. The last customers left the shop. "Well, I guess we better get to work."

We rose to our aching feet and walked over to the store. By now, the city was quiet. All of the vendors were packing up their stands after a long day's work. Everyone seemed to be heading inside to their homes for the night.

"Hello!" Benjin shouted through the doorway.

"Come in!" The woman called from behind the small granite counter. "There is a lot of work to be done!"

Her accent was thick and sharp, but I couldn't tell where she was from. She was small, like me, and had her gray hair tied tightly in a bun on the back of her head. She wore a green button down dress that matched the boy's uniform, with a straw-colored apron draped over it. The floors had decorative mosaic tiles, some with dainty flowers painted on, alternating with plain sage green tiles. The walls were the color of cream, with long narrow paintings hanging.

"What would you like us to do?" Benjin politely asked.

"The girl can wash dishes. Little boy will clean the tables and sweep. You men will fix my bath upstairs and the squeaky front door!" She ordered.

"What's wrong with your bath?" Laago asked.

"It leaks! It leaks every day! Waste of water."

"I can fix it. Benj, you can work on the front door," Laago decided. He could fix just about anything. Benjin nodded in agreement and went to work on the door. "Can you take me to the bath?" Laago asked, following the lady upstairs. The boy from earlier emerged from the kitchen and handed Luka a broom. It was taller than he was.

"I'll clean the tables, you just worry about sweeping, little guy." He patted him on the head and started collecting dishes.

I walked myself into the kitchen. There were piles of dirty cups and dishes. How did such a tiny tea shop have so many dishes? I groaned, then rolled up my sleeves and got to work, eager to finish and finally get to rest. We probably walked about fifty miles today. At this point, my body was actually beginning to grow accustomed to traveling.

When we began our journey, my feet stung with every step and my body ached nonstop. Fortunately lately my feet only begin to hurt closer to sunset, after we did the overwhelming majority of our daily trek. I looked down at my arms as I scrubbed the dishes. I was always so pasty white in Tinshe, but now my arms were beginning to brown. My hair was always long, but now its waves reached past my belly button. My mindless thoughts were interrupted by the boy, as he carried more dirty dishes into the kitchen.

"These are the last of them." His voice was smooth. "My name is Ain."

"Nyla," I answered, too nervous to make eye contact.

"Where are you traveling from?"

"The outskirts. We are headed to Huang to work on a fishing boat."

"I've never been on a boat before." Ain leaned against the counter next to me and folded his arms, staring off into the kitchen.

"Neither have I."

"Are you scared?"

"Not really."

"I heard fishing is one of the most dangerous jobs because the weather in the South Ocean is so unpredictable. A lot of boats that head out don't make it back."

"Are you trying to scare me?"

"Oh, no! I'm sorry, I-"

"I'm just joking. I don't care, I already said I am not scared." Our eyes briefly met, before I looked back down at my dishes and he gazed out at the kitchen.

"Well then you must be a lot braver than I am." He smiled. I thought back to our journey. I was only sixteen, but had taken the lives of men, snuck through enemy territory, and traveled hundreds of miles with my life constantly under threat.

"I'm probably braver than most people you know," I realized, not even meaning to say it out loud. My face reddened.

"I like your confidence, Nyla." Though it was a simple compliment, it was none I had ever heard before. He turned around and began drying the dishes as I set them down.

"Don't you have to finish closing the store?"

"It's fine. It's not like my mother would fire me." He chuckled. "Who are those boys you are traveling with?"

"Those are my two brothers and our friend."

"Are they single?"

"Uh, yes," I responded, realizing Ain preferred men. "But I think they're only interested in women."

"Yeah, yeah. That's what they all say." He laughed. "Which ones are your brothers?"

"The taller one is my older brother Benjin and the little one is Luka."

"I've never seen anyone that tall. What a hunk!" He raised his eyebrows. "What about the other guy?"

"That's Laago. He's been Benjin's best friend since they were kids."

"They're both so handsome..." Ain gushed. "Let me guess, you have a crush on Laago?"

"No..." I blushed. "Well, I don't know." Normally I wouldn't be so honest, but something about Ain made him seem trustworthy. I felt my guard dropping.

"Tell me everything!"

"I've known Laago since I was really young, but I never really got close with him until this trip. Back home, I always thought he was just some goofball that Benjin liked to kill time with. I never realized what a great guy he is. I once mentioned to him I loved bongamelon, then today he surprised me with one and even remembered that I said I hadn't had one since I was a kid. He's sweet and caring, but..."

"But what? He sounds like a great guy. If you don't snatch him up, maybe I will!" Ain tossed his rag onto the counter.

"For as long as I have known him he's been bouncing around girls. He dates one, then cheats on her, and moves onto the next. Besides, Benjin wouldn't be happy."

"Hm..." He pondered, his waist leaning against the counter. "People change."

"I thought so too, then the other day I think he got with some girl from a village we passed through." I sighed, aggressively scrubbing a dirty pot.

"What a pig!" Ain exclaimed. "I think you're too pretty to wait around for some man."

"Boys don't seem to notice me. I've never even had a boyfriend, or anything remotely close," I admitted.

"That's their loss!" Ain picked up his rag and continued drying the dishes. "I've never had an actual boyfriend either."

"Really?" I was surprised. Ain was such an attractive and outgoing guy, I would never think that he would have trouble with that.

"Yeah, most guys seem to just want to have fun. No one wants to stick around for a relationship. Every time I give someone a chance, I think, this time will be different. Then I just end up feeling used."

"I'm sorry, Ain. They're missing out!" Our eyes met and he smiled. I passed him the last dish to dry and threw my sponge in the sink.

"I like you, Nyla. I wish you weren't just passing through." Ain threw his arm around my shoulder. "And I think you should do whatever your heart wants."

"Hey, Ny!" Laago shouted as he bursted through the kitchen door shirtless, holding his soaking wet shirt in his hand. He paused, looking at Ain. "What's up?" He nodded at him, staring at his arm around my shoulder.

"Why are you wet?" I asked.

"Had a little trouble with the bath. It's all fixed now. Are you done in here? I can help you finish up."

"Nope, Ain helped me. We're all done." Ain pulled his arm down and headed to the door.

"It was nice talking to you, Nyla!" He winked, heading back into the restaurant.

"What's up with him?" Laago scoffed.

"What do you mean? He was just helping me with the dishes."

"Seemed like he wanted to do more than just the dishes."

"You're crazy." I laughed, realizing how oblivious he was.

"It's not funny," he countered in a chiding tone.

"What's your problem?"

"What's my problem? You almost got assaulted just the other day and now you're just out here letting a stranger touch you?" He stepped closer to me.

"He's not interested, Laago, but he did say that you and Benjin were his type!" I retorted, storming out of the kitchen.

"Nyla!" He called, following me out. He tried to grab my hand, but I ripped it away and stormed out the front door of the tea shop, right past Benjin who sat on the floor fixing it and Ain who sat against the wall next to him, flirting. Laago chased me out of the store, but I ran into the park and hid behind a tree.

I heard him calling my name in the near distance, but I sat hidden in the darkness, weeping. I didn't even know why I was crying. How dare he say that about me? As if I casually flirted with men and allowed them to encroach upon me. He was the one constantly with a new girl! My near-assault had nothing to do with anything! It wasn't my fault. I felt my blood boil with rage.

"Nyla!" He called, finally catching sight of me. I buried my face in my knees and wrapped my arms around. Laago collapsed onto the ground next to me and put his hand on my shoulder.

"Don't touch me!" I snapped and hit him in the chest with my fist, before I could even stop myself.

"Okay!" He backed off, scooting away to give me space. "I am sorry. I am so so sorry, Ny. I don't know what came over me- that was uncalled for," he acknowledged. I wiped my tears and looked up at him. His eyes were welling up.

"Why did you get so mad?"

"I don't know," he stammered, wiping his eyes.

"Well, I'm not waiting around while you figure it out!" I jumped up and stormed back towards the tea shop, leaving him sitting there on his bottom. I didn't even look back.

As upset as I was, I couldn't help but smile. In such a brief conversation, Ain helped me in more ways than he would ever know. I had been bottling all my emotions up since the plague and forgot how nice it was to talk to a friend openly and honestly. I finally felt a surge of confidence in myself. All along, I thought I was the one confused with my feelings over Laago, but it wasn't just me. Laago had been sending me mixed signals because he was just as conflicted.

I walked back into the tea shop. Benjin and Ain were sitting at a table having an intense conversation. Ain was leaned in, his face resting in his hands, completely involved in whatever story Benjin was spewing. Luka was sprawled out on the floor, already asleep.

"What just happened?" Benjin asked.

"Nothing." I shrugged. "I'm tired."

"Me too, let's go to bed." Benjin stood up and stretched. "Where's Laago?"

"Not sure." I continued towards the staircase, with Ain leading the way. Benjin picked up Luka and followed behind me. We walked up the narrow wooden staircase to Ain and his mother's home.

"Your room is right here," he said, opening the door. There was one bed, big enough for the three of us to squeeze in. Laago would have to sleep on the floor and to be honest, I didn't care. I stared out the window that overlooked the bonsai tree and park, but I didn't see Laago.

"Thank you, Ain. For everything," I said, giving him a hug.

"I'll see you in the morning." He crept out and gently shut the door behind him.

"Seriously, what happened?" Benjin worried. He began pacing in the small room. "Should I go find Laago?"

"He got mad that I was talking to Ain, even though Ain doesn't even like women."

"Ain's gay?" Benjin slapped his forehead, finally realizing why Ain seemed so interested in his story. "But why did Laago get mad?"

"I don't know, Benj."

"This is exactly why I told you to stay away from him! We are on a mission right now, Nyla. We can't be fighting over stuff like this," he hissed, before storming out the door. Normally, I would never dare to argue with Benjin, but instead, I followed him back down the staircase.

"It's not my fault!" I snapped back, keeping my voice low. "He's the emotional one that couldn't handle me talking to someone. He slept with someone the other day. Did I yell? Did I make a scene? No! I shut my mouth and kept it to myself."

Benjin's face dropped. I quietly scampered back up the stairs before he could respond and jumped in bed with Luka, covering my face with a pillow. I wish I could lock the door so both Benjin and Laago could sleep outside for the night.

I laid there for a while trying to fall asleep, but I was too frustrated. I tried taking deep breaths, which would help for a moment until I got lost in thought again. Just knowing Benjin and Laago were out there talking made me anxious. I don't know how much later, but I eventually heard the door squeak open and the boys slip in, but I pretended to be asleep.

The next morning I was the first to wake. Benjin was wrapped around Luka and Laago was sprawled out on the floor in his drawers. I slipped out the bed and crept downstairs to the tea shop. Ain and his mother were already awake as well, sitting at a table with hot tea.

"Good morning, Nyla. How did you sleep?" Ain asked.

"Really well actually!" I grabbed a seat next to him. His mother got up and disappeared into the kitchen to prepare for the morning rush.

"So what happened last night with Laago?"

"He got jealous of us. He totally freaked out!" I gossiped.

"I knew it!" Ain's laughter bellowed. "I saw him look at my arm around you!"

"He ended up apologizing, but he didn't admit to why he got so jealous."

"What do you mean? He obviously likes you..." Ain's eyebrows raised as he sipped his tea.

"I think it's more complicated than that. We would never work as a couple," I said, leaning back into the chair.

"Why not?"

"I don't know... I don't think Laago could ever stay faithful in a long term relationship. I don't think he would even want to. And even if he did, we are both under a lot of stress right now."

"You need to find a new man. One that sees you for the amazing woman you are."

"You barely know me, Ain!" I laughed. "What if I'm actually a mean girl?"

"Nyla, you look like you couldn't hurt a fly!" A customer walked in, so Ain got up to greet them.

I left the tea shop, not wanting to steal a table from a potential guest. I sat outside under the bonsai tree and observed people in the park. The sun was just rising, so the streets were still mostly quiet. I watched a young man exercising, sweat pouring off his body. He had long black hair, tied in a bun on top of his head. Every time he jumped up, it bobbed.

My eyes drifted to an elderly couple walking through the grass park. The old woman wore a long white silk tunic that flowed to her ankles, with blush flowers stitched in. They held hands and looked to the sky, watching birds bounce from branch to branch. I didn't hear them speak, instead they just smiled, appreciating each other and the beauty around them. I sighed and looked away, back at the tea shop. Benjin walked out the front door, swiping his hair out of his face.

"Morning!" He took a seat next to me.

"Morning," I replied. I always hated fighting with Benjin.

"I'm sorry about last night."

"I know, I am too."

"You have nothing to be sorry about, Nyla. I-"

"Can we just put this behind us and move on?" I interrupted. "Like you said, we are on a mission."

"Yeah, about the mission..." He shook his head, biting his lip. "I have a bad feeling."

"What do you mean?" I turned my body to him.

"I don't really know, I couldn't sleep last night. I am worried Ahkpi and his militia will invade sooner than we expected," he whispered, careful to not let anyone hear him.

"I'm sure you're just anxious. We all are," I reasoned. I put my hand on his arm and squeezed it. Laago strolled out of the tea shop, munching on a piece of bread.

"Hey!" He shouted. "Why the long faces?" Laago took a seat next to Benjin.

"I'm worried about the invasion. At this rate, we won't make it to Huang for another two days," Benjin fretted.

"Isn't that right on schedule?"

"Benjin is worried they are going to invade sooner," I explained.

"I see." He stroked his chin with his fingers. "So what do we do?"

"I think we should not stop moving until we reach Huang. If we leave now, we can get there before midnight tomorrow," he said. "I'll go wake Luka."

I could tell Benjin already made up his mind, there was no point in trying to sway him. Before we could even answer, he got up, leaving Laago and I alone. I felt unbelievably awkward. Just as I went to get up, he spoke.

"I hate that I made things awkward," he blurted out. "I don't know what came over me yesterday. I think this long journey is just really getting to me. I just wanted to say I am sorry again for acting like an ass."

"It's okay." I brushed his words aside. "I think we should just focus on reaching General Pago."

"Agreed. Are we good?"

"We're good," I said, finally looking up at him. His smile was contagious. By the time Benjin came outside with Luka, we were both hysterically laughing.

"What's so funny?" Benjin called over, already chuckling too. "You take a bite of holiva root again?"

"It's going to be a looong day," Laago sputtered between laughter.

We got up from the bench and headed inside to the tea shop to gather our belongings. I dreaded saying goodbye to Ain. Though my time with him was so brief, I felt like I knew him my whole life. Ain made me wonder whether past lives were real, because if they were, we were definitely best of friends. I always had trouble opening up, but with him it felt so natural. I didn't worry about sounding dumb or how I looked.

"Maybe one day you can come back to our tea shop."

"I will, I promise," I said, as he wrapped his arms around my body.

I wished I could tell Ain why we were really in the Republic of Terlu. I felt ashamed that I couldn't warn him and his mother to flee north before the war starts. But even if I could, the reality was that Ain's family was the working class. They could not afford to just get up and leave their life behind. If they knew, it would just add unnecessary stress to their lives, over something unpreventable. Perhaps ignorance was bliss after all.

We headed out, with my bow on my back and arrows on my side, into a new day. The sky was clear, there was not a cloud in sight. It was definitely hot, but not the type of hot that made it hard to breathe. Before long, the streets were filled with people, hustling around in every direction.

I stared down at my boots, they clunked with every step. They were worn-down and bore scars of the countless miles behind us. I felt my blisters hitting into the hard soles, sending searing pain from my toes to my calves. It would not be long before the boots began to really fall apart.

My trouser shorts now hung loosely on my legs. I wondered if they simply stretched out from overuse or if I was gradually losing weight. I dug into my bag and pulled out a piece of bread. The last thing I wanted was to be even skinnier, but the relentless days of travel had exacted their toll. Even Benjin and Laago, once robust with muscle, had become leaner shadows of their former selves. When I looked back up, I didn't see the boys.

"Benjin?" I shouted, but I was too small to see over the heads of everyone passing through the streets.

I jumped up, expecting to see Benjin's head floating above the bustling crowds, but I did not see him. I quickly began weaving my way through people, my heart pounding with anxiety. The thought of being lost in a foreign city filled me with dread, especially considering we had no time to spare. I tried to take deep breaths and remind myself that we were to follow this road straight to Huang, and that the boys would have no reason to deviate, but no amount of rationalizing settled me. I continued to call out Benjin's name, but heard no response. My voice dissipated amidst the sea of people and I was far too small to push my way through.

I ran down the street until I reached an opening. Another bonsai tree stood firmly in the center of the road, surrounded by a wooden bench on each side. I jumped into the tree and climbed to the top, hoping for a vantage point to spot the boys. As I scanned down the road, I caught sight of Benjin's head bobbing along through crowds of people, with Luka perched on his shoulders. I felt no relief, because between them and me stood about fifty people bustling along in every direction of the street. I climbed down from the tree, ready to take off after them before they got too far, but a hand grabbed me, pulling me back.

"Hey! No climbing on the republic's property!" A guard yelled.

"I'm sorry, I lost-"

"Save it!" He barked, dragging me down the street, away from the boys. Spit flew from his mouth with every syllable. "Kids like you don't belong in these parts."

"I didn't kn-"

"What did I say?"

"Excuse me!" Another voice rumbled from behind me, this one far less intimidating than the last. "Is my granddaughter causing problems?" I turned my head to see an old man with a big belly in a long hemp tunic. He had a long gray beard that bobbed as he spoke.

"Oh! I am so sorry..." The guard stuttered, releasing me. "I didn't realize she was a member of the Ritu family. Please-"

"It is no worry," the old man replied, smiling. "I apologize for my granddaughter." He placed his hand on the small of my back and we turned away, walking down the street towards the boys.

"Thank you, sir."

"Personally, I think the guards are a little too strict, but it is best to abide by the republic's rules and avoid trouble." He looked down at me, his eyes were warm and inviting. The sun shone on his bald head.

"I lost my brother and I couldn't see over the crowds to find him." I looked at the people flooding the street in front of me. How was I ever going to catch up to Benjin?

"Ah, I understand." He stroked his beard. "We all get lost sometimes, but if you know where you want to end up, you will find your way."

"We were headed to Huang..."

"To reach Huang you will have to travel down this road for many miles. It is unlikely that your brother will veer from it." The old man's voice was soothing. I knew we had to travel mostly down this road, because it was the closest main road to the Bay of Suhai.

"That's what I thought, but when I lost them I got nervous. It is my first time in this city."

"Fear tends to cloud judgment." He smiled down at me. "I always love meeting new visitors. Don't let one grouchy guard give you the wrong impression."

"It's okay, I know I don't fit in here. My clothes are tattered, my hair is raggedy, and I haven't bathed in days. Had I been wearing a smooth and silky dress like every other wealthy person, I probably wouldn't have even been bothered by any guard."

"I think it is wise to not waste your precious time on things that do not matter."

"If I was rich I would dress nice," I admitted. My clothes were stained and smelt. There was nothing wise about that.

"I always thought I would too." The man laughed, his hands on his stomach. I looked at his hemp tunic, it was covered in holes like my clothes.

"You're rich?" I doubted, weaving around a man who carried a wheelbarrow of potatoes.

"I suppose it depends how you define rich."

"Where I come from, it means having a lot of money," I innocently explained. Once again, the man laughed.

"You are a funny young one." He looked up at the sky and a single cloud drifted over us. "But then, yes, by your definition I was once rich."

"What happened?"

"I realized it meant nothing."

"What? Money is everything! Without it, we would starve!"

"Without food, you would starve. Money is just a mineral that we decided to fight and kill each other for. Who is to say gold is worth more than any other rock?"

"I don't know... It's definitely prettier."

"Perhaps it is," he mused, "but I once had more money than one could imagine and not only did it bring me no relief, but it riddled me with anguish. It monopolized the most precious currency I had: my time and my thoughts, and left little room for life's true treasures. Every waking moment was devoured by how to increase my money, how to protect it from thieves... In this empty pursuit, I lost sight of what was really important."

"So what did you do?"

"I gave it back."

"To who?"

"To the Republic of Terlu, to the people, to the children with no mothers." He threw his arms up, gesturing to those around us. "I bought land and built parks, I paid for bonsai trees to be planted along these roads... I bought homes for soldiers who had none."

"Wow... Most people would never give away their money."

"Perhaps, but most people also don't experience having that much wealth, so who are we to decide how they would choose to spend it?"

If I were rich, what would I spend it on? Maybe I would build a nice home by Kiuyah's, for me and the boys to settle down in and live peacefully, away from all the wars and hardships. I wouldn't need much, nor want much, but just enough to live a simple life. One with stability and ease.

"How did you become so rich?" I asked. The old man's eyes drifted to his feet and mine followed. He was barefoot, his feet blackened with dirt.

"I was born wearing ragged clothes, much like yours. I came from the outskirts and traveled into the city every weekend to sell my village's produce, and I was good at it too," he winked. "One fateful day, a wealthy man took notice of my skills and offered me employment. His belief in me transformed my life. Khatch Ritu was the most dedicated worker the world had ever known. He never settled down nor had children, instead he devoted his life to his work. He became like family to me and provided me with everything I now possess. I was able to save a lot of money and send it back to my village, before I ultimately ended up taking over his business when he passed."

"It must have been hard for you to lose him."

"It was." The man sighed. "Though I believe it was what I needed to truly learn."

"Learn what?"

"He fell gravely ill shortly before I embarked on a business trip to the Empire of Gala. It was a long journey, but potential rewards were immense. I expected to triple my profits. Well, the trip was a success, so I began the long voyage home. The whole time I thought of how excited I was to share the news with him, I did it. I really made something of myself. But when I got home, he had already passed. I even missed his burial."

"I am so sorry. I am sure he would have been so proud of you."

"His nurse told me the whole time on his deathbed he was asking for his son, but Khatch never had children of his own. He was talking about me. Here was a man, with everything he could ever want in this world at the tip of his fingers, but on his deathbed he longed for nothing more than my presence."

"None of the money mattered."

"So I gave it all away." We passed through the next opening in the road. This time, I looked at the bonsai tree with a different appreciation. It was one man's selfless decision to use what he had to make the world a better place. "Every time I see these trees or the parks or the families the money has helped, it reminds me of him. He left behind a seed of a legacy, I was just the one who planted it."

"He must be so proud."

"You have a very old heart." He smiled as he rustled my hair. "I am very glad we crossed paths."

"I am too," I said, remembering that I was still lost from Benjin. "I bet you would really like my brother."

"Perhaps one day we will cross paths again, but for now, you should make haste and find him." He rummaged through his pockets and handed me a small piece of paper. "Take this, in case anyone else tries to start trouble with you or your brothers. Best of luck on your journey to Huang."

"Thank you for everything." I slipped it into my boot and waved goodbye, as I ran off into the crowd. It occurred to me that I never asked him for his name.

I weaved between people with a new found confidence. Instead of waiting for someone to move, I pushed my way through. I didn't care if my bag bumped into someone or if I stepped on someone's shoes, just like how they didn't care if they banged into me. I ran through the streets with my arrows bouncing on my hip.

I thought about the nameless old man and his mentor, Khatch Ritu. Though I suppose he wasn't so nameless, if the guard knew him as a member of the Ritu family. I would call him Mister Ritu... It had a nice ring to it. All of my life, I have always assumed money was the answer to all my problems. Although it may be able to solve a lot of them, the deepest issues seem to be incurable by gold.

By now the sun was behind me, causing my anxiety to resurface. I did not want to be traveling alone through the streets in the dark. The crowds already began to lessen. I tried to focus my energy elsewhere, on Benjin, Luka, and Laago.

Laago... The thought of our awkward fight made my face blush. Even when he tried to talk about it, I just brushed it off and avoided saying how I truly felt. I wanted him to admit why he got so mad, even if it would just cause more problems. I know it is easier this way, but-

"Nyla!" Benjin's voice floated through the crowd.

"Benjin?" I jumped up, throwing my arms in the air.

"I see you, don't move!" Before I knew it, he threw his arms around me and hugged me tightly. "What happened? I practically had a heart attack!"

"I don't know, I got separated from you guys. I couldn't see over the crowds of people." It felt so nice to be reunited, even if I was only separated for one afternoon.

"Nyla!" Laago shouted, carrying Luka on his back.

"Miss me?"

"More than you would ever know."

As the sun set behind us, I reflected on my good fortune in having the people I did in my life. I didn't grow up with a drunk father or an absent mother. I may have lost my mother, but I know she would have done anything for me. I never had a brother who bullied me or a friend who backstabbed me. Admittedly, I only had two friends, but Juu and Tasi were the best two friends I could have asked for. I thought of Nonna, who was always down the hall, waiting to feed me cookies and listen to me rant about my day. I even thought of Laago, who was always there with a smile on his face and jokes up his sleeve.

Reflecting on this made me feel warm and loved, but it also broke my heart. I felt pain for all the children, like Laago, who were abused by their parents. I felt the suffering of those who never had guidance or came home to a tight hug. I felt the agony of those consumed by loneliness, whether they were surrounded by people or not.

"I love you guys," I announced.

"I love you too," Benjin replied, too tired to even question it or turn around to me.

"Love you, Ny."

We all dragged our feet through the night, half-asleep but constantly moving forward. I looked to the moon and prayed to Eura. I felt guilty for not praying in a while, but it just didn't feel right. Did I deserve protection from the gods and goddesses when my hands were stained with blood? I was no god, who was I to take a life? I begged Eura for forgiveness and asked for her protection. Not just for myself, but for all those dear to me. From Benjin to Nonna, and even Kiuyah and Bao. I prayed for their longevity, for their happiness, and for this war to be over before it truly began.

"Why wasn't the moon hungry?"

"Why?" Benjin humored Laago, already sighing.

"Because it was already full!" He chuckled to himself. I then prayed for Laago to find better jokes.

# CHAPTER TWELVE

# FROM DUSK TO DAWN

"**H**OW DOES YOUR BICEP feel?" Benjin asked, breaking the silence. We had practically been sleepwalking for a few hours. The moon was directly above us now, illuminating the empty street. The lanterns that lined the road emitted a soft yellow light. As always, Luka laid on Benjin's back, sleeping.

"Better," Laago replied, as he stretched his arm. His thick scab was slowly turning into a deep scar. "I think I finally have most of my mobility back, but it definitely feels weaker."

"Our legs must be pure muscle from all this walking, but we haven't been able to work on our upper body." Benjin flexed his arms. "It's impossible to not lose weight when all we do is move."

"When we get to Huang, maybe General Pago will help us out and give us food or coins," Laago said. "Otherwise, I don't know if we will make it to the Island of Aara."

"If he is as good of a man as Bao said, I am sure he will do the right thing."

"Well, hopefully he can at least give us a boat to get to the Council of Five, because I don't know any other way to get to the island."

"I was thinking we could swim!" Benjin laughed. "After all, you said your arm is all healed up."

"Yeah, nothing like a quick million mile swim. Maybe if we are lucky, a storm will engulf us and save us the trip."

"I don't understand why the Council of Five stay on an island in the middle of the Great Ocean. What's the point of having them, if they are cut off from the world? They claim to represent us, but they don't even know the injustices that occur across the world!" I argued.

"Where else would they go? The rest of the world's land is already inhabited. If the Council of Five moves to a pre-existing kingdom, they will seem biased and lose credibility. The purpose of having a Civil Council is to be a mediator. Keeping them in the center of the ocean protects them from potential corruption," Benjin explained.

"In theory, it sounds logical, but that doesn't mean it is practical," I countered. "Where were they when the plague hit? Or when Najin's militia stormed the south?"

"It frustrates me too, Nyla, but that is why we are on this journey, to reveal the brewing atrocities in the world. Unfortunately for the west, we are more cut off from the Council of Five, which is why things have been able to get as bad as they are. Tinshe doesn't have the resources to reach the Island of Aara, Najin made sure of it. We have no formal army, no navy. Meanwhile, representatives from the Empire of Gala and Chao Binh seem to be able to easily reach the council. Lucky for them, there isn't much internal or external conflict in the east, or at least none of which I know of."

"There is always peace in the east because Empress Jhena and her powerful army make sure of it," Laago said.

"Once we reach the Civil Council, they will make sure all of the countries send in forces to protect Tinshe and restore balance in the Suhai Empire," Benjin promised, though it sounded like he needed to hear that more than me.

My whole life I heard of similar empty promises. *Najin will send medicine and resources to help Tinshe through the plague!* Yet, instead, they sent troops to police and control us. *The resistance will restore peace in the Suhai Empire!* When in reality, they sit in tunnels, cowering. Benjin's naivety grated on my nerves, but I kept it to myself. I was too tired to argue and what good would it do anyway?

"General Ahkpi's militia would crumble before the army of Gala. I hope we have front row seats for their surrender," Laago said.

"I don't," I whispered. "I want to be as far away from that as possible."

In the distance, the outline of two figures illuminated from their lantern as they approached us. By the heavy steps of their boots, I knew it was more guards, patrolling the streets. The Republic of Terlu valued safety and because of it, they had very low crime rates.

"Why are you kids out so late?" One of the guards asked, who didn't look much older than Laago.

"We have to reach Huang by tomorrow for a fishing job," Benjin said.

"I've never seen anybody use a bow or an axe to catch fish. There was a reported break in not too far from here. Empty your bags," he ordered, his mustache bouncing on his lip.

"With all due respect, we are on a tight schedule. We will lose our job if we do not make it to Huang."

"Empty your bags," the other guard repeated, holding his lantern in front of us.

I pulled out my bag and dumped the contents on the floor. A few old dried wheat strips, some of Luka's belongings, a painting of my family, and a bag of coins from Nonna. Benjin set Luka down and dumped his bag out too, as did Laago. The guards dropped to their knees and sifted through our belongings. One of them opened my bag of coins.

"Where'd you get this money from?"

"Our Nonna gave it to us so we could afford food on our journey," Benjin explained as the guard rose to his feet, still holding our bag of coins. He glanced at the other guard.

"I would hate to have to take you kids to the station for questioning. And considering you are the only ones out on the streets this late, suspiciously close to the robbery, it doesn't look too good for you kids. I can tell you're not from around here," he said, his eyes judging our dirty clothes.

I looked up at Benjin anxiously, but his expression made me realize we had no choice but to let this man rob us. To the guards, we were just poor kids with no protection. Without this money, we would have to travel all the way to Huang with no food. Suddenly, an idea came to me. I reached into my boot and pulled out the piece of paper the old man gave me when I got lost.

"Here!" I handed it to the guard, not even knowing what the small piece of paper said.

The guard held his lantern to the paper, his eyes narrowing as he read. Suddenly, his eyes widened, as he nudged the other guard to take a look. Benjin and Laago glanced over at me, clearly confused. I forgot to mention my encounter with the kind old man.

"I am so sorry to disturb you children. We had no idea. Please, carry on!" The guard handed me the paper back and dropped to his knees, putting our belongings back into our bags.

"There's no need for an apology, sir..." Benjin responded, still completely bewildered. The guards handed us our packs and were on their way. Laago's head turned to me as they passed us. Once they were far enough away, he threw his hands up.

"What just happened?"

"I met a gentleman when I got lost and it turns out he holds a lot of power in the republic." I unfolded the piece of paper and analyzed it. It was a travel document that stated we were family of Mister Ritu, authorizing us undisturbed travel within the republic! It was signed by Khatch Ritu himself.

"Why didn't you tell us?" Benjin stammered, reaching for the slip of paper to see for himself.

"He gave that paper as I left, I just put it in my boot without even looking at it. He said if we got into any trouble, to use it."

"Authorized by Mister Khatch Ritu..." He read aloud. "Who is that?"

"He was the wealthiest man in the republic!" Laago remembered. "He made military equipment for the army."

"When he died, his fortune was passed down to the man I met. He gave it all away to the people of the republic, because he realized money was worthless."

"Money is a lot of things, but not worthless. We almost would have starved if those guards took our money," Benjin countered.

I shrugged my shoulders. I knew he wouldn't get it. I didn't even really get it, but I wanted to. Perhaps no one could truly understand, unless they find themselves in the same position as the old man found himself in.

We continued walking, the moon sinking behind our backs. Clouds began to form in the sky, releasing a soft drizzle upon us. The rain was cold, which contrasted the humidity. It stuck to my body uncomfortably. Even so, I dreaded the sunrise, because it would fill the streets with people and slow down travel time. The further we made it under the moon's watchful eye, the better. I glanced at Benjin, whose hand was clenched around the scroll tied to his chest. I was glad I wasn't responsible for carrying that, even the thought of it gave me anxiety. The fate of the Republic of Terlu and Tinshe, tied to some boy's chest with a vine.

As the sun rose, the humidity intensified. My mouth was dry and each step shot pain through my feet and up my calves. Poor Benjin had been carrying Luka through the night, before he finally set him down and made him walk on his own. My eyes kept falling shut and I would shake my head trying to fight it off, but it would only wake me for a few seconds, until my eyes drifted shut again. I felt as though I was walking through a cloud, my body began to feel weightless, no more pain in each step. The buildings and streets around me began to fade into darkness, until I saw nothing but black. I wasn't scared, I actually felt unimaginably safe and completely at ease.

Around me stars began to emerge and glow, some with a gentle white light emitting, others radiating soft hues of yellow, pink, or blue. My body was drifting through the cosmos, towards a faint round light. I smelt a familiar scent, the perfume of my mother drifting through our apartment. Looking down, I did not see my body, just more darkness speckled with twinkling distant stars. As my body floated through, I realized the small circle of light in the distance was the moon. Eura was calling me home.

But once the inviting moon finally felt to be within reach, I began falling backwards, quickly, but I had no body, no arms to stop me from falling and nothing to grab onto anyway. All the stars began to vanish, hurtling into the distance and leaving me engulfed in an empty, black void until I finally hit the bottom. I stared into blackness and began to feel very cold and damp.

"Nyla?" I heard a familiar voice crying in the distance. Suddenly I felt my body shaking. "Can you hear me?" The voice called again, it sounded scared.

"Let's get her out of the rain!" Another voice called. It was Laago. I heard thunder roar in the distance and rain pelting against the ground around me and hitting my body. My eyes drowsily opened and I saw Benjin's face, but it was cloudy.

"She's opening her eyes!" He cheered in relief.

"Benj..." My eyes drifted shut.

"It's okay, Nyla. You're safe," he promised, as I fell back into the darkness.

It felt like I passed out for hours, but when I finally opened my eyes, the sun was still up. I was lying between Laago's legs, my head resting on his chest. He was asleep, as were Benjin and Luka to our side. We sat in an alley, hidden under a building's roof from the sun's unforgiving rays.

"Hey..." He whispered, awake from my sudden movements.

"What happened?" My head was pounding.

"You passed out from the heat exhaustion. I guess traveling through the night wasn't the best idea."

"I must have dreamt I was floating in space."

"That's kind of how I felt when I was high off the holiva root." He smiled.

"Was it raining?" My clothes were drenched and sticking to my body.

"Yeah, it went from drizzling to a storm within minutes. That's when you collapsed." Laago hit Benjin's arm to wake him. He immediately perked up once he realized I was awake.

"I'm sorry..." I blurted, knowing that time was sensitive.

"There's nothing to be sorry about, Nyla. You always act so strong that I sometimes forget you are a lot smaller than Laago and me. I wasn't thinking."

"How long was I asleep for?" I asked. Benjin rose to his feet and stood at the edge of the alley, to see where the sun was.

"Not long. Maybe an hour?"

"Really? It feels like I slept for days..." I rubbed my forehead, trying to soothe my throbbing headache.

"How do you feel?" Laago asked.

"I feel achy, but I am okay."

"Take as long as you need." Laago petted my hair, gently pulling it off my face. As much as I would love to stay and rest, I knew it was a bad idea. For each hour that passed brought us closer to the invasion.

I took a deep breath and pulled my body off Laago's chest and sat on my butt. My headache intensified and my ears rang. I put my hands on the ground and leaned forward, lifting myself onto my knee. My vision doubled, I saw four arms in front of me. I exhaled heavily and pulled myself to my feet, leaning onto the wall in front of me for support.

"Nyla, I don't think you should push yourself." Benjin's voice faded as my vision did. I felt myself collapse on the ground, my head hitting into the stone alley floor and when I finally awoke, it was night.

As I reopened my eyes, I felt a cool breeze. I was bouncing, almost floating through the streets. My neck was too tired to lift my head, but I saw a dark night sky speckled with stars. Suddenly, I realized I was being carried on someone's back while I was unconscious. As exhausted as I was, I immediately began to panic, I shrieked and slammed my hands on whoever was carrying me.

"Calm down, Ny!" Laago shouted, dropping me to the ground. I sat on the cold sandstone, wheezing in an attempt to regain my breath.

"You're okay!" Benjin dropped to his knees, hugging me.

"I'm sorry, I-"

"There's nothing to apologize for. When you passed back out, we realized you were probably down for the day, so we decided to just carry you."

"You actually don't feel much heavier than Luka." Laago smiled. After all this walking, I couldn't imagine having to carry another hundred pounds on my back. It is unbelievable how strong Benjin and Laago are.

"Wow. I passed out at midday... You were carrying me for hours."

"Good thing you're so tiny, Ny."

"Feel that? That's the ocean breeze. We will be at Huang before you know it!" Benjin exclaimed, holding his arms up and embracing the wind.

"Well I guess we should get going." I rose to my feet and stretched my legs.

My head pounded with every step, but it didn't matter, we had to keep moving. I wouldn't be able to live with myself if my own weakness led to the fall of Terlu. As horrible as I felt, the cold sea winds invigorated me. We were so close.

Since we entered the walls of the republic, we followed the one main sandstone road that stretches from the southwestern gates all the way to Huang. It was clear we were finally nearing the port because the road was now hugging the coastline, whereas before it ran through the city and was lined with stores and parks. I could hear the ocean in the distance, its waves crashing and receding.

"So what's our plan when we get to Huang?" I asked.

"Track down General Pago and give him the scroll." Laago shrugged.

"I don't think it will be that simple..." I warned. I looked at Benjin for assurance. Luka was hanging from his back, napping as always. "What do you think, Benjin? You always have a plan."

"I wish I knew, Nyla, but I have never been to Huang so I don't know what to expect. I think we are going to have to wing it," he simply said. For once, Benjin's words did not soothe me. Instead, I felt more anxious.

"Just be ready to fight!" Laago's daggers danced in his hands, as he practiced his handling.

"Absolutely not." Benjin chuckled. "Walking into a military-occupied area with weapons would be suicide. When we get to Huang, we will just ask around to find out where General Pago is. I'm sure someone will help us."

"Are they really going to tell a bunch of random kids where their highest-ranked general is?"

"No, but they'll tell General Pago's niece and nephews where he is." Benjin winked, his famous grin filling his face.

"So I guess we aren't going to work on a fishing boat in Huang anymore?" Laago's laughter roared. "I like this, now we are practically royalty."

"We are Bao and his wife Ona's children, here to surprise visit our uncle."

"Since when did you become so good at lying?"

"When the fate of the world began to depend on it," he responded, clenching the scroll tied to his chest.

As the lanterns of Huang began to shine in the sky, the streets became more filled. Not overfilled, but just enough people to make me feel comfortable. Walking through an empty militia occupied port, like how the Port of Eura was, was eerie and unsettling. Although it was night, it was still early enough and in a bustling port like Huang, the streets never sleep. Men pushed wagons full of produce, couples skipped past us on their way home from dates, and a few soldiers were standing guard.

The coast leading to Huang contrasted the smooth sandy coast by the Port of Eura. There were massive dark-gray rocks lining the water, separated from the road by a stone fence that reached my hip. It's not that it wasn't as pretty, it was just different. Everything here was far more industrialized. Before, we traveled on a bumpy dirt path. Now, we walk along a smoothly paved sandstone road.

Already I could make out the large stone dock protruding into the ocean. Not too far into the water from it stood a tall lighthouse, its light scanning the water. I have heard about lighthouses, but this was my first time actually seeing one.

"How do they get the light to shine on the water like that?" I asked, to no one in particular.

"I believe it is the reflection of a fire that sits inside the top part of the lighthouse," Benjin said, his finger pointing at the light emitting from the top, then followed it along down into the water. "But I am not really sure. I've never seen something like this." We all stared in wonder at the light as it scanned the water.

"Someone must be in there controlling where the light shines," Laago guessed.

"Fresh produce!" A man was shouting on the side of the road. "Produce here!"

"Does he sit out here all night?" I whispered to Benjin.

"You kids look like you could use some food!" He called over to us. "I got the freshest produce for the best price!" My stomach growled.

"No, but thank you sir." Benjin pulled his pants pockets out, showing they were empty of coins. "Actually, do you know where General Pago is stationed?"

"He's somewhere in Huang with his troops." The man pointed towards the port.

"Any idea where in Huang?"

"If I knew stuff like that, I wouldn't be on the side of a street selling produce, kid."

"Thanks anyways," Benjin said, catching up to us. "It was worth a shot."

"Why do you want to know where the General is?" A man inquired, walking behind us. He had a long black pipe hanging from his mouth.

"We came to surprise him, we are family," Benjin lied.

"The army has a headquarters right off the port, you can't miss it. I am sure if you kids go there, you will find him. Not sure if the guards will let you in though."

"Thank you!" Benjin exclaimed. The man nodded his head, smoke billowing out of his mouth.

"Watch out for those men," the man cautioned, before he turned away and began walking in the opposite direction. I looked forward and saw the three men walking down the street towards us. I turned around and realized everyone else already fled the street.

"Get behind me, Nyla," Benjin whispered, handing Luka to me. I walked in Benjin's steps, praying to Eura that his large stature would deter anyone from harming us. The moon's light shined on Laago's daggers as they sat in his back pocket, ready to be used.

"Well, well, well," a voice barked. "What do we have here?"

"Just passing through to Huang," Benjin responded, his axe hanging from his holster on his hip. One of the men walked right up to Benjin and sized him up, but Benjin towered over him. The man's arms were crossed, resting on his chest. The other two men stood behind him, their arms crossed as well.

"Just passin' through, eh?" He let off a creepy toothless smile. The moonlight shone on his bald head.

"We are working on a fishing boat in Huang," Benjin calmly elaborated, trying to de-escalate the situation. "We don't mean any harm."

"You hear this?" The man bellowed, turning to his two fat friends. "These kids say they don't mean any harm. Good thing, I was shaking in my boots!" Benjin went to step around him, but the man moved in front of him. "I am sick of dirty people coming into my city and stealing our jobs. Every day, boats come to this port, filled with people from who knows where. All dirty, stinky, poor people. They come here and fill our streets with grime! No wonder our taxes keep goin' up!" Spit flew from the man's mouth as he spoke.

"Listen..." Laago spoke up.

"I'm sick of listening." The man shifted over, his face right in Laago's. He flicked his wrist, revealing a rusty metal blade. "You don't come to my city and tell me. I'll tell you!" The man sneered. I watched Laago's hand grip his dagger in his back pocket and thought he would strike. Instead, he stepped back and tried to resolve this peacefully.

"I am from Terlu, I grew up in the northwest outskirts."

"So go back to your pile of dirt town. We don't like your kind here," the man hissed, his arms flailing his poorly made weapon. His two friends stepped forward. Laago swiftly hit the man's hand, knocking his blade to the ground, and pulled his dagger out to the man's throat. Benjin ripped his axe out of his holster and held it tightly.

"Tell your friends to back off or I'll cut your head off!" Laago demanded, his hand clenching the man's jaw.

"You're bluffin'. I see it in your eyes, you couldn't hurt a fly!" The bald man sputtered, trying to breathe.

"Look!" Laago held his dagger in the man's face. "You know how a dagger gets blood on it? You want your blood on it too? It wouldn't be the first and it won't be the last."

"Alright, alright. Boys, back off!" The toothless mugger blurted. Both of his friends listened and stepped down. Laago released the man, who began to fall backwards, but his friends caught him. "Dirty outskirters..." The man mumbled as he reached for his blade, but Benjin stomped on it, causing the man to stumble back. Benjin picked up the blade and ran to the edge of the street, throwing it into the ocean with all his might.

"Maybe you'll think twice before you mess with some dirty outskirters!" Laago howled.

"Get 'em!" The bald man hissed.

His two friends pulled their own blades out and charged at Laago. Benjin turned around, running back over with his axe. I grabbed Luka and ran towards a produce stand that was deserted as soon as these thugs came prowling through. I sat with Luka's face in my chest, covering his eyes and ears from the fight. I watched the boys intensely, ready to prepare my bow at any given moment.

One man barreled towards Laago, who swiftly shifted and dodged him. He faced the man's back as he stumbled forward, his blade dropping to the ground. Laago lunged forward and tackled him, wailing on the back of his head with his fists. The other man went to grab Laago off his friend, but Benjin grabbed him by the collar and hit him right in the jaw. I watched the lights go out in the man's eyes, his body went limp. Just as Benjin released the man, letting his body fall to the floor, the bald man came from behind and threw a rock at Benjin's head. Immediately, blood began to pour out.

"Stay here!" I ordered Luka, as I jumped up and prepared my bow. The man leaped onto Benjin, but he was small and couldn't knock him to the ground.

"Benjin!" Laago panted, rising up from the other man's body. He grabbed the bald man and tugged him off Benjin, throwing him to the side. Benjin clenched the back of his head as it gushed blood. "Are you okay?"

"What?"

"You're bleeding pretty badly!" Laago shouted, but Benjin did not respond. He stumbled over, falling onto the road. Laago knelt beside him. "Benj, it's me, Laago. Can you see me?"

"I..." He mumbled. "I see..."

"Stay with me," Laago kept repeating. I watched the bald man crawl towards his friend's blade.

"Stop!" I warned, as I prepared an arrow. The man looked up at me and raised his hands. "If you move, I will release."

I watched the man's eyes glance back to the blade before he grabbed it off the floor and went to lunge at Laago, leaving me no choice but to release an arrow. It launched into his thigh, almost reaching halfway through. Laago turned around, his eyes widened with shock, as the man yelped and fell to the ground. I flung my bow onto my back and ran to Luka.

"Come on, Buba. We have to go!"

"What happened to Benji?" He began to cry.

"Benji got hurt, but he is okay." I carried Luka over to the boys. "We should go- let's leave now before any guards stroll through."

"I think that rock got him good, Ny."

"I'm okay..." Benjin mumbled, stumbling to his feet. "We have to get home."

"Home? You mean Huang?" Laago helped him stand.

"Huang..." Benjin wrapped his arm over Laago and stepped forward. "Why does my head hurt?"

"You got hit in the head with a rock."

"Ouch," Benjin groaned, looking at his bloody hand.

"Next time Benjin says we travel through the night what do we say?" Laago shook his head.

"Do you think he'll be okay?"

"It depends if it stops bleeding. Either way, the only help we can get is in Huang."

"We need to get to General Pago," Benjin mumbled. I looked at Laago and we both shrugged, slowly moving forward.

"You're bleeding too, Laago!" The scab that covered his bicep wound was ripped open.

"Don't worry about it, it doesn't hurt," he assured me, though I know he wouldn't admit if he was in pain anyway.

The rest of the walk to Huang was painfully slow. We planned to be there last night, but between me collapsing and this fight, we fell behind schedule. By the time we reached the port, it was almost dawn. Benjin treaded forward, each time he raised his leg it was a struggle. Most of his weight rested on Laago and though he didn't complain, sweat poured down his red face. Not only did he travel for a day nonstop, but he carried me for part of it and now Benjin, who was much bigger than him.

"I think his bleeding stopped..." I analyzed his head, but he was too tall for me to tell for sure. Laago didn't respond, instead he just focused on moving forward.

It was clear we finally reached Huang because there was stand after stand of produce, meats, and any goods you could imagine. Although the sun was not yet up, it seemed like the whole port was wide awake. Large wooden caravels were docked, unloading pallets of goods to be shipped east. And to think we were so excited to reach the port and try their infamous delicacies. Now we just needed to get through.

"Your friend is injured!" A woman called over to us, spotting the blood that stained Benjin's shirt. She wore a long white apron over her beige tunic and a white cap on her head. "I am a nurse, I can help him."

"Three men tried to mug us last night and our friend got hit in the head with a rock."

"It looks like the bleeding has slowed, but I can't tell if it stopped," she examined. "Follow me."

We followed her down the road that hugged the coast. She was a trim woman, pretty but not striking. She moved quickly, weaving through the crowds of people. Finally, we arrived at a small sandy-colored tent with its doors left wide open. There were around ten cots placed throughout. She pointed to one.

"Sit here," she said.

"What happened to him, Suqa?" Another woman asked, as she tended to a soldier's grotesque wounds.

She worked quickly to wrap clean bandages around his arm, which was covered in burns so severe that it left flesh exposed and spanned up to his elbow. His face was expressionless, he blankly stared into the ceiling of the tent. I shuddered at the thought of what may have caused such a horrifying injury and when I turned to look away I noticed that Luka's mouth was agape. In his few years of life, he hadn't been exposed to such a thing. I turned him away, hoping he would forget what he saw, but I knew my attempts were futile. Already he had seen too much on this trip. A month ago, he was an aloof kid with contagious laughter. At home, he loved to perform for guests. Our dining room table was his stage and we were his audience.

It suddenly dawned on me that he rarely spoke anymore and the childlike wonder had escaped his eyes. Instead, he spent his days quietly trudging along. We understood that within this journey we would sacrifice a lot, but never would I have agreed to sacrifice Luka. Another pure, innocent child now engulfed in our plagued world.

"A mugger hit him in the head with a rock. He seems mildly to moderately concussed."

"How deep is the wound?"

"I have to clean off the blood to see." Suqa grabbed a cloth from a bucket of water and rang it out. The three of us stood anxiously, watching the nurse tend to Benjin's head.

"I am okay," he said. "Just dizzy."

"You are a tough kid." She smiled as she cleaned his wound. "It's deep, but no bone is protruding. Does this hurt?"

"Yes!" Benjin winced.

"Good. If it didn't, then we would be in trouble," she said as the other nurse handed her a kit. "I'll sew you up."

"How long is that going to take?" Laago fretted.

"Why, you got somewhere to be?" Suqa laughed.

"Actually, yes."

"Give me five minutes," she said with a sigh. "Where are you kids from?"

"We are visiting our uncle, General Pago," Laago lied. "We know he is in Huang, but other than that we are kind of lost."

"You're related to the general?" Her eyes narrowed, likely not believing our story, until she seemed to realize it was not a concern of hers. "He shouldn't be too hard to find. Many high ranking officers tend to remain tucked away, but General Pago likes to stay in the middle of the action. He actually came by here last week to check up on his nurses."

"You're army nurses?" I asked.

"We are."

"Do you get to travel around with the troops?"

"I have been stationed in Huang for quite some time now, but yes, I go wherever they send me."

"That sounds awesome!" Laago naively remarked.

"It may be nice here, because our troops are just here to patrol, but I am usually stationed in a conflict zone. If they send me somewhere new it means a lot of men and women got injured..." Her voice was dry and lacked emotion, as she casually stitched Benjin's wound.

"I'm so sorry, I wasn't thinking. I am sure you have had to experience a lot of pain."

"It's my job, I wouldn't change it for anything. I had wanted to be a nurse since I was little."

"That's very honorable." I always admired nurses, from their bravery to their quickness and strength. When someone got hurt, they were the first ones to respond. Throughout the plague, Tinshe's nurses were overworked and exposed. Most of them didn't survive very long. I could never be a nurse, I don't have the courage.

"All done. You seem to have a grade two concussion, it should mostly wear off within a day or two," she assessed, dropping her dirty tools in a bucket. "Make sure he keeps his head clean and let his body rest. Any strenuous activity will only prolong his injury."

"Thank you." Benjin strained a smile. "I already feel better."

"Well, go find your uncle. I am sure he'll be excited to see you." She wiped her bloody hands with a clean cloth.

"A man told us we might have luck finding him at the headquarters. Do you know which direction that is in?"

"Walk east through the port, it is on the water. It's a tent like this, but much larger. You shouldn't miss it."

"Thank you!" I shouted over my shoulder, as we walked out of the tent.

Our eyes scanned the bustling port town, looking for signs of this supposedly obvious headquarters. As we ran east through the port, I felt a surge of emotion. Weeks ago, I stood on the production line, simply putting a screw in a piece of metal, day after day, hour after hour. Today, I ran through the streets of the Republic of Terlu with my brothers and lifelong friend. The idea of simply working in a mundane factory day after day became an unimaginable concept. I don't think I could ever go back to my old life after this. The world is meant for so much more than just surviving. I want to travel, to love, and to learn. I don't want to just get by. I want to thrive.

"I think that's it!" Laago shouted, pointing at a large tan tent. We all picked up our speed, eager to finally relay the news.

When we arrived outside of the headquarters, we quickly realized it was surrounded by armed guards. Men stood at every corner, armed with long swords and intimidating demeanors. There was not a single opening in the tent other than the door, not even a window to crawl through. Though it would be naive to think that we could sneak past these guards, even if we tried. I followed closely behind Benjin, who took charge despite his injury.

"What's our plan?" Laago whispered.

"Just act like we are supposed to be here and hopefully no one will question us."

"I don't think that's going to work..." I sighed. I doubted the army headquarters takes walk-ins. As Benjin approached the entrance, two of the guards shifted in front of the door, blocking us from entering.

"Hello, we are here to surprise our uncle," Benjin calmly explained, but the guards didn't even make eye contact. Instead, they just blankly stared away towards the ocean. "Our uncle is General Pago. We just traveled a very long way to see him."

They continued to ignore us and I remembered the note the old man gave me. If it worked with the other men, perhaps it would work here as well. I reached into my boot to find it, causing one of the guards to pull his sword from his hip. It was a long iron sword, curved at the tip and its handle neatly wrapped in leather. The man was merely average height and size, but he had an intense look to him. I could see why they chose him to guard the great General Pago's temporary headquarters.

"No, it's just a note!" I held out the small piece of paper, signed by Mister Ritu himself. The guard took it and without even looking at it, he crumpled it up and tossed it on the ground. As he did, the other guard stepped forward.

"Leave," he declared, his hand tightly squeezing his sword handle.

"I understand you are doing your job, but we have to speak to General Pago," Benjin pleaded.

"If you continue to refuse orders we-"

"It's okay, we are leaving." Laago grabbed Benjin and pulled him back.

"What are you doing? We have to get in there!" Benjin argued.

"We are smarter than them. We will find another way in."

"How? There are two guards on every side of the building!" Benjin was livid, but I just felt defeated.

We made it all the way here, further from home than I had ever been, just to be turned away. We crossed the street and walked onto a small wooden dock that was lined with long row boats. A boy, around my age, sat in one of them, patching a hole in its side.

"So what's your plan, Laago?" Benjin sat on his butt and rested his chin on his fist.

"Well..." He joined him on the ground. "General Pago can't stay in there forever."

"We don't even know if he is even in there right now," I pondered aloud.

"So maybe we can catch him on his way in!"

"Your optimism astonishes me," Benjin groaned, tracing his fingers along his wound. "We don't have time for this."

"Why do you guys need to see General Pago?" The boy sat up in his boat and faced us. He had dark olive skin and brunette curly hair that was tightly shaved on the sides and sat like a mop on top of his head.

"Don't worry about it," Benjin called over his shoulder, paying no mind to him.

"Well, if someone needed to speak with General Pago, I would tell them not to waste their time here for him, because he is out today," the boy said, as he wiped his hands off with a stained cloth and continued working.

"Where can we find him?" Benjin spun around so quickly that he almost knocked me off the dock.

"Why do you need to see him?" The boy tinkered away, as it was now his turn to ignore us. He wore sandy-colored pants with paint stains on his thigh and rips at the knee. His white tunic was covered in grime and rolled up past his elbows. He was filthy. How could he have any idea where the Republic of Terlu's army general is?

"Listen." Benjin walked over to the front of his boat and crouched down on one knee. "I know this sounds crazy, but you need to trust me. Take us to General Pago."

"Why?"

Benjin looked over his shoulder to Laago, Luka, and me. Laago shrugged, simply giving Benjin support to do whatever he thought was right. There were two possibilities, either this kid somehow knew where General Pago was or he didn't. If he did, he could help us find him. If he didn't, we would have to hope he keeps his mouth shut and continue our original plan, waiting for General Pago to show up here.

"We were sent here from Tinshe to deliver a message to him."

"What does it concern?" The kid sat up and set his rag on his shoulder.

"Enough with the questions!" Laago snapped. "We are running out of time!" The boy stared intensely at Laago, Benjin, and then me.

"Okay." He rubbed his chin.

"Okay, what?" Benjin anxiously asked. The boy stood up.

"I will take you to General Pago."

# CHAPTER THIRTEEN

# WHEN TWO WORLDS COLLIDE

"How do you know where General Pago is?" Benjin asked, as we followed the boy past the headquarters and down the road.

"I have worked under him for years. He keeps a pretty consistent schedule."

The boy quickly weaved through the streets, dodging the vendors and quick-walking citizens of Huang. He was a little shorter than Laago and thinner in stature, but what muscle he did have was well-defined. He clearly did manual work for a living. The back of his neck was burnt, probably from working long hours. I noticed a long blade with a golden handle sticking out of his belt, which was fastened tightly to his hip. It was rare to see a poor boy with such a fancy sword.

"Are you in the army?" Laago asked.

"Not technically, but if they need me to fight I will!" The boy shouted over his shoulder. "So you guys traveled all the way from Tinshe to give General Pago a message? That's a pretty long journey, it must be pretty important."

"Yeah, it is," Benjin admitted.

"Well, I am guessing it is not good news."

"Why are you trusting us?" I blurted out. The boy turned around to me and laughed.

"Probably for the same reason you are trusting me. I have been around, I know when people are lying to me." He shrugged. "Besides, if you are trying to pull a fast one, General Pago will have you thrown in prison for life for wasting his time." Once again, he glanced back and chuckled. He had a handsome smile. For some reason, I did trust him, though I didn't even know his name.

"What's your name?" I was embarrassed that we didn't ask sooner. We were so focused on delivering this message that we forgot basic manners.

"Jon Li. What's yours?"

"I am Nyla. These are my brothers, Benjin and Luka, and our friend, Laago," I pointed.

"Nice to meet you all!" He quickly turned down a street corner, leading us to a narrower unpaved road. Homeless people leaned against the buildings and shoeless children played with a ball. Laago and I looked at each other.

We had uncovered the poorer side of Huang, it reminded me of home. No freshly painted walls and flower pots. I grabbed Luka's hand and squeezed it, but he didn't need to be comforted, he was more occupied watching the game the children were playing. The irony made me laugh. I spent my whole life in poverty, living in a forever too hot or too cold apartment that rarely had water and skipping meals. The children on this street were me. Well, not literally me, but versions of myself. And here I was, judging them. Three young boys chased the ball. They had what many would consider nothing, yet their smiles and contagious laughter showed otherwise.

"Here we are!" Jon shouted.

It was a small soup kitchen, with a broken front window and dirty floors. As we walked in, many people called his name to greet him and embraced him with warm hugs. Everybody seemed to not only know him, but adore him.

"He's like a celebrity over here..." Laago whispered. Jon motioned us to follow him through a ratty curtain leading into a back room.

"These kids need to speak with you."

General Pago immediately rose from his chair, eyeing us down. He was sitting at a small round table with five young children. It seemed he was reading to them.

Like Jon Li, he had black hair that was shaved on the sides, but his was not as curly and long. He has stubble on his face and heavy bags under his eyes. His face had a deep scar stretching from his eyebrow to his hairline. General Pago was average height and build, and wore a white collared shirt tucked into his forest-green pants, which were cuffed at the bottom and rested neatly on his shiny brown boots.

"What can I do for you?" His voice was deep. He didn't just speak, he rumbled. It felt as if we weren't just interfering with story time with a bunch of children, but an important meeting with the President.

"We-we were sent here from Tinshe to deliver a message to you," Benjin stuttered.

"Well, let me have it." General Pago reached out his hand. "You kids traveled all the way here from Tinshe?"

"Yessir."

"How long did that take you?"

"A bit over two weeks, sir." Benjin pulled the scroll from under his shirt and untied the twine. General Pago took it from his hand and studied the seal that closed the scroll.

"Who gave this to you?" His eyebrows raised.

"May we please speak to you alone, sir?" Benjin glanced towards the two guards that stood behind the general, then down at the young children sitting around the table. I watched General Pago eye Jon Li, who stood in front of the curtain. Jon gave him a subtle nod and just like that, the general raised his hand, signaling his guards to leave. They took the children and headed out the tattered curtain. Only Jon remained.

"Take a seat," he ordered, motioning to the flimsy chairs. General Pago sat back down in his child-size chair and peeled the scroll open. As he read the message, his eyes widened. He sat there for a minute, rubbing the scruff on his chin, before he finally looked up at us. "Okay."

"Okay?" Benjin asked, confused by his reaction. General Pago abruptly stood up.

"Jon, take them to the headquarters. I will be there shortly, but I need to make a stop along the way." Without a moment to waste, the general of the Republic of Terlu's forces was out the door.

"Let's go!" Jon ordered. We all followed him out the door and into the street. As we were about to turn the corner, Jon stopped and turned to us. "Are we at war?" He asked, but we all just stood there, unsure of how to respond. "I knew it." He sighed, as he turned back around and headed down the street.

I felt a weight lift off of me knowing that everything we did finally paid off. The blood, the pain, the tears... We sacrificed so much to reach Huang. But we did it, we made it to General Pago. Maybe we were only successful from a weird stroke of luck- bumping into Jon Li- but we were successful nonetheless. There are more people living in the Republic of Terlu than I could count, yet our path led us directly to him.

"Do you believe in coincidences?" I pondered aloud.

"You just read my mind, Ny."

This time, as we strolled up to the headquarters, Jon led the way. The same guards who once blocked our way moved over without hesitation for him, allowing us to enter seamlessly. I watched Laago make a face at the guard as we passed through.

Inside the tent was one long dark spruce table, lined with beautifully carved matching chairs with amber-colored cushions. The walls were covered in large maps. There was one of the world, one of the Republic of Terlu, and many of the other empires. A large metal lantern sat on the center of the table, lighting the room.

"Take a seat." Jon sat right next to the head of the table. I sat towards the middle, with Luka on my lap, in between Benjin and Laago.

"What's going on, Nyla?" Luka whispered.

"I think the general wanted to meet with us somewhere safe to talk about the news." I reached down and squeezed his hand. The relief I experienced quickly passed, now I felt unbelievably nervous.

"Don't be nervous," Jon replied, as if he read my mind. "General Pago may seem intimidating, but he is a good man. I just can't believe they sent a couple of kids to relay such an important message."

"Neither can we." Laago smiled.

General Pago barged through the tent with two men and a woman following him closely behind. He took a seat at the head of the table and the three others took seats next to him. The general pulled his chair in and rested his arms on the table, folding his hands.

"Tell me everything."

"I don't know where to begin..." Benjin stammered, as we all looked at each other.

"From the beginning."

"General Ahkpi of Najin claimed he moved his militia into Tinshe to help us recover from the plague, but he lied, it was to exploit us and seize any resources we had left. Shortly after his invasion, he ordered for the Protectors to be executed, but he failed, because one escaped," Benjin revealed. "His name is Amu and he founded the resistance. He sent us here to warn you of the upcoming invasion. Your brother, Bao, trained us. He brought us all the way to the Port of Eura, which is now fully occupied by Najin's militia. As we traveled here, we encountered many militants. They are slowly moving hundreds of soldiers closer and closer to your walls. Perhaps even thousands!" Benjin exhaled.

As he spoke, one of the men ferociously wrote every word he said in a thick leather book, he must be the scribe. The woman sat still, her arms crossed against her chest. She had long black hair pulled back in a tight bun. She was a bit tall for a woman and had a fierce look to her. Her eyes were sharp, glaring at us from her seat, like an attack dog. The other man's mouth was agape.

"Bao?"

"Yes, he trained us for many days underground in the Forest of the Earth before he led us through the tunnels to the port. He is a great warrior and an even better man. He spoke very highly of you."

"How long until the militia reaches our walls?"

"Days," Laago said. He abruptly stood up and approached the hanging maps, tracing his finger along the route we took from the Port of Eura to the outer walls. "Around here was the last point where we bumped into militant scouts." General Pago looked at his two advisors, his face sullen.

"I already sent orders for scouts to patrol and find the exact coordinates of General Ahkpi's troops. They should be back before night falls. Chief Sakra, relay the news to the west wall and prepare for the invasion. I want every troop at the wall. Send out a force to bring as many outskirt villagers safely behind our walls and evacuate anyone from the wall villages deeper within the republic for protection. I want no citizen within twenty miles of the wall. We can house them in schools, kitchens, and vacant apartments," he ordered, before he turned to the woman. "Chief Kholok, our eastern navy is to be moved to the southwest. We must protect Huang, if it is penetrated, the supply chain for the entire country will fall."

The chiefs rose from their seats and bowed, before filing out the door without a word said. My eyes followed Chief Kholok in awe, amazed by how much power she had. In Suhai, women could work, but none bore titles as great as hers.

"Shall we inform President Suin?" Jon asked.

"It is already done. He is preparing to make a statement tomorrow, when we have a better estimate on when the invasion will begin. There is no need to worry the people until we have answers," General Pago spoke with great ferocity. "I welcome you children into our home to get some rest. Your bravery and sacrifice will not go unnoticed. I understand from the scroll that you must leave for the Island of Aara. I want my son, Jon, to accompany you. He knows the ocean well and I trust him more than anybody. I will give you a boat and supplies for the journey. You will leave at dusk."

My jaw dropped at the revelation that the boy we found tinkering away on a boat and covered in grime was the son of the republic's general. None of us uttered a word, because what was there to say?

"I just don't understand how General Ahkpi obtained so much power. Where was Emperor Nahkon of Suhai through all this?" Jon stammered in disbelief.

"He's a mere puppet, a fool..." General Pago shook his head.

"Why did you not act on this, if you knew he was an inept leader? We could have prevented this!" Jon slammed his fist on the table, rattling the tent.

"What good would it do, boy?" The general hissed. "If I sent my soldiers into Suhai it would be an invasion. It would look just as it does when General Ahkpi's militia storms our walls. Thousands would die, another meaningless war that history would blame on greed. If Emperor Nahkon is overthrown, it must be by the people."

His words were spoken with an intimidating intensity. Deep down, I knew he was right. As much as I would love for General Pago to bring his troops into Tinshe to save us, it was not the right way. Before Jon could muster a response, the general left as quickly as he came, leaving us alone with Jon and the silent scribe.

"I will lead you to our home, where you can rest before we depart."

We all got up and followed Jon to the door. As we walked down the road, we already saw many troops headed west towards the wall. There was no way people wouldn't realize trouble was brewing.

"I didn't know General Pago had kids," Laago wondered aloud.

"He didn't, but he took me and my sister in shortly after we lost our parents. My sister and I lived on the streets during the plague and were regulars at the soup kitchen he frequented. For some reason, one day General Pago asked if we would like to live with him. I owe him everything."

"I am sorry for your loss. We lost our mother and two sisters in the plague too," I said.

"I don't know a single person who hasn't lost someone from the plague," Jon said. "It really makes you think... Life can be taken just as easily as it is given."

I looked at the many people we passed in the streets. Jon was right; I was certain nearly every person here had lost someone during the plague, and sadly, most had lost even more. We hurried past two old men diligently shining shoes on a street corner. One moment you were alive, and the next, you could be dead.

We passed by the soup kitchen from earlier, with the same kids playing out in the street. They were so young, so full of life. I envied their lightheartedness and wished Luka could join them. Instead, he had to waste away fighting to end some greedy man's war. We turned down the next street and Jon ran up stone steps to an apartment.

"Here we are!" He shouted over his shoulder as he opened the door. It looked unassuming on the outside, it was on a typical street with potholes and more barefoot children, but had flower pots on the front steps and freshly painted window sills. Though it wasn't necessarily a bad area, I was still shocked that the highest general of the Republic of Terlu's army lived on an ordinary street. Laago and I looked at each other and shrugged. "Jin?" Jon called down the hall.

"Is this whole place yours?" Benjin asked, looking up the dark spruce stairwell. The building was five stories high, and standing in the entry room of the apartment, you could look up and see the ceiling of the building.

"We just use the first floor and the roof. The general allows local families to live on the upper floors for free, just to help them get on their feet," Jon said. "Make yourselves at home."

The general seemed like a genuinely good man, a quality that was rare in those who had so much power. Luka jumped out of my arms and ran down the hallway that was lined with a long ornate maroon rug.

"Hello!" A soft voice called from the hallway, "I am Jin." She stood in the doorway, holding Luka's hand. She wore a long pale green dress that was cinched at the waist. Her feet were bare and dirty.

"I see you have already met Luka." Benjin grinned. "I am Benjin and this is my sister, Nyla."

"Laago!" He smiled and waved, introducing himself.

"It is nice to meet you all. What brings you here?" Jin had long hair so dark it was almost black. It was curly like Jon's and was perfectly pulled back by two wooden hair sticks, decorated with emeralds at the tips. Her skin was not as browned from the sun as her brother's, but still had a natural olive glow.

"I think we should sit down for this," Jon said, his voice filled with heaviness.

Jon led us down the hall to the first room on the left. A beautifully crafted spruce archway led us into a living room. Two of the walls were covered in books, from the floor to the ceiling. On the wall opposite of the archway sat an enormous stone fireplace, with two tall brass candle holders on each side. Above the fireplace, an old detailed portrait of General Pago, Jon, and Jin hung in a thick gold frame.

"We got that portrait done a few months after he took us in," Jon mentioned after noticing me staring. "It was then that I knew he would never put us back on the streets. It was the most relieved I ever felt."

"It's beautiful," I admired, though I did feel a pang of jealousy. I wished I had a painting like that of my family. I carried a small one that was done by a street vendor on the south coast of Tinshe, but it was nowhere near as well done as this one was.

Benjin sat on the long satin couch across from the fireplace. It was made of the same wood as the staircase and archway, clearly a theme in their home, and the cushions were deep red. Luka climbed onto his lap and nuzzled his face into his chest. He had been growing like a weed, his clothes were becoming shorter and shorter on him.

"Look at all the books, Benji!"

"How many do you think there are, Buba?"

"A million!" He squealed.

"Definitely more than ten!" Laago joked, joining them on the couch. "Take a seat, Ny." He patted the cushion next to him. Jon and Jin both sat on the reading chairs on each side of the couch.

"There's no easy way to say this, Jin, so I'll be straightforward. They were sent from Tinshe to warn us of an imminent invasion. General Ahkpi's treacherous militia is encroaching upon us."

"No..." She trembled. Her face turned ghost white, her hands shakily covered her mouth. "You're lying."

"They will be at our walls within days." Jon leaned back in his chair and ran his hand through his curly hair. "War is upon us."

"How does Najin's militia have the power to invade our republic? Are they even backed by the Suhai Empire or Emperor Nahkon?"

"I don't know, Jin. From what I have heard, they sound powerful, but I doubt they have the numbers to storm our walls."

"Well they wouldn't plan to invade us if they didn't think they could pull it off," she snapped. "Where's dad?"

"He should be home soon. I am leaving with them at nightfall to the Island of Aara. We have to get help, not only to protect our empire, but to destroy the militia and kick them out of Tinshe."

"There's no need!" She jumped from her seat. "Why cross an entire ocean when we can send troops north to recruit help from Yana?"

"Traveling through the unforgiving Qaran Desert, only to traverse the ice-covered and snow panther-infested mountains of Yana, is no safer of a journey," he said, shaking his head. "Besides, when has King Zabar Mazraat III ever provided aid? Very little of his mind was spared since the passing of his son, the first prince. He's as mad as

General Ahkpi, only he cowers away in the north while the second prince muddles their name."

"I don't care about kings and princes. I care about my family and little more," her voice rose even louder. "You promised that you would never leave me!"

"All will be well, Jin. It is the Great Ocean, not the North nor South."

"Storms know no boundary between oceans. You think you are invincible!"

"I have to do this!" Jon shouted, his patience finally wearing thin. "What type of man would I be if I did nothing?"

"A living one," Jin cried, as she stormed out of the room. Jon sat for a moment, rubbing his forehead. None of us knew what to say.

"I am sorry you had to hear that." He threw his hand up in defeat. "After we lost our parents we became inseparable. It's like we are two parts of a whole. I know it sounds crazy, but if she gets hurt, I feel it. I know Jin seems really upset, but she will prevail. She is one of the toughest people I know."

"Believe me, we understand. We all have lost more people than we can count." Benjin leaned forward and put his hand on Jon's shoulder. "Go talk to her. She needs you."

"Thank you," he said, rising to his feet. "There is a bath down the hall, if you guys want to clean up before our journey."

"I would kill for a bath," I admitted. My whole body felt like it was covered in dirt and sticky sweat.

I followed Jon down the long hallway. It was lined with tall windows that were partially covered with draping maroon curtains, open just enough for a little light to shine through. At the very end of the hall, rested the bathroom. Jon twisted the knob on the tub, letting the bath water run.

"Did the first prince of Yana pass from the plague?"

"No, I believe it was slightly before the plague hit. There are rumors that he was poisoned by his brother, Prince Xan."

"His own brother?" I gasped. "Why?"

"I suppose the second prince wanted to become the first." He shrugged. "I wouldn't doubt it, I have never heard a good word spoken of him."

"That's terrible."

"It is, and now, he will one day be king. Imagine that." He pulled a towel down from the shelf and handed me a fresh bar of pink soap. It was in the shape of a field daisy. "I don't mean to be rude, but do you not have any clean clothes?"

"No…" I blushed. I was wearing Benjin's raggedy old shirt. I looked like a dirty street kid. Well, I suppose I was a dirty street kid.

"Jin has many of dresses. I'll grab one for you."

"No, I'm okay." I waved my hand. I could not imagine myself wearing one of her fancy dresses, I would look ridiculous.

"How about I grab you one of my shirts and leave it at the door?" Jon smiled, sensing my awkwardness. "You can borrow it while we clean this one." He turned off the bath water, before he walked out and shut the door behind him.

I stripped down and got in the bath. I dunked my head underwater and began scrubbing myself with the soap bar. Dirt floated off me. For a moment, I laid in the tub and imagined I was Jin. She was a beautiful girl, living in a perfect home. I was scrawny and short. The only clothes I owned other than these beaten down trousers were Benjin's. I had no home. I worked in a factory from the age of eight, until I had to traverse across the south coast for the sake of Tinshe, with nothing to my name beyond the clothes on my back.

I began to weep. What did I do to the gods to deserve a life of pain and suffering? I was tired, home sick, and I wanted to give up. My feet were blistered and my body ached every day. I had men's blood on my hands. As my tears flooded the tub, I began to feel overwhelmed with grief. I sat in the bath crying- crying for the lives I took, crying because of my envy towards Jin.

I cried because I felt ungrateful for my brothers, Laago, and all of the wonderful people in my life. I cried for Kiuyah and her lost love, just as I did for Bao and his. I even cried for all of the lives yet to be taken from the invasion, for all of the boys who would not return home to their mothers, and for all of the men who would not return to their wives…

CHAPTER FOURTEEN

# THE CALM BEFORE THE STORM

W E ALL SAT AROUND the dining room table, anxiously waiting for General Pago to arrive with an update. It was a long sturdy table, meant to host many people. I thought of all the important meetings that must have been held there. I stared out the large windows that engulfed two of the walls. The window behind the head of the table opened to the garden. Tall plants and vines rose far past the window, almost blocking any light from shining through. Out the wider window, across from me, sat the backyard. It was a small grass area, fenced in by fat green and purple-leafed bushes.

I watched three young girls, who I assume to be the upstairs tenants, play hide and seek. They reminded me of Luchi, Dalia, and myself. My heart began to feel heavy, so I looked away. My eyes met with Jon's who sat next to the head of the table, in front of the window. An enormous chandelier loomed over us, twinkling from the sunlight that passed through the window so beautifully. It was made of bronze and held a dozen half-melted white candles.

"You guys must be tired," he said.

"We are used to running off no sleep." Benjin faked a smile. He sat across from Jon, with Luka to his right. "How's Jin?"

"Better. I feel like she is most upset because she knows it is for the best that I go with you all." He ran his hand through his thick hair.

"Smells delicious, Litia," General Pago's voice echoed through the front entry. I listened to his boots stomp through the kitchen as he complimented the cook, a small-framed woman who lived two floors up. General Pago walked through the archway and into the dining room. We all instinctively stood up and greeted him. "Please, take a seat. Where's Jin?" He asked, as she waltzed in.

"I'm here." She stood on her toes and kissed him on the cheek before she took her seat next to Jon, across from Luka.

"Have you briefed your sister?"

"Yessir."

"I am postponing your departure until tomorrow night. I have been informed by Chief Kholok of a storm passing through the Great Ocean. Tonight you will get some well-deserved rest." We all sighed in relief. Finally, a night to relax. General Pago popped open a bottle of red wine and poured himself a cup. He held the bottle over Benjin's glass. "You are one of the tallest boys I have ever seen. What do they feed you?"

"Tiger duck and wheat fertilizer," Benjin joked. General Pago's laughter roared through the room, bouncing off the walls.

"He's funny too." He stood up and filled Jon's glass, then Jin's, before he made his way over to mine and Laago's, only skipping over Luka's. "I have some tartar berry juice for you, boy. Litia, let's get the boy some tartar juice!" He stomped into the kitchen with a now empty wine bottle, only to come back with a new one and a mug filled with juice for Luka, before he signaled for Jon and Jin to help bring the food out. They were both quick to rise.

"Thank you, Mister General!" Luka exclaimed, taking a gulp of the sour-yet-sweet juice.

"Please, call me Roan." He took a seat at the head of the table, "Litia, take a seat."

Litia walked in, carrying another clear glass bottle of violet wine, and took a seat across from me. She had short black hair that ended at her chin and straight bangs that covered her tiny face. She wore a light blue skirt that ended just above her knees, with a dainty white apron draped over it and her cream-colored blouse. Jin placed a dish of green dumplings in front of me, followed by Jon with a dish of juicy meat skewers and assorted root vegetables.

"What's life in Tinshe like?" Jon asked, as he served himself a plate.

"Before or after the plague?" Laago chuckled.

"Both."

"It was nice before, definitely better than where I grew up in the outskirts of Terlu." Laago bit into a meat skewer, talking with his mouth full of food. Its juice dripped down his chin and he wiped it with his shirt without a second thought. I shrunk down in my seat, embarrassed by his lack of table manners.

"Which outskirts?" Litia asked.

"Northwest."

"I am from the northeast."

"Oh, wow. I have never been that way. What's it like up there?"

"It was peaceful. I lived by the water, about an hour south of Eura's Harbor."

"Why did you leave?"

"There was no work. My village may have been nice, but not nice enough to starve in." She took a long drink of wine. "I came here when I was twenty. What about you, why did you leave?"

"Absent mother and abusive father. I ran away when I was eight."

"That must have been difficult to overcome."

"If I didn't leave, I would be dead by now. My pops hit me so hard it would knock me out."

"How did an eight-year-old travel from the northwest outskirts all the way to Tinshe?" General Pago curiously asked, sipping his wine.

"I ran," he said, which was the simple truth.

"You are a tough kid." General Pago leaned back in his chair, studying Laago.

"I would be nothing without Benjin and his family. They found me and took me in. His parents treated me like their own." He put his hand on my shoulder.

"May I ask where your parents are now?" General Pago looked at Benjin.

"We lost our mother and two sisters to the plague." Benjin mushed the food around on his plate with his fork.

"What about your father?" Jon asked, as he bit into a purple potato.

"We thought he abandoned us after our mother passed, but the last Protector revealed that our father disappeared when he went to get Tinshe help from General Ahpki and his militia. He was a part of the resistance."

Though I spoke with pride, a feeling of guilt lingered closely over my head from the years of anger I had towards him. Even if it was all internal, I still felt horrible for assuming my brave father abandoned us. I hoped that wherever he was, he had not given up on us as we did to him.

"Your father was a brave man," Jon admired.

"And an honorable one, for the last Protector to bestow such a monumental duty upon him," the general said. "Does Amu have any indication of what may have happened to him?"

"One day Amu stopped sensing his energy, so he assumed my father was killed, but we believe he may be imprisoned in the Mountains of Shiren," Benjin explained, setting his fork down. He had not taken a bite of food yet. General Pago leaned forward in his chair.

"And what makes you think that?"

"Bao told us that the Suhai Empire does not keep high threat prisoners within its walls. Instead, they are shipped to the maximum-security prison in the east, which is secured by Empress Jhena's elite military." He set his fork down and looked at General Pago. "I know it may sound crazy, but we know in our hearts that he is still out there."

"Interesting..." General Pago ripped off a piece of bread and ate it. He was a hard man to get a read on. "If he was a major contributor to the resistance and got caught, he could have been classified as a domestic terrorist and sent to the Mountains of Shiren by General Ahkpi, but would it not be easier for him to just..." His voice trailed off as his eyes met Luka's. "I suppose it could be possible," he concluded, though it was clear he was doubtful.

"Empress Jhena of Gala is a good and honest leader, if she was informed, would she not free him?" Jon suggested.

"The empress will be preparing her army to cross the Great Ocean to fight in our war. How much more could we ask of her?" Jin scoffed.

"Anyone wrongfully imprisoned by the militia will be freed and instead it will be General Ahkpi serving a life sentence, but these things take time. Who knows how many innocent men and women are detained?" General Pago sighed. The reality may be harsh, but I am glad he was honest with us. I was tired of false hopes and lies. "In the end, the good will always prevail." He raised his glass and we all followed suit. Luka leaned onto Benjin, dropping his head in his lap.

"Are you tired, Buba?" He whispered.

"You must all be exhausted. Jon will make room for you boys in his room and Nyla, Jin has plenty of space for you." I anxiously glanced over to Benjin.

"There's more than enough space on the roof for you too, Nyla," Jon offered, cutting my moment of panic short. It was just like when he offered me one of Jin's dresses, he seemed to know what I was thinking without me saying a word.

"I thought you would be relieved to finally have some time away from the boys." General Pago chuckled.

"We prefer to stick together." Benjin twirled Luka's curls as he peacefully napped on his lap. Jin stood up and began clearing the empty dishes.

"Let me help!" Laago stood up.

"No, no..." Litia took the plates from Laago's hand and shooed us away. "You kids go upstairs and get some well-deserved rest."

We followed Jon up the staircase, which was lined with a maroon rug decorated with intricate gold patterns. When we got to the top floor, I looked down the stairwell. It had elegantly carved wooden railings and a large golden chandelier hanging above. It truly is a beautiful building, despite looking so average on the outside and being in a poorer side of town.

"Welcome to my home," Jon said, as he pushed open the metal hatch to the roof.

It was beautiful. To our side stood a large stone room, which once may have been used for storage, but had since been renovated as Jon's own home. It sat atop of this tall apartment building, with red vines growing up its outer walls, with small pink berries hanging in bundles. In the center of the roof, most adjacent to the hatch, sat a fire pit that was lined with black stones and surrounded by four handcrafted benches made of the same material. It separated the stone room from the garden, where lush green plants overtook the roof's outer perimeter, blocking the view of the city and creating its own hidden oasis.

"This is my garden, everything up here feeds the entire apartment. All of the produce you ate today was grown right here." He proudly picked a handful of berries and held them out to us.

"They're so yummy!" Luka squealed, smacking his lips.

"You do all of this yourself?" Laago asked.

"Some of the kids downstairs help me water the plants and weed if I am stuck at work, but I prefer to do it if I can. Oftentimes, it is my favorite part of the day." He led us from the garden and towards the stone room. It was as if a home from the outskirts was picked up and dropped on the roof of this apartment building. He opened the door and led us inside.

"You barely ate any dinner," I whispered to Benjin.

"My head is killing me." He held the back of his head, where the stitches sat. "I just need some rest."

"Sorry, it's a little messy. I have been working a lot of long days lately."

He walked over to the windows and pushed them open, which pulled a breeze of fresh air through. Though his room had little furniture, there was clutter everywhere. Against the wall opposite of the door sat a large wooden desk with no chair. It was meant to be used standing and was covered in tools, trinkets, and newspapers.

A large bookcase sat to its left in the corner, spanning across both walls. The majority of it was filled with novelty and trifle items, not books. In the other corner hung a woven hemp hammock that swayed in the wind from the now-opened windows. Through the doorway, I watched Jin as she climbed through the hatch with a bundle of blankets in her arms.

"If it wasn't supposed to storm before dawn I would set you all up out here, so you could sleep under the stars, but inside will have to do." Jin laid the blankets on the floor.

"Whatever works for us, we are easy. I just can't believe you have all these tools!" Laago's face lit up as he examined the different equipment scattered around. "What type of work do you do?"

"Pretty much any job that no one else in the army wants to do." He laughed. "If something is broken, I fix it. If something is dirty, I clean it."

"I did maintenance for our apartment too. Some days were definitely better than others." Laago shook his head.

"Yeah, I mostly don't mind. I have learned so much since I started working for General Pago, I am just really grateful for the opportunity. I've been sent all over the republic and its outskirts to fix military machinery and to help with other maintenance jobs."

"And you got all of these awesome tools out of it!"

"Well, most of these tools are borrowed technically, but they've been borrowed for years now," Jon said with a wink.

"Back in Tinshe, I had like three tools, but I was responsible for the whole apartment building!"

"Wow, I don't know how you managed. You must be crafty!" Jon handed him a tool. "Check this one out."

"Looks like Jon found a new friend." Jin rolled her eyes. Benjin sat down on the blankets with Luka wrapped around him.

"Can I see your cut?" I dropped to my knees.

"What happened?" Jin asked.

"He got hit in the head with a rock by some muggers."

"But Benji's tough!" Luka squealed.

"You know it, Buba," Benjin said I pushed his hair back and examined the stitches.

"It doesn't look infected... How does your head feel?"

"Jon is prone to bad headaches, he has suffered from them since he was a kid. Maybe he has a root that can help alleviate the pain," Jin offered.

At the other side of the door sat three clay pots with plants in them. I recognized one to be a mingh root, which is a plant found in the east that is used for treating wounds. If you squeeze the liquid from the root onto a cut, it can prevent infection.

"I told you I am fine." Benjin smacked my hand away.

"I'll get a fire going outside," Jon said.

"Let me help!" Laago followed him outside, and I was quick to follow, knowing my worrying was only irritating Benjin.

I took a seat on the cold stone bench. The sun was finally setting, taking the humidity with it and replacing it with a cool sea breeze. I watched Laago make a teepee with the logs in the fire pit. He held them in place as Jon filled the center with kindling. Once his structure was sound, Jon began rubbing flint and steel, sending sparks onto the small twigs and leaves.

"What do you do out here for fun?" Laago asked, carefully blowing on the small flame.

"I am usually up here fixing army equipment or patching boats at the dock for extra coin. I recently got into carving wood paddles too, they sell for cheap but coin is coin." Jon took a seat across from us, satisfied with his fire. "If I get off work early enough I try to run over to the soup kitchen. That place has always been like a home to me."

"He asked what do you do for fun, don't bore him to death," Jin teased.

"Sounds like fun to me!" Laago smiled.

"Sometimes I go fishing."

"Benj and I used to fish all the time off the south coast. Have you caught anything good around here?"

"Oh yeah, the Bay of Suhai is loaded with fish. That's why Huang was founded, it was originally just a fishing town. Over time it became so prosperous, making it one of the world's greatest ports," Jon explained. "I once saw a whaleshark not too far off the coast when I was out in the water."

"No way! I heard those things are mean."

"I never got out of the water so fast."

"It was probably just a turtle whale," Jin scoffed.

"A turtle whale? Off the coast of Huang? Yeah right..."

"Benj's father once told me about a navy ship that sunk in the Bay of Suhai, every man got plucked from the water and eaten whole by a swarm of whalesharks!"

"All but three," Jon corrected Laago.

"You know the story?"

"It was ten years ago. Chief Unq was deep in the bay late at night, practicing rescue drills with his men when his head officer warned him of an approaching storm. Chief Unq was a stubborn man, he did not believe her, that is, until just before morning light when the wind picked up and the waves tripled in size. The chief finally allowed the ship to change course back to Huang, but by then it was too late. They were stuck in the eye of the storm."

"I never heard this part of the story!" Laago sat on the edge of the bench. "What happened next?"

"A massive wave formed, almost the size of this building, and crushed the ship. Many drowned." He soberly looked up from the fire. "When dawn came and the storm weakened, many of the men were already gone. That is when the whalesharks came."

"How did anyone even survive?" I asked.

"The officer who sensed the storm was coming found a large wooden panel floating in what was left of the wreck and crafted it into a raft. She took Chief Unq and one other survivor and paddled across the bay with a piece of wood as her oar."

"Wow, tough lady. I would've left Chief Unq there to get eaten by whalesharks," Laago admitted.

"Well, he wanted to be, but the officer physically forced him onto her makeshift raft because he wanted to go down with his ship. Once they got closer to shore, a fishing boat saw them and brought them to land. Chief Unq immediately resigned from his position."

"Rightfully so. If it wasn't for his arrogance, none of those men would have died."

"When he stepped down, he appointed the officer who saved him as the new chief of the navy and she has been leading ever since."

"Chief Kholok?" I asked, remembering her from our meeting at the headquarters.

"Yes." Jon nodded. "Chief Unq took his own life exactly one week after the incident, he couldn't live with the guilt."

"That's terrible..." Laago said, regretting his initial harsh comments on the chief.

"He served in the republic's navy since he was sixteen, he put his heart and soul into his work. Chief Unq had no wife, no children... His family was his crew," Jon solemnly spoke. "The chief may have been imperious and stubborn, but his intentions were pure. In fact, those qualities were why Chief Unq was such a successful leader to begin with- he was unwavering."

"Oftentimes a man's greatest strength is also his greatest weakness," I reflected, remembering words my father once told me.

"It's true," Jon agreed, "but when the people heard of the tragedy, they acted like Unq himself caused the storm. They rushed to form opinions without understanding the situation. This tendency is the root of a lot of strife in this world. You could look at the navy ship sinkage and blame Chief Unq. Or you could try to understand that he was just another human being, one with immense responsibility. Most people couldn't fathom being responsible for an entire navy, yet that was a burden the chief shouldered every day. He never made any severe mistakes, until he did, and once that happened, it was as if he didn't spend the last forty years of his life fighting for the people of Terlu."

"I feel like a jerk," Laago admitted.

"Don't. Our brain was designed to jump to conclusions. If every decision we ever made took us hours of research and contemplation, our species would have died out hundreds of years ago."

"I suppose that's true. Instead, we just have to train our brain to be more sympathetic automatically," I pondered aloud.

"Maybe." Laago leaned back on the bench and rested his arm behind me. "Or maybe it's okay to have an initial negative reaction, but to just take a moment to think before we speak. That way we can understand why someone else may have a more hateful opinion and help guide them to see things clearer too."

"I like that, Laago." Jon grabbed a thick log and placed it on top of the growing fire. "The initial intruding thought is not the cause of misunderstanding others, but deciding whether or not to listen to that thought is. Instead of pretending those negative thoughts don't exist, we can acknowledge them and recognize they are wrong, then formulate a new, truer opinion before we speak."

"That was well said," Laago complimented.

"I'll let you in on a secret." Jon leaned forward in his seat. "Our army engineers are working on creating metal ships. They'll be able to withstand much stronger storms than the one that decimated Chief Unq and his crew."

"I heard something about this while we were traveling here. Apparently the engineers in the Empire of Gala are working on something similar?" Laago's eyebrows scrunched.

"Yes, it was actually there where the idea originated. Our republic and the Empire of Gala have always maintained a tight alliance, so every year our top engineers and scientists would come together and share ideas. Years ago they sent us the concept of these ships and both of our governments jointly began funding their creation. But when the plague hit, the budget was cut to zero and the project was halted."

"That's incredible. Do you think it will start up again soon?"

"The general thinks Empress Jhena never actually stopped the research, but instead continued to work on the ships in secret. They weren't hit hard by the plague, due to their secure borders and strong government. I don't see why they would stop working on such an important project, especially with all riches the empire has to waste."

"Empress Jhena rules with an iron first." Jin huffed, her arms crossed. "If you ask me, she has way too much power."

"Wouldn't that be a breach of your alliance?" Laago asked.

"Not technically, because they are not bound by anything to inform us on all of their actions. But, I suppose, morally speaking it is. Our government spent a lot of money on it the year before the plague and now the Empire of Gala is reaping the benefits of all that research. I wouldn't be surprised if the ships hit the water within a year or two."

"Shouldn't President Suin do something about that?"

"The Empire of Gala is far too powerful for us to intervene. It may be to our benefit to just keep Empress Jhena on our side and let it happen. Our republic is still recovering financially from the plague. We will reach their level of technology eventually, it just might take some extra time."

"What a time to be alive! Metal ships... Wouldn't that be a sight to see?" Laago shook his head.

As we sat under the moonlight, the wind began to howl. The fire crackled and sputtered, its bright wild light illuminating our faces. I watched Laago's eyes, lost in the fickle flames. He aged a lot in the weeks since we left our homes, though I suppose we all had. Even Luka, who slept soundly with Benjin inside, his body once small and soft was now stretching and hardening. His naive toothy smile was replaced with a deep gaze. He was beginning to see the world for what it truly was.

"So how long have you two been together?" Jin broke the silence. I nearly jumped from my seat, my face beet red. Laago erupted in laughter, not budging from his comfortable position.

"We are not..."

"Ten years," Laago sarcastically interrupted.

"You're not actually dating?" Jin made a face.

"No!" I immediately responded, not giving Laago a moment to joke. It still hurt to think of him like that. As much as I loved him, dating him would be a lost cause. No matter how into me he seemed, when another girl strolled by he drooled like a foxdog waiting for dinner.

"What, Ny, I'm not good enough for you?" He teased me.

"Not gonna lie, I assumed you guys were together too," Jon admitted.

"What? Why?"

"As long as you have been here you have been glued to each other's sides. At dinner you sat next to each other... And look at you now!" Jin laughed, pointing at Laago's arm resting behind me on the bench.

"Come here!" He playfully grabbed me. "Give your boyfriend a kiss!"

"You wish!" I slapped his hands away. The metal hatch to the roof flung open, and out climbed General Pago. Laago and I immediately put our hands to ourselves and sat up straight.

"What a beautiful night!" He called over.

"The wind is starting to pick up," Jon commented.

"Mind if I join?"

"Of course not, sir," Laago enthusiastically responded.

"Please, call me Roan." General Pago walked over and took a seat next to Jin on a bench. "Where are the other boys?"

"They're asleep. Benjin's head was hurting him," Jin voiced. "He has a concussion."

"Within my walls?" The general shook his head. "What happened?"

"Some guys tried to rob us and one of them hit Benjin in the head with a rock," Laago explained. "But one of the army nurses saw that he was injured and stitched him up."

"And to think you kids were going to leave for the Island of Aara tonight..." He rubbed the scruff on his chin.

"I'm sorry, sir. We didn't want to worry you," Laago admitted.

"Worry me? It is my job to worry. We are at war, boy. If people don't tell me the whole truth, I cannot successfully do my job. I can't just know the big picture; I need to know every detail," his voice echoed through the rooftop. "Tell me, how was your journey here? Did you meet much opposition?"

"Long!" Laago sighed. "Once we passed the Port of Eura we didn't see many militants, other than a few scouts."

"Were they good fighters?"

"We ambushed the scouts pretty easily, but one got me good in the bicep." Laago rolled up his sleeve, revealing his wound. It partially healed back over, leaving the skin surrounding it pinkish-white in color. "That didn't feel too hot."

"I remember the first time I was struck. Before then, I thought nothing could take me down." My eyes drifted to the scar stretching across his eyebrow. "And you, Nyla?" He leaned forward on the bench. "Have you been struck?"

"No..." I responded, unsure of my answer for a moment. I may not have been physically struck, but living every day in fear of my life made me feel as though I have.

"A man tried to take her in an outskirt village, but Benjin nearly beat him to death. The man wasn't even a militant," Laago hissed. I shuddered at the thought of Quacho.

"Good brother. I would do the same," Jon added, meaning the words more seriously than they sounded. I watched him glance at Jin. She was a beautiful girl living in the shadier side of Huang. I had no doubt that she has had her share of interactions with vile men... I don't know of any girls who haven't.

"I am sure Nyla could hold her own," General Pago said.

"I'm not sure that I could have, I didn't have my bow on me."

"How many men's lives have you taken with your bow?"

"More than I would have liked to," I said with a gloomy sigh. Jin's eyes widened.

"You've actually killed people?" Jin's eyes widened. She sounded disgusted.

"We had no choice, it was kill or be killed," Laago snapped back defensively. "We wouldn't have made it here without Nyla. We did what we had to do to get help for Tinshe and to warn the Republic of Terlu."

"There's always another way..." Jin said.

Another way? If only we thought of that before the hundreds of wars that have plagued our world. I looked down at her neatly ironed pale green dress and her bouncy black curls that were pulled back so perfectly with her elegant wooden hair sticks. How easy would life be from a position of such privilege?

"Don't be naive, there is no other way. War is a part of life, whether we like it or not. Though only the insane enjoy killing, the rest of us only do it only out of necessity. We do it to protect our daughters, our sons, our wives..." General Pago shook his head. "I remember each face I have slain. I would forget my own name before I forgot theirs. Never has a day passed where I did not mourn for them."

"I thought I was just weak for thinking that." I felt tears begin to form in my eyes, but I wiped them away, before they had a chance to fall. Laago instinctively put his arm back around to comfort me. "I see their faces every night when I try to sleep. There was so much blood. They were militants, but they looked so young. They were just boys, no older than Laago."

"Though the burden may not go away, it will become easier to carry."

"I hope I never have to take a life," Jon said with a sad grimace. He was one of those who understood our suffering without having to experience it himself. "I am sorry you guys had to go through that, but I am thankful you did. By taking a few lives, you saved many."

"Can I ask you something, Gener- I mean Roan?" Laago's voice grew soft.

"Go on, spit it out, boy." General Pago grinned. He had a way with words.

"It's about Bao..." He hesitated, unsure if he would come off as nosey. "Do you miss him?" Laago soberly asked. General Pago sat still for a moment, his eyes gazed into the fire, deeply thinking.

"I never had a brother, until my sister wed Bao. She was my only sibling and we were very close. People often mistook us for twins, not just because of our relationship, but because we looked very alike too. When Ona passed..." He paused again, rubbing his scruff. "When Ona passed, I was devastated. It was the hardest thing I ever lived through. But then, Bao shut me out and would not speak nor look at me. Not only did I lose my sister, but I lost my brother... And I don't know what I did for him to hate me- I try to understand- I know he was suffering, but he was my brother..." He drifted off to silence. The words were too painful for him to say.

"Bao feels horrible for closing you out, he could barely speak of you without getting emotional. He said you looked too similar to Ona for him to bear, but I could tell he really loved you by the way he spoke of you." I reassured him.

"I cannot force the man to be in my life."

"But you can at least try. Once all of this is over, we would like to visit Bao again. You should come with us," Laago offered, not trying to sound pushy.

"Perhaps if the timing is right," General Pago concluded.

"I'll take it!" Laago smiled. "Life is too short to have regrets, I think you should be honest about how you feel," he squeezed my shoulder as he spoke. Storm clouds quickly rolled in from the south, covering the night sky and blocking the stars' flickering lights. As they did, rain began to pelt down.

"I think we should call it a night," Jon shouted, jumping up from his bench.

"You kids get some sleep, I'll see you in the morning." General Pago headed towards the hatch with Jin and they disappeared into the building.

I followed the boys back into Jon's room. Benjin was deeply asleep, his body cuddled around Luka as usual. Jon jumped into his hammock, as it wavered in the wind drifting through the window. The rain noisily bounced on the tin roof above us, but it didn't sound chaotic, it just drowned out the noise of the city around us. When I laid next to Luka, I closed my eyes and pretended I was in a rainforest. Behind my head sat three clay pots with plants, filling my nose with the scent of mingh root. Laago sat next to me and stretched his back before laying down.

"I'm glad we got to spend one night like normal people before we have to leave again," he whispered, careful to not wake the boys.

"I don't want to leave..."

I thought of the five of us drifting through the Bay of Suhai and into the Great Ocean in a small wooden boat. I thought of the navy ship that was obliterated in a storm ten years ago. I remembered Bao's words, when he said if we sailed through the bay we would be sitting ducks, targets for the militia.

"We will be okay," he said, as he wrapped himself around me.

Normally I would push him off to hide my true feelings, but his body felt so warm and comforting, like a big blanket over me. His chin rested on my head and I felt his heart beating against my back. Without even realizing it, I grabbed his hand and squeezed it, pulling it towards my chest.

# CHAPTER FIFTEEN

# A SCARED LITTLE BOY

W HEN I AWOKE IN the morning, I was alone. I laid there for a moment, tangled in the blankets and my eyes blurry. I thought of last night: of Jin and her fancy dress, of General Pago and Bao, and of course, of Laago. It felt like every time I thought I was over him, he would crawl back and engulf my mind. I tried to think of all the reasons we would never work as a couple, but I kept making excuses. He flirted with every woman. But don't most men? Benjin would be uncomfortable if we dated. But Benjin is overprotective of me; he would be uncomfortable with anyone I end up dating.

I sat up and rubbed my eyes, but no matter how hard I tried, they were still blurry. I crawled out of bed and stood in the doorway, stretching my legs. The blue sky was speckled with white fluffy clouds. Jon's garden looked bright and vibrant from the heavy rain that stormed the city last night. As I walked through the rows of plants, I gently ran my hand along them, touching and admiring the different types of produce. The plants felt strong and full of life, I felt their energy pulsating into me. If I had a garden like this in Tinshe, I would be considered rich.

"Ny?" Laago called, lifting the hatch up. Something in me felt so at ease, surrounded by all these plants. I chose not to answer. Instead, I continued walking down the row, until I reached the edge of the building. My body felt so light, as though it was slowly drifting through the air. Between two tall fignut bushes rested a view of the city, like a painting on a canvas. I stood there in awe of the sight, I never knew a city could look so beautiful. It made me think of my mother and her striking beauty that always caused people to stare. I heard Laago's footsteps behind me. He stood there behind me for a minute before letting out a sigh. "It's beautiful, isn't it?"

"It is," I whispered.

"Litia cooked us breakfast, I don't want to be rude." Laago reached his hand over to my shoulder.

"Why do you always do that?" I asked, not allowing my gaze to break from the city skyline.

"Do what?" He pulled his hand back and brushed it through his long wavy brown hair, pulling it away from his face. His eyes squinted from the sun shining through the clouds, but remained locked on mine.

"You're always there. You always sit next to me, you put your arm around me..." I looked down at my dirty boots, feeling my face begin to blush.

"You always sit next to me, too." He grinned.

"I like being around you, but it's confusing," I admitted. "I feel like you send me mixed signals."

"I'm sorry," Laago said with a sense of guilt. "You're right. I'll give you space."

"Is that what you want?" I felt my head get hot.

"I don't know, Ny. What do you want me to do? We are stuck together day and night, it's natural for us to get close, but I don't want to complicate things with Benjin. He's given me everything I have." His voice trailed off. "...Especially with everything going on right now, is it really the time?"

"I feel like it will never be the right time- but it was always the right time with all those other girls. With Atheti."

"Are you serious right now? Is that really what you want?" He flung his arms up. "For me to make a move on you while I am high off holiva root? We don't even know if anything happened, I could've passed out for all we know!"

"No, I just want you to make up your mind!" I turned around and started to walk away, but he grabbed my arm, pulling me in.

"You know I love you," he whispered into my ear, my heart racing. I pulled back, but only enough so I could look up at him. Everything in me wanted to grab his face and kiss him, but as I leaned forward to finally do it, his face began to change. His skin faded to gray, until he was the color of stone. "Nyla..." His voice grew filled with fear, as his features began to sag.

"Laago!" I squeezed him tighter, but it was no use. His body slowly turned to ash in my arms, until all that he was dissipated into the wind, leaving me alone. "Please... Please don't leave me!"

As I collapsed onto the floor, the ground gave way beneath my feet, plunging me into a bone-chilling ocean. This was no ordinary sea of waves- it was an abyss. I fell deeper and deeper in, regardless of how hard I swam. A faint voice echoed in the distance, but I could not decipher who it was. Water rushed into my face and down my throat, suffocating me. Finally, I gave in to the current, allowing myself to be sucked under.

"Nyla!" Benjin called louder, shaking me. I jumped up, almost smashing my head into Benjin's chin. I was asleep, it was a dream. "I was going to let you sleep in, but I didn't want you to miss breakfast."

"Benjin!" I shot up, gasping for air.

"Did you have another nightmare?" His eyes were filled with worry.

"No." I shook my head. My whole body was sticky with sweat.

"Alright, I'll see you downstairs," he replied. Though there was hesitation in his voice, he walked himself out of Jon's room, giving me time to collect myself.

I sat there for a couple minutes, still lost in my dream. It felt so real- the way Laago spoke, the warmness of his touch... Even when he disappeared from under my fingers. I felt the breeze that took the last of him away from me, leaving me in despair.

My forest-green shirt was sitting by my feet, neatly folded. Jon must have washed it and left it there while I was sleeping. I slipped Jon's shirt off and put mine back on. It smelt fresh and clean, reminding me of when I was younger, when my mother would wash my clothes. I stood up and walked toward the doorway. I tried to shake off my dream, but I had a pit in my stomach. Benjin was right, it was no dream, but a nightmare.

It was just past sunrise. The sky was cloudy and gray, the ground still wet from the storm. The plants were a lush green, satisfied from a long night of much needed water. I remembered the beautiful view of the city between the fignut bushes and ran over, eager to see if it was real. But when I turned the corner, all I saw was more tall plants that blocked the view. I climbed through a row of purple corn and pushed the plants aside to create an opening, but the view was dissatisfying and mostly just revealed gray rooftops that lacked color, all less appealing than Jon's. I looked at the apartment building across the street, its walls lined with windows.

Each window held a different story, some were closed with thick curtains, others were wide open allowing a cool breeze to flow through. I watched a young boy sit at a windowsill, his head laying on his arms as he gazed down at the kids playing in the street below him. I imagined he was a shy boy with a strict mother who never let him outside. Instead he had to stay inside and practice math. His mother wanted him to become a doctor, to get them out of this side of town, but he wanted to be an artist.

I shook my head, waking me from my daydream. I didn't want to be rude and miss breakfast. I jumped through the hatch and headed down the staircase. As I scampered through, I turned my head and caught a little girl, perhaps three years old in age, sticking her head out her doorway. Her brown eyes were wide with curiosity as I walked by. I did my best to smile back, but it was a pathetic attempt. I could not shake the feeling of impending doom.

I could smell breakfast before I even reached the bottom of the stairwell. Hints of cinnamon lingered through the hall. In the kitchen, Litia stood over a large simmering pot, its steam rising into the air. She moved swiftly and effortlessly, grabbing pinches of spices without even looking. Benjin and Laago hovered closely over her.

"Have you kids ever had street stew? It is a classic here." Litia grabbed a bowl and filled it.

"No, but it smells delicious!" Laago smiled, taking it from her.

"It's a mixture of leftovers, but we use sweet spices to brighten them up," she explained, handing Benjin and me each a bowl. "Eat up."

We all took a seat at the dining room table. No candles were lit, but instead a soft morning light shined through the windows and brightened the room. I still felt off from my dream. It felt too real.

"Where's Luka?" Benjin immediately stood back up.

"Probably out playing in the courtyard. I saw a bunch of kids out there earlier," Laago assumed, slurping down spoonfuls of stew. "This is delicious!"

"I'm gonna go look for him." Benjin looked out the window, scanning the courtyard for Luka's bouncy curls, before he headed out through the kitchen.

"He's always so worried about you guys. We are in the home of the republic's general, I am sure Luka is safe." He looked up at me. "Don't tell me you are worried too?"

"I'm always worried." I let out an awkward chuckle, as I got up from my chair to help Benjin.

"I guess it runs in the family."

I looked up and paused as I passed under the stairwell, my eyes fixated on the massive chandelier hanging five stories above me before I heard Benjin's voice drifting through the living room. I stood hidden behind the wall by the doorway, eavesdropping.

"What are you doing in here, Buba?" He sat beside Luka on the floor, who was laying on his stomach and flipping through some book. "Breakfast is ready, we don't want to be rude."

"I'm not hungry..." Luka mumbled, his eyes glued to the pages.

"What are you reading?" Benjin slid the book over so he could see it too. *The Pain of War...*" His eyes widened as he flipped through. Though I couldn't see much, I saw paintings of burning villages and somber men consuming the pages. Benjin abruptly shut the book, leaving an air of heaviness between them.

"I was looking at that!" Luka yelled, grabbing it back from him.

"I don't know if you should be seeing this." Benjin went to comb his hand through Luka's curls, but he slapped his hand away.

"Why? I see it everyday with you guys!"

"I know, and I am sorry for that. What you have experienced is not normal, especially for a kid your age. I have tried so hard to shield you from certain things, but I know you are too smart for that. But just because you have seen some bad things, doesn't mean you are ready to see all of the bad things." Benjin took the book back from Luka. "You want to limit the amount of bad things you see, so your mind doesn't begin to normalize them. Remember, just because bad things happen, doesn't mean that it is normal. We have to focus on the good."

"I want to go home."

"Me too." Benjin put his hand on Luka's back. "Maybe you should stay here while we travel to the Island of Aara. You would be safe and can play with all of the other kids in this apartment..."

"No!" Luka jumped up and wrapped his little body around Benjin. I felt tears stream down my face. "Please, don't leave me! Don't leave like mommy and daddy!"

"I will never leave you, Buba. I promise." He kissed the top of his head. "Now go get some breakfast before you wither away." Luka lifted himself up and ran out of the living room, right past me without even noticing.

I peered back through the archway and saw that Benjin sat unmoved on the floor, holding the book and sobbing. My big brother, who once seemed so unbreakable... Before I could even think, I ran over and collapsed against him, squeezing him tight.

"It feels like we are failing him," he cried.

"He'll be fine."

"I wish mother and father were here."

"Me too." I wiped the tears streaming down my face and looked at him. "But we have to stay strong for them."

"We should go eat, I don't want anyone to grow concerned." Benjin rose to his feet and held out his hand for me. I grabbed onto him and he pulled me up effortlessly.

When we came back to the dining room, Luka's cheeks were full of stew and he was giggling away at Laago's antics. I looked up at Benjin, whose eyes were still red and teary, but he put on a fake smile and kissed the top of Luka's head as he took a seat beside him. Oh, to be a kid again, where your world collapses for a moment, only to be forgotten when a friend makes a silly face.

"Let's see who can fit more stew in their mouth!" Laago sputtered between spoonfuls, racing Luka.

"Don't make a mess." Benjin blew on his breakfast.

"Sorry, pops!" Laago grinned, his mouth full with stew seeping out.

"How do you like it?" Jon breezed through the doorway, grinning at Laago, whose face turned red for a moment.

"It's delicious!" Luka turned around, showing his cheeks were full too.

"I can tell." Jon chuckled. "Did you guys sleep well?"

"Definitely!" Benjin responded cheerily. I looked down at my bowl, embarrassed of my dream from last night. "Have you heard anything new from General Pago?"

"I was actually just at a meeting with the chiefs. The western walls are secured, the gates are closed, and the scouts predict General Ahkpi's troops are still a day away."

"What a relief!" Laago sighed.

"Are we still expected to leave at dusk?" I asked.

"Yes. I prepared our boat this morning. It is a small rowboat, but I have traveled many miles in it over the years."

"A rowboat?" Benjin's eyebrows raised at the thought of us rowing across the entire ocean. "Shouldn't we take a sail?"

"A sail would give away our position, while a rowboat should be able to sneak through virtually undetected," Jon explained. "Besides, I can handle the majority of the rowing. My body is conditioned for it, for me it is no different than walking."

"Okay," Benjin hesitantly agreed. He bit his lip anxiously. "I don't have much experience with boats, especially in such open water."

"The North Ocean is hostile and ruthless, between its erratic waves and freezing temperatures, it is a deathtrap for those who are not truly prepared. When our navy sends boats up there, the soldiers call it the graveyard shift, because so many boats have sunk up there. The South Ocean itself is known to be tamer, as it is warmer and less choppy, but the problem there is the quick-forming storms that sailors claim can overtake a blue sky in seconds."

"You're not a very good salesman..." Laago fidgeted in his seat.

"My point is, the Great Ocean is the most welcoming of all oceans, hence the name, and it looks like we will have clear weather. Though it is a long voyage, we will be safe. I have enough boating experience for all of us."

"Good." Laago finally sat still, crossing his arms across his chest.

"There is something we need to discuss," Jon leaned forward in his chair, clasping his hands together. "After speaking with the chiefs, General Pago decided it is best if Luka stays here with Litia and Jin."

"No!" Luka immediately shrieked, jumping up in his chair and slamming his fist on the table. "I am coming too!"

"I'm sorry, but it's for the best if you stay back," Jon calmly spoke. "General Pago will be out fighting alongside his men. I heard you are a great fighter, and I need you to keep Jin and Litia safe for me while I am gone. You need to be the man of the house for us. I don't trust anyone else. Could you do it for me?" He looked into Luka's eyes pleadingly. We all intently watched Luka, who sat there thinking this offer over for a moment with his face all scrunched up.

"Okay," he finally agreed. "I will protect them."

We all sighed a heavy breath. I was relieved Jon encouraged him to stay back, because the thought of bringing Luka worried me sick. The stakes were too high and he would only be a distraction.

"Will it be safe here?" Laago asked.

"We won't let these savages get past our walls, nor will we let them return to the Suhai Empire," Jon reassured him. "We crush their army and hold the militants accountable for their war crimes. We will not let General Ahkpi get away with this."

"How does Ahkpi sleep at night?" Laago shook his head, with his face showing disgust.

"In his twisted head, he probably thinks his actions are justified," Benjin said.

"Are you defending him?"

"No, I'm obviously not." He rolled his eyes.

"Putting yourself in the mind of your enemy only gives you advantages," General Pago's voice rumbled from the kitchen. He joined us in the dining room, with a hot bowl of stew in his hands. "The boy is right. To us, Ahkpi and his militants are destructive tyrants, but to them, they must be doing what they believe is right. No sane man would serve his life just to watch the world crumble and fall."

"How can raiding cities, stealing food, and murdering innocent civilians be a good thing?" Laago snapped.

"Why did General Ahkpi move his forces into Tinshe?" General Pago took his seat at the head of the table and blew on his stew.

"To extort the people and rob us of our resources."

"From our perception he did. But he claimed he did it to redistribute wealth, food, and medicine," Benjin explained.

"By distribute do you mean steal?" Laago scoffed.

"Well, that is what his militants ended up doing, but was that Ahkpi's intention?" Benjin pondered aloud.

"Any true leader would have control over his soldiers. I believe it's all a part of his agenda," Jon argued, bringing up a good point. I shook my head in agreement.

"What do you think, Nyla?" General Pago asked.

"I've never seen anything good come from the militant's occupation. But... When I had to kill those two militants in the tunnels, I didn't feel good about it. I didn't even feel relieved. I just felt horrible, because they just looked like boys to me. They looked as scared and confused as we did."

"Boys that would have killed us."

"But they were just boys," my voice choked and I felt my eyes well up with tears. "Here we are, spitting on them for their violence, while we act the same."

It was an epiphany. I never even noticed the hypocrisy of our actions until now. How could I have been so blind? Everyone was silent for a moment. When I finally looked up from my empty bowl, I caught General Pago smiling.

"That, my dear, is the paradox of war. You are not the first to get lost in this and you are certainly not the last. When I was a young private, I watched three of my fellow soldiers take advantage of a young woman. They ordered me to be the lookout. Instead, I ran to my officer. I'll never forget his reaction. He looked up from his newspaper, threw it on the desk, and told me to shut my mouth and mind my own business. When I went back to the barracks that night, I got my buttocks whooped for being a rat."

"No way..." Laago gasped.

"But once I got my beating, I didn't regret that I reported the crime to my officer. I only regretted not protecting the poor lady at that moment. Instead, she thinks I just ran away and left her there to be taken advantage of. It makes me feel sick. When I became General, I swore a zero tolerance for that type of barbaric behavior, but I am one man and cannot control the actions of every soldier."

"You cannot compare our army to the militants. One is clearly tyrannical," Jon countered.

"I think it's good to have awareness. There are two sides to every story, no matter how hard it may be." Benjin shrugged. I saw my father in the words he spoke, who always looked to understand the evil in the world, no matter the situation.

"That's not awareness, it's delusion." Laago chuckled.

"It's perception," the general corrected. "I am aware some citizens of the republic have had a growing taste of dissent towards our army. There's been protests, riots..."

"Those people just want Terlu to burn. Who protects them from invaders? Who protects their freedoms? We sacrifice our lives for those ungrateful bastards." Jon's face turned red, his voice spat with rage.

"It is our duty to protect their ability to have an opinion; it is not our duty to control their opinion. That wouldn't be a democracy, but a militaristic dictatorship. We would be no better than the militants storming our walls."

"I disagree." Jon crossed his arm and rolled his eyes.

"And that is okay, but one day, I believe we will see eye to eye." General Pago slurped his stew. "Life would be easy if everything was black and white, but it isn't. It would be easy if there was one side to every story, but there isn't. There's rarely even two. It is more like three, or four, or five..."

"I know that, but I am not excusing any tyrannical behavior just because it can be justified in some backwards way." Jon's response was met with silence for a moment, as the general leaned back in his chair and let out a heavy breath.

"My sister and I grew up on the streets. We lived every day in fear, whether it be for our safety, for shelter, or for hunger. We could have succumbed to anger and despair, as many children do in such circumstances, but we didn't. Like all of you here, who endured rough upbringings, whether it be from the plague or life itself..." His voice trailed off in a moment of reflection, before he continued. "We persevered, no matter how fiercely the world seemed to resist us. General Ahkpi, too, had a similar upbringing. I once met him at a western leadership meeting, shortly after he was appointed general. He exuded charisma and charm. He possessed a deep understanding of world history and was well-versed in cultural knowledge. Did you know Anuk Ahkpi is from Tinshe?"

"No..." I whispered in disbelief.

"Then why would he seek to destroy it?" Laago asked.

"Like me, Anuk sought refuge from a life of poverty in the army. And like me, he rose through the ranks- from bottom up- until he became the army's general. But even when I met him and he told me of these things, I sensed a profound dissimilarity between us," he explained. "When I reflect on my time in the military, I found solace in the lives I changed for the better. It's the reason I endured the relentless hardships of sleepless nights, prolonged absences from home, fighting to survive... But when he spoke to me, he bragged about how many men he had slain and how many women he conquered. His perception of the world was shrouded in darkness and despair, he did not believe in the people. Why is that?"

"Because you used the hardships of life to be able to better understand those around you, even people like General Ahkpi, but he used it to separate himself and lose sight of why he joined the army in the first place. He let fear overrun his life," I voiced, the words flooding through my mouth like water through a broken dam.

"When I think of Anuk, I think of the little boy who slept on the streets of Tinshe, scavenging for scraps from waste bins and drinking from murky ponds. The little boy who witnessed his mother get stabbed and held her in his trembling arms until she passed. When I think of Anuk Ahkpi, I see the same scared little boy, only now, he is concealed behind the facade of a general's uniform adorned with fancy medals."

"Is all of that true?" I gasped. The general solemnly nodded.

"So what is your plan then, for the war?" Laago asked.

"We will fight, but we will not fight out of hatred, it will be for peace. With that, I know the gods will be on our side and protect us." He pulled a scroll out of his pocket and slid it across the table towards Benjin. "It is President Suin's official message to the people. It is being dispersed to the people as we speak."

Benjin carefully opened the scroll, his eyes scanning the document. He cleared his throat and began to read the president's words aloud to us.

"It is with a heavy heart that I must inform the people of our great nation that General Ahkpi of the Suhai Empire has declared war against the Republic of Terlu. He did not do so honorably, as if unnecessary war could ever be. Instead, it was a cowardly act executed behind our backs, bypassing not only our government but also the Civil Council and our world's esteemed leaders. He led his treasonous militia to our western wall, dishonorably shattering a longstanding alliance between our two nations.

General Ahkpi did not do so out of necessity nor desperation, but rather from a deep well of greed and selfishness. General Ahkpi did not see the devastating plague as a time to unite, but instead, as a time to take advantage of those around him. He rallied the people of Najin, convincing them that the innocent men and women of Tinshe were somehow to blame for the plague that swept our world." Benjin paused and exhaled sharply. Tears were welling up in my eyes and a lump engulfed my throat. After a moment, he gathered his strength and continued.

"Two years into the plague, General Ahkpi moved his treasonous militia south into Tinshe, claiming they were there to provide aid to the less fortunate, who suffered the most from the plague. But General Ahkpi is not an honorable man and his words concealed deceit. He used his militia to pillage and torment the innocent civilians of Tinshe, who had already suffered enough loss. General Ahkpi ordered for their Protectors, the men who peacefully protected Tinshe for centuries, to be executed.

The people of Tinshe have been targeted for simply being born on the wrong side of the Suhai Empire. Emperor Nahkon has abandoned his people and relinquished all power to General Ahkpi, by idly sitting by and allowing him to act in such a horrific manner. In the name of the justice and equality that our republic has fought hard to preserve, we would like to formally apologize for not recognizing the signs of a genocide earlier. People of Tinshe, we will not sit idly by as your emperor did and allow this to happen. General Ahkpi's reign of terror has gone on for too long.

Now, he has moved his troops east in an attempt to destroy our republic. But General Ahkpi is a fool if he thinks our great republic will fall to cowards who target women and children. Together, we must unite and fight off the evil that is trying so desperately to overturn our world. For all it takes for the evil to win, is for the good to do nothing. I am issuing a mandatory evacuation of all citizens who reside on the western front and the coastline of Huang. Our troops will be dispersed throughout the republic, to inform everyone of their evacuation zone. Please do not hesitate to ask them for help, they are here to aid the people. All elderly and disabled citizens will be personally assisted later in the evening.

Emperor Nahkon, I personally call to you, not as a President, but as a citizen of our free republic. No more blood needs to be shed. No more mothers should have to lose their sons in vain. On behalf of the people of both the Republic of Terlu and those in the Suhai Empire who have no voice, we demand you dishonorably discharge the general of your militia or to relinquish your power and resign immediately. General Ahkpi, on behalf of the people of both the Republic of Terlu and the Suhai Empire, we demand you recall your troops to Najin and resign in disgrace," Benjin shakily concluded, as he set the scroll on the table and wiped his eyes with his shirt.

President Suin's words left me speechless. He sounded like a true leader, bravely defending the people of his republic and even the people of Tinshe, who he owed nothing to. Our own emperor didn't just abandon us, but he threw us to the whalesharks. I believe his crimes against our people are just as severe as General Ahkpi's.

"Not a word about us, huh?" Laago broke the silence, as he leaned back in his chair. "We risked our lives for the people."

"It is safer this way." Benjin shook his head. "The less attention we get, the better."

"The president only did so to protect you. Putting your names on that message would have been a death sentence. Once the war is over, you will all receive the recognition you deserve, but until then, it is wise to lay low." General Pago stood up, grabbing his now empty bowl. "It is time to get to work. There is much to do before you all leave at dusk. Jon, take them with you to evacuate the Korja district. Bring the citizens to the Ritu family's central estate." Jon eagerly rose to his feet.

"Can I ask you a question?" Laago followed General Pago into the kitchen with a stack of the dirty bowls. "Do you really believe in gods and goddesses?"

"Doesn't hurt to." He set his bowls in the sink and rinsed off his hands. "I have to get back to work, but I should be home before dusk. Make sure you are not late as well." General Pago headed out the kitchen and through the front entrance of the building, off to his next meeting.

"How about you stay with me, Mister Luka? I could use some help around here, I am cooking as much as I can for the evacuated families," Litia crouched down and reached for his hand. "I need someone to test the honeydew pie for me..." Luka's eyes widened as he eagerly looked up to Benjin for an answer.

"Of course, Buba. Be sure you are on your best behavior for Miss Litia." He picked Luka up and gave him a kiss on the cheek. "Ready?" He looked at Jon.

"Let's go!" He headed towards the door before pausing. "Just to be safe, everyone should have a blade on them."

"I don't go anywhere without mine." Laago grinned.

"Should I bring my bow?"

"No, it may intimidate the citizens, but you should bring your blade."

"I don't have one."

"How have you traveled all this way without a dagger?" Jon's mouth was agape, his expression bewildered. "I think everyone should carry one, especially girls. Here, come with me."

I followed him up the stairs to his room. My mind drifted to Quacho and his skinny pale body. My hands turned ice cold and my stomach churned, I wanted to throw up. After we left that village, Laago promised he would get me a dagger, but our time ran short and we had little opportunity to shop at the markets. I fantasized what could have happened if I had one with me when Quacho tried to assault me. I could have sliced his little friend clean off his body.

"What are you smiling about?" Jon asked as he held the metal hatch open.

"Nothing." My eyes widened, embarrassed that such a sick thought brought me pleasure.

"It must have been an interesting experience to travel from Tinshe to here. You probably got to see so much."

"I feel like I have only seen such a small portion of the world."

"To think most people live their whole life without leaving their city... It's a shame," Jon said as he rummaged through his bookcase. "Will you return to Tinshe when the war is over and your father is freed?"

"I don't know... I would like to continue to travel, maybe go all the way across the Great Ocean to the east, if I don't have to already go there to find my father."

"I wish I could do that too."

"You can."

"I can't leave Terlu, I have too much responsibility here. The general has given me so much, I cannot abandon my duties."

"One day the general will be gone and it will be just you. Would you regret living your life for someone else?" Jon's eyes met mine, I never noticed how vibrantly green they were.

"You are far wiser than most sixteen-year-olds."

"Like you're so old." My face scrunched up. "Aren't you like sixteen too?"

"Sixteen?" He laughed. "I sure hope I don't look that young! I'm eighteen."

"You're only two years older!"

"And those two years are full of growth, both physically and mentally," he said as he pulled a steel dagger out of a pouch and guided my fingers around its black leather handle. "How does it feel?" Jon stood close to me. He smelt earthy, perhaps of sandalwood.

"I'm afraid I won't know how to use it."

"When the time comes, I think you'll know exactly what to do," he assured me as we climbed back through the hatch. "Jin has an extra thigh holster you can have, since you don't have a belt." As he stepped down the stairs, his long sword bounced against his leg.

"Let's see your new blade!" Laago called up the staircase. I pulled it out of its pouch and waved it around. "Look at you, you've got a nicer weapon than we do."

"Now I just have to figure out how to use it."

"It may be small and light, but it is sharp and strong. Take advantage of its speed," Benjin explained.

"You have two options, stab or slice!" Laago grinned.

"Here, Nyla." Jon handed me Jin's holster. "Make sure you fasten it tightly so it doesn't slip off of you."

"Thank you." My hands awkwardly fumbled as I tried to buckle it around my thigh.

"Let me help you." Jon crouched down and pulled the smooth leather strap through the buckle and squeezed. I felt my face blush. My eyes drifted away from Jon to Laago, who was subtly rolling his eyes. I quickly looked away and tried to ignore him. "Is this too tight?"

"No, I don't think so."

"Good. Is everyone ready to go?" Jon headed out the door and down the steps, with all of us following closely behind. "We will take my boat. It'll be much faster."

As we followed Jon through the city streets, I watched the people of Terlu. The air felt different, everyone seemed tense and anxious knowing war was imminent. Mothers ran by with their crying babies in arms, lugging suitcases behind them. Businesses were being boarded up with wooden planks and blinds were pulled down. Soldiers were in the streets, trying to create order in the mayhem.

Jon's boat was one of the only ones still left at the dock. I could see military boats spread throughout the bay over the horizon, all hovering close to shore, carefully blocking the entrance to the port. We all jumped in without speaking, the overwhelming chaos in the city was already wearing us down. Jon began to row, pumping the oars back and forth. Though he wasn't a big guy by any means, he was much stronger than he appeared.

"The Korja District is just northwest of here. It is definitely a rougher side of the city, but I am sure we will be fine. I imagine most people haven't evacuated yet and some people are probably planning to not leave at all. We need to convey the significance of the situation without terrifying them. I think we should split up into teams of two to cover more ground."

"Laago, want to go with me?" Benjin asked. Laago quickly glanced at me before meeting Benjin's stare. A fake smile plastered across his face to hide how he truly felt.

"Sure!" I felt the hesitation in his voice.

"Looks like it's me and you, Nyla." Jon nodded. "Most of the citizens know where the Ritu family's central estate is because it is almost like a tourist attraction, so as long as you inform them that it is their evacuation home, they will know where to go. It's a large red and gold mansion surrounded by gardens, northeast of Korja. Our main job is to encourage people to leave and to make sure they don't bring unnecessary things. Let's limit each person to one or two bags, depending on the size."

"Okay, so send them to the central Ritu estate and limit what they bring. Anything else?" Benjin clarified.

"Remind them to hide their valuables and to seal their homes. Comfort them and keep an eye out for thieves. You'll be fine, just follow your instincts."

"What if people don't want to listen to us?"

"It's a mandatory evacuation. Either they leave now, willingly and with their belongings, or they are forced out by our troops tomorrow. Oh, and here." Jon pulled two metal badges out from his pocket. "Fasten these on your shirts. They're official military badges."

"We look like we robbed soldiers!" Laago laughed, pinning the badge to his worn out shirt.

"It's better than nothing. Besides, I never wear one and I haven't had problems. I take military boats right off the dock and no one asks a single question."

"Being the general's adopted son probably helps," Laago jabbed.

The water was choppy, still rough from last night's storm. Jon carefully steered our boat into a worn-down dock, unaffected by the strong current. It was made of spruce wood, with cracked planks hanging on by rusty nails. He swiftly jumped off the boat and tightly tied it to the dock with a thick brown rope. The dock met a short sandy shoreline. There was a tall wooden staircase surrounded by big overgrown bushes that led up a steep hill to the Korja district.

"Let's hope this dock doesn't blow away," Laago joked.

"If it does, it'll be a long walk home." Jon held out his hand to Benjin, helping him onto the dock. "The Korja District is four blocks wide and most buildings are only a few stories high. Nyla and I will take the two western blocks, you guys can take the east. Meet back here an hour before dusk."

"Got it." Benjin nodded in affirmation.

"Team Laajin!" Laago high fived Benjin. "Or Bengo... I'll have to work on that."

"More like Team Benjin and Other!" He laughed.

"You wish, Benj."

"Nyla, be careful." Benjin put his hand on my shoulder. "Pay attention to your surroundings and stay close to Jon."

"Thanks, father!" I raised my eyebrows. "I'll make sure to keep Jon safe."

"I'll do my best to keep up with her," Jon called to them as we followed the smooth sandstone road away from them. "Alright, see you guys before dusk. Don't be late!"

"Got it, chief!"

And we were off. I stayed glued to Jon's side, fearing I would get lost in the crowd. He was a true city boy, it seemed he knew every nook and cranny of Terlu. As we moved through the mobs of people, I felt my anxiety grow. I did not worry of myself, but of Benjin and Laago. They didn't know the republic like Jon did, what if they got lost?

"They'll be fine." Jon looked back and smiled at me, grabbing my hand.

"How did you know I was worrying about them?"

"Just had a feeling."

He weaved through the crowd and into an apartment building, about three stories high. The apartment buildings here remind me of home, though they are a bit nicer. Perhaps it was the smell- the scent of people and life. Each apartment was not just a place to sleep in, but a home full of life and stories. If the walls could talk...

"Attention! There has been a mandatory evacuation issued by President Suin and General Pago. You are to report to the Ritu family's central estate, where you will be housed and fed until further notice. We are limiting possessions to one bag per person." His voice was loud and firm as it echoed through the hall, catching the attention of the ten or so people. It even caught me off guard. Everyone fell silent.

"What about my mother? She's too old to walk that far!" A woman cried.

"General Pago will be sending troops tomorrow at dawn to assist any elderly that cannot evacuate on their own. That is the only circumstance in which you may remain home until then."

"You can't kick us out of our homes!" A man shouted.

"I understand your anger, but we want to ensure that we can protect everyone. We can't guarantee that if people are too close to the wall."

"That delusional militia isn't making it past our wall! This is ridiculous!"

"We have to prepare for the worst, sir. Everyone must be out before dusk, otherwise you will be forced out," Jon stressed. The people began to murmur as they headed back to their apartments, hopefully to begin evacuating.

"I don't think I am cut out for this..." I whispered to him.

"I used to hate public speaking too, but you get used to it." He banged on our first apartment door. "Direct orders from the President and General, open up."

Jon sounded different, his voice was deeper, sterner, and a bit intimidating. Even how he stood changed, before he slouched like a typical boy, but now he stood firm and tall. The door slowly creaked open and on the other side stood a man with a messy overgrown beard and long unbrushed hair that stuck out in every direction.

"It wasn't me!" The man fretted, his face was ghost white.

"We are here to inform you of a mandatory evacuation issued by the President."

"Oh, right... I heard about that..."

"You must evacuate before dusk or else you will be forcibly removed. Report to the Ritu central estate." Jon stepped back. "So I would be out before then, especially if you are hiding something." He smirked, nodding to me that it was time to move on. As we walked away, I couldn't help but glance back at the man, who stood there unmoving. I tugged on Jon's shirt for his attention.

"Shouldn't we see what he is up to? He was awfully sketchy..."

"We have much bigger things to worry about."

Most of the apartments we went to were uneventful. Some people had already left, others tried to fight the orders. After Jon's reasoning with them, most agreed to leave, especially knowing the military would force them out eventually regardless. But everyone seemed scared. All of the children cried, the mothers were on edge, and the fathers deeply worried. Many of these homes were family heirlooms, passed down from generation to generation. They lived their whole lives in the Korja District, their children were born here and their parents have passed here.

I expected this would be challenging, however, it turned out to be difficult in ways I could not have imagined. Jon tried to comfort the people of Korja, but we had no guarantee of anything. No answers, just hopeful promises. Unfortunately, from what I have learned over the years, promises tend to be broken. We did not know if the militia would break through the secure walls of Terlu. We did not know if these citizens' homes would be destroyed. All we could do was hope for the best. And hope can be a frightening thing to cling to.

I mostly stayed quiet, practically hiding behind Jon. It felt wrong for me to be there in a situation so intimate, as if I was invading their privacy. I could tell everything was wearing Jon down too. As we made it to the second, then third apartment building, his knuckles grew red from knocking and his words became briefer.

"Mandatory evacuation to the Ritu family's central estate. Be out before sundown or be forced out in the morning." He walked away, leaving the woman standing in her doorway, mouth agape.

"It will be okay, miss," I said in an attempt to console her, as her three screaming kids ran around behind her. "The military will provide both shelter and food. Just bring any important and necessary items with you. You can bring one bag per person." She slowly nodded her head, still shocked by the orders. "It will be okay." I reached out to hold her hand, but she pulled me in and hugged me tightly, weeping into my shoulder. She sputtered words between tears, but I could not understand her.

By the time I caught up with Jon, he was headed to the top floor. He pushed his hair out of his face and looked at me with a sad smile. Sometimes, one look can say more than a hundred words ever could. I knew he truly understood how I felt. It seemed we both carried the burden of other peoples' pain more than some might.

"Having fun?" He pursed his lips together, rubbing his temples.

"Not at all."

"Me neither." He sighed as he knocked on the door. "My head is killing me."

"Who's there?" A man's voice called.

"Open up! I have orders from President Suin and the general."

"Hold onto your boots, boy." An elderly man with a hunched over back opened the door. "What, they sent two pups to deliver important news? This better be good."

"There's a mandatory evacuation. The Korja District must be vacant by dusk. All citizens report to the Ritu family's central estate."

"Over my dead body!" The man went to slam the door on our faces, but Jon stuck his hand out.

"Leave by dusk or be forced out at dawn by the military," he declared, as he dropped his hand and began to walk away.

"I'll tell you who the real tyrants are..." The man mumbled as he shut his door.

"It's as if we are throwing them over the wall to feed the militants. Gods forbid we try to protect our citizens!" Jon spat.

"Listen..."

"No one respects the government anymore. No one respects the military." He threw his hands up as we headed to the next door. When he got angry it seemed to take over his whole body. "Everything we do is for these people and yet they're so ungrateful!"

"Jon, you're focusing too much on the few hostile people. Most people are just scared, but they seemed to appreciate us."

He did not respond and that was okay, because I knew that just as the people of Korja were engulfed with fear, so was he. It had not been long since Jon found stability from the plague that left him a homeless orphan and now the militia wished to take that from him. He knocked on the next door, feeling a bit weaker than he was before.

As he spoke to the remaining people of the apartment building, I couldn't help but think about the last few weeks. Everything I did was for the good of the world. If I went through what I did and was shamed for my actions, I would be devastated. Jin's disgusted reaction to me killing those militants was enough. I couldn't blame her though, because if you told me a year ago that I would take a life, I would have reacted similarly.

"I'm sorry I snapped." Jon bit his cheek as we headed back down the stairwell. "It wasn't right for me to take my frustrations out on you."

"It's okay."

"I feel like no matter what I do, being affiliated with the military always casts a shadow. Some people hate us and I don't understand why. I know some soldiers do bad things, but most people join the army to help the world, not destroy it."

"I understand."

"I feel like you rarely say what's on your mind. What do you actually think?"

"I don't know." I looked down at the stairs as I walked.

"Nyla, you look like you're always thinking. Just be honest."

"I think a lot of citizens, regardless of where they live, have had bad interactions with people in power- whether it be politicians, soldiers, or their bosses. So it causes a natural distrust," I reflected, thinking of my own experiences in Tinshe. "We don't know what the people here have been through and we do not know what they have seen. I understand if they feel weary. But in response, it cannot anger those people in power, instead they have to understand this and use it to mend the barrier. If you fight fire with fire, where will that get you?"

"We will all get burned." Jon nodded his head in agreement.

"I don't think it is the responsibility of the people as much as it is the soldiers and officials. I think the people in power need to step up and be the bigger person, otherwise this issue will never heal."

"Perhaps you are right," he said as we stepped outside of the apartment and into the street. The sun was starting to break through the clouds, shining its warm rays down onto us. I looked up at him and our eyes met. "I like when you're honest."

"Well, to be honest, I'm used to Benjin or Laago talking over me." I quickly looked back at the ground.

"Get off me!" A woman shrieked. My eyes shot back up and I saw a man pull a woman's bag from her.

"Hey!" Jon's voice roared. "Stop!"

The man did one final pull before ripping it from the woman's hands and fleeing down an alley. Jon jumped over the apartment steps and bolted after him, weaving in and out of people. I did my best to follow him, but he was fast. He turned down the alley after the man and jumped over a pile of garbage the man knocked over behind him.

As I turned the next corner, I almost smashed into Jon, who was stopped dead in his tracks. The man stood with a long steel sword pointed towards us. He had a sour grimace on his face and wore ragged clothes.

"Carry on, kids!" His lips curled. "Go on now, scram." He raised his sword closer to us. Jon raised his badge.

"I'm ordering you on behalf of the republic's army to drop your weapon."

"Ha!" The thief fake laughed. "A couple of kids playing soldier. Well, I ain't playin' with yous. I'll slice your pretty little head clean off, then your girlfriend's."

Before he could even finish his sentence Jon pulled his sword from his belt and hit it against the man's sword, hard enough for him to lose balance and have to take a step back. But before he regained his footing, Jon lunged forward and grabbed the man's wrist, twisting it back until he dropped his sword. The thief dropped the woman's bag and swung his fist at Jon, but he swiftly ducked and slammed his shoulder into the man's chest, knocking him onto the ground. I ran forward and grabbed the man's fallen sword, so he couldn't recover it.

"You're not very good at playing thief," Jon sneered.

"That's him!" The woman ran behind me pointing her finger at the man. A soldier followed closely behind her.

"You are under arrest!" He shouted, as the man tried scrambling to his feet to run away.

"Looks like you have things under control." Jon nodded to the soldier as he walked away, tossing the stolen bag back to the woman.

"Thanks, kid. You should think about joining the army someday."

"Yeah, I'll think about it." Jon raised his eyebrows and kept walking to hide his grin. "We should get back to the dock."

The sun was just beginning to fall in the sky, though it was not yet setting. It ended up being a beautiful day out, despite last night's storm. The sky was painted with soft white clouds, but the shy sun would poke out and shed some light down, warming us up from the cool sea breeze. Its rays casted a golden hue against the building walls.

"Jon, how do you always know what I am thinking?"

"Because I am a mind reader." He looked over to me and smiled.

"That's what it feels like."

"I don't know, I've always been like that. Growing up, my mother called it my intuition. She was the same way, it really felt like she was reading my mind growing up. It made it difficult to get away with anything."

"Wow, I wish I had that." Jon could take one glance at me and know what I was thinking, even if I tried to mask it. I could never figure out what Benjin or Laago were thinking.

"It can sometimes be hard to shut off. Like before, the weight of every person's baggage began to weigh me down. My head was spinning by the time we got to the last apartment building. I have gotten debilitating headaches from it since I was a kid."

"That must be really difficult to cope with, but there is some good in it too. You seem to really understand people."

"I used to hate it, I thought I was cursed. Especially during the plague, when everyone around me was suffering, I felt like I was suffocating. That's why when General Pago took me in, he built me my own place on the roof. He knew I needed complete solitude to maintain inner balance, so the pain of everyone around me wouldn't drown me."

"I did think it was a bit odd you lived on the roof like that."

"What, you don't like my place?"

"No, it's just-"

"I'm just playing, Ny." My face blushed, Laago was the only person to ever call me that. It almost felt wrong to come from anyone else's lips. "Have you ever had a honey-glazed sweet potato stick?" He walked up to a food stand, engulfed by a delicious aroma.

"No..."

"We'll take two." He tossed the vendor some coins before handing me one.

"I feel bad, I have no money," I said, hesitant to take it.

"It's on me."

"Thank you." I bit into it, its sweetness overrunning my tastebuds. "It's incredible!" I had never eaten something so flavorful. In Tinshe, we ate to survive. Ingredients like honey were rare to come by and even if a store had it, I would never be able to afford such a delicacy.

"My favorite part of working for the army is trying food in new places."

"I am sure there are so many delicious choices out here."

"Hey!" Jon called down the staircase to Benjin and Laago, who were already at the dock. "Looks like they made friends," he commented as we made our way down.

Two girls were with them. One had long black hair pulled into a side braid, almost reaching her waist. She had bangs that she gently pushed aside on her forehead, covering her eyebrows. I could see her bright smile from here. She stood in front of Benjin, her hands clasped behind her back. My jaw dropped when I realized Benjin was smiling too. Not just a polite smile, but an authentic happy smile covering his face. His eyes were glistening in the sun.

"How'd it go for you two?" Benjin asked.

Laago sat towards the edge of the dock with a tiny girl, no taller than me, whose legs hung over the dock. He was so focused on their conversation that he did not even notice Jon and me. She started to laugh flirtatiously and dropped her hands onto his leg. My heart was pounding.

"It went well!" I bragged, faking my cheerfulness. "Jon even stopped a crime."

"No way, what happened?" Benjin's eyes widened.

"It was just a mugger, nothing serious." He shrugged, before changing the subject. "Nice to meet you, ladies!"

"Oh, I don't mean to be rude. This is Kalah and Suta, they live in Korja and work at a flower stand together."

"It is a pleasure to meet you." Kalah bowed her head.

"Hiya!" The tiny girl called over to us, as she kicked her feet about in the water. She also had her hair pulled back into a braid, but hers sat on her back. The girls wore matching scarlet aprons.

"It seems we have a little time to spare before dusk... Nyla, would you like to come with me to get another sweet potato stick?" Jon smiled.

"Sure!" I quickly responded, eager to be anywhere but here. I turned around and began climbing back up the flimsy wooden staircase that connected the dock to the smooth sandstone road. I felt my face flush red with jealousy. Jon ran to catch up with me.

"Benjin looks happy."

"I haven't seen him smile like that since the plague hit."

"Really? I figured he had a bunch of girls back home. He's a good looking guy."

"There was a girl from Kosi whom he dated for like ten years, but her family fled Tinshe during the plague, and he never saw her again. We don't know if she is alive or not."

"The unknown is a tortuous place." His eyes drifted shut for a moment. While he stood here with me, his mind was sent back in time, perhaps to a memory stuck deep within his heart. "Not knowing, I mean. I would rather know, good or bad, rather than be stuck in the purgatory that is the in-between."

"Me too," I replied. I sensed a familiar longing in him, one that often plagues Benjin as well, but it didn't seem to be a story that he was ready to share.

"Back for more?" The man running the stand asked.

"Yes, please. We'll take two more." Jon handed him coins.

"Lucky girl! My wife never buys me things," the man joked as we walked away.

"What about you, do you have a girlfriend?" I asked.

"No." He bit into his sweet potato. "I have had a few over the years, but none really lasted."

"Why not?"

"I'm always too busy with work. It seems girls tend to dislike being your second priority." Though he grinned, something in the way he spoke makes me believe he was holding back from telling me the whole picture. But that was okay, it wasn't my business anyway. We stood at the top of the staircase, looking down at the dock.

"I don't blame them. What's the point of having a boyfriend who is never there?"

"Ouch!" He laughed, leaning against the wooden railing. The sun was just beginning to set. "What about you, have you ever had a boyfriend?"

"No," I admitted.

"Why not?"

"I don't know, it just never happened. Boys never seem to notice me." I shrugged, feeling sorry for myself, until Jon let out a big howl of laughter. My head jerked back and my ears turned red; I couldn't help but feel defensive.

"Maybe it's because you have a ten-foot-tall personal bodyguard who could squash any guy who looks twice at you." He looked down at my brother, who stood towering over Kalah.

"Benjin?"

"No, Luka," he joked. "Look at Benjin! He is undeniably intimidating."

"No way, he's a gentle giant."

"Yeah, I know that, but most suitors wouldn't take that risk," he guessed. I never even thought about that. Perhaps Benjin did scare boys away, without either of us realizing it. There was no way he would do it on purpose. Or, maybe that was just an excuse and boys really didn't care for me. "Well, either way, they are missing out," Jon said as he tossed his sweet potato stick over the ledge and headed down the staircase. I stood there for a moment, caught off guard by his sincerity, before I ran down the stairs to catch up with him.

"Time to go?" Laago asked, rising to his feet. He held his hand down to Suta and pulled her up.

"Come visit me soon," Kalah said. Her voice was smooth and sweet.

"I will," Benjin lied, before he stepped into the boat and took a seat.

I jumped in after him, watching Laago say his goodbye to Suta out of the corner of my eye. She stood on her tiptoes and kissed him on the cheek. I turned around and looked at the sunset, trying not to boil over with jealousy. It was like a watercolor painting across the sky. The ocean was a deep blue, its surface shimmering from the sun's rays. Laago got in the boat as Jon began to untie it from the dock, pushing us off into the ocean as he jumped in too.

"What a beautiful sunset..." Benjin remarked.

"The sun may set a thousand times in our lives, but each time feels like the first. It never gets old," Jon affirmed.

"I wish we could have hung out with those girls for a little longer, Benj," Laago groaned. "They were fun. It felt like the good old days for a moment."

"Except in the good old days, one of them would wound up having her boyfriend show up and chase us down a few blocks." Benjin chuckled.

As I gazed at the setting sun, I reminisced of my childhood. Every year on my birthday, Juu and Tasi would sleep over. We'd play make believe all day, then bake a cake with my mother. We would stay up until sunrise gossiping and giggling. My father used to tell the best stories about evil spirits. He would shut off the lights and we would all huddle onto the balcony, with Luchi too, and squeal in fear. Dalia was very little, so she was too scared to listen. Whenever my father would blow out the candles, she would run to my mother and cover her face, knowing the stories were beginning.

"The good old days..." I sighed longingly. Benjin reached over and put his hand on my knee. It was no secret that memories brought back more sadness and pain than anything else.

We pulled up to the dock, the side of our boat scraping against the wooden planks. Jon jumped out first and tied our boat back to the dock. We quickly followed Jon off the boat and through the streets towards his home. I immediately noticed the city was empty, there was not a soul in sight, meaning the evacuation was a success. Huang was a major access point to the Republic of Terlu, making it an obvious target for the militants. If they could secure Huang, the republic would quickly fall.

"It's a ghost town," Laago marveled. Doors were hastily covered with wooden boards, windows were nailed shut. Potted plants and decorations were all brought inside. There were no food stands to be seen.

"I've never seen Huang so empty," Jon sputtered in awe, stepping up his front stairs. General Pago swung the door open.

"There you are!" He ushered us in. "Get your things together. It's time to go."

"Yessir," Jon replied.

"Benji!" Luka squealed, running over to us.

"Hey, Buba!" Benjin scooped him up and gave him a kiss on the cheek. "How was your day?" He asked, carrying him up the staircase with us.

"Fun!" He cheered. "We made a bunch of pies!"

"You made or you ate?" He tickled Luka's stomach.

"We made and ate!" Luka giggled. "They were so yummy."

"I hope you saved one for me."

"I ate them all, Benji!"

"All of them?"

"Mhm, a hundred!"

"No..."

"No wait, it was a thousand!"

"That's a lot of pie, Luka!" Laago chimed in, as we walked through the hatch and onto the roof.

We all began getting our belongings in order. I felt tremendously anxious. All I had was my bag and my bow, but I still felt as though I was forgetting something. I looked over to Luka, who did not seem to yet understand the severity of the situation. I dreaded the idea of leaving him behind, even if it was for the best. We were family, we had to stick together.

"You're going to watch after Jin and Litia for me while we are gone, right?" Jon sat on his knee in front of Luka.

"I will keep them safe." He pulled his baton from his belt loop and smacked it against his hand.

"I am glad I can count on you. Thank you." He rubbed Luka's head and stood back up. "Is everyone ready?"

We all filed back downstairs. My arrows bounced against my hip. I rubbed my hand through them for comfort. Each step down the stairs I felt more and more nauseous. General Pago stood by the front door waiting for us.

"I do not want to arouse any suspicion, so I will not join you to the dock," he declared. "Litia, give them the food."

"Here!" Litia hustled over to us, handing Jon a bag. "This should be more than enough."

"You should arrive at the Island of Aara in two and a half days. Jon will navigate you towards the Hua Stream, which will swiftly pull your boat to the island."

"What's that?" Laago asked.

"It's a really strong ocean current that will practically launch us directly to the island. If we paddle on top of that, we may even make it there in two days flat," Jon estimated.

"Be safe and follow your instincts." General Pago put his hand on Jon's shoulder, then pulled him in for a hug. The door swung open and Jin ran in.

"Jon!" She yelled, grabbing onto him and squeezing him tight. "I thought I missed you."

"I would never leave without saying goodbye, Jin."

"You better be back soon!" She glared at him. "Promise me."

"I promise," he said, stepping towards the door.

"I love you so much, Buba." Benjin squeezed him one more time before he set him down. He did his best to hold back his tears and put on a brave face for Luka. "We will be back before you even know it."

"I love you too, Benji," his voice grew quiet. I dropped to my knees and wrapped myself around Luka, kissing the top of his head. "Bye bye, Nyla."

"Love you." I rose to my feet and nearly walked out the door, but before I did, I took the old painting of my family from my bag and gave it to Luka. I wanted him to have it. "We'll see you soon, Luka. Be a good boy while we are gone." He took it in his hands, rubbing his little finger along the edge, before turning to Litia.

"Can I have more pie, Miss Litia?" Luka pleaded. I couldn't help but smile at his innocence.

We followed Jon out the door and began running towards the dock. It was dark out, but Jon could navigate through this city blindfolded. I knew how he felt, leaving his sister for the first time, as I had never left Luka for longer than a day's work. I felt a lump grow in my throat at the thought. Although we know it was for the best, it did not hurt any less. For Jon, it would be much easier for him to just stay behind and protect Jin, but instead he was sacrificing his own wishes for the greater good. I looked over at him as we ran through the streets, but his eyes seemed focused on what was in front of him, not behind.

I felt a heavy weight in my chest, a familiar one that I have carried for the majority of this wretched journey. Fleeting moments of security and comfort were full of false hope, as they were always closely followed by suffering and hardship. Darkness engulfed the sky, not even the moon dared to shine. Though it looked eerie, I knew it was for the best. The darker it was, the safer we were from the militants. I looked solemnly out at the vast ocean. Once we set sail, we were at the mercy of her will. Anything could be out there, waiting for us beyond the horizon.

Laago jumped down into the rickety wooden boat and held his hand out to me. The boat rocked as I stepped in, but the water was calm and still. I prayed the rest of our journey would be so. Benjin stepped on next, taking a seat in the middle of the boat. Jon followed, untying our boat and pushing off the dock to begin the next chapter of our journey. He sat down at the back of the boat and picked up the oars, rowing us deeper into the black abyss.

# CHAPTER SIXTEEN

# ACROSS THE GREAT OCEAN

W E WERE DEEP IN the Bay of Suhai when the sun finally began to rise. I felt nauseous, hot, and sticky, but most of all, I felt trapped on this tiny boat- a mere speck in the Great Ocean. Even with General Pago's assurance, Bao's words still echoed in my head: *A boat in open waters? You will be as vulnerable as a fish flopping on dry land. Like sitting ducks!*

As much as I respected General Pago, I still felt weary. What if, to him, we were just pawns in his game of war? If it would help keep his republic safe, surely he would sacrifice some kids. And I couldn't blame him, it was his duty to protect his people. No...

I looked over to Jon, who laid next to me. He rowed through the night without a single complaint, only allowing Benjin to take over about an hour ago. General Pago would never put his son in danger. He viewed Jon and Jin as his own, his only surviving family beside Bao. I tried to ignore my negative thoughts, but instead they just multiplied. I gripped onto my flimsy bow, our only form of protection.

"When the sun reaches its highest point, it will be overwhelmingly hot. It is best for us to over hydrate now, otherwise we will face the consequences later." Jon pulled a military grade water purifier from his forest-green backpack. "Fortunately for us, we have an unlimited supply of water."

"I don't like the idea of drinking ocean water..." Benjin said. "How does it work?"

"A team of army engineers designed it for our navy. I know this long tube has three separate chambers. I believe that one is for removing minerals, another heats the water, and the third condenses it back to its liquid form. Here, feel it. It's heavier than it looks." Jon handed it to Benjin, who fumbled it around in his hands and examined it.

"I really want to jump in and cool off." Laago dragged his hand in the cold water alongside the boat.

"I wouldn't. We have lost many great men and women in our navy to the Great Ocean. The current is unbelievably strong and fast, which is useful to us in our journey, but unforgiving for those who are not prepared. There are underwater whirlpools under this stream and caves that can suck you in. Once the current has a hold of you, it will not let you go." I shuttered at Jon's words. "Not to mention the whalesh-"

"I'll take my chances," Laago interrupted. He stood up and unbuttoned his pants to pee over the edge of the boat. I could tell Jon's endless knowledge and wisdom irked him. Laago never did well with authority, especially coming from a kid younger than him.

"You sure are stubborn." Jon chuckled. I held my breath for a moment, unsure how Laago would react, but instead he just laughed.

"Yeah, I am, aren't I?" He sat back down in the boat.

"If you had to get through a path and you had the choice of getting Laago to move over or a giant boulder to, you would have a better shot reasoning with the boulder," Benjin joked.

"Laago's skull is thicker than a boulder," I chimed in.

"Alright, alright." He waved his hands in defeat. "Point taken. I'm waving my white flag!"

Here I was, worrying for my life, but also laughing at the boys' antics. I looked over to Benjin, who stood up to stretch his legs. His body was practically as long as the boat. The sun's light kissed his face, gradually turning his cheekbones and nose a soft pink. Benjin laid back down in the boat, his eyes slowly shutting. He looked so peaceful, his hands rested behind his head and his legs hung over the boat's edge. Since I saw him with that Korja District girl, his smile seemed a bit brighter. Maybe he realized there were other fish in the sea afterall.

My thoughts were interrupted by Jon. Though he didn't say anything, I felt him staring at me. Not an empty or blank stare, but more of a deep gaze. I quickly looked down at my feet. What was he thinking? I glanced back up. My confusion must have shown in my face, because he began to grin.

"What are you looking at?" I snapped defensively, feeling my face redden.

"You."

"Why?"

"I don't know," Laago interrupted. His head rested on the boat's edge, his arms dangling in the water up to his elbows. "Maybe because we are all stuck on a boat the size of a coffin together- there's only so much to look at."

"You're cute," Jon said, ignoring Laago. Benjin flinched, his eyes quickly shot open. Laago lifted his head, curious to see what Jon would dare to say next. "The way you look at Benjin reminds me of Jin."

"Was little Nyla admiring her big ol' brother?" Benjin's suspicious glare quickly faded to a toothy smile. He rolled over and reached for me, but I smacked his hands away. "Come on, give your brother a hug."

"It's too hot for that!" I wiped the sweat dripping off my forehead.

"Sounds like it's someone's time of the mo-" I hit Laago in the bicep with all my might before he could finish his sentence. "Ow! Watch my wound, it's not fully healed yet!"

"You deserved that one." Benjin laughed.

Our boat was cruising through the ocean, we barely even had to row. At this rate, we would arrive at the Island of Aara in no time. Though it didn't necessarily feel like it, every wave we passed brought us a moment closer. As the day dragged on, my anxiety faded. The further we traveled, the safer we were. Or so I thought.

Laago fidgeted in his seat. Every time he shifted from one side to another, the wooden plank he sat on squeaked. He stood up, stretched one leg and then the other, before sitting back down again. He slapped his hand on his thighs and beat his head, humming to an old folk song, over and over again. I tried to tune him out, but the more I did, the more I focused on his obnoxious behavior. Benjin and Jon seemed to not even notice it.

Benjin laid with his butt on the boat's floor and his legs dangling over the edge. His eyes were shut, but I don't think he was asleep, perhaps just daydreaming. I'm sure his head could use the rest, considering the concussion, which is something he would never do unless he was forced to. Benjin really shouldn't be exerting himself if he wanted his injury to heal properly.

Jon pushed the oars back and forth. He took back over from Benjin only a few hours after they originally rotated. He was even worse at sitting still than Laago. Once he stopped rowing, he didn't stop talking. I think that's why Benjin surrendered the oars back to him so quickly, he knew it was the only way to get some peace and quiet. My arms would have fallen off if I rowed that long, so would any sane person's, but Jon didn't seem to mind. He actually seemed to enjoy it. His eyes wandered all around, flickering between the ocean and the sky. Most people would get bored of staring off to the ocean after a whole day of rowing, but I think Jon really appreciated the beauty of the world around him.

Laago abruptly rose to his feet again and stretched down to touch his toes, rocking the boat. He then swung his arms up to the sky, extending them upwards, and then back down. Once he felt he was done with that, he began twisting his back to crack it. His eyes bounced around too, but definitely out of boredom, not appreciation for the nature around him.

"Let's play a game!" Laago decided.

"Anything to stop you from fidgeting," I said.

"What do you want to play?" Benjin sluggishly sat up, rubbing his eyes.

"I dunno." Laago shrugged.

"Two truths and one lie?" Jon suggested.

"How do you play?"

"It's as simple as it sounds. You say two truthful statements and one lie, then we try to guess what the lie is. We used to play this a lot in Huang."

"Sounds easy enough. I'll go first." Laago plopped back into his seat, rubbing his hands together. "Okay, I've never had a fried egg, my mom is a harlot, and I have had over twenty girlfriends."

"You've eaten a fried egg at my house. That's the lie!" Benjin wagged his finger.

"Your mom is a-" Jon gasped, only to be cut off by Laago.

"Yup, that's how I was born. She was knocked up by one of her clients." He smiled, surprising me.

"Wow, what was that like growing up?" Jon asked.

"I never met her, she dumped me on my pops when I was born. My mom never wanted me to begin with," Laago admitted.

His words may have sounded dark, but I don't think they were meant to be. He did not sound upset or angry, more so just stating the truth. It seemed he had accepted it. In the past, he never mentioned her. Now, he was not only opening up about it, but doing so bluntly and seamlessly. Perhaps our journey helped Laago become a more confident man, who knew something like that did not define him. I envied his self assurance.

"I am sorry. That must have been rough," Jon said.

"If Laago had good parents, he would have never fled the outskirts. We would have never met each other," Benjin emphasized. "Life would be so boring without you."

"It's true, I dropped two absent parents and picked up a loving family. I consider myself lucky."

"Love you, brother." Benjin hit his fist against Laago's knee.

My heart suddenly felt warm and full. When Laago had opened up to me about his parents, I perceived it as a tragedy, a disadvantage that held him back. But it wasn't one, because he did not allow it to be. Instead, he chose to view it positively, as a gift. It was a conscious decision he made. It served as a reminder that nothing was good nor bad, until you decide which it will be.

For Laago to say that what he experienced as a child was worth it for the love my family brought him was an honor. Little did he know, we were just as lucky to have him in our lives as well. I couldn't imagine life without him. He had always been there for my family. If my parents weren't home, he would help Benjin watch Luchi, Dalia, Luka, and me. If our apartment needed a repair, he would put us to the top of his list and push back his other appointments.

"Are we just going to ignore the fact that Laago's had over twenty girlfriends?" Jon commented.

"Probably more like thirty to forty," Benjin estimated, rubbing his chin.

"Who knows!" Laago shrugged. Jon's jaw dropped at their cavalier manner. "Your turn, Benj."

"Hm, let me think." He looked out to the ocean. "I can hold my breath for four minutes, I am allergic to sage, and I hate being so tall."

"There's no way you hate being tall," Jon scoffed.

"You're allergic to thyme, not sage," I revealed. A wide grin spread across Benjin's face.

"You caught me."

"Why on Earth would you hate being tall?" Jon exclaimed.

"My neck hurts from always having to look down."

"Oh, boo-hoo. Poor Benj, always having to look down on the common-folk," Laago teased. "Cry me a river."

"I would kill to be taller," I said.

"Believe me, I would give you a few of my inches if I could."

"At least you're a girl, so it isn't a big deal," Jon consoled me.

"It doesn't matter what gender you are, being perceived as weak all the time isn't fun."

"Anyone who thinks you are weak is sadly mistaken. You are tough as rocks, Ny."

"Let people think what they want and don't concern yourself with their foolish opinions. Good people do not judge others for what they cannot control." Jon's words came from his heart. They were genuine and true.

"The kid is right," Laago agreed. He put his comforting hand on my back. "You're up, Jon."

"Okay, ready?"

"Ready."

"I hate being in tight spaces, I was voted most likely to teach a teacher in school, and I once fought off a fuji ox with only a paint-brush and a match."

"The last one is a lie!" Laago shouted eagerly, but Jon shook his head. "You're messing with us."

"I swear it."

"Well, you have to tell us about it now."

"I was doing work for the army in the northern outskirts about a year ago. I believe I was up there for a month. Well, one day I found myself with some time to kill, so I headed towards the coast to overlook Eura's Harbor. What I didn't know was that about two days before, a boat came to transport twelve fuji oxes to a farm and two of them escaped."

"No way!" Benjin shook his head. "What happened?"

"So I pull off the main path and am in the middle of peeing in the woods when I feel like something is watching me. By the time I but-ton my pants back up and turn around, a fuji ox is running full steam at me and I can tell he was not happy. A million thoughts immediately pop in my head, with one underlying theme, how in-the-Urliq can I get this thing to back off?" Our eyes were wide, enthralled in his story. "I reached into my back pocket, hoping for a blade, but all I had was a dirty ol' paintbrush from work. But I remembered I had a box of matches on me and stuck one to light the paintbrush on fire. As the beast was about a foot from me, I waved my inflamed paintbrush in its face and it turned around so fast it nearly tripped over its own feet."

"You are full of it!" Laago rolled his eyes.

"Believe me or not, but it is true." Jon shrugged. "I'll tell you, that was the last time I went anywhere without my dagger."

"I would've pissed myself!" Benjin laughed.

"I probably would have, had I not just gone."

"So which is the lie?" I asked.

"I already forgot the other two," Laago said.

"I don't actually mind tight spaces, in fact, I find them kind of comforting," Jon said. "Your turn, Nyla."

"Someone else can go, I'll pass."

"Everyone else already went."

"Come on, Ny, give it a go," Laago insisted.

"Alright, let me think," I surrendered. "I have never broken a bone, I am very flexible, and I hate turnips."

"Has she broken a bone?" Laago looked at Benjin curiously.

"No, she hasn't." Benjin rubbed his chin. "I don't remember if she likes turnips, though."

"I've never seen Ny eat one, now that I think about it," Laago pondered. He looked over at Jon, who shrugged.

"Sorry, boys, I am no help on this one."

"My final answer is turnips!" Laago roared.

"Wrong, I actually like turnips," I said. "I'm less flexible than you, Benjin, you know that!"

"Of course I knew that!" He smacked his hand onto his forehead. "So does Nyla win?"

"There's not really a final winner, but since she stumped us, she goes again until we get it right. Then the rotation continues."

"You heard the man." Laago nudged me.

We played round after round, as the sun gently set in the sky. The sunset was beautiful, it engulfed the entire horizon in front of us. Long thin clouds stretched across the sky, partially covering the orange sun, as it melted into the sparkling blue ocean, turning the sky pink and purple. A flock of white seabirds flew over my head, flapping their feathery wings into the distance. I laid next to Benjin and nuzzled into him. The sun's heat was being replaced by a cool sea breeze that hit against my sunburnt cheeks. I fell asleep listening to the hums of their voices, as they talked and joked into the night.

Floating through the water felt peaceful, almost therapeutic. The boat gently rose and lowered over the water, like I was a child being rocked to sleep. I slept peacefully through the night and did not wake until the sun began to rise over the horizon. There was still no land in sight, just crashing waves for as far as the eye could see. I slowly lifted myself from the bottom of the boat and slid into my seat, careful to not wake Benjin.

"Good morning, sunshine," Laago chirped. "How did you sleep?"

He was rowing gingerly, helping the boat smoothly sail through the strong current. I looked over to Jon. He was curled up in a ball, knocked out. They must have rotated while I was asleep. I must have been pretty tired to not wake when they walked over me.

"Pretty well, surprisingly." I reached my arms up and stretched my back.

"Luckily it didn't get too cold last night."

"Yeah, I don't know what we would've done."

"Freeze?"

"I guess that would've been our only option." I chuckled. "How long have you been rowing for?"

"A couple hours," he said with a calm look in his eyes.

"I wouldn't last thirty minutes."

"It's not as bad as it seems, it's actually a bit soothing. Besides, I think you are underestimating yourself."

"I don't know about that." I raised my arms and flexed my lack of muscles.

"I forget how tiny you are sometimes." Laago grinned.

"It is peaceful out here." My eyes drifted back to the rising sun.

"Now it is. Before, when you were all asleep, the stars were my only light. The moon wasn't even there to guide me. It felt so eerie, like we were sailing into a void."

"Are you afraid of the dark?" I teased. When our eyes met, he shook his head, a mischievous grin forming on his lips as he averted his gaze. "What?"

"It's nothing."

"Tell me."

"In another life..."

"What?"

"I think we were together in another life."

"What do you mean?"

"Don't overthink it." He smirked and shifted his gaze to the rising sun. "I feel strangely at ease here."

"You can't just change the subject!" My face blushed.

"I have felt anxious since I got on this boat, but last night, when I was rowing, I began to really panic. I had a really bad feeling that something was going to happen. It loomed closely over, practically suffocating me. Have you ever gotten that?"

"Yes, many times. This trip has been one big panic attack for me."

"I knew you would understand. My heart was pounding and my body was sweating, then suddenly, I had a moment of clarity."

"And what was that?"

"It dawned on me that whatever happens, happens. I accept it." He looked back at me, his eyes focused and his face serious. "We have all been anxious this whole trip, fighting back at the world with every ounce of power we have in us. And while I think that is a good thing, we have to accept that we cannot control everything."

"You're confusing me."

"I am trying to say that I accept whatever my fate is and with that, my anxiety has disappeared. I feel at ease, my heart is calm. I think you should do the same."

"But what if something bad happens?"

"Well, then, it happens." He shrugged.

"I don't want to accept that."

"I understand," he sympathized, "but you will feel a whole lot better once you do."

I sat there for a moment, deep in thought. Laago did not appear to be someone who was plagued by such deep fears, but I suppose anybody would be in our situation. Though I didn't really understand exactly what he was saying, I think I understood his point.

The odds had been against us throughout the entirety of this trip. Of course, it doesn't mean we should give up, we have to keep fighting, but it would be naive to think that nothing would ever go wrong. Blind optimism mirrors insanity, we could not deny reality.

"I don't want to think of all this."

"I'm sorry if I am rambling nonsense. I think my filter is off from exhaustion." He stood up and leaned over me to tap Jon, waking him. "If I have to row a minute longer, I might actually pass out."

"Morning already?" Jon grumbled as he sleepily sat up. He rubbed his eyes and looked up at the sunrise.

"How'd you sleep?"

"My arms feel like lead." He stood up and stretched, before slowly switching seats with Laago, careful to not tip the boat. "If my arms don't get bigger from this trip, it'll be a waste."

"Maybe one day you'll be big like me!" Laago flexed his arms.

"I'd look like an ape if I had arms the size of yours on my body," Jon joked.

"Wouldn't that be a sight to see?" He laid back with his head resting in his hands and closed his eyes.

It was bewildering to me how Laago could go from deeply serious to lighthearted at the drop of a hat. His moods changed like the tides. I sat there for a moment, my eyes fixated on him. His breathing slowed to a quiet hum as he seamlessly fell asleep. He must have been exhausted. Both he and Benjin looked so innocent while they slept, I wished I could wrap my body around theirs, like a shield protecting them from everything in this world.

"Have you been up long?" Jon asked, picking up the oars to row.

"No, I awoke at the first morning light."

"Good, I'm glad you got some sleep. I think we will make it to the island by noon."

"It looks like were are making great time then. I can't wait to get off this boat," I said. "But I feel terrible you have to row again, especially when I haven't contributed at all. I'm useless."

"Don't say that. I think you are plenty useful. Plus, you are a great company." He had a warm smile. "And at the very least, you are much nicer to look at than those two." I felt my face blush.

"Oh, please!" I quickly turned my head to the ocean, hiding behind my hair.

"I'm sorry." He chuckled. "I just like when you get all embarrassed like that."

"You're..." I whispered, confused. "Making fun of me?"

"No!" He raised his hands, dropping the oars for a moment. "I mean what I said, honestly, I enjoy your company. I like being around you. I just meant that your reactions make me laugh sometimes."

"You guys are confusing." I shook my head.

"Was Laago messing with you too this morning?"

"I don't even know," my voice fell so quiet that even I could barely hear it. "You seem to always understand people so clearly, but I can't even understand what someone means when they're saying it direct-ly to my face."

"Perhaps you do know, you are just not ready to accept it." He winked.

"Perhaps."

"Can I ask you a question?" He asked. "When this is all over, where do you imagine yourself?"

"With my father, brothers, and Laago. Somewhere beautiful... And safe." My eyes drifted to the waves, glowing from the rising sun's light. "In a small cottage, surrounded by lush green forest. We would live off the land- hunting, farming... There would be a lively village within an hour walk from us. Close enough for us to attend a monthly festival, but far enough for us to be away from the problems that plague the world. Maybe I could run a stand there on the first day of every week, selling pelts or crafts."

I imagined a small stone cottage with a thatched roof and a tall chimney that poked out, sending plumes of smoke billowing into the sky. The air smelt rich of pine, for our home was surrounded by towering trees with deep green leaves. Not too far in the distance, my father and Benjin chopped wood, carefully stacking it in a neat pile to keep us warm through the winter. Luka sat beside Laago, who crouched over a fire lined with stone. As he added another piece of wood, he began to blow on it. A bright smile spread across Luka's face as the fire ignited.

"That sounds wonderful."

"It would be a long time before I could ever get there."

"Yes, but you can," Jon assured me. "Oftentimes, the idea of where we are versus where we want to be can feel overwhelming," he mused. "Like us sailing across this ocean. It may sound frightening at first, or maybe even absurd. The ocean is far too vast, we have never sailed so far... What if a storm comes? What if one of us falls ill? What if, what if, what if? But what if it is beautiful? What if our lives are forever changed? The only way we will find out is if we set sail. After that, the rest is solved, one row at a time. Eventually, you may wonder why you ever worried at all."

"You have a way with words," I said. Most boys did not speak half as eloquently as Jon did. "Where do you imagine yourself?"

"For the longest time, I wanted to follow in General Pago's footsteps. Whether it was some sort of divine intervention or a mere coincidence, I thought it was my destiny to become the next general of Terlu's forces." His eyes squinted from the bright sun. "But I don't know if that is my path, or if it is something I just feel pressured to do as a repayment to the general for his generosity. All I know is that I want to help people, but I don't know how."

"You would make a great leader, Jon," I remarked. "It is one thing for a man to be a skilled fighter, but it is rare for them to also possess such charisma and compassion. I think you should just follow your strengths and see where it takes you."

"Fighting used to excite me. I loved playing with weapons since I was young, but my time in the field changed my perspective. I've been sent to many outskirt villages ravaged by raiders, where I witnessed boys as young as Luka, filled with the same rage that once engulfed me. I have watched the violent cycle continue, because unlike how General Pago saved me, no hero came down to save them. I don't want to be another soldier sent to gods-knows-where to kill gods-knows-who. It's senseless and it does not address the root causes of the violence. It only fuels more resentment, which erupts into even deadlier conflict."

"What do you mean?"

"Consider the Khurayl Raiders of the Qara Desert for example, who are notorious for extorting the northwest outskirt villages for as long as time itself. Every so often, we deploy our troops out to fend them off. Many raiders die, as well as our soldiers and innocent villagers. Once the raiders retreat, our troops go home. But the resentment and hostility always grows, like an untamable fire. The people are angry, as are the soldiers and raiders. It is never too long before a new wave of raiders storm through, in an even more desperate attempt that is fueled by the loss of their loved ones. And so, the cycle continues."

"You think that the war against the raiders isn't solving any problems, but instead just fueling the violent cycle?"

"I am not saying that war is a bad thing, but it is not a means to solve problems; it is only beneficial in containing them. By continuously devastating the raiders, it only causes more problems in the long term. I am not condoning their actions, but to figure out a permanent solution, we have to at least try to understand them."

"So why do the raiders raid?"

"The Khurayl Raiders were actually founded by escaped slaves from the Kingdom of Yana, a country that still lives in the past. They tried to seek refuge in the Republic of Terlu but were denied by the government to avoid international conflict. Not even the outskirt villages would accept them. They ultimately settled in the Qara Desert, where life is anything but welcome. The land is hostile, unsuitable for farming. To keep their people fed and alive, they resorted to raiding the same villages that denied them refuge."

"So this hundred year quarrel could have been avoided if someone just accepted these refugees to begin with?" I asked. "Can't the government do something to help now?"

"The relations between our people and the raiders are quite strained, making it nearly impossible to convince them to allow the government to spend the people's tax money on those who have stolen and killed members of their community."

"If it is impossible-"

"I said it was near impossible. Sometimes, the government has to intervene and do what is right, even if the people cannot see the situation clearly yet. The problem is that elected officials care too much about public opinion, so they avoid taking action that may cause dissent."

"Maybe one day it will be you who will rebuild the bridge that now lies in rubble."

"Maybe," he said, drifting off to thought. "Though I don't believe there was ever a bridge to begin with."

I laid back down in my seat, stretching my stiff legs out over the edge of the boat. My eyes wandered over the horizon, as I daydreamed of the future. I struggled to imagine myself working any job, let alone one as esteemed as what I imagined for Jon's bright future. My stomach was too weak to be a nurse and my voice was too timid to be a leader. All I knew was I long for a life of comfort, where I did not fall asleep to my anxiety nor wake fearing what the new day would bring.

When the sun finally reached its peak, I noticed a small glimmer in the distance. It was faint, disappearing behind the waves, only to reemerge when they receded. It seemed Jon had noticed too, because he dropped the oars and stood against the boat, holding his hand over his eyes to block the sun's strong beams. He brushed his hair back with his hand to get his curls out of his face.

"What is that?" I asked, slowly rising to my feet.

"Whatever it is, it isn't good," he bluntly responded. "General Pago assured me our route would be clear." Jon leaned over and wacked Benjin to wake him, his eyes not lifting from the speck over the horizon.

"What?" His body swung up. Jon silently pointed, as worry began to fill his face. Laago was sitting up too now, finally awake. Both of them were squinting now, trying to make out the mysterious object.

"It's probably nothing," Laago said, but I sensed panic in his voice.

"Nyla, prepare your bow," Benjin ordered. "Everyone, get down."

I fumbled around for my bow and grabbed my bag of arrows. The boys dropped down from their seats and squeezed onto the floor of the boat. I prepared an arrow on my bow and pulled it back, not yet launching it. I waited for us to drift closer, it could be anything. A lost fisherman, a pile of garbage drifting through the sea... Seconds felt like minutes, minutes like hours. The sun continued to beat down on us, as if she wanted to burn us.

"I think I see land in the distance!" Laago pointed out a small land mass resting in the distance. I could see a tall tower with a gold pointed roof sticking up, passing through the clouds.

"It is! That must be the Island of Aara," Benjin responded, giving us a moment of relief. "But still, what is that in the water?"

"It looks like it is moving towards us..." Jon mumbled under his breath. We all sat there silently, squinting off into the distance. We were so close to the island, we just had to make it a little further.

Jon rose back up to his seat and began rowing the boat aggressively. For us to reach the island, he had to turn the boat and row it parallel to the foreign object in the water, bringing us closer for a moment before we could pass by it. I slid down from my seat, nestling between Benjin and my seat, which separated me from Laago.

"Jon, you should get down."

"We need to get closer to the island. I'm not waiting around to find out whatever that thing is." His eyes were focused, his arms pumping the oars back and forth, sending us cruising through the water.

As we rowed closer, it became clear that the glimmer was a small boat. I could not make out much detail, but it appeared to have a few people in it. We all sat silently, focused on the boat as we moved towards each other. In an ocean so vast, why must we cross paths with strangers? I squeezed my bow tightly, with an arrow balancing on its string.

"It seems to be moving faster now too," I whispered.

"Do you think they see-"

As Laago spoke, an arrow flew into the side of our boat with such great ferocity that it rocked us back and forth. Jon dropped the oars and sunk back into the floor of the boat. My body instinctively flinched, releasing my arrow. It flew into the ocean, disappearing underwater. I slapped my forehead. I already had limited arrows and now I just lost one, leaving me with only eight.

It was too far out for me to make out anyone on the boat just yet, especially with the sun's rays blinding me. I dropped my head down, using the boat's wall to shield me from the barrage of arrows. I felt trapped knowing that I could not hide behind Benjin or Laago. They were helpless.

"Take a shot, Nyla!" Jon scowled.

"I can't see anyone yet. I have to wait for them to get a little closer."

"We're sitting ducks!" Benjin hissed. Another arrow flew over our heads and into the water behind us. "Gods, what are the militants doing out here?"

"Keeping anyone from reaching the Council of Five!" Jon covered his head with his arms.

"But then why are they so close? The council will know they are here." Laago shook his head. "It doesn't make any sense. That would just prove to them that General Ahkpi's militia is treasonous!"

"Maybe they don't care if the council sees them..." Benjin wondered aloud.

Still crouching out of sight, I released an arrow. My legs were shaking uncontrollably. I peaked my head up and was finally able to make out three men. Their boat was gaining on us, heading directly our way. They were determined to kill us. I cursed under my breath.

"I am going to have to stand to make a shot."

"No, absolutely not. You can get hit!" Benjin argued, his voice wavering. Another arrow punctured the side of our boat.

"You got this, Ny." Laago put his hand on my back.

I took a deep breath and waited for the next arrow to fly over my head before I quickly jumped up. I thought back to my training with Bao: "An arrow is launching into the future. If you aim where your target was in the past, you will surely miss. Whenever you launch an attack, whether it be a punch or through a weapon, do so with anticipation of where your opponent will be, not where they are. Getting caught up in the past is a dangerous thing for a warrior."

I could not aim for where the militants were, I had to aim for where they would be. I locked eyes with one of the men and released, before quickly dropping back down. I covered my eyes with my trembling hands and held my breath. Just as a panic attack began to consume my mind and body, I heard a sharp cry from across the water.

"You hit him!" Benjin's jaw dropped as he peaked over the boat.

"Great shot, Ny."

"Now you just need to make two more," Jon anxiously added.

Okay, just two more. I could do this. I balanced the next arrow on my bow and slowly rose up, but Laago pulled me down just as an arrow grazed my side. These were clearly trained archers, their precision was terrifying. Their arrows were painted black with red fletching and were far nicer quality than any I had ever seen.

"Gods!" Benjin winced, grabbing onto me. His hands were sweating.

My heart was pounding through my chest, it felt like it was about to burst. But I had to do this, I knew I could. If I failed, all our training and miles walked under the blistering sun would be for nothing. Images of my father bombarded my mind. Just like us, he put his life on the line for the people of Tinshe. Only he never made it.

I rose as quickly as I dropped back down, releasing an arrow at my next target, only to miss. Another arrow flew over my head. Benjin flinched, reaching his hand out to me. Everyone held their breath, their eyes anxiously darting back and forth between me and the militants. I peaked over the side of our wooden boat and took a deep breath.

Not only were the boys' lives in my hands, but the entire Republic of Terlu and my home's fate did as well. For Nonna, for Bao, for Kiuyah, for Mister Ritu and for General Pago... We had to make it to the Council of Five, there was no other option. After everything we had been through to make it this far, I could not fail us now.

I released the next arrow and dropped back down, but this time, I did not break eye contact with the militant. I watched the arrow rip through his chest, his eyes bulging out in shock as he fell back. It was a clean shot, there was no way he would survive it. For once, I felt no guilt, only relief.

"Just one more!" Jon whispered.

I only nodded in response, for I knew if I spoke I would fall apart. My mouth was unbearably dry and my hands were clammy, but I had to focus. It was just one more- I could do one more.

I looked over at Benjin. His eyes were blind with panic, his tall body scrunched down against the bottom of the boat. He wasn't accustomed to not being in control. Jon's legs were shaking as he intensely stared over the boat's edge at my last target. But Laago, he sat crouched beside me with his hand on my thigh and a comforting smile. His brown eyes were as warm and inviting as ever, just as they were the night we danced under the moon drinking wheat beer.

"You can do this, Ny. If anyone can, it is you. You can accomplish anything you put your mind to. I believe in you!"

As he spoke, an arrow pierced into our boat, its black tip protruding through the wooden panels. As they moved closer to us, their arrows penetrated deeper. I locked onto my final target. He was short and pudgy, with no hair. Another arrow flew over Jon's head, grazing his curls. It was my time to strike.

I leaped up, took aim, and released. The arrow flew through the air and grazed past him. I quickly released my next arrow, I had no time to wait. This one would hit him, I felt it in my bones. As I felt a sense of relief rush over my body, Laago jumped up and pushed me over. I fell over onto Benjin, who shoved me off of him.

"I hit him!" I cheered, lifting myself off the floor.

"Laago!" Benjin shrieked, as the color drained out of his face. I turned around to see an arrow had pierced through Laago. It was stuck deep within his chest. I dropped back down to the floor, my body numb.

"But... I hit him..." My voice cracked.

Blood poured through his wound, staining his shirt and puddling beneath him. Laago looked down at the arrow that stuck through his chest. His eyes were wide and his mouth agape. He moved around anxiously, his hands trembling. Benjin ripped off his shirt and held it in a ball over Laago's wound to stop the bleeding.

"You did, but the bastard had already released another arrow!" Jon panted. He anxiously looked back at their boat, which was now slowly drifting towards us, void of a captain.

"It's okay, Laago. It is going to be okay, just stay with me!" Benjin's attempt to stay calm was a failure. Laago lifted his hand and squeezed Benjin's. "Jon, row! We have to get to the island, they will be able to help us!" He cried. Jon began to ferociously row the boat, his arms flying. But I couldn't move, I was paralyzed. I failed- I did this. It was my fault.

"It's okay..." Laago mumbled. "It's okay."

"Keep talking and focus on my voice. We are going to get you help."

"Benj..." His voice was eerily calm. "It's okay. When I told you I would come with you guys, I understood what could happen."

"Don't say such things! You are going to make it through this."

"Listen." He slowly reached over to me and grabbed my hand, his eyes locking with mine. "I would do it again, in a heartbeat..." He kissed my hand softly.

"Laago... I'm so sorry," I sputtered as tears streamed down my face.

"There is nothing to be sorry about, Ny." He squeezed my hand. His words were slow, he struggled to speak. "I promised your father that I would always protect you all, no matter what... Your family gave me everything. It was an honor to know you, to love you... You changed my life. I love you with all of my heart, more than I could ever find the words to say."

"Laago!" Benjin wrapped his arm around his shoulder, still squeezing his shirt drenched in blood over his wound. "I love you so much. Please, hold on. You can't leave me. We are so close."

"It's okay, Benj. I'll always be with you guys." He smiled.

"No, don't talk like that! You are going to be okay."

"Jon, I need you to do me a favor."

"What is it? I'll do anything!" His eyes were wide.

"Promise me that you'll take care of them."

"Of course, I promise."

"What we do for love..." Laago whispered, as his eyes shut for a final time. Benjin kissed his forehead, his tears falling into Laago's hair.

We were nearing the island. So close, yet so far... A moment too late. The warmth had left Laago's body, leaving the air freezing cold. I saw a group of people gathered on the shoreline, waiting for us to reach land. I assumed them to be guards of the Civil Council.

As we were pulled into shore a gong was struck, its deep bellow marking our arrival. A flock of white seabirds dispersed from the island, flying over my head and towards the ocean. People in soft beige cloaks surrounded us, as they carefully pulled Laago's cold body from our boat. They all spoke at once, flustered in a panic. I sat still, unmoved, with my arms wrapped around my legs and my chin resting on my knees, struggling to believe any of this could be real.

Benjin followed the men from the shore up a long cobblestone staircase, lined with ivy bushes. Though I heard nothing but white noise, I watched him move frantically, yelling between cries. They were headed to a tall mossy building that resembled a miniature castle. It looked as old as the island itself. This wasn't happening, how could the gods be so cruel?

We were so close. I blankly stared into the distance, I could not move. I knew Jon was still with me and I felt the boat rock as he climbed closer. I watched his mouth move, but I heard no words. I heard nothing, just a deafening silence. He reached over and put his hand on my back, but I did not feel his warmth. It was as if I entered a void, a black abyss where I could not feel nor hear anything. This wasn't happening.

The choppy ocean looked no different than the dull sky, which was once so vibrant. The only way I even knew I was alive was from the ice that filled my veins, freezing my heart over. It was over. I had no strength to go on. The one who brought color to my world was ripped from me. And it was my fault.

I felt a loud agonizing cry erupt from deep within me. It was sharp, piercing, and horrific, as if I was stabbed in the chest. My wailing exploded, shaking the world around me and causing Jon to fall back on his bottom. His eyes were wide with fear, unsure of how to handle me.

I stumbled forward, crawling to the edge of the boat. I felt like I was going to vomit. I grabbed onto the side and hung my head over the water. I could not go on like this. I pushed myself over the edge, headfirst into the water. It was shallow, my head slammed into the rocky bottom. I staggered deeper into the cold ocean on my knees. It was my fault. If I didn't miss...

Waves began to crash on me as I stumbled further into the water, slapping me in the face, but I felt nothing. Once I reached a point where I could not stand, I threw myself forward and allowed my wails to be muffled and suffocated by the ferocious waves.

But as my vision faded to black, I felt a hand grab my collar and drag me up. I fought violently to break free, but they wrapped their arms around my chest and pulled me above water. My body felt weak, battered, and defeated. I surrendered, laying limp.

Jon dropped my body on the shore and began pushing down on my chest, trying to clear my lungs of water. He was panicking, tears flooded down his cheeks. He was both yelling and crying, but I heard nothing. Just piercing silence. It was as if I was a mere spectator to my own life, because I could not feel my body. I was just a shell of a human.

"Let me die..." I begged, as water flew out of my lungs.

## CHAPTER SEVENTEEN

# A WORLD WITHOUT COLOR

M Y EYES SLOWLY DRIFTED open, it felt like I was floating on a cloud. Everything around me was blurry, but I could see that I was in a room made of stone, laying in a large white bed with thick white blankets and fluffy pillows. I quickly realized it was night, because no light shined through the window, only darkness. A single candle's flame flickered beside my bed.

"You're awake," a soft voice called. I tried to turn my head, but it sent a sharp pain down my neck. "Please, don't move!" Jon rose from a wooden chair and stood over me.

"What..?"

"Stay still. You need to rest." He dropped to his knees and rested his arms beside me on the bed. I could tell he was at a loss for words.

"What happened?" My mind felt fuzzy and my body hurt.

"You may have a concussion from hitting your head and you are a bit cut up from the rocks in the water."

Suddenly, everything came flooding back to me. I shot up, dropping my head in my hands. The image of Laago laying there, sputtering his final breaths stained my mind and shattered my heart. What we do for love, he cried, before the gods took what they had no reason to.

"Laago..."

"It's not your fault, Nyla. There was nothing we could have done. I am so sorry." He reached over and grabbed my hand, squeezing it. The scrapes on my hand burned from his touch. I sat still, unable to process reality.

"Where's Benjin?"

"He had to take care of a few things, but he should be back soon."

"I failed us." I began to cry, burying my face in the blanket.

"No, Nyla. If it wasn't for you, none of us would have made it here to warn the Civil Council. You saved us."

"But at what cost?" I blubbered between sobs.

Jon pursed his lips, his face sunken. Instead of trying to change my mind or prove me wrong, he just sat beside me as I cried. He knew there was nothing to say that could alleviate the pain I felt.

I thought of Laago, his beautiful brown eyes and warm smile. The way he pulled his hair back into a bun when he was too hot. No matter how many times he pulled it from his face, it always seemed to fall back down, only for him to brush his hand through it again. His contagious laughter was a melody to my ears, brightening the darkest of days. I don't believe he had a bad bone in his body. I believe even his hotheaded youthful days just stemmed from him not understanding his emotions. All Laago ever wanted was to be accepted and loved.

The door swung open and there Benjin was. He stood there for a moment, his face sunken. It may have been dark, but I could see his eyes were full of pain, red and puffy from many tears shed. He ran over to me and collapsed on the bed, wrapping his body around me. He wept like a baby, allowing his body to go limp. We sat there for hours, sobbing until the sun began to rise. Jon sat in his chair quietly, staring at the wall. I had no idea what thoughts tormented his mind, but he did not dare to sleep either.

A soft knock at the door captured our attention. Jon quickly rose to his feet, motioning us to stay in bed, but I do not think Benjin nor I would have budged either way. Even my heart was so broken that it struggled to beat. As he walked to the door, I noticed his hand was resting on his sword. I wondered if he even realized or if it was an unconscious habit.

"Yes?" He called as he opened the door, his voice sounding strong and deep.

"Here!" A small boy, who appeared to be in his early teens, handed Jon a wooden tray. He had eyes so brown they looked black and dark hair shaved so short he was practically bald. He wore a beige tunic that ended just above his bony knees and thin tan sandals that seemed to be held together by a single thread.

"Thank you." He nodded. It had a pot of tea, still steaming, and three cups.

"We hope you will come for breakfast, but we understand if you do not." He stared at the ground as he spoke, his eyes not moving from the floor. Jon looked over his shoulder at Benjin and me.

"Come by then and I will let you know our answer. For now, they need rest," Jon's voice quieted to a whisper. The boy bowed his head and began to walk away, before Jon called after him. "Excuse my manners, I did not ask for your name."

"I have none."

"You don't have a name?"

"No, sir."

"Oh..." Jon paused. "Well, thank you for the tea, bud!" As those simple words fluttered thoughtlessly from his mouth, I saw the boy's eyes widen and his cheeks redden. Jon gently closed the door, not noticing the effect such a simple exchange had on this stranger. "A boy with no name..." Jon mumbled to himself, as he set the tray at the end of our bed.

Jon poured a cup and handed it to me, but I waved it away. My stomach was in knots, tossing and turning. Benjin took it and placed it in my hands, wrapping my trembling fingers around it. It felt warm and had a familiar sweet scent. Jon poured a second cup, handing it to Benjin, before serving the last cup for himself.

He sat back in his chair and blew on his tea, his eyes zoned out on the dark spruce wooden floor. He had bruises that were beginning to form on his forearm and bicep. He looked exhausted, I could see dark bags forming under his eyes, but I knew I did not look any better.

"You should take a nap," I whispered ever so silently, my voice cracking from dryness.

"Don't worry about me." Jon plastered a fake smile on his face. "Do you like the tea?"

"Yes," I lied, taking a sip. It tasted like nothing to me.

"Well, drink up. You need it."

We sat there for a while, quietly sipping the warm tea. I stared down into my cup and watched the steam rise into the air, before it slowly dissipated. No matter how hot my cup was, my hands were freezing. I looked at my brother, his eyes were sunken with defeat. He looked different, almost unrecognizable. His heart was taken and replaced with a lump of black coal.

"Benjin, where were you yesterday, before you came here?"

"I stayed by Laago's side until they made me leave. Then, I attended an emergency meeting with the Civil Council."

"I am sorry you attended that. It should have been me," Jon earnestly apologized.

"It was my duty to. We have come so far, Laago would have wanted me to finish the job."

"I understand." He solemnly nodded. "What did they say when you informed them of the inevitable war and of General Ahkpi's treasonous militia?"

"They seemed shocked. I guess they heard rumors, but didn't realize how bad it has gotten, especially when I told them of the Republic of Terlu's upcoming invasion."

"Who knows, they could already be at our walls." Jon rubbed his chin. "I hate not knowing." I felt a pang in my chest. I hoped Luka was safe.

"What did they say of the militants who-"

"They captured their boat and checked the bodies," Benjin interrupted, not wanting to even hear the rest of Jon's sentence. "They were high ranking militants, clearly a part of some sort of elite special forces. It appears they were sent to assassinate the members of the Civil Council."

"That's an awfully bold move," Jon said. "What were they thinking? Did they really think they'd get away with this?"

"I don't know." Benjin shook his head. "But now I am even more worried about Luka, Jin, and General Pago. If General Ahkpi would go so far as to order for the Civil Council members to be assassinated-"

"I don't even want to think about that," Jon interjected. "Besides, Roan can carry his own. Luka will be safe in our home, I am sure of it. It is so discrete, it looks like any old apartment building. The militants would never find it, let alone breach our walls."

"More surprising things have happened. I am never underestimating my enemies again."

"What I don't understand is why would they have only sent three militants here? This island is well protected," Jon pondered aloud.

"It was a sneak attack. General Ahkpi must have known there was no way he would be successful if he attacked head on."

"Did you speak of the Protector who returned to Tinshe, only to be assassinated?" I tugged on Benjin's shirt. The council must have given him a new one, it was a blackened tunic that had silver embroidery along its collar.

"They said before he left, there was a big fight. When he did not return from the routine check up to Tinshe, the Civil Council assumed it was because of the altercation."

"What do you think of that?" Jon prodded.

"It doesn't sit well with me," Benjin admitted. "I wanted to ask what the argument was about, but it is not my business."

"I am sure there is more to that than they would admit, even if you had asked. But we have more important things to worry about."

Benjin sighed, setting down his empty tea cup. Just as he laid back against the pillows, there was another knock at the door. Jon jumped up from his seat and headed over to open it. The same boy from before stood in the doorway with his head bowed.

"A meal is prepared in the great hall," he announced. Jon looked at Benjin, who looked at me.

"I know you don't want to, but you both should eat something," Jon said.

After a moment's hesitation, Benjin pulled himself out of bed and held his hand out to me. I surrendered, grabbing onto his hand. I felt disgusting. My hair was knotted from the rough salt water and my clothes were wrinkled.

"What happened to your hands?" Benjin asked, analyzing the little cuts and scrapes that engulfed my palms, stretching all the way up to my elbows. "Your head is beat up too!" He gently rubbed his thumb across my forehead, sending a shooting pain down my body.

"I fell off the boat." I anxiously looked at Jon, who quickly looked at the floor and said nothing. It seemed he didn't tell Benjin, thankfully. He had no need to hear about that.

"We will grab a bite and head back here," Jon said, changing the subject. He held the door open for us. "Quick and easy."

The three of us followed the boy through a long hallway with stone walls and candlelit sconces. We descended a narrow spiral staircase with steep steps that led us to an open room with a massive iron door, which was guarded by two men in beige robes, armed with embellished broadswords. As our boots tapped against the cold gray tile floor, I gazed up at the colossal bronze chandelier suspended above us, hanging beneath a high ceiling adorned with a detailed mural of the world map. Tinshe looked incredibly far from the Island of Aara on a map this grand.

We continued through the room and down a wide hallway, passing under a large archway that was ornately engraved with ocean waves. A delicious aroma filled the air, leading us to the great hall, where five round tables were positioned throughout, draped in maroon cloths. The centers of the tables were crowded with tall golden candlesticks whose lit flames slowly dripped wax, surrounded by pure porcelain dishes and crystal wine glasses.

Tall, narrow windows lined the cobblestone walls, overlooking the ocean and stretching upwards towards the lofty ceiling, where a single golden chandelier hung over the central table, which rested closer to the back wall. Behind this table, an enormous painted glass window depicted the five original Civil Council members, sitting at a feast in this very room. It was surrounded by smaller glass paintings that were too distant to discern.

"Hello!" A voice boomed. It came from a man in a forest-green robe. He walked towards us with his arms stretching wide. "Allow me to introduce myself. I am Nahksona Rykima of the great Republic of Terlu! It is a pleasure to finally meet you two." He extended his hand out to Jon, eagerly shaking it, then grabbed onto mine, softly kissing my knuckle.

Nahksona Rykima had dark brown hair, buzzed on the sides and slightly longer on top, similar to all the men of Terlu's forces. His skin was glowing, a deep olive tone. He had light brown eyes and a bright white smile, that was almost too perfect. His cheeks were stained from years of smiling.

"The pleasure is ours, Mister Nahksona Rykima of Terlu." Jon bowed his head.

"Please, call me Nahksona." He patted Benjin on the back. "It is nice to see you again, I hope you got some rest last night. Please, follow me. You must be starving."

Nahksona walked with a cool stride, almost bouncing as he stepped. He led us to a table and took a seat with us. With a snap of his fingers, three servants quickly emerged from the kitchen. One pushed a wooden cart of drinks, another pushed one of food, and a third led the way. The three of us exchanged glances, already feeling uncomfortably overwhelmed. The servants began to pile food onto our plates and fill our glasses: one with tea, another with water, and a third with a yellow juice.

"Let us know if you need anything at all," one of them insisted, before they all bowed and disappeared back into the kitchen.

"To selflessly sacrificing your lives to protect the innocent people of our empires and republics." He raised his glass. We all followed suit, sipping the sweet juice. But it felt wrong without Laago here with us. I looked over to Benjin and caught him wiping a tear as it fell down his cheek. "What are you waiting for? Dig in."

"Thank you, sir," Jon said.

"Benjin told me you are the son of the great General Pago. Is this true?"

"Well, adopted, but yessir." Jon smiled. "Do you know him?"

"Of course! I served with Chief Sakra, it was he who introduced us. Your father is a great man, one of the best. A born leader!" He spoke a mile a minute in between bites. "In fact, I pestered him to run for office. He didn't listen to me, of course, but I believe he would make a great President!"

"Wow, he never mentioned that." Jon's eyebrows raised.

"Why, yes! Wouldn't you agree?" He asked, without even giving Jon time to respond. "Is he still quite the ladies man? Roan would show up late to every event and the women would flock to him! Sakra would be red in the face, because he spent all day trying to win one over, then Roan would stroll through and steal all the attention without even trying!"

"Really?" Jon awkwardly chuckled, learning a new side of his adoptive father. He bit into a potato wedge.

"Oh, here I go again, revealing too much. Roan used to call me the fly he can never seem to swat!" Nahksona erupted into laughter. "That was a nickname that stuck no matter how hard I tried to shake it."

The more Nahksona spoke, the more my head ached. It was a piercing pain that was so sharp it almost blinded me. It felt like my brain was going to burst and crack through my skull. I set my fork down and reached for a sip of water, hoping it would help cool me down, but my hand was trembling and I did not want to draw attention to myself, so I gave up before I even took a sip. My head was spinning.

"Rykima!" A woman in a maroon robe called as she walked gracefully through the archway. "I can hear you from outside."

"Sagtra!" He welcomed. "This is Jia Sagtra of Gala."

"Hello," she said. "I hope he hasn't talked your ears off, but who am I kidding?"

"It is an honor to meet you." Jon quickly stood and bowed.

"Oh, please, take a seat!" Jia responded, as she sat next to Nahksona.

She had beautiful straight black hair that reached past her waist. It gently rested on her back, not a single piece of hair out of place. Part of it was pulled away from her face and into a thin braid that sat on her chest, stretching to her stomach. She wore a deep red lipstick that matched her maroon robe.

"You have beautiful hair," I accidentally remarked aloud.

"Thank you."

When she smiled, she did not show teeth, but instead her lips just slightly raised. She had a beauty mark on her upper cheek, below her dark almond-shaped eyes. Jia Sagtra of Gala was fiercely beautiful, reminding me of my mother.

"In the Empire of Gala, the higher your ranking, the longer your hair. Sagtra is one of the few granted permission to grow it this long," Nahksona explained.

"I heard Empress Jhena's hair reaches the floor," Jon said.

"It does."

"You're all cut up. What happened?" Jia Sagtra's eyebrows raised.

"I fell off the boat when we arrived," I lied.

"It must have been a hard fall, even your forehead is cut up. We will have a healer look at that after we eat."

"Yes, miss."

"Please, call me Jia," she spoke cordially, but her eyes were sharp, like daggers. "I wanted to thank you all, on behalf of Empress Jhena and the Empire of Gala. Though she does not yet know all that you have endured to make it here, I know that she would send you her highest regards. What you have accomplished is no small achievement. It should be carried with pride and celebrated."

"We did what anyone would do in our position," Benjin earnestly replied.

"No," she interjected. "Even after only hearing a brief summary of your journey, I know you all survived unimaginable hardship and stress. I give credit where it is due and you should too."

Her words struck deep within me. I looked at Benjin and a lump began to form in my throat. Though to some he may have looked fine, I knew he wore a mask to hide his true emotions. He swiftly rubbed his eyes and plastered a convincing smile across his face.

"Thank you, Jia. It truly means so much, especially coming from a member of the Civil Council." His response was true, coming from his heart.

"Have you seen Ban yet today?" Nahksona asked Jia.

"Not since yesterday's emergency session."

"He seems to be taking this harshly."

"Was he wearing the blue robe yesterday? I believe he is the representative of Suhai?" Benjin recalled.

"Oh, yes. How rude of me!" Nahksona looked to Jon and me. "I assume you will be formally introduced shortly. He is Tsalen Ban of the Suhai Empire."

"He did appear quite shocked when I informed you all of General Ahkpi's atrocities," Benjin observed.

"Ban served with General Ahkpi. He was actually quite fond of the general. But, worry not, he will come around." Nahksona waved his hand and leaned back in his chair casually, crossing his legs. Jia shot him a look, her eyes narrowing. "Oh, look at me, always saying too much."

"Rykima, go find Ban. It is rude for him to not introduce himself to our guests, especially since they come from his homeland."

"Yes, yes!" Nahksona jumped up and smiled. "Tonight at sunset we will hold a funeral service for your dear friend. It will be arranged for you to visit the monk first, because some decisions must be made, but certainly not until after you bathe! How senseless of me? Jia, please, have the boy show them to the bathhouse!" He spoke dramatically, always waving his arms around. Once he finally left, it felt like an ocean after a storm.

"I imagine you could all use a nap after that one." Jia looked at me. "Are you feeling alright?"

"I think I am just tired."

"If you are done eating, I would like to show you to the healer."

"Yes, miss."

She abruptly stood up and began walking towards the archway. I looked at Benjin, unsure of if I was supposed to follow her. Even so, the thought of leaving my brother's side made me anxious. But he just shrugged, surrendering to the council's will. Whatever they say is the law, whether it is the start of a war or for us to take a bath.

"Are you coming?" She called over her shoulder to me.

I quickly jumped up. She was not large physically, in fact, she was thin framed and below average weight, but I felt very intimidated by her. The words she spoke seemed to conflict with the stern look on her face, which gave me great unrest. I had to be sure to keep my guard up. Though the members of the council bore esteemed titles, I have learned that meant very little to a person's character.

I followed closely behind her down the hall and through the big open room. Jia walked quickly, her eyes focused in front of her, not straying from her path. The two guards at the front entrance stood unmoving, their hands resting on their swords. She raised her hand, snapping her fingers once, and the nameless boy from earlier emerged from out of nowhere.

"Take the two visitors to the bathhouse," she ordered, not even breaking stride as she spoke.

"Yes, miss." He bowed his head and shuffled away.

"Worry not, Nyla. You will be sent to the separate women's bath-house after your visit with the healer." She knocked twice at a door and it immediately creaked open.

"Miss Sagtra of Gala."

A frail old woman with thick curly gray hair sticking in every direction stood bowing in the doorway. She wore a long beige dress that dragged on the creaky wooden floor behind her as she slowly crept. The bottom of her flowy dress was decorated with dainty white embroidered patterns. An off-white sweater was draped over her upper body, leaving her collarbone and shoulders exposed.

"Our guest fell off her boat on the way in. She has minor cuts and bruises from her hands to her elbows, as well as her forehead and knees. I fear she may be concussed."

"Oh, my..." The woman grabbed onto my hand and led me to a narrow bed with a wooden frame. Her hand was bony and cold. " I will remedy her injuries, Miss Sagtra."

"Have the boy send her to the bathhouse after your work is done."

"Yes, miss." She bowed, but Jia was already out the door.

"Thank you for seeing me," I whispered. My head was pounding as I spoke.

"Of course. I am a healer and I love what I do. However, I differ from most of my profession."

She sat next to me on the bed. There was a brick fireplace in front of us, with sweet smelling smoke. A large black pot hung over it boiling. It was a small cozy room, with bookshelves lining the walls and a desk sitting in the corner, with papers stacked high. Drying plants were hung from the window, which was left slightly open, allowing the ocean's cool breeze to sneak through. Clear glass jars of plants, seeds, and herbs were all neatly lined up on shelves.

"How so?"

"I do not just heal physical injuries, but emotional wounds as well. Our body cannot heal if our mind is in shambles," her voice was soft. She gently touched her hands to the scrapes on my head. "A fool could see your head is injured, but I want to know why."

"I fell off the boat," I plainly spoke.

"Why?" Her eyes are the color of honey, warm and soothing.

"Because I fell." My body tensed up, sending shooting pain up my neck. "I don't know what you want from me," I snapped defensively.

"There is something you are not ready yet to face, but remember, you are not lying to me, you are only lying to yourself."

The woman lifted herself to her feet and grabbed a long wooden spoon to mix her bubbling pot. She threw a handful of herbs in and began churning it. I felt tears begin to well up in my eyes. She reminded me of Jon in a way, she saw right through my words and into my heart. I hated it.

"What is there to say?" I sighed. "I wanted to die. I killed the man I loved most and it left the world colorless. Does this make you happy?"

"No..." She set her spoon down, staring into her pot. "It fills me with sadness." She turned to me, her eyes wet like the ocean.

"Why are you crying?" My face scrunched up.

"I cry for you, because you will not." She sat down on the bed and wrapped her arm around me gingerly. I tried to scoot away as her tears fell, her openness made me uncomfortable. As I pushed away, she squeezed me tighter, and for a frail old woman, her grip was tight.

"Leave me alone!" But as I yelled, my voice cracked, erupting into a heavy wail. She opened the lid, forcing my tears to flood. I buried my face in her chest, sobbing my eyes out, like a child. She smelt of cinnamon, sweet and comforting.

"Thank you for opening up to me. I sensed the hollowness in your words by the coldness in your gaze. Though you said little, I heard the echoes of your pain. What you endured crushed your soul, but do not let it darken your heart. There is always hope. The world is still bright and full of color, if you look in the right places." Her eyes drifted out the window to the blue sky melting into the ocean. "But what you feel is genuine and real. Allow yourself to be hurt, to mourn... Take off your mask and be free."

I didn't respond, I couldn't. When my mother and sisters passed away, everyone told us to stay strong. They said my brothers and I were tough, that we could make it through it if we kept our chins up. I was only ten years old, but I still recall a neighborhood lady telling me it was time for me to step up, to shoulder the responsibilities that my mother once carried. They said we should be grateful to be alive. Though their words were well-intended, they only left me feeling even lonelier and apprehensive of the future.

But why didn't anyone tell us that it was okay to hurt? It was okay to cry, it was okay to mourn. I was tired of painting on a brave face and acting strong. My chest was painfully heavy and my lungs wheezed. I gazed at the fire, but all I could see was Laago. He was like a flame, he could be right in front of you, but you could never have him. If you reached in, you only got burnt. But if you sat close, you felt his warmth deep within your soul. Above all else, he was there to bring light to our world.

"Love is not always about possession," she whispered to me. "It is about appreciation. The feelings you have, the memories you shared... Those will stay with you forever, warming your heart like this fire."

"I can't erase this feeling of guilt. I failed him."

"An event occurred that you had no control over."

"I did, I was the only one who could have protected him!"

"You are not responsible for the actions of the bad men who killed your friend. It is not your fault. What you did was selfless and that is the essence of love. You risked your own life to protect him."

"But he dove in front of me."

"He chose to do what he believed was right. It was his will. He valued you so greatly that he decided to sacrifice his life for you.

"I wish he didn't."

"But he did, so you must accept the decision he made. It doesn't have to be now, these things take time, but when you are ready."

She brushed her hand through my hair, pulling it back from my face. "What do you know of the Koba moon?"

"It is when the moon is at its closest point to the Earth."

"In simplest terms, yes, but what do you know of the spiritual aspect of it?"

I thought back to my dream of my mother, when she revealed to me that the Koba moon was when she was closest to us. The last Protector, Amu, mentioned the Koba moon as well. He believed the moon goddess herself ordered him to wait in the tunnels for us, so he threw his life away to please her.

"Are we closer to the spirits?"

"We are always close to the spirits, they live among us until they are ready to cross. Yet most people's minds are too cluttered, their souls too chaotic, and their hearts too weak to sense the energy of their deceased loved ones. So when they die, we assume they are gone forever. But they are here, as real as you and me." She stood up and walked towards her pot, mixing it just before it could boil over again. "The Koba moon heightens humans' energy, as well as strengthens the spirits, allowing us to more clearly see what was in front of us all along."

"Do you really think I will be able to talk to them?"

"That is up to you." She smiled. "You choose what your limitations will be in life. Don't allow this to be one of them." She stood and walked towards her almanac, hanging over her desk. She traced her fingers along the dates, following the path of the moon. "Fortunately for you, the Koba moon is quickly approaching. When it does, you should be prepared to speak to those who hold your heart hostage and find the closure that you deserve."

"Closure..." I shook my head. I couldn't even think about that right now. How could I have closure if I could not even accept what happened? Every time I thought of my future, it was with the boys, all of them. Without Laago, that dream was gone.

"I know." She turned around and began rummaging through a cabinet, moving glass bottles around, before grabbing one. "Here."

"What is it?"

"It is bark from an akni tree, native to the Sacred Forest of Akta," she explained. It was brown, with no physical features setting it apart from any other type of bark. "Boil this as you would tea and drink it on an empty stomach at the height of the Koba moon. Once heated, it will glow like gold as its strong spiritual properties are activated. However, only consume it if you are mentally prepared to face those you have lost. The bark of an akni tree bridges the barrier between you and the spirits, giving you the ability to interact with them as you may in a dream. But beware, misuse can lead to a permanent disconnection from reality, like being stuck in a dream."

"What if I am not ready?" I fumbled the bottle around in my hand, analyzing the bark.

"You must face yourself before you face those who have passed. When the time comes, only you will know. Trust your instincts as you always have, they exist to guide you."

"I suppose..." I looked out the window to the Great Ocean. "I have nothing to lose anyway."

"As long as you live and breathe, you have everything to lose," she countered. A soft knock on the door interrupted her. "Enter!"

"I was sent to bring our guest to the bathhouse." The same boy from earlier stood in the doorway, staring at the floor.

"Grant me a moment longer," the woman said.

She pulled a blue tinted bottle from a shelf and shook it, before pouring some of the cream onto her hand. She grabbed my hand and began rubbing it on my cuts, up my arms, ending at my elbows.

"What is this?"

"It is an ointment for your wounds, to prevent infection. Though I am not very worried about your external wounds." She tapped her temple then her chest, before she rubbed the rest of the cream on my forehead. "I worry for your mind and heart. Please do not neglect them in your healing process."

"Thank you, miss," I said before gasping. "I never asked you for your name!"

"You sweet soul. It is the great goddess, Eura, who we should all thank!" She bowed her head. "My name is Taara of the Sacred Forest of Akta."

I rose to my feet and followed the boy out the door. I slid the small glass bottle of bark into my boot. Right outside of Taara's room was a side door to exit the main building. The boy held it open, motioning me to walk through. The air outside was warm, it seemed summer came early to the Island of Aara. We walked down a cobblestone path, surrounded by beachy bushes.

"To the left is the women's bath, to the right is the men's. I cannot take you any further." He bowed his head.

"May I ask you something?" I turned to him. "Why do you not have a name?"

"Servants to the Civil Council cannot bear names."

"Does that bother you?"

"I..." For a moment I thought he was about to look up at me, but he quickly stopped himself and dropped his head back down to the floor. "It is an honor to serve the Civil Council."

"Hey, Nyla!" Jon called over, emerging from the men's bathhouse. He walked over to us, with his hand resting on his sword. His hair was still damp, water droplets fell down his forehead. By the time I looked back at the kid, he was gone. "What are you doing out here?"

"I was just brought here to bathe."

"That kid is interesting, right? It's like he is a slave ..." Jon whispered to me, but his words made me anxious. Who knows if we were being listened to and the last thing I would want to do was disrespect the Civil Council.

"I feel sorry for him," I admitted.

"Me too," Jon said. "Well, focus on yourself for now. The bathhouse is beautiful, I think you'll be amazed."

"I'd be okay with bathing in the ocean at this point." I tried to joke, as I walked towards the building.

It was made of cobblestone with strong iron doors, matching the main building. I struggled to pull open the door, but when I did a waft of steam floated out. I stepped into the bathhouse and took off my shoes. I had the room to myself.

The floor was made up of white and lavender mosaic tiles, with beautiful patterns. The tiles reached from the ground to a couple feet up the walls, before elaborate paintings began, which stretched all the way up the high cathedral ceiling. At the very top, directly above a large in-ground bath that sat in the middle of the room, was a single skylight that casted warm beams of light into the water and reflected an array of colors from the painted walls. I grabbed a towel from the rack, it was white and fluffy. I placed it on the ground beside the bath, then slipped my clothes off into a pile and stepped into the warm water. Steam drifted up my body and into my face. It smelt like rose petals. I closed my eyes and submerged my body, slowly exhaling.

For a brief moment I felt at ease, until I lowered my head underwater as well. I quickly shot back up, immediately trembling from flashbacks of being beaten by the ocean before Jon pulled me out. I felt my heart rate accelerate and my body temperature rise. I tried to drown myself in front of Jon and I still haven't uttered a word of it nor apologized to him. He must have thought I went mad. My hands cupped my face as I sat in the beautiful bath, worrying about everything that has occurred over the last few days. My guilt, my rage, and my tears began to pour out of me. I ruined everything, we were so close to arriving at this island safely...

As I laid there swallowed by self-pity, it dawned on me that I was incapable of being alone with myself. I quickly got out of the water and dried myself off, throwing my dirty clothes back on before running out of the bathhouse. I need to find the boys. Every time I was alone, dark thoughts flooded my mind and drowned me. I needed to escape myself. As I swung the door open, Benjin was just leaving the men's bath as well.

"You look like you saw a ghost." He stepped towards me, reaching his hand towards my forehead. "Are you feeling alright?"

"Yeah, it was just hot in there," I lied.

"Done already?" Jon emerged from the bushes surrounding the path.

"What were you doing over there, weirdo?" Benjin chuckled.

"Check this out!" He motioned us to come over. We stepped over a couple bushes before we reached an unkept path that was being overgrown by moss. Jon pulled back the branches from trees that hung over us, making just enough space for us to squeeze through. "Look."

"Wow," Benjin gushed.

He placed his hand on his heart and closed his eyes. His mouth moved, he was whispering something to himself that not even I could hear. I squeezed around him to see the view. The path diverged into a small clearing. We stood on a steep cliff, overlooking the ocean. The sun sat high in the sky, sending her rays down onto the sparkling water. A flock of white seabirds rested in the distance, floating over the gentle waves.

"I wonder why the path isn't maintained, it is so beautiful here," Jon said.

"There are not many visitors here, and when there are, they are probably focused on pressing issues and not here for leisure," Benjin assumed, finally reopening his eyes. I saw a tear float down his cheek.

"It takes just one moment, one breath, to appreciate nature." Jon shrugged. I heard a twig snap behind me and quickly turned around.

"Pardon me. Your attendance is requested." The nameless boy bowed before us, his beige tunic falling off his scrawny shoulder. It was almost eerie how quietly he moved.

"We'll follow you, bud," Jon responded, his hand on his sword.

Without saying another word, the boy turned and began to walk up the overgrown path. We followed him back inside the main building, down the hall and into the entrance room, which was heavily guarded by men in beige robes. As we passed them, I couldn't help but feel bad. Perhaps they saw their service as an honor, but to me they wasted their lives away, standing still in one spot.

Instead of walking through the room and down the hall towards the dining hall, the boy turned left, standing before large engraved wooden doors that sat opposite of the entrance to the building. Two guards stood in front and did not even look at us before swiftly opening the doors.

"Hello?" Jon called, frozen still.

It was a dimly lit room with no windows. A long marble table stretched across, lined with sturdy chairs with thick leather cushions. A small desk sat in the corner, stacked high with papers. Other than that, there was no furniture, just candles.

"You may enter," a voice called. "I am Okurai Sari of Chao Binh."

"Hello, Mister Sari. It is a pleasure to see you again." Benjin bowed his head.

"Yes, take a seat." His voice reminded me of a hissing snake. The man was bald and pudgy, wearing a gold robe. He sat at the table's head. "I met Benjin briefly the other day, shortly after your arrival to our island, but I have not met you. What is your name, boy?"

"Jon Li."

"I have been informed you are the son of General Pago. Is this true?"

"He adopted my sister and I after we lost our parents in the plague."

"A true man. I have yet to have the honor of meeting him," Mister Sari spoke coldly, with no emotion, which contradicted the kind words he spoke. "I hope you have enjoyed your time thus far on our island. The food is quite divine, is it not?"

"Yessir." Benjin smiled, but I saw in his eyes it was ingenuine. Our friend was dead and this man dared to ask us how we liked the food?

"Why were we summoned here?"

"We sent a representative to the Empire of Gala to inform Empress Jhena. They should arrive at the Port of Gala in three days, leaving their estimated arrival to the Capital one week from today. We sent three men to Huang shortly after we spoke. Their duty is to report back to us with an update on how the republic is holding up and whether or not the walls were penetrated."

"Okay."

"We also sent a representative to the Kingdom of Yana to report to King Zabar Mazraat III, as well as to Prince Xan, second Prince of Yana. For their troops to reach the Republic of Terlu will likely take just as long as Empress Jhena's." He leaned forward in his chair and rested his elbows on the table, clasping his hands together. "All and all, it will take upwards of two weeks before the Republic of Terlu receives reinforcements. How long do you think the republic will hold?" He looked at Jon.

"Our walls will not fall."

"Good." He leaned back. "Which brings me to my next question. Where will you go?"

"Home, to fight in the war," Jon sternly responded.

"I suppose you could..." Mister Sari rubbed his chin, his eyes unmoved from Jon. "But I fear that would only waste your potential. Though we have sent a representative to the Empire of Gala, I would like you to strongly consider meeting with the empress personally to give her a firsthand account of your experience with General Ahkpi's militia."

"Why?" Jon asked. Mister Sari held up one finger.

"A firsthand account will increase her trust." He raised a second finger. "Hearing the tale of your journey and service to the people will gain us her compassion. These are two important components to ensure she provides the Republic of Terlu, as well as Tinshe, the maximum support she is able to spare." He raised a third finger. "And who would refuse an offer to meet with the empress of such a great country? Very few outsiders have met her in person."

"So you want us to encourage Empress Jhena to send more troops west?"

"Would it not be in your best interest? Either you can go, as one mere man, and foolishly risk your life in the war, or you can use your position and intelligence to lead a thousand more men to battle." He threw his hands up.

"It does make sense..." Jon looked to Benjin. "What do you think?"

"We would have a stronger impact on the war if we convince Empress Jhena to send more troops." Benjin agreed.

"So that settles it," Mister Sari said. When he spoke, it was directed solely to the boys.

"Well, what do you think, Nyla?" Jon turned to me.

Thoughts of Luka immediately flooded my mind. Traveling east to the Empire of Gala meant it may be weeks before we were reunited with him. The thought of abandoning him in the Republic of Terlu broke my already shattered heart, but I could not be selfish. I had to remember the thousands of boys in Terlu whose lives were in danger- this may be the only thing that can save them. Though Luka may not understand now, in time he will come to appreciate our decision.

"I think we should go to the east."

My eyes wandered to Mister Sari, but he avoided eye contact. I suddenly remembered Kiuyah's words- she was from Eastern Chao Binh and said it was very traditional there. Women lived to serve men and were viewed as lesser. I suddenly felt very uncomfortable. It was clear this man did not respect me.

"Okay. We'll do it." Jon looked at Mister Sari. "How will we find Empress Jhena?"

"I sent a letter with the representative, informing her of your arrival," he revealed. Mister Sari assumed we would not be able to turn down his offer to meet with the empress in person. "I requested for her to send one of her men to the Port of Gala to meet you and personally escort you to the Capital. I will also give you a sealed scroll, to deliver to Empress Jhena. Your trip will be sponsored entirely by the council, so no more sleeping in barns." He placed a small bag of gold on the table.

"You don't have to do that. It is our honor to serve the people, truly!" Jon earnestly replied, but the councilman pushed the bag closer to us. Benjin leaned forward and took it, tying it to his belt beside his axe.

"You will be compensated for the work you have done thus far as well in due time." Mister Sari slowly stood up. "I believe the service for your friend is at dusk. You best go and prepare yourselves."

We rose to our feet and bowed. A guard opened the door and the same nameless boy stood still, looking at the floor. We followed him out the door, as we led him to our room.

As relieved as I was to know the council would cover us financially, I couldn't help but feel a knot in my stomach and a tight feeling in my chest. I thought of Laago, a boy who came from nothing and then continued to sacrifice the little that he did have to protect those he loved. He overcame so much in his life, severe physical and mental abuse, living on the streets alone as a child, and raising himself. He could have given up and become a bitter and angry person, but he didn't. He refused to. Laago fought against the life he was dealt with every bone in his body, but his time was cut short. His beautiful soul, his pure heart... I longed for the day we could be together again, but in the meantime, I knew in my heart that he was taking care of my mother and sisters, making them laugh and warming their souls. Jon put his hand on my shoulder.

"How are you feeling?" He asked, as we entered our room.

"There are no words I could use to say."

"That is okay," Jon assured me. Benjin flopped onto our bed and buried his face into the thick white blanket. "You've barely spoken today. How are you holding up?"

But Benjin didn't answer. Instead he laid still, blocking himself from reality. I didn't have the strength to be there for him. Every step I took and every fake smile I painted on my face took all of the energy

I could muster. I felt a dark cloud blanket over Benjin. His heart was weak and broken. I sat on the edge of the bed and looked out the window. If Laago was still with us, we would have likely spent the day at the beach, playing in the waves.

"I'm going to get ready for tonight." Jon stepped into the bathroom, leaving the door cracked open. "If you need me, let me know."

Though I sat next to Benjin on the bed, it felt like we were an ocean apart. Even when we lost our mother and sisters, Benjin never faltered. He stayed strong and took over the responsibilities they left empty. But losing Laago was different. He was the only person Benjin was truly honest with, even when it pained him. It's a lot easier to open up about your insecurities to a good friend than a parent or sibling. I'm sure Benjin told Laago things he would never consider sharing with me. When I put my hand on his back, I realized his body was trembling. Benjin sat there quietly weeping into the blanket until he fell asleep.

# CHAPTER EIGHTEEN

# EVERYTHING TO NOTHING

"HAVE YOU EVER HEARD of an akni tree?" I asked, walking into the bathroom. Jon stood in front of the mirror, shaving his face. The razorblade danced along his neck, before he flicked it away just beneath his chin. He turned to look at me, his eyebrows raised and his head tilted. I took a seat on the toilet next to him.

"Yes, why?"

"Supposedly the bark has spiritual properties?"

"Akni bark has been illegal in the Republic of Terlu for ages." He turned back around to the mirror, carefully sliding the razor across his cheek. "What sparks your interest?"

"Why is it illegal?"

"Because it makes people lose their minds," Jon stated, matter-of-factly. "I'm surprised you don't know about it."

"Is that the drug that collapsed the Onumi Empire?" Benjin called over, who must have woken from his nap when I left the bed.

"That and economic turmoil due to hyperinflation," he explained as he wiped the shaving oil off his face and leaned against the doorway.

"Is there anything you don't know?" Benjin sat up on the bed. "Give us a history lesson, Mister Jon."

"It all started around five hundred years ago, with the last true king of the Onumi Empire, King Nao III. The Onumi Empire was once a leading country, their economy dominated the west. It was King Nao III who globalized trade, truly uniting the west with the east for the first time in history. He opened trade with Emperor Jheman, first of his name, ruler of the Empire of Gala, who is actually the great ancestor of Empress Jhena and is whom she is named after. If it wasn't for King Nao III, the Empire of Gala may have never become as prosperous as it is now. Emperor Jheman even named a city after Nao and sent him one of his sisters as a wife." Jon shook his head. "Sorry, I am getting off topic."

"No, please, keep going. I love it!" Benjin chirped. The sudden burst of his old self threw me off. His inner strength never ceased to amaze me.

"King Nao III wed Beira of Gala, and they had a son, but she died during childbirth. Emperor Jheman later arranged for another sister to be the new wife of the King of Onumi, with whom he had two more sons," Jon explained. "Around twenty years later, Prince Nao IV, the king's first son, went on a diplomatic trip to the Empire of Gala. During his return, he visited the Sacred Forest of Akta, seeking a tree that allowed communication with the dead. He desperately wanted to speak to his deceased mother. According to the legend, he blamed himself for the death of his mother and carried that great burden with him."

"That's terrible."

"Unfortunately, it only gets worse. Prince Nao IV went behind the native healers' backs and stole seeds of the tree from their sacred land and brought it back to the Onumi Empire. Some say they cursed him and his empire, because things quickly fell to pieces once he returned."

"What happened?"

"A couple things. One, the Onumi Empire may have seemed prosperous, but apparently they had been in serious debt for years. King Nao III had just been inflating their currency, never actually solving the root of the problem. It was a bubbling pot about to explode and send their currency plummeting to zero, being completely worthless."

"What a moron!" Benjin exclaimed. He rose to his feet and walked into the bathroom, joining us. He stood towering behind Jon and began fixing his hair in the mirror. "What was he thinking?"

"Many men are foolish when it comes to money, they spend more than they bring in. That's a major problem with monarchies, it just takes one fool to ruin a nation." Jon's words may have been harsh but they were wise. "I think that's why Prince Nao IV had been in the Empire of Gala, his country was bankrupt and he needed money- fast. Either way, it was a lost cause. He returned home to his father rebuilding their perfectly good castle, while their people were starving. Prince Nao IV slipped into despair. Once the akni tree grew from the stolen seedlings, he tried the bark and went insane. He lost his mind."

"Did he ever regain his sanity?" I asked.

"No, his addiction consumed him," Jon solemnly said. "It is said that he burnt down their castle with King Nao III, the queen, and his two half-brothers trapped inside. He set fires all across their empire with a group of fanatics, burning it to the ground. The whole time he screamed and cried, saying he had no choice, because the empire would fall either way. Then, he killed himself."

"So that's it?" Benjin's jaw dropped. "He just killed everyone?"

"Everyone in the castle died, but not in the empire. The wealthy fled to the Kingdom of Yana, but unfortunately, the common people had no choice but to flee to the Qara Desert and start anew. These were the first known people to create permanent settlements there and eventually became known as the Qarans. They are often confused with the Khurayl Raiders, though they share no similarities in culture nor history."

"You're a walking history book." Benjin left the bathroom and laid back in bed. "It really is the Lost Lands of Onumi, huh? No one even talks about their history."

"Yeah, it has kind of become forgotten. I guess it is just too dark for people to want to remember." Jon trailed off in thought before refocusing. "Why are we talking about this again?"

"I was just wondering..." I lied, hesitating to reveal the bark the healer had given me. What if they were opposed to it and impulsively discarded it? I needed time to make a decision of whether I would use it or not, then I could tell them. Jon shrugged it aside and moved on.

"I wish I had formal clothes to wear. It feels inappropriate attending a service without proper attire." Jon looked down at his wrinkled shirt and stained pants.

"I've worn this outfit for so long that it feels a part of me." I shrugged, rising back to my feet. I slid next to him in front of the mirror. "My hair looks like a rat's nest." I shuddered at the sight of myself and sat back down on the toilet.

"There's a bunch of stuff in here. When I saw the razor, I couldn't help but shave my face. I was looking like a rat myself." Jon pulled open a drawer under the sink, handing me a brush.

"I'm okay," I said, waving my hand. I was struggling enough as it was to just sit there and hold a conversation. The thought of doing anything made me want to collapse in bed, like Benjin. I had no energy to take care of myself.

"Here," he called as he stepped behind me and began to gently brush through my knotted hair. "Just tell me if I am hurting you."

"You don't have to do this..." But Jon didn't respond to my comment, instead he just quietly hummed. I closed my eyes, zoning out to his voice. I felt safe with him, a rare feeling that usually took years for me to develop with a new person. Having someone brush my hair for me reminded me of being a helpless child, but as embarrassed as I was, it felt nice having someone care for me. "Thank you."

"I loved brushing Jin's hair when she was a little, but she won't let me anymore."

"No, I mean thank you for everything," I whispered. Though my eyes were shut, I felt him softly kiss the top of my head. It surprised me, but not from a place of discomfort. It felt innocent and sweet. We sat there in silence for a moment, as he stroked my hair.

"All done," he boasted. "You look great." He set the brush back in its drawers and swung his hands up, walking into the bedroom. I sat there for a moment, still feeling his warmth. He jumped on the bed, startling Benjin.

"Where's all this energy coming from?" Benjin couldn't help but grin at Jon's contagious smile.

"We get to meet the Empress of Gala! Do you know what that means?"

"Uh, we get to rally for more troops?"

"Well, that, but we can find out if your father is imprisoned in the Mountains of Shiren!" Jon exclaimed. Benjin's hand swung up, slapping into his own forehead.

"How am I so stupid?" He gasped. "I was so focused on Laago that I forgot about my own father."

"You're not stupid, you're mourning." Jon sat next to him. "But it is happening. We will finally find out what happened to him!"

Sitting in the bathroom, I began to cry. I buried my face in my shirt to muffle the sound as tears flooded down my cheeks. I, too, was blinded by the loss of Laago to see what was right in front of us. When we tell Empress Jhena of the atrocities led by General Ahkpi, she will undoubtedly free our father. We can finally be with him again.

I rose to my feet and stood in front of the mirror, still choked up. When I looked at my reflection, I felt strange, as if I was a mere spectator outside of my own body. I look a lot older than I remember, my face was thinner and my eyes more narrow. I was no longer a bright eyed kid with an innocent smile. I survived things I could have never imagined as a child. I had seen things that changed my world. But inside, I felt even more lost and scared than ever before.

A sudden knock at the door interrupted my thoughts. I quickly wiped my tears and splashed water on my face. I didn't want anyone to worry about me, it only made me feel uncomfortable. I just had to get by. Jon opened the door, allowing the nameless boy to enter. As always, he stared at the floor and avoided making eye contact.

"The high monk would like to see you before the service begins." He bowed and extended his arms out. In his hands laid a neatly folded dress.

"What is this?"

"A dress for Nyla to wear," he spoke, with his head still down. I watched from the bathroom doorway as Jon took the dress from the boy's hands, letting it unravel onto the floor. It was a pale blue dress made of silk, with long bell sleeves and a cascade collar.

"It's beautiful!" Jon commented, running his hand along the bodice.

"It is," Benjin agreed. "What do you think, Nyla?"

"I don't want it."

"It is a gift from Master Sari." The boy's head shot up. "It's the color of your empire."

"Tell him I said thank you, but I have no need for it," I said. "The only gift I will accept is arrows. My supply runs short."

"But it was a gift," he repeated, his voice shaking. "Master Sari-"

"We will tell him," Jon assured him. "Do not worry."

"Then that settles it." Benjin tossed the dress onto the bed and motioned me over. "Let us see this high monk you speak of."

We followed the boy through the hall and back down the spiral staircase. This time, the guards held the large iron entrance doors open for us, revealing a beautiful view of the main stairs that led down to the ocean. It was like a painting, soft fluffy clouds striped across the light blue sky that melted into the deep blue water. I wish Laago was here to see this.

"This is as far as I am permitted to take you." The boy abruptly stopped walking. "Follow this path to the tower, where the monk is waiting for you." He pointed towards the tower, which stood in grandeur and overlooked the island. It was tall, made of cobblestone, with a gold pointed roof.

"Thanks, bud." Jon patted the boy's back, before he turned off the main path and began down the smaller stone path. The boy's eyes widened and his body tensed up, he seemed surprised to be touched- even in such a casual manner. I bet he never gets thanked for his work either.

I followed behind the boys, admiring the island. We passed through a neatly arranged flower garden, surrounded by lush green grass. There was a slight incline in the path, because the tower rested on a hill, with a cliff separating the island from the ocean. A warm breeze flew through the flowers and up the tower's cobblestone walls, rattling a large open window that marked the top floor. I noticed a young man who sat leaning against the windowsill.

He wore a white robe, similar to the ones the council wore, but he seemed far too young to be a member. He had wavy white hair that was neatly parted down the middle, reaching his shoulders. His skin is so pale that it glows in the sun's light. He looked so lonely, as he longingly gazed over the horizon. Something about him deeply intrigued me. Though it was too far for me to see his eyes, I saw him turn his head to us. I quickly looked away, but out of the corner of my eye I watched him disappear from the windowsill. I looked at the boys, but neither seemed to notice. We walked in silence, because it was clear Benjin did not want to talk. Besides, there was nothing worth saying anyway.

When we approached the tower, it seemed the door was not shut. Without knocking, Jon pushed it open and walked in. As always, his hand rested on his sword. The ground was made of aged wood and our heavy boots caused it to creak loudly as we entered, sending its echo up through the tower. There was no furniture, just holes carved into the walls with melting candles, mirroring the design in the main estate. I looked up at the spiral wooden staircase that stretched up the cold cobblestone walls.

"Hello?" Jon called. "We were requested to speak with the monk."

"Yes, come upstairs," an old voice echoed.

This time Benjin led the way, crouching under the next layer of stairs. Most buildings were not meant for someone as tall as he is, especially in an old tower like this one. Light shined through the small circular windows that lined the walls, offering a glimpse of the island. As we climbed the staircase, the main estate appeared to look smaller and smaller.

"Look!" I stopped. A bird's nest rested on the other side of the window. Three small eggs laid unattended in it.

"I wonder what type of eggs those are," Jon pondered, analyzing them. "They are too small to be seabird eggs..." He continued up the stairs to catch up to Benjin, who did not even stop to look.

"It is a lovebird nest," the man answered as we stepped into his room. He sat on the floor in a deep orange robe with his legs crossed beneath him. There was a small bookshelf behind him, barely half full, and a wooden ladder stretching against the wall through a hole leading to the top floor. The only other furniture was a low table with a teapot and a small stone board with different colored crystals resting on it. "If you kiss an egg, it serves as good luck to your love life."

"I've never heard of that," Jon replied. "Are you the monk?"

"I am what they call a monk," he spoke purposefully, each word that left his mouth was intentional.

"I am Jon Li, from the Republic of Terlu." He bowed his head. "This is Benjin and Nyla, who are from the Suhai Empire."

"My given name is Hosdayel of Kito, a small island north of the Kingdom of Yana, but you may call me Day. How are you, my children?"

"Good, sir. How are you?" Jon sat down on the floor before him, then Benjin and I followed suit. It was cold, a draft floated down from the open hatch that led the attic above.

"I am." He smiled, his eyes bright. "I heard news of your travels as well as your terrible loss. I wanted to offer you my condolences."

"Thank you, sir."

"How are you handling this loss?" Day's words felt so sincere that they pierced my heart. Jon's eyes got lost in the floor for a moment before rejoining with the monk's.

"Not well, sir," he admitted. "Though I am the last who should speak." He looked over to Benjin, who just blankly stared out the small circular window.

"Thank you for your honesty. Many men pretend to be at ease when their mind is on fire..." His eyebrows raised as his lips curled to a slight smile. "But then no one will know to bring a bucket of water to remedy the flames. I think there is much bravery in admitting vulnerability. This is a safe space, you do not need to build walls."

His eyes drifted to Benjin, but my brother did not budge. I heard a loud thud above us, causing me to flinch. Jon's hand instinctively reached for his sword. We were not alone.

"What was that?"

"Ko!" The monk called. "Do not be shy, come greet our guests."

I heard another thud, before a man jumped down from the hole in the ceiling and swiftly landed on one knee, with one fist against the hardwood floor. He was the man I noticed sitting in the windowsill on our way in. He was so beautiful, his features almost looked feminine. His hair was as white as snow, it looked so pure and soft, without a single piece out of place. The white robe was draped over him so elegantly, he almost looked fake- like a doll. Though as beautiful as he was, I felt a great sadness in him. He had sharp eyes as blue as Benjin's, but they were missing something. They felt... Empty. He slowly rose to his feet and spoke, his voice soft and gentle.

"I am Zarak Yoko of the Kingdom of Yana. It is an honor to meet you, Nyla, from the Suhai Empire, and Jon Li, from the Republic of Terlu. And Benjin..." He clasped his hands. "It is a pleasure to see you again."

"You as well." Benjin nodded, momentarily breaking his gaze from the window.

"Are you a member of the council?" Jon asked, clearly confused as well. He looked far too young to be a part of such a grand and noble council, yet he wore the cloak and even had the emblem of the Kingdom of Yana pinned to his chest to prove it- a snow falcon with a winter rose hanging from its beak.

"Aye, I represent my kingdom." He leaned against the bookshelf.

"Ko replaced the last representative of the Kingdom of Yana five years ago, when he was just sixteen." He looked lovingly at Zarak Yoko. "I have mentored him since he was young and did not let him leave the kingdom to serve without me."

"It is truly a pleasure to meet you, Zarak Yoko of the Kingdom of Yana." Jon stood up to bow, but he waved him to sit back down.

"Zarak is fine." His eyes drifted to the window, joining Benjin's lost in the ocean's waves. His energy felt very different from the other members of the council we have met so far. Jia Sagtra of Gala, Nahksona Rykima of Terlu, and Okurai Sari of Chao Binh had strong personalities. I could tell they were born leaders from a single conversation with each of them. Zarak Yoko of Yana seemed too soft to lead. "It must have been a long journey across the sea."

"About two and a half days."

"Did you follow the Hua Stream?"

"Yessir." Jon nodded. "It made rowing significantly easier, the current practically pulled us here."

"I'm sure your arms are sore nonetheless."

"That's the least of our worries," Benjin quietly interrupted. I felt a great surge of irritation in his voice. Zarak's eyes widened in shock for a moment, before quickly narrowing.

"Oh, gods..." He slowly slid his back down the wall, dropping to the floor. "I am becoming one of them." He rubbed his forehead and shook his head.

"One of who?" Jon asked.

"Everyone wastes precious time dwelling on the little things, so they never have to face the real issues. Whether it stems from fear, laziness, or disinterest..." He leaned back against the wall, his eyes drifting to the ceiling. "I suppose it is all the same at the end of the day."

At first impression, the blank gaze in Zarak's eyes could be mistaken for detachment or his vague response as boredom, but I think his mind may actually be flooded with thoughts and worries, creating a wall between him and the world around us. His quickness to empathize with us reminded me of Jon, who was hypersensitive to emotion- arguably to a fault.

"It's true," the monk agreed. "Small talk feels easiest, but we are here to discuss the truth. I will be leading the service for your friend at dusk, so I would like to focus on him and you all for a bit."

"What more is there to say?" Benjin sighed, pushing his hair out of his face.

"Whatever will begin lifting the weight off your shoulders. It is not your burden to carry."

"I was supposed to protect him and I failed to. Now Laago lays dead because of it. It is my burden," Benjin snapped. His words stabbed through my heart like daggers, tears began to flood my face. "Nyla..." He hid his eyes behind his hands, ashamed of his outburst.

"If I made the shot..." I cried. Benjin got up and wrapped his body around me. No matter how much pain he was in, he always put it to the side and protected me before himself.

"You did everything you could, while I sat there and did nothing."

"I was the only one who could have done something." I buried my face in his chest. "I'm sorry. It should have been me."

"No." Benjin grabbed my face and stared into my eyes. I could see his heart wanted to say more, but his mind stopped him. "It should have been the militant."

"It is not your burden. Laago sacrificed himself for all of us. We will carry it together, forever honoring him," the monk spoke softly. "Did Laago believe in the gods?"

"No," I responded, wiping the tears from my face. "He didn't."

"That is okay. The gods don't care whether you bow for them or not." He raised his hand and gently tapped against his heart. "This is all that matters. His heart was good, so the gods will look favorably upon him. He will find himself a seat at the eternal table, beside the great gods and goddesses in Qalia."

"How narcissistic would the gods be to only accept those who swoon for them?" Zarak contemplated aloud. "Some of the most religious people are also the furthest from the gods... They can be more lost than those who openly denounce them."

"The gods are good, just, and all-knowing. They will see Laago for who he is, the purest essence of his soul. Worry not."

"They owe him that much," Benjin interjected. "After not protecting him."

"Yes, they do," the monk calmly responded. "Now, tell me about Laago. I want my speech to be true to him."

We sat in silence for a moment. Benjin continued to desperately stare out the window and my eyes remained lost in the floor. I thought back to the old days, before we left Tinshe and dove into the unknown. Laago was always at my home, with a smile on his face. He just wanted to be happy and have a good time. He never complained, no matter how heavy his work schedule was. His basement apartment was dark and damp, barely a home, but he was nothing short of appreciative of it.

"He was always there with a smile." I shook my head, thinking of all the dumb jokes he has cracked over the years. "And he always had something funny to say. He was the type of person you always wanted around, no matter what was happening. He was a rock."

"He was." Benjin looked over to me, tears streaming down his cheeks. His eyes were smiling in memory of his dear friend, though his heart was deeply wounded. "I would swing by his place after crappy days at work and he always had a way of making me forget why I was even mad in the first place."

"Mother and father really loved him."

"So did Luchi and Dalia," Benjin winced. "I cannot fathom telling Luka..."

"I don't want to even think about that right now. He'll be devastated."

"What we do for love..." Benjin mumbled. "His last words said more than a whole life ever could."

"How could he say something so beautiful while something so ugly was happening?" I shuddered. The image of him taking his last breaths, with an arrow deep in his chest, barraged my mind.

"Death is many things but ugly," the monk voiced. "It is not the opposite of life, but the essence of it. It is not the end, but a new beginning. They are two parts of a whole, one just as inevitable as the other. Do not fear it, as you would not life, because to fear the inevitable would mirror insanity. Your friend knew this, which is why his heart was open enough to focus on the love that led his life, not the fear that could have so easily engulfed it."

"We can live by love or die by fear," Zarak declared.

"I just feel so lost. I don't know how I am supposed to go on without him," Benjin admitted. "I have all of these emotions whirling around inside of me like a volcano that is about to erupt."

"And that is okay. There is nothing wrong with feeling negative emotions," the monk said. "Emotions exist because they are meant to be felt, it is in the name. Pretending they do not exist may feel better in the moment, however, it will only cause you more inner turmoil overtime. Allow yourself to face these terrible feelings head on."

"The weight of them is crushing me." Benjin buried his face in his hands. "I end up losing everyone I love."

"We all do. That is life. We live every day knowing that one day will be our last, but that is not a reason to stop living. In fact, it may be a reason why humans are so ambitious. We have so many wants and needs. Nothing is ever enough, so we strive for the stars, though we know that one day we will return to them."

"Aye." Zarak nodded in accord. A loud bang on a gong interrupted our conversation, sending shivers down my spine. I anxiously looked at Benjin. "It is time."

"Ko will lead you to the service." The monk slowly rose to his feet. "I will meet you all there shortly."

"Thank you for your time, sir." Jon graciously bowed before him.

"It is I who should be thanking you all for your time. It was an honor to talk with you young heroes." He leaned over and put his shaky hand on Benjin's shoulder. "You have come so far. Do not surrender now."

"Ready?" Jon held his hand out for me and pulled me to my feet. We stood still for a moment, our eyes lost in each other's. His emerald green eyes shone in the window's light. They were full of sadness, I could feel it.

"I have no choice but to be."

We followed Zarak down the steep spiral staircase and out the door. My head was spinning from our long conversation; it delved far deeper than I was prepared for. Both the monk and Zarak forced me to think about things that I tried so desperately to avoid. I felt lightheaded and nauseous, physically and mentally exhausted. I was not ready for the service, though I don't believe I could ever be. But for Laago, I had to try to stay strong, even if it cost me my life.

The sun was slowly falling from the sky, preparing to finally set for the night. Its golden rays reflected against the water, causing a shimmer in the deep blue waves. Under different circumstances, I was sure it would have looked beautiful, but it just made me feel sad to see such a view without Laago. All I saw was gray.

Zarak walked ahead of us, silently leading the way. I appreciated that he did not try to start small talk, because none of us were in the mood for it. I looked over to Jon, my mind filled with worry. He rubbed his forehead and exhaled heavily, trailing behind us. Neither he nor Benjin have been speaking much at all, which made time move painfully slow. I slowed down and walked beside him.

"Are you okay?"

"Don't worry about me, Nyla." He looked at me and pursed his lips, his eyes squinting from the sun. A small fake smile grazed his face in an attempt to hide how he truly felt. "Just have a bit of a headache." He finally admitted. I could tell him to take care of himself first or to not push himself too hard, but I saw no point. Any response I could muster felt half-hearted or ingenuine.

We walked down the main steps, which overlooked the shoreline. I could see that people had already begun to gather. My heart rate accelerated and I began to sweat. I dreaded having to talk to them. Since we arrived on the island, it had been one thing after another. I just wanted to be alone with my brother, so I could try to process all of this.

The water was still, not a single gust of wind breezed by. The waves ever so gently drifted into the shore, as if they were softly kissing the sand. Four of the council members were already here, with their long robes draped over their bodies, brushing against the sand as they walked. They watched us as we stepped down the staircase, led by Zarak. I heard the echoes of Nahksona's voice, as he rambled loudly to Jia Sagtra of Gala. Her dark eyes were deeply focused on us, I am sure she did not even hear a single word that flooded out of his mouth.

"Welcome!" Nahksona shouted, abruptly ending his one sided conversation with Jia. He waved his hands theatrically, as if we didn't already see him.

"Hello," Zarak calmly responded, finally reaching the end of the long staircase. "Monk Day will arrive shortly."

"Beautiful day, is it not?" Nahksona's blindness to our pain left a distaste in my mouth. What a beautiful day to say goodbye to a lifelong friend, whose life was cut violently short.

"How are you feeling?" Jia stepped in front of Nahksona, blocking his ignorance from us.

"Been better," Benjin honestly answered. Though Jia did not respond, her eyes did. She tilted her head and softly looked at us, her eyes saying more than words could.

"My condolences." Mister Sari held his hand out to Benjin, firmly shaking it. He shook Jon's hand next, before turning his back to us and gazing at the water.

Of course, he did not even look at me. I watched disdain grow in Jia Sagtra's eyes. Not only was a fellow member of the council a woman, but the most powerful leader in all of the lands was too. By discrediting me due to my gender, he was also disrespecting the Empress Jhena of the Empire of Gala. I reckon she would not look fondly upon Mister Sari.

"What a shame it is to meet under these circumstances," a man in a deep blue robe rumbled. "I am Tsalen Ban of the Suhai Empire." He had brown wavy hair that freely rested just above his shoulders with stubble across his face, eerily similar to Laago's.

"It is an honor to meet you, Mister Tsalen Ban of the Suhai Empire." Jon bowed his head. "I am Jon Li, from the Republic of Terlu, and this is Nyla, from the Suhai Empire."

"The honor is mine." A smile crept across his face. "In times as dark as these, it is important to remember that it is people like you who represent our wonderful empire, not the traitors. Suhai is ours, not theirs. Let them think what they want, because justice always prevails in the end."

Before I could reply, the crowd's murmuring halted to complete silence. I looked up to Benjin, whose eyes had joined the others, drifting to the wooden staircase. The nameless boy stood still at the top of the stairs, frozen in time. He was wearing a white ceremonial gown that drowned his tiny body and a tall white cone-shaped hat with a sheer veil over his face. He looked like a spirit.

He held his arm stretched high in the sky, clenching the stem of a small brass bell that twinkled in the sun. The boy swiftly flicked his wrist, shaking the bell a single time, and traveled down a single step. I clenched my chest as the echo of the bell flew down the stairs and past us on the beach. His eyes were locked forward, not straying from the sun. He rang the bell and took another step. None of the council members dared to move. Even Nahksona stood still, not uttering a word, with his emerald green robe fluttering in the wind.

The boy slowly continued this process until he reached the bottom of the seemingly endless staircase. He stood there for a moment in silence. I watched him inhale deeply, before he abruptly spun around and dropped to his knees, bowing before the stairs. As my eyes drifted upwards, I noticed Monk Day appeared, standing before us at the top. I could swear he looked directly at me, with a sad grimace. He began to slowly raise a golden box with colorful stained glass sides into the sky, until his arms were stretched out completely. Its glass shimmered in the sunlight, casting a small rainbow. He stood there for what felt like an eternity, before finally taking his first few steps down the stairs. As he walked, his cloak glided down the steps behind him.

When he reached the bottom, he leaned over and put his hand on the nameless boy's head affectionately, who hesitatingly raised his head, still avoiding direct eye contact. Monk Day put his hand under the boy's chin and slowly raised it, forcing him to look at him. I felt his anxiety from here, but Monk Day warmly smiled, trying to comfort him. I heard Mister Sari scoff to himself, appalled of Monk Day's inappropriate behavior, which caused me to smile ever so slightly. The boy's hands trembled as Monk Day handed him the golden box, its beautiful colors shimmering under the evening sun. He then walked over to us, only to stop once he stood directly before Benjin, Jon, and me. The boy trailed behind him in the distance, holding the bell high with one arm and hanging his head low. The box rested in the palm of his other hand.

"Today we are joined together not only to mourn the loss of a selfless hero..." He paused and released a heavy breath, his eyes solemnly stuck on Benjin's. "But to celebrate life. Yesterday, Laago of the Suhai Empire's soul decided it was time to leave behind his physical body and begin his next chapter in the afterlife. While some may feel he left us too soon, know that the eternal clock that binds us all is never late nor early."

I felt a pang in my chest. Not only did Monk Day name Laago as a man of the Suhai Empire, but he bore him a great title. Very few people are of their country, unless they are royalty or of high nobility. People like Benjin and I, even Jon who is adopted by the great general of the republic, are merely from our countries, not of them.

The boy rang the bell once, holding it in the sky. Monk Day's head slowly turned to look towards the stairs. A man I had never seen stood there. He was thin and bald, wearing a beige cloak. He had a dark brown leather strap wrapped from his shoulder to waist, with a large golden drum hanging in front. His left hand gripped a wooden stick with a ball attached to the end. As soon as his foot touched the first step, he slammed his stick against the drum, its intense sound sending goosebumps down my spine and rattling my bones. Then, my heart sunk so deep into my chest that I feared I had lost it forever. Four men carrying a large wooden canoe emerged from over the horizon. I clenched onto Benjin's arm as they stood on the stairs.

The men began to slowly tread down the steps, with the weight of the boat distributed on their backs. They wore similar cloaks to the bald man, except theirs ended just above their knees. As they traveled down, I saw the white cloth that mercilessly covered Laago's body. Jon gently placed his hand on the small of my back, a subtle yet warm act that comforted me more than words could.

The closer the men traveled to us, the heavier my heart felt. It pushed against my lungs and caused me to struggle to breathe. Every time the man hit his drum I felt the lump in my throat move further and further up, until it choked me. The men passed through us, separating Benjin, Jon, and me from the council. I watched the sweat slide down their faces as they slowly lowered the boat into the sand. It sat between us, with its front tip facing directly at the setting sun. I could now see it was elegantly crafted, with birds carefully carved throughout, appearing to be dancing in the sky. Monk Day stood directly behind the boat and motioned us closer.

"This boat carried the original members of the council to the Island of Aara, nearly five hundred years ago. It was handcrafted in Eko, by a world revered craftsman. Since then, we have coated it in wax from the Chitiro tree, meaning it cannot burn."

I gingerly ran my hand along the boat's edge, but I was too hesitant to go any closer. I felt denial boil within me. The lump hiding under the white cloth was not Laago. He was my everything... How could he now be reduced to just an empty body? He was so much more than that.

But Benjin... Benjin collapsed into the sand, his face buried in the cloth and his arms wrapped around what was once his best friend. The helpless cries that poured out of my poor brother shattered my world.

"Laago..." He sputtered between breaths. "I couldn't protect you... My brother..."

As the words left his mouth, they pierced me. I dropped down beside Benjin and wrapped one arm around him. My other hand slid under the cloth and squeezed onto Laago's hand. It did not feel like him- it was cold and empty. Jon stepped closer and placed his hand on Laago's leg. His eyes were closed, but tears slowly rained down his face as well.

"Let it out," Monk Day finally spoke. "All of your grief, fury, and hopelessness... Expel it from yourself. Scream, cry, and curse the world around you. Let it all out!"

As he spoke the bald man began to steadily beat his drum, his stick quickly rattling against its head. Benjin's cries slowly rose to a yell, exploding into an agonizing scream. He cursed the militants for murdering Laago, General Ahkpi for tearing our home apart, and the plague for killing our family. He cursed at himself, for failing to protect Laago, and even the tides for not carrying us quicker from harm. He slammed his fists into the sand before he finally buried his head in his hands and wept like a baby.

"I can't do this anymore!" He cried. "I can't pretend to be strong. I surrender." He dropped his hands and raised his head, his face looking up at the sky, wet with tears. He panted to catch his breath.

"Thank you," Monk Day said. "You deserve to release some of your pain. Thank you for being vulnerable with us."

"I love you so much. I can't do this without you." Benjin flung his arm around me and pulled me in, kissing the top of my head. I crawled onto his lap and wrapped my arms around him tightly. I sat there for a moment crying, refusing to open my eyes.

"Now that you have released, we will let go," the monk said.

"No!" Benjin lunged forward, tightly grabbing onto the edge of the boat. "Please..."

"Release him. Let Laago return to the warm arms of our Earth," Monk Day spoke slowly and with intention. "He deserves to lay in peace." Benjin paused for a moment, seeming to take his words to heart. Finally, he crawled over to Laago and hovered over his body.

"I love you, Laago. Please... Say hi to our mother and the girls for me." He kissed Laago's forehead through the cloth. "I'll be with you again one day."

He looked down at me. Though my eyes were wide with defeat, I knew what I had to do. I rose to my feet and stood beside Benjin. I took a deep breath and wiped my endless stream of tears before leaning over Laago. I placed my hand on his shoulder and began to whisper in his ear.

"You always saw the beauty in me, even when I could not. You taught me how to love myself. Thank you for that. I love you more than I ever told you, but I bet you knew it anyway. You knew you were my first love... And perhaps you'll be my last." I thought of all the times we had, all of the smiles shared. "But as much as I want to be with you right now, I am not done with this life yet. Just as you taught me, I won't give up. I will keep fighting. I will for you... And you will live through me, Laago. I love you." I kissed his forehead and turned to Benjin, hiding my face in his chest.

The nameless boy handed the golden box to Monk Day, before drifting back behind everyone. The members of the council stood quietly at the other side of the boat. Nahksona looked at me with a sad grimace. Jia Sagtra looked at the ground, her head bowed and her hands clasped together. The bald man slowed his drum roll, beating it once every few seconds. As he did, the four carriers stepped forward and began to push the boat into the sea. I felt a piece of me leave as they did their final push, sending the boat sailing with the tide. The boy with no name knelt before me with my bow. I anxiously looked over to Benjin.

"I can't." I shook my head.

"It should be you." Benjin put his hand on my shoulder. "It's what Laago would want."

My hands trembled as I picked the bow up. The boy dipped an arrow in a pouch of liquid that hung from his side. He quickly swiped it against a black stone, sending sparks flying. He did it once more, igniting the arrow, before handing it to me. I placed the arrow on the string and pulled it back.

I closed my eyes for a moment and envisioned Laago. His goofy smile, his soft hair, and his warm eyes... I opened one eye and focused on the boat as it slowly drifted away. I released an arrow and watched it cut up through the air before it fell, hitting straight into the hay that surrounded his body. It instantly ignited.

I instinctively closed my eyes and dropped my bow on the ground, but something in me made me almost immediately reopen them. I would stand by Laago through everything and that included his physical self's final moments. I did not wipe my tears, nor did Benjin. Instead, we allowed them to flow as we said goodbye to our dear friend. A strange feeling began to fill me- a sort of emptiness. Zarak caught my eye, his white hair shimmering in the setting sun's rays.

His eyes were lost in the flames that danced in the burning boat. I watched a single glimmering tear roll down his cheek and drop onto the cold sand beneath him.

"His ashes will be collected for you," Monk Day assured us. "For now, accept this."

He held the golden box in front of us, its stained glass reflecting in the light. My hand trembled as it lifted open the box, revealing Laago's daggers. I hesitated to pick one up, to hold something he once held so tightly. Benjin's hand swung up and clenched his chest as he gazed at the weapons.

"The leather strap he used to tie his hair with is here as well." Monk Day picked it up and slid it onto my wrist. It loosely hung on. I finally reached into the box and took a dagger, tracing my fingers along the blade. Its leather handle was worn-down and faded, and there was a small chip in the edge of the iron blade. Benjin followed suit and took the second dagger. His eyes studied it for a moment, before he brought the blade to his mouth and softly kissed it.

"Thank you." His eyes drifted up, meeting Day's.

"They belong to you," he sincerely replied.

Benjin and Monk Day drifted into a conversation, but my mind felt too weak to contribute. I slipped off my boots and stepped towards the water, allowing the waves to crash onto my feet, the cold ocean foam sticking to my toes. The fire had subsided in the boat, leaving a faint trail of black smoke behind. My eyes drifted up as a flock of white seabirds flew overhead, twirling in the sky. The sun had finally set, leaving me in darkness.

"Ah, seabirds..." Zarak's voice called from behind me. "It is said they serve as good luck." He stepped beside me in the water, clenching onto his white cloak to keep it from dragging in the water. I tried to respond, but no words left my mouth. I felt my anxiety grow as he stood behind me in silence. "I know what it feels like to lose everything."

"You do?" I asked skeptically, as my hands fidgeted with Laago's blade.

"I do." He slowly nodded his head. "I did not come to this island by choice."

"When I first saw you, I was surprised you were a member of the council... You don't seem to fit in."

"To many, it would be an honor." He turned to me, but his stare felt too intense, I had to look away. "But to me, it was a punishment."

"Why were you selected as a member of the Civil Council? All the others were high ranking officials before they were sent here, but you, you're so young."

"Aye, it is true. Jia Sagtra of Gala was the grand advisor to the empress. Okurai Sari of Chao Binh was chief of relations between the west and east. Nahksona Rykima of Terlu was the grand diplomat, and Tsalen Ban of Suhai was master of coin." He looked back to the ocean. "All of them shared a life of experience in politics and economics."

"And you?"

"Me? I suppose I was a nuisance."

"King Zabaar Mazraat III could have chosen anyone, why would he not choose someone that actually wanted this?"

"He could have," Zarak agreed, "but it was not him who chose. It was his son, Prince Xan."

"He was the second prince until his brother passed, right?" I asked, trying to mask my knowledge of the rumors Jon once shared with me.

"Aye, Prince Zabar Mazraat IV passed shortly before the plague. May he rest in peace." His tone changed, he sounded on edge. He closed his eyes for a moment and quietly whispered a few words to himself. "Now, Prince Xan is heir to the throne."

"You sound displeased with that."

"Careful now." I could swear for a moment he almost smiled, but as if a wall came down, his face went blank. "I live to serve King Zabar Mazraat III. Whoever succeeds him will have my loyalty as well."

"Did you know him personally?"

"I did. My father was the Grand Duke, ordered to succeed the king in the event of tragedy until his son was of age and fit to rule."

"Was?"

"He passed suddenly, just before Prince Zabar IV."

"Do you believe in coincidences?" I asked, knowing there was more to this than what appeared at surface level.

"I do not." Zarak released a heavy sigh. "And Prince Xan knows that, which is why it was easier to cast me away here than to deal with me there."

"Zarak Yoko," Tsalen Ban interrupted from the shoreline. "How surprising it is to see you!"

"Tsalen Ban." He turned around to face him, but before he walked away, he whispered, "be wary of who you entrust."

"You'll catch a cold if you stay in the water all night," Jon called over, interrupting my thoughts. He stood in the sand, carrying my boots. I looked down at my legs and saw they were covered in goosebumps.

"I did not realize how cold it had gotten." I shivered as I stepped out of the water.

"You're shaking," he observed, his expression filled with concern. He tenderly rubbed his hands down my arms, trying to warm me. "I know things have been really hard for you, but I am so amazed at how strong you have been."

"I don't feel strong." I avoided eye contact and looked down at the sand.

"Every step you have taken is a step forward, and that is something to be proud of. Give yourself some credit for once."

"I'm sorry you had to see me like that..." I said, stepping away from him. I glanced down at my hands, which were still scraped up.

"No." He stepped in front of me. "I am so thankful I was there. I don't want to think about what could've happened..."

"Me too," I agreed, looking down at Laago's dagger. I reached into my thigh holster and took out the blade Jon lent me back at his home in the republic, replacing it with Laago's. "Here."

"It was a gift." He waved his hands. "Keep it."

"I have no place for it," I insisted, placing it in his hands anyway. "Besides, you should have a close range weapon as well."

"Alright," he quietly replied, as he stuffed it into his waistband.

"How are you holding up? I know it was hard to leave Jin and General Pago."

"I have no choice but to be hopeful..." I felt the desperation in his voice. Benjin walked over to us, joining our conversation. The members of the Civil Council had drifted up the staircase one by one, finally leaving just us on the beach.

"So this is it..." He interrupted. "Tomorrow we sail east to the Empire of Gala."

"Imagine that." Jon shook his head.

"If you told me a year ago- no- one a month ago that I was sent by the Civil Council to personally meet Empress Jhena...." Benjin chuckled to himself. "I would ask how much holiva root you have been taking."

"Less than a week ago I didn't even know an entire militia was marching to my republic's walls." Jon looked to the moon. It was a small sliver in the sky. Benjin put his hand on Jon's shoulder.

"General Pago is a true leader. There is no one who I believe in more. The Republic of Terlu will not fall." Benjin's words were spoken with unwavering intensity.

"I know," Jon whispered, but his voice was filled with uncertainty. "I think I'm going to call it a night." He stretched his arms.

"We'll meet you there," Benjin said.

We stood there for a few moments in silence, watching the waves crash. The crescent moon was slowly rising, leaving the stars to illuminate the dark night sky.

"I know you really loved him." Benjin looked down at me, his eyes wet with tears. "And whether he realized it or not, he loved you too." He wrapped his arm around me and pulled me in, kissing the top of my head. As if the walls to a dam exploded, tears began to flood down my face.

"I loved him so much," I sputtered between sobs, nestling my face in his chest.

"I know..." He whispered ever so softly. "I understand the pain you feel." His eyes drifted onto the ocean, his gaze lost at sea. He began to mumble to himself.

"What?" I asked, looking up at him.

"I was just wondering," he pondered aloud. "What would Laago say if he was here with us right now?"

I looked off to the ocean, its waves tumbling before us. They were controlled by a distant force that pushed and pulled on them continuously, no matter how far apart they were. Laago may not be physically with us, but his spirit will live with us eternally. And one day, I believe our souls will be reunited.

"Why wasn't the moon hungry?" I asked, unable to hide my grin. A smile immediately spread across Benjin's wet face. "Because it was already full."

"That's exactly what he would have said." He wiped his tears with his shirt. "Come on, let's try to get some sleep."

# CHAPTER NINETEEN

# THE IMPENETRABLE WALL

W E WERE AWOKEN BY knocking on our door. Benjin and I immediately sat up, but I was still half asleep. Jon jumped up from the ground and grabbed his sword, wielding it in one hand. Wearing only his underwear, he swung the door open.

"What?" He groaned to the nameless boy who stood at our door.

"Your attendance is requested."

"What time is it?" Benjin asked, rubbing his eyes.

"Four hours until dawn."

"This can't be good," Jon muttered, throwing pants on.

We all quickly dressed and piled out the door. It was eerily quiet as we followed the nameless boy through the hall. There was not a single sound beside the stomping of our boots as we stepped down the narrow spiral staircase. Though silence pierced the air, twice as many guards blockaded the door. I felt my stomach twist and turn. Something was off. I looked to Jon, his fingers rubbed his forehead anxiously. I held Laago's dagger to my chest for comfort.

The boy stopped before two guards who stood before the meeting hall. Without a single word exchanged, they opened the doors, revealing the long wooden table. Only this time, all of the council members sat around it. Nahksona rose from his chair and stared at us silently, even he did not dare to speak. He sat back down and shook his head in defeat. Jia Sagtra sat to his left and Mister Sari to his right. Their eyes were fixated on a map of the world. Tsalen Ban stood with his back towards us, leaning over the table. Only Zarak stood away from it. He leaned against the wall with his arms crossed. Mister Sari cleared his throat before speaking.

"Our scouts have reported back," he spoke plainly, as if we were merely discussing the weather. "General Pago and his troops held their ground against General Ahkpi's western attack."

"This is great news!" Jon eagerly responded.

"But-" Mister Sari held up his finger, silencing Jon. "The northern wall has been infiltrated."

"How is this possible?" Jon stuttered. "General Ahkpi could not have moved thousands of troops that far north undetected."

"It was not the militia," Zarak revealed. He stood up from the wall and joined the others around the map. He pointed to the northern wall of the Republic of Terlu and dragged his finger north. "At first, there were reports that the Khurayl Raiders of the Qara Desert led an attack on the-"

"That's impossible," Jon said, shaking his head. "It would be suicide."

"Aye, it would be," Zarak agreed, tossing a pendant on the table.

Jon reached over and grabbed it, his hand shaking. It was unmistakable; a silver coin etched with a snow falcon, the token given to every Yanian warrior before his first battle. As soon as he held it before his eyes, they widened.

"How can this be?" He gasped.

"King Zabar-"

"He is no king and you know it," Zarak interjected, addressing Mister Sari. "Prince Xan has controlled every aspect of the Kingdom of Yana since Prince Zabar Mazraat IV passed."

"King Zabar Mazraat III wears the crown," Mister Sari spoke coldly, his eyes narrowing.

"And Prince Xan pulls the strings," Zarak hissed.

"Men..." Nahksona waved his hand. "Enough." Zarak and Mister Sari stood still for a moment, their eyes filled with fire.

"Regardless of who made the order, the northern wall of Terlu has been infiltrated," Jia Sagtra finally spoke, "and there will be repercussions for the invasion, as well as betraying the council."

"Aye, by giving Empress Jhena even more power. I cannot envision that having any foreseeable consequences."

"What good are your words, boy?" Nahksona said.

"I told you my attendance was unwanted." He rolled his eyes and leaned against the wall, slowly sliding down onto the floor. "They burnt every village from the Port of Eura to the walls of Terlu... Killed all the men..."

"Are there any survivors?" Benjin gasped, thinking of all the villagers who welcomed us with open arms, from Kiayuh to Petota. But Zarak just shook his head, staring at the floor.

"None yet, but once the Empire of Gala's forces move in there will be a full search. Any survivors will be rescued."

"Those poor villagers," Jon shuddered as he spoke, "they did no wrong; they were innocent."

"We did not call you here to drown your minds with the misfortunes of war." Nahksona sat back down and clasped his hands, resting his elbows on the table. "A boat is being prepared for you. It would be best if you left now. The sooner you meet with Empress Jhena, the less lives will be taken."

"And with you, take this message for the empress." Mister Sari pulled a sealed scroll from his cloak and placed it on the table. "It contains verification that you are who you say you are and of the unfortunate updates of the war."

"We are ready to leave," Benjin assured the council. He took the scroll and tucked it into his belt.

"Allow me to travel with them." Zarak quickly rose to his feet.

"A councilman does not abandon his post." Mister Sari chuckled. None of the other council member's dared to speak.

"I serve no use here. What would be a better show of urgency than for a councilman to show up at her doorstep?"

"No councilman has ever left the Island of Aara since being sworn in. It would be an abomination."

"The fact no councilman has ever left this island is an abomination of itself."

"The answer is no," Mister Sari said, his voice rising with intensity.

"Zarak has a point," Nahksona countered. "A councilman would have the strongest influence on the empress."

"This is treachery!" Mister Sari threw his hands up. "What next, we abandon our robes and switch to peasant clothes?" His eyes glared at me.

"We swore an oath," Tsalen Ban argued, agreeing with Mister Sari.

"And who did you swear yours to, the council? Or General Ahkpi?" Zarak retorted, before turning to Jia. "What is your vote?" I felt the desperation in his pleas, they sent chills down my spine.

"It is true; we swore an oath to not abandon our post," she said, her eyes analyzing the map before her, "but Zarak is not. Our post is wherever we can best serve the people. Voyage east to the Empire of Gala and represent those with no voice."

"Traitors!" Mister Sari snapped. "All of you!" He stood up abruptly, slamming his palms onto the table.

"My only oath is to the people." Zarak looked at us. "We will leave within the hour. The boy will bring you to the docks when it is time." He knocked once on the door and the guards swung them open without hesitation.

"If you leave this island you are no councilman to me," Mister Sari growled.

"I never wanted to be," Zarak mumbled to himself as he walked out, his white robe dragging on the floor behind him.

"Well!" Mister Sari looked at us. "Leave! We have no more use of you here." He shooed us towards the door. I clenched onto Benjin's arm.

"Okurai Sari!" Nahksona threw his hands up. He looked exhausted, with dark bags under his eyes. "Enough!"

"Is that all you say?"

"What more is there to?" He brushed his hair out of his face before collapsing back into his chair in defeat.

"Your behavior is what is treachery," Jia Sagtra sharply spoke. Her eyes laid heavily upon Mister Sari, but he just chuckled as he hurriedly gathered his things together.

"Treachery was the moment a woman was permitted to serve in the council."

"I must have forgotten, us women get too emotional to be able to make rational decisions. We shout, we get red in the face, and we slam our fists onto tables like a child." Her eyes narrowed.

"Traitors," Mister Sari hissed over his shoulder as he stormed out of the room, pushing between Benjin and Jon.

"Okurai!" Tsalen Ban called after him, before following him out the room.

"I'm sure this is not how you envisioned the Council of Five to be." Jia Sagtra sighed, rising to her feet. "But where there is government, there is squabbling. It seems one cannot exist without the other."

"It is embarrassing, truly. I apologize on behalf of Mister Sari." Nahksona raised his hand to his chest in sincerity. "Some men are stuck in their old ways."

"Though it does not excuse his behavior, I suppose it helps explain it," Jia responded, as she approached us. She stood before me and put her hand on my shoulder. "Do not allow his words to cast shadows upon your accomplishments thus far. For every stride a man makes, we must tread three. Even as a member of the Council of Five, I still encounter nonsense. Yet the louder their complaints grow, the better job I know I am doing. Do you understand me, dear?"

"I believe I do."

"Good." She turned her back to me, not wasting a moment. "Now, be gone. Time is not our friend."

"Thank you both, for everything." Jon bowed before Nahksona and Jia Sagtra. "You were more than hospitable."

"Save your thanks, for it is us who owe you them." Nahksona extended his hand to Jon. "I believe when our paths next cross, your names will have become common in households across the west. But for now, stay safe." Nahksona shook Benjin's hand, then mine.

The guards held the door open for us, as we passed through one by one. The air felt heavy, and the building narrower as we raced down the hall to our room. My head throbbed, but there was no time to rest. To my surprise, ten arrows laid outside our door, bound together with twine.

"Looks like you got another gift, Nyla," Jon remarked as he picked up the bundle and observed their fine craftsmanship. Their shafts were hewn from dark wood, their fletching alternating between midnight blue and black. The arrowheads were sharp and black, but would soon be stained red. I found myself wondering how many lives would be taken with these ten pointed sticks.

"These'll suffice," I said, accepting the gift. It had no indication who provided them, though I held doubts it was Mister Sari, given his belief that a woman was not fit for battle. Perhaps the nameless boy informed someone else of my need, though now was not the time to dwell on such trivial matters.

Benjin swung our bedroom door open and we all piled in, frantically preparing to leave the island. Fortunately for us, we had all been traveling light so there was not much to pack, which alleviated a drop of stress from a bucket that already overflowed.

"This is the journey that never ends," Benjin muttered aloud as he threw his bag over his shoulder.

"Maybe that's for the better," I whispered to myself. So far, Laago's journey was the only one that came to a close, leaving the odds not in our favor.

Jon paced back and forth in the tiny room, his boots thudding on the wood floor and his sword clanking against his hip with every step. His sage green eyes were wide with worry, fluttering with panic. I am sure I looked the same when we all started this journey in the streets of Tinshe, but not anymore. I have learnt that worrying does nothing but blind you from fate.

"I hope they send a messenger to Terlu to inform General Pago of our trip east." His eyes darted around the room. "I don't want him or Jin to worry about us not returning."

"They will." Benjin sat on the edge of our bed, awaiting the nameless boy's inevitable knock on our door.

"I wonder if they put enough rations in our boat."

"They will," Benjin dryly replied, his chin resting on his fist. They were both anxious, but showed it differently.

"They didn't mention anything about the weather..." Jon nervously looked out the window, but it was too dark to make anything out. "I hope-"

"It is what it is," Benjin's voice slightly rose in aggravation. Jon stopped pacing and froze.

"It's not," he sternly said. Before another word could be said, there was a knock on the door. Benjin shot up from the bed and unlatched the door.

"Is it time?"

"Yessir." The nameless boy stood before him, eyes glued to the ground as per usual. Benjin turned and looked at Jon.

"You ready?"

"Ready as I'll ever be." Jon slid past him out the door. Benjin put his hand on my shoulder.

"How are you doing?" Benjin asked such a simple question- one that you hear a thousand times in your life- but somehow each time I hear it, it becomes harder to find an answer. My eyes drifted up to his and my lips pursed. "I know," he replied, answering his own question.

"Will it ever get easier?"

"They say time heals all wounds..." He stepped towards the open door, his back to me. "But it never did for me."

We followed the boy through the hall and down the spiral staircase. He, too, seemed more anxious than usual, if that was even possible. The slightest creak in the floorboards practically sent him flying. I clenched my bow as we walked, a habit I had picked up on this wretched journey. I did not feel safe in this world without a weapon anymore.

As we traveled through the large open room leading to the front doors of the castle for the last time, I did not feel sad. On all of our other stops throughout this trip, from Bao to General Pago, my chest hurt leaving. It felt as though the moment we got comfortable, we would be thrown back to the whalesharks. Any sense of safety was fleeting, often leaving us quicker than it stayed. But this time, I felt relieved to leave this gods' forsaken island. Nothing good came of this place for me. Two guards in beige robes nodded to us as we passed through the heavy iron doors for the final time.

There was a soft breeze in the air. It was still night but it was already warm out, so I knew when the sun did rise, it would be a hot spring day. I turned around and took one last look at the castle. There was something inscribed in the stone above the doors, but it was in a language I did not recognize.

"Come on, Nyla," Benjin called from the stairs that led to the dock.

"This is as far as I am permitted to take you." The boy bowed before Benjin and Jon.

"Thank you, bud. You have been a great host to us." Jon returned the bow, but as he rose back upright, a grin spread across his face like a wildfire. He grabbed the boy and pulled him in for a tight hug. "Take care of yourself." Jon released him and headed down the staircase, but the boy stood frozen still.

"It was nice to meet you," Benjin said as he followed Jon. I smiled at the boy as I passed, but I don't think he even noticed me. As soon as I took my first step down the stairs, I heard him dart away.

"Why'd you hug him?" I overheard Benjin ask Jon.

"I dunno," Jon replied. "I felt like he needed it."

"I bet that was the first time someone's hugged him in years."

"What a sad truth..." Jon shook his head. "The tides appear to be in our favor," he called down to Zarak, who was already waiting by the dock, with his long white robe wavering in the breeze. Monk Day stood by his side. Their backs were towards us, as they stared out into the vast ocean.

"Aye." Zarak turned to face us and extended his arm out, firmly shaking Jon's.

"The gods will be as well." Monk Day smiled. "I have these for you." He handed Benjin and I two small brass containers. They had seabirds etched in gold, flying above ocean waves, towards a sun with long rays, similar in style to those that decorated the wooden boat that we sent Laago off in. We opened them up in unison and I felt my heart sink.

"Laago..." Benjin gasped, clenching his heart.

"Now your friend will not only be spiritually within you, but physically as well. Laago's legacy will continue to live on through you."

"Thank you." Benjin brought the urn to his chest and squeezed it tightly. I stood there, my body unmoving and my eyes lost in the ash that was once my love.

"It is an honor to be a part of your journey." He reached up and put his hand on Benjin's. "Remember, no burden is yours to carry alone.

By ourselves, we may be weak at times, but together, we can weather any storm." As always his words were warm, but they hurt my heart nonetheless. Benjin didn't respond, he couldn't. I saw tears welling up in his lapis eyes, before he quickly wiped them away.

"It's time," Zarak decided. He swiftly pulled off his robe and held it out to Monk Day. "I suppose I have no use of this now."

"I will keep it safe for you, but please, keep your pin. It is a token of your country, not solely of the prince." The monk's hands shook as he removed the pin of the snow falcon from Zarak's long white robe. They joined hands for a last time and Zarak accepted the token of his people, before stepping into the wooden row boat. Monk Day called to him. "Be wise, Ko. Remember all that I have taught you."

"How could I forget?" Zarak leapt back out of the boat and embraced the monk.

He was tall and slender, towering over Monk Day. Zarak looked so different without his robe on, but still so beautiful. He wore fitted gray pants that disappeared into his black boots that reached just above his knee. He had an off-white short sleeved jacket that fit him loosely, but not in a sloppy way. It was a button down, but he wore it open. It looked carefully handcrafted, with gold stitching around the edges. Under it, he wore a tight black shirt with the sleeves rolled up his forearms, tucked into his pants. Zarak's sword hung from his black leather belt with a silver buckle draped around his waist. It was thin and lightweight, opposite of Jon's heavy broad sword. Zarak pulled a single black glove from his pocket and slid it onto his sword yielding hand.

"I am so proud of the man you have become. I love you like my own, Ko."

"I am who I am because of you." He let go of Monk Day and stepped back into the boat. "I will see you soon."

Monk Day turned away and began slowly walking towards the stairs, his body creaking with every step. As he passed me, I noticed his eyes were red, stung with tears. I found his relationship with Zarak touching. He viewed the young councilman as a son. If it was true that he followed Zarak to the island, as he once said, it must be so hard for him to watch him leave to the east. I'm sure living in that tower would be lonely without him.

Just as Jon began to push our boat into the water, I noticed someone running down the steep staircase, but it was too dark for me to see. None of the boys seemed to notice. They were all focused ahead, on the seemingly endless ocean before us, dividing us from the Empire of Gala.

"I think someone is running over to us." I carefully rose to my feet, as the boat rocked back and forth, and squinted my eyes. Jon turned around, still knee deep in water.

"It's the boy..." He muttered in confusion. "What could he possibly want?"

"Nothing good, that's for sure," Benjin assumed, as he tied the bag that held our urns to his belt, out of fear a sharp wave could knock the remains of our beloved friend overboard. In it, he also tossed our coin bag and the sealed scroll for safekeeping.

The nameless boy jumped down the final three steps and into the sand- not taking a moment to breathe. He darted through and did not stop until he stood before Jon, his hands grasping his knees as he bent over, gasping for air.

"Is everything okay?" Jon nervously asked.

"Wei Ten..." He sputtered between breaths. "My name... is Wei Ten."

He shakily reached forward and grabbed Jon's hand, only to put a folded up piece of paper in it. The once nameless boy tightly squeezed Jon's hand around it before letting go and bolting away, back up the stairs from where he came.

"Wei Ten..." Jon whispered as he watched the boy run up the stairs and disappear into the darkness. He shoved the piece of paper into his back pocket and gave us a final push before jumping in. We slowly drifted out to sea, officially beginning our next journey. Jon grabbed a hold of the oars and began to row, while the rest of us sat in silence, eager to hear what the paper said.

"Are you going to read it, Jon?" Benjin impatiently asked.

"Let's see." He set the heavy wooden oars back down and pulled the piece of paper from his pocket, carefully unfolding it. "It looks like some sort of letter... Dated almost a year back."

"To who?"

"It's written to Tsalen Ban of the Suhai Empire," Jon mumbled aloud as he skimmed through it. "Seems to be from an old friend." Suddenly, his eyes widened and his face went white.

"What's it say?" Benjin shot up in his seat, intensely staring at Jon.

"It's informing him of the plans to invade the Republic of Terlu." He slapped his hand onto his forehead in disbelief. "It's signed by General Ahkpi."

"What do you mean?" Zarak's eyebrows rose. He lunged forward and ripped the letter from Jon's hands. "You will be pleased to hear Prince Xan of the Kingdom of Yana, true heir to the throne, has agreed to move troops to penetrate the northwestern walls of the Republic of Terlu... His allegiance to the militia will not go unrewarded... In exchange for his aid, he requests capture of a traitor, returned to him alive... Once spring brings false hope of summer, we will be the ice that thaws the once great walls, cracking them to their core."

"He knew it all along," Jon's voice rose in intensity, his face red with rage. "The bastard conspired with General Ahkpi!" Benjin grabbed the paper from Zarak, his eyes darting from line to line, confirming the treachery that rang in his ears.

"This is unbelievable," he stammered. "He's a traitor."

"And I am a fool..." Zarak grimaced, drowning in disbelief.

"We have to go back." Jon reached for the oars, but Benjin grabbed his hands.

"No, this is even more reason to reach Empress Jhena! Even the council is compromised. We cannot go back."

"But what about the other councilmen?" Jon looked to Zarak for guidance.

"Tsalen Ban is a traitor and will be rightfully punished, but not yet. None of the councilmen will be harmed, I am sure of it. Benjin is right, meeting with Empress Jhena is of the utmost importance-our main priority. The Republic of Terlu needs her military backing so our arrival to the Empire of Gala cannot be delayed any further. Ban is not going anywhere, he would not leave that island unless he is dragged out by his hair."

"None of the councilmen will be harmed?" Jon mocked. "General Ahkpi sent a boat of trained assassins to the island!" He looked at me to back him up. "We have to go back, right Nyla?"

"It's you." I looked at Zarak, his crystal blue eyes glimmering in the moonlight. "You are the traitor to Prince Xan that General Ahkpi wrote of."

"Aye, I am surprised the hot-headed prince is so concerned of me." He crossed his legs and rubbed his chin. "I presume that was the cause of your encounter with the militants in the ocean. They were sent to capture and deliver me to Prince Xan. He must be enraged to know they failed. You saved my life."

"You are a walking target..." Terror overtook Jon's face. "General Ahkpi will not stop until you are captured."

"We are all walking targets, Jon." Benjin laid back down and nestled himself between my seat and his. There was an eeriness in his tone, he almost sounded completely indifferent. "We have been since the moment I killed that militant in the streets of Tinshe and we will be until both General Ahkpi and Prince Xan's heads sit on spikes before us." His eyes drifted shut before Jon could even respond.

Jon let out a grumbled sigh and began rowing ferociously to blow off some steam. Benjin had to understand that his ability to cope with such life-threatening fears did not occur overnight. Nor did it take days, more like weeks. Like us, Jon went from his comfortable home to being thrown into fire in a matter of a day. The only difference was while we were forced into it, he did so willingly. When Benjin took that militant's life to defend me, he did so knowing it meant there was no turning back, but also knowing there was no other choice. But Jon, he chose to embark on this journey with his own free will. His sister, Jin, begged him to not go. He did not owe anyone anything, yet something deep within him pushed him to venture out into the unknown, knowing full well that it could result in him making the ultimate sacrifice.

"We are better fighters than them, Jon." His eyes remained closed. "I have looked their militants in the eyes- they're just boys. They fight because they are ordered to; we fight because if we don't, our entire world will burn to ash and because of that, they will never prevail."

"Will is not the only weapon in war," Jon cautioned. "If General Ahkpi and Tsalen Ban were directly corresponding, then he is probably aware of our little excursion now..."

"The general and prince must think the stars have aligned for a traitor to the crown, the son of an enemy general, and two wanted terrorists to all be sailing together on the same boat," Zarak surmised.

"I hope your arrows are ready, Nyla," Benjin chimed in.

I looked down at my pouch of arrows, a blend of both seasoned and freshly crafted. I pulled one out and delicately ran my finger down the wood and to its worn-down point. There was a bit of dried blood still stained on the tip. I wondered whose it could be... I wondered how many men's lives I have taken thus far. There were the two militants in the tunnels, the one drunkenly passed out against the wall at the Port of Eura, and the bastards who stole the fire in my heart. Were there more? I shuddered and quickly put my arrows away. Whether there were more or not mattered not, because there would be more to come. I would kill every man from here to Prince Xan's throne if it meant I could personally launch one of my little arrows into his blackened heart.

"What does Prince Xan look like?" I pondered aloud.

"Like many of the northerners, his hair is white as snow, but Prince Xan is royalty, so he does not have it flow free as mine does. While it stretches down his back, the top is pulled into a warrior's bun." Zarak chuckled softly to himself. "Though he has won no battles."

"Does he fight alongside his people?" Jon asked.

"Aye, he does, but behind six of his royal guards."

"Like a true king," Benjin scoffed.

"He uses a sword so heavy he could barely lift it." Zarak sighed. "But we were young then and I have heard he has trained heavily since. He has the body of a fuji ox, so it is about time he learns his stance. I hope he finally puts up a good fight."

"It sounds like you-"

"Believe me when I say, I will personally see through the end of Prince Xan," he interrupted.

"That's a bold statement." Benjin sat up in his seat, a little too interested in Zarak's words. "You said he is guarded by six men?"

"At the least." Zarak's eyes locked onto Benjin's. "That is, when he is not in his castle protected by an entire army."

"Take my axe."

"This is between Prince Xan and myself."

"He murdered Laago- my brother," Benjin's voice boomed with intensity. "We will head to Empress Jhena as planned. Once we convince her to bring more troops west, we will bring Jon and Nyla back to Huang, so they can reunite with Luka and wait out the war. But you and I, we will head north and see to the end of Prince Xan, so we can end this war before it ends us."

"No!" I voiced, only for Benjin to speak over me.

"I am not wavering."

"Benjin, I am coming with you."

"Nyla, it is not safe..." He shook his head, waving his hand. "And what about Luka?"

"What about all the boys who will die at the hands of Prince Xan? What about all the boys who have already perished? The war is in its infancy and entire towns lie in ruin," I argued. "I am not wavering either. You need my bow."

"He has elite personal guards-"

"Give me six decent arrows and there won't be anyone standing between us and him."

"Take my sword as well," Jon demanded. "I have no use for it in Huang."

"So it is decided," Benjin reluctantly conceded, yielding to our demands. "Once we depart from the east, we shall head north to the Kingdom of Yana."

"And then what?" Jon fretted.

"We put Prince Xan's head on a spike where it belongs."

# Book II
# Coming Soon

Subscribe to my newsletter via
www.virginiamaryarts.com
or follow @VirginiaMaryArts on
Instagram to be the first to hear
about Book II's release date.

If you enjoyed the world of Across the
Great Ocean, please leave a review on
Amazon to help support me as an
independent author.

# About the Author

**MEET VIRGINIA MARY,** poet and author of the Across the Great Ocean series, and a lover of backpacking, photography, cats, & all things outdoors...

When she is not working on her fantasy series, you can find her somewhere in the sun, sipping her favorite tea & smelling the flowers.

INSTAGRAM @VIRGINIAMARYARTS
WWW.VIRGINIAMARYARTS.COM

Made in the USA
Middletown, DE
06 July 2024

56646837R00205